BANANA ROSE

ALSO BY NATALIE GOLDBERG

Writing Down the Bones
Wild Mind
Long Quiet Highway

BANANA
ROSE

NATALIE
GOLDBERG

Natalie Goldberg

BANTAM BOOKS

NEW YORK TORONTO

LONDON SYDNEY AUCKLAND

AUTHOR'S NOTE

Though there are certain similarities between Nell Schwartz's life and my own, and I've set this novel in familiar locations, *Banana Rose* remains a work of fiction. All of the characters are the product of my imagination, and their actions, motivations, thoughts, and conversations are solely my creation. I've drawn inspiration from my own experiences, but neither the characters nor the situations in which they find themselves are intended to depict real people or events.

BANANA ROSE

A Bantam Book / March 1995

Grateful acknowledgment is made for permission to reprint from the following:
Line from "Do Not Go Gentle Into That Good Night," from Dylan Thomas,
Poems of Dylan Thomas. Copyright © 1952 by Dylan Thomas. Reprinted by
permission of New Directions Publishing Corp. Two haiku from *Haiku, Volume
One,* by R. H. Blyth. Copyright © 1949, 1981 by R. H. Blyth. Reprinted by
permission of The Hokuseido Press.

Chapter 47 was first published under the title of "Lakestone, Minnesota" in
The Sun, *November 1988.*

Library of Congress Cataloging-in-Publication Data
Goldberg, Natalie.
Banana Rose / Natalie Goldberg.
p.   cm.
ISBN 0-553-09527-7
1. Jewish women—New Mexico—Taos—Psychology—
Fiction. 2. Taos (N.M.)—Fiction. I. Title.
PS3557.O3583B36   1995
813'.54—dc20   94-34476
                                                      CIP

Published simultaneously in the United States and Canada

Bantam Books are published by Bantam Books, a division of Bantam Doubleday Dell Publishing Group, Inc.
Its trademark, consisting of the words "Bantam Books" and the portrayal of a rooster, is Registered in U.S. Patent
and Trademark Office and in other countries. Marca Registrada. Bantam Books, 1540 Broadway, New York,
New York 10036.

FOR ROB STRELL,
MY LONGTIME FRIEND,

AND

ROMI GOLDBERG,
MY SISTER

If we have no soul
Something aches in us anyway
Heaves our breath
Pumps our blood

Sun thrown across tree tops
Do you see New Mexico?

Wind storms crack across it
Days break against it
I hurt for dry dirt
Big sky
Bell in a tower
Sage across the eye

Burnt land
Old sand carcass
Your rosebuds are hardening
Your leaves turning
My heart burning

BANANA ROSE

PREFACE:
CREMATION

She had sent me a postcard just before she got in her car. "I'm finally coming home! I want to be near that blue sky again. Just like a raven or a magpie. I want to soar with that land. You were right. Give me that and I'll be sane."

Even that Tuesday, a week after the accident, I couldn't believe she was dead. How can a life be there and then gone? All day Sam and Daniel gathered piñon and cedar. They piled it into a funeral pyre near the pyramid that Sam had built years earlier as an experiment. He'd heard that pyramids had magical powers.

I thought over and over again about what must have happened on the road that night in Kansas. It was a thin two-lane highway. Midnight was full of stars and the dry stalks of corn. She was in her Volkswagen. There were two semis, one driving ahead of her and the other thundering east. With the last slow insects of summer stuck on the windshield, she tried to pass the semi in front of her but her timing was off.

Here my mind always stopped. I didn't want to think about the crash. In a few hours I was going to see her for the last time.

At sunset, we carried the coffin to the pyre and placed it on the piñon and cedar logs. Then we stood in a circle on the mesa, where we could see 360 degrees. We could see three hundred miles away. There were no trees, only sagebrush. People said it was like the Mind of God: empty. Daniel, Anna's brother, opened the coffin. Each of us took a turn speaking to her. Then we each placed something in the coffin that we wanted her to have.

Blue went first. She gave her a pinecone. "Anna, honey, we'll miss you. Nell wanted you back so bad. Remember when we ate posole together by the wood stove that October long ago? You sure had pretty gray eyes." Blue paused. She swallowed. Suddenly the finality of what we were doing seemed to run through her whole body. "I hope we will meet again in the next life."

We couldn't actually see her. She was wrapped up like a mummy. The funeral home in Kansas had prepared her for the long ride home in the back of Blue's red Subaru.

I gave her a bouquet of sage. "Oh, god, Anna, I'm going to miss you! Where are you? I can't believe you're gone. I pray to the sky and the heavens that they take you. Lift you like you were flying."

The sun radiated purple and white rays behind silver clouds in the west. Just as Daniel placed in the coffin all the hair that he had shaved off his head that morning, there was a huge clash of thunder. Lightning shrieked across the southwest part of the sky. We saw rain in the distance, tall and blue-gray, the kind the Indians call Long Walking Man. To the east, over Taos Mountain, night began its black climb over the Sangre de Cristos.

We closed the coffin. Daniel's hands were in tight fists at his sides, and his eyes stared straight at the coffin that held his sister. Blue's face was soft, taking it all in, looking from me to Daniel and then over to where Anna was. Sam held his right elbow with his left hand, swaying slightly, grinding the heel of his black boot in the dirt. I was the only one crying.

Over the coffin we erected her tipi, the one she had lived in on the mesa before she moved to the rim, where I met her. I could imagine her stooping to crawl into the low tipi opening, her black high-top sneakers the last things that would disappear.

Anna was my best friend. She was a writer and had almost finished her first novel. She'd left New Mexico and gone back to Nebraska because she was born there, but she had never stopped being a part of us. I always wondered how long she'd last in her native state. Eventually, I knew, she'd have to come back to her real home.

Daniel doused the end of a cedar log in kerosene and set it on fire. The rainstorm in the southwest turned into a double rainbow, reaching all the way from the Rio Grande gorge to The Pedernal in Abiquiu. Everyone saw it and smiled. Then Daniel knelt and lit the bottom edges of the canvas tipi. I was amazed how quickly the material caught. I somehow thought we'd have more time. I wanted more time with Anna. The flames became huge. We all stood back from the immense heat. Why did she die? None of it made sense. I was still alive. How much longer in this life I didn't know—years or days or minutes? But now I had to live that time without Anna. The moon's full face rose over Taos Mountain.

Anna was burning. We smelled her through the cedar, the canvas, and the pine box. It was a clear and awful smell. We all breathed it in deep. It was the last of her and her smoke now entered our bodies. Something huge and blazing pink rose over the east. A spaceship? Someone said it was Venus, though I never saw Venus look quite like that before.

If I had had any doubts about the cremation, at that moment I knew we did the right thing for Anna. She was in our breath and we were all very close to her. Sam prayed that we do good acts with her life that we now carried within us. Blue passed around a Mason jar of rose water and each of us drank slow and deep.

It took all night for the fire to burn down to embers. In the last hour, Daniel took his sleeping bag ten yards away and lay on his back looking up at the sky. Sam hardly spoke at all. He and Blue watched that the nearby sage didn't catch fire. And for a long time I sat on the ground, hugging my knees, rocking back and forth, repeating, "Anna, Anna," slowly, like a mantra under my breath.

Late the next morning, Sam bent over the ashes and picked out the bone chips, his fingers rubbed blue-black. He put the chips in a green jar. He even found a chunk of Daniel's blond hair untouched among the black cinders.

Days later, we scattered the ashes and bones in her favorite places. By moonlight, I placed some under a ponderosa where Anna had fallen asleep one night. I threw one bone over the Rio Grande bridge that she had walked across one early morning, pretending to fly. And one chip of a bone I secretly dropped by the curb in front of Rexall Drugs on Taos plaza. She would sit at the soda fountain there and sip Coke with ice after she taught writing at the hippie school behind the Church of the Hand-maidens of the Sacred Blood. We also met there a lot for malts. Weeks later, I found a chip in my pocket when I was cutting across Kit Carson Park. I left it near a cemetery stone we once leaned against.

Daniel took some back to Nebraska and I kept two in a jar on my fireplace mantel. Someday I plan to leave one of those near the place where she died, where we saw the angels. And maybe sometime I'll get to the Missouri again. That's the one place I know for sure Anna wanted her ashes thrown.

And some bones just sat there near the pyramid for anyone to take. I imagine they are still sitting there, untouched.

PART

1

1

The first time I saw him, he was standing in a corral. He wore a red shirt and had both hands on a brown leather saddle that he had just taken off the back of a black quarter horse. I was walking along the dirt shoulder of the two-lane highway, on my way to meet a friend a mile down at the Texaco station. A lawn separated the corral from the road by about two hundred yards. The grass belonged to the Sheepskin Company. It was early October and the grass should have been yellow—after all, it was New Mexico—but the company had hired someone to take care of it. I was walking west, but my head was turned north, looking at the amazingly green lawn and noticing the horse and the man with the saddle. Not watching where I was going, I stepped on the teeth of a rake, a big one, and its handle jolted up and hit me hard in the head, right between the eyebrows. I saw stars, lifted my left hand to greet them, and then I fell backward.

The next thing I remember was sitting under a cottonwood on the lawn. The man from the corral was handing me a bottle of water. His arms and face had freckles, his red hair was shoulder-length, and his eyes were a quiet hazel. I thanked him, took two sips, and said, ''I better be going.''

''Are you okay?'' he asked.

"Sure, thanks, I'm fine."

He went back to the corral. I let the cottonwood hold me a little longer and watched him lift a bale of hay. Then I stood on the miraculous two feet that I had just been knocked off of and began to take a step. With the first step that my left foot took ahead and away from my right, my mouth began to whistle "Yankee Doodle Dandy." It was in tune and I knew all the notes, even though I had never whistled before in my life. I swung my arms and marched away from the cottonwood toward the Texaco station.

The second time I saw him was two weeks later on a Friday night at the Elephant House in Talpa. Every Friday night the commune celebrated the beginning of Shabbos, the Jewish day of rest. Only two of us in the house were Jews, but it was the non-Jews who especially loved to celebrate it. It saved all of us in the commune. Each week we could easily have killed one another, but on Friday night we lit the candles and forgave the hair left in the tub, the mud on the floor, and the fact that Celeste didn't know one thing about the *Tibetan Book of the Dead*. We fell into one another's arms, ate a huge pot-luck dinner, danced, and sang gospel and old Beatles songs. The Shabbos became bigger and bigger until half the hippies in Taos came to one or another of our Friday nights.

On this particular one, the man from the corral came. I walked into the kitchen after taking a shower, rubbing my wet hair with a yellow towel, my head cocked to the right, and I saw him across the long room. He'd gotten the time wrong and come an hour early, so he was helping Carmel cut up celery. They laughed about how Friday night was like a salami. I didn't get the joke. Actually, I wasn't really listening because time had suddenly stopped. I saw him across the room, and I heard water running far away, and his laughter, too, was water.

We said hi to each other, and I walked through the kitchen and into my bedroom. I sat down on the bed. I got up. He was one room away. I put on my socks. I remembered I had to take the cheesecake I had baked out of the fridge and put strawberries on it. "Oh, hell," I said to myself. "Just get dressed and go in there. You don't even know him, and you probably don't want to."

I marched myself into the kitchen and opened the refrigerator. I didn't look at anyone. I didn't want anyone to know I was in love. I wasn't in love, for goodness' sake! There were now about eight people milling around. I bent to get the strawberries from the lower shelf.

Carmel yelled out, "Hey, Banana Rose, you have on one red sock and one white. Is that a Shabbos tradition?" Besides Happiness, whose nonhippie name was Jane Berg, I was the only other Jewish authority in the house. Everything I did on Shabbos was considered significant. I looked down, flustered. Nearby, I heard him say, "So that's her name." I stood up, shut the refrigerator, and turned with a professorial air. I raised my right hand, my index finger pointed. "Yes, if Shabbos falls on October seventeenth, it is proper for all Jews to have on one red and one white sock. Deuteronomy, chapter twelve, verse eight, line three."

He laughed with everyone else. I liked him; he appreciated my jokes. But I couldn't act like I liked him. I acted like he was a wooden frame on the wall. I talked to everyone but him. I thought if I didn't know his name, he wouldn't exist. Nevertheless, this man whose name I didn't know was blurring my heart like a forest of wild roses. I couldn't see anything else, though I looked everywhere else but where he was.

At six, the sun set and we lit the candles. There must have been thirty-five of us in the big kitchen. Blue came from up Talpa hill. I remember her dog Bonnie pawing at the door. Blue brought posole, a corn dish we all loved, and she had on a babushka. That week she was reading a Russian novel and the peasant woman wore a babushka. She decided "babushka" would fit in with Shabbos. Big Allen was there and brought out his flute. Tiny William took his fiddle out of its case, but it wasn't yet time for music.

"When I light these candles, we can let go of everything and enter a time of peace," said Happiness as she flicked the match. There was silence in the room. I snuck a peek at him. He wore a pair of square glasses with the left stem taped on. Happiness then said the prayer over the wine. We passed a goblet around and everyone took a sip.

We took the napkin off the two challahs and thanked God, King and Queen of the Universe, for bringing forth grain from the earth. We passed the braided egg bread around. Each person took a hunk, enough to put a crumb in everyone's mouth and wish them "Good Shabbos."

"You can't miss anyone," I called out as people hugged and fed each other.

There he was. I'd already fed everyone else. Suddenly, I wasn't feeling so robust. "Hi, Banana Rose." He beamed at me. "I'm Gauguin." He laughed, grabbed me, and gave me a big hug. Flustered, I hugged him back. We stepped away from each other, then he dropped his last piece of bread in my mouth, put his hands together in prayer position, and bowed. I bowed too. I still had the bread in my hand. I put it in his mouth.

Tiny began playing his fiddle. Gauguin went over to a black case in the corner and unsnapped it. He pulled out a trumpet. I wondered, Did he play his horn in Harlem or on the south side of Chicago? Did he shoot up heroin, stay up all night, and wear dark glasses? He joined in the homemade music. Happiness brought out our pots. Some people grabbed the utensils on the table. Paul and Ellen played hand drums. Blue hit a spatula against a wooden chair. A spatula! It was perfect with her babushka. Her eyes looked like she'd eaten chunks of turquoise for lunch—they were that blue. Her hands were so worn, you'd think they belonged to an old woman, but she banged her instrument with the vigor of a young girl.

I felt shy for the rest of the night. No matter where I was—washing dishes, hitting a wooden spoon against a glass to the rhythm of "Amazing Grace," biting into cheesecake, talking to Lightning about his hurt foot, or listening to Fine Point whisper in my ear, "Banana Rose, I have a new lover. She lives in La Madeira, but anytime you want me you can have me"—all that time, I knew one thing: Gauguin was in the room. He played his gold trumpet, and when he wasn't blowing, he tapped out the rhythm with his hand against his thigh.

It was 11:30. I was tired from the effort I'd made to appear not to notice him. Without waiting for everyone to leave, I went into my bedroom, threw off my clothes, and fell into a sound, dreamless sleep.

At 3 A.M. I woke abruptly and had to go to the bathroom. I didn't want to get up, but I knew I would never get back to sleep if I didn't go. I trudged through the kitchen in my long white T-shirt. The hall between the kitchen and bathroom was wide enough to hold a mattress, where guests stayed overnight. As I went down the hall, I noticed someone lying there. I didn't much care. I was tired. People often needed a place to crash after Shabbos. When I came out of the bathroom, the person on the mattress was sitting up in his sleeping bag. It was Gauguin.

"Hi," he said.

"Hi," I said, raising my hand and heading for the kitchen.

"Why don't you sit down and talk a minute?" Gauguin asked.

I sat down on the edge of his bed. In my head a voice thundered, I want to hold him, be with him, and in my body I felt a howling of coyotes. I said to myself, Go ahead, Nell, just ask him to sleep with you.

While my mind was thinking all this, my mouth was making small talk with Gauguin. "Yes, Taos Pueblo has Indian dances several times a year. They're good. You should go to see them."

I counted in my head, "One, two, three . . ." As I opened my lips to speak, Gauguin said, "I know this seems odd, but I'd like to sleep with you."

For a second, I wasn't sure whose mouth those words had come out of, but then I said, "I'd like that too." Suddenly shy, we both got up, walked through the kitchen and into my bedroom.

As soon as we sat on the bed, Gauguin called me "honey" and "darling" and "baby." I thought to myself, Who is this hick? Gauguin told me later that he'd thought to himself, What am I doing with her? She has such a heavy New York accent.

When Gauguin and I finally emerged from the bedroom late the next morning, people in the kitchen teased us. "Hey, Gauguin," Happiness said, "we were afraid the coyotes carried you off. All we saw on the cot was your crumpled sleeping bag." She yelled into her bedroom, "Hey, Light, we were right! Coyote Banana carried him off."

Gauguin smiled and ran his hand through his long red hair. It was the color of beets or maples in the fall.

"Do you want to go rose hipping?" I asked. We were eating yogurt with bananas and granola. He rubbed his bare foot along my calf. I looked at him and then tossed my eyes down to the yogurt.

"Sure," he said. "I'll do anything with you."

I took two plastic bags out of the cupboard, and we headed for the higher Talpa Road. We stopped in at Barela's candy store. Gauguin bought me a stick of red licorice before I could say, "You don't buy anything here. You just stop in." The licorice alone could have given me dentures for the rest of my life, all the candy was so old. But I decided to shut up, and when Gauguin wasn't looking, I chucked the red candy into a ditch.

A week before, there had been an unusually cold night and the temperature had dropped to freezing for a few hours in the early morning. That was good. Rose hips have the highest vitamin C after first frost. They grew along one side of the dirt path where we walked. Above them hung small wild green plums. Beyond was a field spotted with cows. Nearby two white horses bent their long necks. I showed Gauguin how to select the darker rose hips. He began a little song about Rose's hips. I smiled and tried to ignore the fact that he was singing about me.

I wore a pair of white pants stained with paint, and as I stood in front of the thornbushes, I felt the sun's heat through the cotton on the back of my thighs. I also felt the season turning, and I knew when I looked over at Gauguin that he felt it too.

Gauguin told me he came from Minnesota. One night, he'd dreamed that he stood on his head at the top of Machu Picchu. That was the whole dream, and it had lasted for hours: way on the top of the Andes, his feet hanging in the sky and his head full of blood, his crown touching the soil where the Incas lived. It was an obvious sign, he said. He had to go there. He was hitchhiking his way to Peru and had taken a three-week job at the corral where I first saw him to get some extra cash. He planned to stay in Taos another week and then continue south.

He's headed for Peru—I'll never see him again! I told myself to calm down, not to panic.

I'll paint a picture of all this after he leaves. Maybe an abstract picture. I began to see it in my mind. There'd be a moon—a yellow one —in the upper-right corner of the paper and I'd layer paint like an explosion in the middle. I'd keep working the colors until I got the acrylics just right. I saw myself standing in my little studio bedroom at the Elephant House. I couldn't paint it realistically; no one would believe the sky and the light at this moment—it was too beautiful. Stay in the present, I reminded myself. Forget about painting right now. Forget about where this thing with Gauguin is going. I turned my head.

Gauguin was squatting near a dead skunk. He motioned for me to come over. I stood and looked down. The skunk's hair was matted and it looked like it had been dead for a long time. My eyes wandered to Gauguin's hair. It was even redder in the sun.

Gauguin was twenty-five years old and he'd already lived with two women. One had filled the house each week with white roses and said to him, "Count how many there are. I want to make love that many times this week." Gauguin had counted twenty-nine roses out loud, and then they got to work. It meant making love at least three times a day. He said he'd been eighteen and so hungry for sex, he could have eaten through a refrigerator door. The other woman he lived with had sewn silk banners and ran off with the man who delivered pizzas for his band. It broke his heart.

He had told me a lot about himself in just that one night. He hadn't gone to college, so he'd had to worry about the draft. Before his physical, he fasted for twelve days and weighed in at 120 pounds. His height was

13

five feet eleven inches. To his amazement, they were still going to take him. He became frantic and demanded to see the army psychiatrist. They kept him waiting on a red plastic chair for three hours. When he was finally led into a tiny gray office down the hall, he was shaking.

"Well, what seems to be the problem?" The psychiatrist coughed twice behind his hand.

Gauguin stood up and came around to the other side of the desk. He put his hand on the doctor's knee, then bent down and whispered in his ear, "I'm queer. I fuck men in the ass."

The doctor jerked up, pointed to the seat across the desk, and said, "Get over there, or I'll have you arrested." After that, everything became very businesslike as forms were filled out deeming him ineligible for the army.

Lying in bed next to Gauguin, I asked, "But weren't you afraid it would be on your record?" I had boyfriends in college who were afraid they wouldn't be able to go to law school if they tried to get out of the draft for dealing drugs.

"Hell, no." Gauguin laughed. "I'd be a lot more upset if I killed people in Vietnam and that was on my record. The only thing I felt bad about was portraying gay people like that, but I knew the army was freaked out about that stuff, so I used it. I was desperate." He seemed in a rush to share with me, and at the same time it felt as though we owned time. He ran his hand slowly along my face.

I picked another rose hip and looked up at the clouds. It was fall. Anything I did—turn my head, bend to lift a pebble, tie my shoe, glance at the pale yellow dirt of Talpa—felt as if I had already done it before in another life. The sky was so blue that only imagining the deepest red could give you a sense of that color blue. Smoke rose from a distant chimney, and the two white tipis way down by the Elephant Mountains were still out. Some hippies declared they would live there all winter, but in late November after a snow I hoped they would give in for warmth.

Last night, I told Gauguin that I'd majored in education in college because my family thought it was a good idea. I didn't know what else to do and my father was paying, so I did what he said. Way down deep, I used to dream of being a painter, but I didn't know anyone who painted. Everyone in my family owned small businesses: a vacuum store, a grocery, a cleaners. My father had a luncheonette. After I graduated from college, I taught full time for a few years in Ann Arbor, but something was missing. Then I moved to Taos and broke free. I decided to give myself a chance at painting.

"Taos is special to you, isn't it?" he asked.

"Yes." I nodded. "When I got here, I felt I could do anything. I teach school part time and try to paint the rest of the day, but it's not so easy. I get tired after teaching, and then there's always something happening here at the commune."

"Show me something you've painted," he said.

I got up from the bed and switched on a light. Naked, I grabbed a white towel and wrapped it around me. I opened the closet door and brought out two paintings.

He sat up in bed and reached out his arms. "Hey, let's see." He looked quietly for a while. I was uncomfortable and shifted around, sitting at the edge of the mattress. I bent over and picked at my big toe.

"I like them," he said, and then he hesitated. "Are they finished?"

"Well, no. That's sort of my problem. I want to finish them, and then I don't. I get scared. What if I finish them, and I really didn't say anything or I don't like them?"

"What's there to say?" he asked. "Just do it." He shrugged. "My father went to art school for two years before he became an architect. I think my father said you just do it."

I nodded. I dropped my towel and got back in bed. I wanted to ask him more about that, but I also wanted to kiss him.

He laid the paintings down gently and put his arms around me. We brought our lips together—his were thick—and we kissed for a long time, not moving, just feeling our bodies naked against each other. Then I put my leg over his. He moved and was suddenly on top of me and inside me. I opened out like spring rain. I bit his lower lip and we went wild. He cried above me, "Oh, Rose!" He tensed and then relaxed. We were quiet for a time. Then he began moving again, slow and soft. And with the wetness of his sperm inside me, I came, my body shuddering, ripples running down my entire length.

Gauguin and I were finished picking rose hips. We walked home with our bags full of those hard fall nuggets that used to be pink wild roses. It was late afternoon. When we got back, we decided to take a nap. We covered ourselves with a yellow wool blanket on my single mattress on the floor. The narrow bed seemed plenty large.

With the heaviness of sleep on our eyelids, I said, as though confessing, "Gauguin, my real name is Nell Schwartz."

"Yeah," he murmured, his head on the pillow.

"You see, I was with a group of friends, toasting marshmallows around a campfire near the Rio Grande. I forgot what we were talking about, but for some reason I said, 'Y'know, I like to look normal. I don't want people to think I'm a freak.'

"This guy named Neon looked up from the fire. 'You never fooled anyone, Nell. We all know you're bananas. I know! Let's call you Banana —no, Banana Rose, because right now is that time of rose sunset.'

"The name stuck." I smiled at Gauguin.

We fell asleep right after that.

We woke in the early evening. Gauguin said he'd been up for several minutes, looking around my room. "Why don't you show me some more of your paintings?" he asked. "And what's that fat black pillow over in the corner?"

"That's a sitting cushion. For meditating. Sometimes we all sit together. Neon, the man who named me, taught Happiness, and she taught all of us." I yawned and then answered his first question, "I'll show you more paintings later."

He moved a bit away from me so he could see me better. "Will you teach me how? I tried to meditate when I was living in the woods in northern Washington, but I wasn't sure what to do.''

"Sure, I'll show you. What were you doing in Washington?''

"It was four years ago. I wanted to learn the trumpet and kept trying to talk myself out of it. Finally I saw one for two hundred dollars in a hock shop, and I bought it. I said to myself, 'You spent the money for this, you're going to go off and learn it.' I had about fifty dollars left. I bought a bunch of supplies, lots of oatmeal, and headed for an abandoned shack I'd heard about. I practiced all day and ate simple.''

"Did you ever have any lessons?'' I asked. "How did you know what to do?''

"I just figured it out. Me and the horn. We became friends. I brought a book along. It didn't help much, though, because I couldn't read notes.'' Gauguin kissed my cheek. "How do you sit? Tell me.''

"I can't tell you. Let's get up and do it.'' We threw on some clothes. I gave Gauguin the zafu, and I used pillows for myself. "Here. You cross your legs like this.'' I crossed my legs. "You put your hands on your knees. Back straight.'' I leaned over and adjusted his chin and shoulders. "Relax. Now you just sit this way. Watch your breath go in and out. Thoughts will come. Keep coming back to the breath. Do you want to try fifteen minutes?''

"How long did you do it the first time?'' he asked.

"For thirty.''

"Well, then let's do it for thirty,'' he said eagerly.

"Okay, if you're sure. Oh, and don't worry if you have trouble staying with the breath. Our minds always wander.''

"Got it. Let's go.''

I smiled. He entered it like a race. Yeah, I thought, a race that goes noplace. There, I made a rhyme. I would tell him when the thirty minutes were up. Of course, when they were finally up, I'd forgotten. I was busy thinking about how much I liked him, about a really good pizza I had a week ago at the House of Taos, about how my foot had fallen asleep. I

17

glanced at the clock. Only fifteen minutes had passed. I wanted to touch Gauguin, but I had to wait fifteen more minutes. I remembered Aunt Ruth had once sued a five-and-ten-cent store because she found a piece of glass in her Coke. I think she collected $5,000. My nose itched. Should I scratch it? Naa, I wanted to show Gauguin how still I could sit.

2

"You know, sometimes I think I ought to change Banana Rose. Sometimes the kids at school call me Banana Split, and when my father heard the name, he said, 'You mean Banana Nose. You always had a big nose.' " I made a face and turned to Blue. "I don't have a big nose, do I?"

"No, sugar." She reached her hand out and touched my arm. "I can't believe your father said something like that. I think you're beautiful, honey. Those black curls all over your head—we ought to count them. There must be eight hundred." Blue moved some hair out of my eye.

I looked at her. "You're pretty beautiful yourself. I like your back best. When you dove into the reservoir once, I remember you reminded me of a leopard, lean and strong. And I like your cheekbones." I brushed my finger along her face.

We sat on two wood stumps outside her house, throwing scraps from last night's dinner to the chickens who pecked near our feet. Sylvester, the rooster, flew into Blue's lap.

I leaned over and petted him. He had those dinosaur kind of feet that could do you in if he wanted to, but he didn't have a mean bone in his body. He was so confident of his own beauty, he didn't need to challenge anyone. I loved his iridescent blue and green feathers.

Blue smiled and said, "Banana Rose is the perfect name for you, but change it if you want. I change my name whenever I think it's right. I'm an ever-changing identity. Once I looked up at the aspens in fall and said 'Golden Fruit'—that became my name that autumn. When winter came, I was Barbiturate. That's because that winter I was determined to see my own face. Every day after I dropped Lightning off at school, I took acid and crawled into the fireplace and sat there, touching the bricks, running my fingers along them."

"How can you find your own face? What did you expect to see?" I scrunched up *my* face. I didn't get it.

"That bricks are put together with cement." She laughed and shrugged. "I don't know. I didn't find anything. And then you can imagine, I'd have to pick Lightning up from school at three-thirty, and he'd want his friend Shannon to come home with him—you know Shannon, the kid who always had his finger in his nose?—and then they'd want to go to Frosty Freeze. I'd sit in the car while they slurped up chocolate milk shakes. This was after I spent the whole day in the fireplace."

We had moved to our garden and were bent over picking rocks from the soil. "Blue, do you think I'll ever see Gauguin again?" He had left two weeks earlier for Machu Picchu.

She stood up. "Sure, sugar, have faith."

I bent down again. That summer we had planted spinach, zucchini, garlic, onions, and tomatoes in the little plot on Talpa hill near Blue's house, next to the long crumbling adobe coop where old Hernandez used to keep chickens. The soil was fertile from the chicken shit.

Some mornings, I went up and meditated in that garden and once in a while Blue joined me. One day we sat so still in the climbing sunlight of dawn that two magpies landed on us, one on my shoulder, one on her right knee. We didn't move; we just let ourselves become one with them. It was in that silent sitting that I suddenly understood that Blue suffered. The pain wasn't about her living alone with her son in a poor dirt adobe. The truth was she was a New Orleans debutante and could have had a trust fund, but when she told her rich daddy that she was going to give it to the Black Panthers, they stopped payment as quick as the light caught on a horseshoe. She didn't care. Her suffering wasn't about money. She just had a storm inside her that kept her from fitting into her genteel Southern upbringing.

"Blue—" I stood up, my hands full of rocks. "Oh, never mind. It was about Gauguin again."

Before Blue moved to Taos, she'd lived with her husband in a big white colonial house. She told me once she was so unhappy, she'd tried to commit suicide. She bought a box of bonbons and went into the garage and turned on her car. As she sat there waiting to die, she carefully ate all the raspberry-filled chocolates first, because they were her favorites. Just as she was about to bite into a maple cream, the carbon monoxide started to choke her. Before that, she had been congratulating herself on what a lovely way she'd chosen to die. She'd even put on a red velvet dress with silver buttons, so she'd look good when she was found. She'd thought she might even float out over Louisiana and wave good-bye. But the carbon monoxide hurt. This was not for her. She turned off the car, got out, and went back in the house. In the living room she finished off the nut creams.

Two months later, Blue was thrown while riding her horse Guinevere. She broke her back and lay for eight weeks not able to move. During those weeks, lying so still, she realized she had to get out of the South or die. As soon as she was better, she picked up her son from school one Friday morning in her big Ford station wagon and headed west for California, where she thought everything was happening. In *Look* magazine she'd read about the hippies in Big Sur, Haight Ashbury, and Berkeley. She drove through hours of flat land, through the sagebrush of West Texas, and finally one evening stopped in Taos. She asked the long-haired attendant at the gas station, "Where's the communes?" and never left town.

We took a break in the shade of the abandoned chicken shack. "You know, B.R., love hurts. I don't know why it should be like that. Even if it's good, it hurts."

I nodded. I was twenty-six. Blue was thirty-one. I believed her. I missed Gauguin.

"Hey, what are you reading now?" I asked her. "I just finished a book by Willa Cather. Ever read her?"

"Didn't she write about Nebraska?" Blue flung two stones across the ditch. "Never been there."

"Me, either," I said.

Blue read a lot: Herbert Marcuse, Simone de Beauvoir, Henri Bergson, Aristotle, Mark Twain, Émile Zola. In winter, she spent whole afternoons at the Harwood library. Her little adobe had poor insulation, and the Harwood was warm. She'd close her eyes and run her finger along the book spines. Wherever her finger stopped was what she'd read for the week. She liked to sit me down and read me a paragraph. I could tell with each book she was realigning her thought system. But it was the novels that really caught her. She read a fictionalized account of the great Spanish matador Juan Belmonte, and sure enough, one day I found her near our garden with a red blanket, coaxing the pigweed to charge her.

She looked up from the pigweed when she became aware of my presence. "Banana, I've got to go to Valencia to train with the young bulls. That's how you begin."

I pointed at the long weeds and yelled, "Watch out! Don't take your eyes off them. They'll charge!"

A week later, I saw her at a party, standing by the guacamole, about to make a *quite:* legs and feet together, perfectly erect, ready for the charge of the bull. It was a dangerous moment, when the matador faced death at the horns of the great animal. Blue stood still and courageous.

The Belmonte book was thick. It took her a month to read it, so for a full month she was wholly a matador. I knew she'd finished it when I asked her one morning to tell me about the bravery of the Andalusian bulls. "Oh, I don't really care about that anymore. Come, see the pink stone I found in the hills." Her matador career had lasted as long as the book.

Then she read something about Stevie Wonder. Of course, she became blind. I tried to reason with her. "Look, Blue—"

"Please, call me Stevie," she interrupted.

"Look, Stevie. Shit, you're *not* Stevie!" I was exasperated.

"How do you know? I'm anything I want to be." She shook her head. "I'm Stevie Wonder. Could you please lead me over to my piano? I can't see the light."

"But you can read. If you were blind, you couldn't read," I again tried to reason.

She turned to me haughtily. "Each person who has lost the use of their eyes is given another gift to compensate. For Stevie Wonder, it was music. For Helen Keller, it was her brilliant mind. I was compensated for the loss of sight with my great ability to read."

I couldn't wait for her to finish that book, because while she was blind, she couldn't drive and I had to take Lightning to school each day.

Sometimes I thought Blue was nuts, but it was the kind of nuts I enjoyed. Plus I knew her kind of nuts also made her wise. I wanted so bad to believe what she said about Gauguin—that he would return. I said good-bye to Blue and walked down the hill to the Elephant House.

Gauguin had stayed with me for five days. He left on a Thursday. I said good-bye to him before I went to work. By lunch, I was surprised how lonesome I was for him.

After school that day, I went home and tried to paint. I repeated the words he had told me: " 'Just do it.' "

I painted the paper all brown, then with red stripes, then blotches of turquoise. I couldn't get anything going.

Suddenly, Blue appeared at my door. "Geez, honey, that's disgusting," she blurted out, and then put her hand to her mouth. "I'm sorry." She paused. "Well, what is it?" She cocked her head trying to make sense out of it. "Is it a dog? A cat?"

"No, it's a helicopter," I assured her. "You're right. It is disgusting. It's entitled, 'Gauguin Left.' " And I began to put away my acrylics, thinking how I hated painting. I didn't know how to do it. Whoever thought of being a painter, anyway? My mother said being a teacher and then getting married was just a fine thing for a girl to do. I wasn't a girl, though. My mother didn't understand. I was a monster. I didn't fit in. I wanted to be a painter.

Blue started to laugh. I turned my head. "I'll buy it if you come down from $2,000 to $1,500," she said.

"Never mind," I said, still grumpy. And then I lifted my brush and stroked a blue line across her forehead. "Ten dollars for this, please." I held out my palm and smiled.

Blue was quick. "It goes for fifty." She put her hands on her hips and pranced around the room.

Then she stopped and turned to me. "He'll be back," she said, and nodded.

3

"Okay, okay, Mom, I know. I'll be real nice to Rita while she's here," I said into the phone.

"Don't just be nice. Knock some sense into her, Nell. We don't know what to do with her. Please do something. You're the oldest. . . ."

I'd heard this all before. I picked at the peeling green paint on the table as my mother harangued me long distance. The more she talked, the more I wanted to murder Rita. I was sitting in the staff room at the Red Willow School. I looked at the clock. In five minutes, I had to go back to my class of fifth graders.

"Mom, don't keep calling me here. I'm at work," I said. "Look, I wasn't put in jail—Rita was. Stop nagging me."

"Well, your so-called commune doesn't have a phone. How am I supposed to talk with you?" my mother demanded.

"Don't. Write letters," I offered brightly.

"Never mind. A mother needs to be in contact with her daughter. Please, Nell—"

"I know, I know. Rita! Take care of Rita. Look, I have to go. Sure, I love you, too." I hung up the phone. It was two days before Thanksgiving. I heaved a long sigh and went to the door of my classroom. Most of the kids I taught had hippie parents. Four of the children in my group of twelve had dropped acid at least once and probably more. Curly-haired Janice had told me her mother gave her acid on her seventh birthday and they tripped together for the whole afternoon, watching the water at the Rio Chiquita.

My mother and I had had trips, too, I thought: to Macy's, to Fortunoff's, to Abraham and Straus, and then always, after the shopping spree, to Micky's on our corner for ice cream sodas.

Just yesterday the kids in class had asked me about my childhood, and I told them about playing school with my grandfather in the living room of the apartment we shared with my grandparents in Brooklyn. Some of them weren't sure what an apartment was—they lived in rambling, run-down adobes surrounded by fields or in communes, and two lived in log cabins up Kit Carson Road. So I described the fire escape off the kitchen, the dark-green-flowered wall-to-wall carpet, the smell of boiling chicken from the apartment across the hall, the sound of locks clicking into place after the slam of the neighboring apartment door, the footsteps of the people in apartment 3C above us, and the silver bugs that scuttled across the linoleum in the kitchen.

I'd say to my grandfather, "Sam, you got your addition wrong. Now go to the corner," and he would stand up, take off his spectacles, and walk slowly to the corner of the room, pretending to weep.

"You were mean," Ronnie called out.

"I was a strict teacher. Sam had to learn to add," I teased.

"And then what? And then what?" they would ask eagerly whenever I talked of my childhood.

Once I told them how my cousins and my sister and I sat out on the stoop.

"What's a stoop?" Mirabai asked.

So I explained stoop and curb, getting the picture just right. I set up blocks like they were steps in front of our apartment house and sat on them.

"When we all were out on this stoop, we'd bend over with stones in

our hands and smash caps.'' I bent over and pretended to smash at
something. I told them about the thin strips of red paper dotted with
infinitesimal portions of gunpowder, and how when you hit the dots just
right, they would ignite with a sharp sound and emit the smell of smoke.
Some of them had played with caps, but they were surprised I had.

Then I explained to them about the newspaper stands on the corners
in the city and how in Brooklyn, when the rain pelted our street, the
drops would bounce when they hit concrete. My sister and I would splash
in the river that ran in the gutter.

"And your sister? Did you love her?" Sage asked.

"Yes, I loved her, but sometimes I was mean to her. I'd hide from
her in the alleys, and she would be scared all alone between high buildings." Emile and Coyote snickered. "But I did love her."

The Greyhound bus was late that afternoon. I stood in the slow Taos rain
that was trying to be snow and waited for Rita. I breathed in deeply and
looked around. I could hardly see Taos Mountain. It was misty gray, like
in a Japanese painting. I'd come to Taos a year and a half before with an
old boyfriend named Nicky. We broke up two months after we got here.
He left, and I stayed on. I'd known it was my home the moment I saw the
mountain.

It figured Rita was late. Even though I knew it couldn't be her fault
—after all, she was on a bus—it felt like her fault just the same. She was
always late. I stuck a piece of chewing gum in my mouth.

Then I saw the bus in the foggy distance. It pulled up in front of me,
and as soon as the door opened, Rita fell out. I caught her in my arms.
The driver threw her knapsack out after her and I caught it.

"Good-bye," he yelled with a good-riddance voice.

"What was that about?" I asked.

"Oh, nothing." Rita waved her hand dismissingly.

"C'mon, it wasn't nothing." Rita had beautiful long black wavy hair
that frizzed out like Jimi Hendrix's, and she always wore silver sneakers.

"I was just singing in the bus a lot, and someone complained, and I asked the passengers to take a vote. I won, and so I kept on singing. Then I lost my wallet in Pueblo, Colorado, where we made a pit stop, and I wouldn't let the bus leave until I found it. After everyone searched for fifteen minutes, I found it in my pocket."

"So you were why the bus was late?" I asked.

"Naw, it was an awful driver. He was so slow." She turned her head around. "So this is Taos. It's so small."

"My car's over here," I said, toting her bag.

I took her to dinner at the House of Taos.

"This restaurant is dark," she said.

I looked around. "It's adobe, and they did a thin wash with straw and sand over the adobe bricks. They have great pizza. Let's get a green chile. It's my favorite."

"This place feels like jail." She made a face.

"Look, Rita, it's a great place. It's not New York, okay?" I felt that old crunch in my stomach. It was a cross between rage and claustrophobia. It made me want to run. I'd been feeling it since I was a young kid, so I bolted from Brooklyn as soon as I could and went away to college in Michigan. Since then, I'd only been back home for a week or two at a time for visits.

"So what was it like in Kearney?" I asked, as a way to shift the energy from Taos.

"How would I know? I only saw a cell. Look at all the weight I lost." She showed me the waistband on her pants.

"Well, let's order a large. You want anything else? A malt, salad?"

"Yeah," she cheered a bit. "Everything. How 'bout a beer?"

"They don't have a liquor license." I made a gesture at a smile.

"Brother! This place is a honky-tonk—"

I cut her off and called over the waitress. "We'll have a large green chile, extra cheese." I turned to Rita and took charge. "Do you want a chocolate malt?" She nodded. "And a salad with blue cheese. We'll share it."

Rita told me how she and four friends had been driving through Kearney at 3 A.M., high on Quaaludes. They were headed for California and had stopped in a café. "You could just see it," she said, slurping her malt.

Just then the waitress placed the pizza before us. Rita pulled some of the cheese off a slice and put it in her mouth. "Five wired freaks from the Big Apple stop for OJ. The café owner took one look at us and called the cops while we were sucking juice at the counter."

"You were wearing your silver sneakers, I presume?"

She nodded, laughing.

"And your hair was way out, no doubt?"

She nodded again. "And Calvin had painted a cross on my forehead. I guess it was still showing." She smiled.

"I guess it was," I said like a lawyer. God, I hated playing the part of the big sister. I had my own life, but around my family I always fell back into the same role.

But I couldn't stop myself. "And so how long were you there?"

"Two weeks. Man, I thought I'd die. Daddy started to cry when he heard. I got one call home when they busted us. Mom screamed, 'This is the final straw!' I don't know what she was so uptight about. It wasn't my fault."

I just nodded. I would have liked to put my hands around her throat. Instead, I paid the bill for the food and we left.

That night Rita wanted to stay up late. I had to teach the next day, so I loaned her my car.

"Careful," I said as I handed her the keys. Why did I have to say that? It sounded so square. I sounded like our mother—but, after all, it was my car and Rita had been known to take Mom's car, run out of gas, and then just abandon it at the roadside.

Rita's eyes glazed over as she took the keys. "Sure."

Maybe I should go with her, I thought. It's her first night here, she just got out of jail. But Rita grabbed her coat and in a flash was out the door.

I went in the bathroom to brush my teeth. I looked in the mirror. Rita and I looked alike, but my nose was bigger. Her chin was wider. She was three inches taller. I don't know how that was possible. After all, she was the *little* sister.

Hey, cut that out, I said to myself. No big, no little. We're both in our twenties.

I squeezed co-op mint toothpaste onto my gold toothbrush.

Happiness knocked at the door. "Come in," I called, and put the brush in my mouth.

We both stood facing the mirror. "So that's your sister, huh?"

I nodded, my mouth full of paste.

"You look alike, but you're different. I mean, I don't know, she seems tough."

I spat out the paste and turned my head to face her. "You only met her for a minute."

"It feels like she's casing the joint or something, and she doesn't look you in the eye." Happiness paused awkwardly. "But hey, Banana, what do I know?"

I just nodded. I didn't want to get into it. I pulled out a long piece of floss and leaned close to the mirror. "Look at this pimple," I said. "It's almost ready to squeeze."

The next day, Rita and I walked into town. My right back tire was flat when I went out to get in the car. Rita swore she didn't know how it happened. She said the car had been fine when she left it in the drive at one in the morning. Luckily, I didn't have to be at school until ten that day.

"Well, Nelly, here we are. Riteey and her sissy. Just the two of us." She took my hand and swung it, like a schoolgirl. "I'm glad I'm coming with you. I'd get bored at that commune. You don't have a phone, a TV, or music. I don't know how you live that way."

We were walking along a narrow two-way road. Taos Mountain wore a necklace of clouds, with the blue peak high above them.

"Gee, Riteey, since you're my sissy, will you fix the tire while I'm at school? Then you can drive and pick me up afterward. Doc's Automotive is near Red Willow." I was feeling better. I wasn't taking all the responsibility. "And then we'll have some time together. I can show you some of my paintings, and maybe you can even pose for one."

"I never changed a flat tire before. I don't know, Nell. Don't you have a friend?" she whined.

"Nope, no friends." I was beginning to enjoy myself. "You have five hours to do it. I'm sure you can figure something out. Right, sissy?" I ruffled her hair.

The sky was so blue, so beautiful. I thought of pointing it out, but I declined. I bet Rita could find something wrong with it. It wasn't L.A. or New York. It had no pollution; it wasn't gray; it didn't smell; it was too big; it was a waste of space.

Just then, Neon pulled up behind us in his electric pink jeep. He had a yellow rubber chicken dangling from his rearview mirror.

"Hey, Banana, need a ride?" He stuck his head out the window, all shaggy with curls like a lion's. His head was too big for his body, he had narrow shoulders and a small chest.

Rita lit up. "Yeah!" she cried, and ran to the passenger seat. The old jeep jangled and jumped and chugged even in idle. We had to speak loudly to be heard. Rita yelled at Neon, "Nell has a flat. I told her I'd fix it while she's at school. Maybe you could help?"

I rolled my eyes to the roof in the back seat as we passed the tortilla shop.

"Sure enough. I'll take care of it." Neon smiled gallantly.

"Hey, why don't we all go to the boogie together tonight? I could pick you up at eight." Neon swiveled his head around to look at me as he turned onto Taos Highway.

"Hey, watch it!" I yelled.

Neon turned his oversize head back slowly. "Banana, you seem nervous. Don't you worry. Neon can drive."

"He certainly can," Rita chimed in as she lit a joint in the front seat.

"Well, don't forget the tire," I said. As I climbed out in front of the school, Neon was handing the joint back to Rita.

"Oh, we won't." Rita waved as they pulled away.

That night, I wore a red dress I had found in the co-op free box two weeks before, and my sister wore lots of jewelry and a skin-tight sweater dress.

"You're fit to kill," I told her. It was a line I'd heard from our father. She smiled in the mirror and applied silver glitter to her cheekbones. We were leaving in a few minutes for the boogie. I could hear Neon's jeep in the distance.

Martinez Hall was across from the Ranchos Church and it was jammed. Everyone I knew was there, including half of my fifth graders with their parents.

Blue walked over and pinched me on the butt.

I swung around. "Blue!" I gave her a big hug. "And Lightning!" I grabbed him. He was wearing his black wool cap. He never took it off—not in school, not to go to the bathroom, not to sleep. He was shy and squirmed away, held up his hand solemnly and said, "Hi." I could barely hear him. The band was tuning up.

"I want to meet your sister," Blue said.

Where was Rita? I looked around. She was gone. I knew where. "You just wait here. I'll find her in a sec."

I elbowed my way through the crowd to the bar in the back. Rita was handing cash to the bartender and reaching for a margarita.

"Rita, I want you to meet some friends." I grabbed her by the wrist.

"Easy, easy. You're going to knock over my drink."

"Rita, promise me you'll only drink three tonight."

"Sure, sis, sure."

I looked around. I'd lost Blue.

The band began its first number. Rita gulped down her drink and began to move. It was always hot in here. Neon danced near me, wearing only a vest, no shirt, and his arms were already gleaming with sweat. Tiny passed by, flinging his head of long straight hair. I liked the pungent smell of bodies mixed with the scents of cotton and leather, the wood of the building, the crisp air outside that occasionally blew in in sweeps of cold through the open side doors. I was happy. I hooked my arm into Rita's when she whirled by, and we moved our hips together for a while.

"Sissy," she screamed in my ear. "This is fun!"

I yelled back, "So Taos isn't so bad?"

She made a face that meant, I wouldn't say that, but just for now I'm enjoying myself.

We danced ourselves into oblivion. Chairs took up space, so the hall had no chairs. If you were in the hall, you were dancing. If you needed a break, you went outside. No one danced as a couple. We each moved to our own energy, communicating with the music, sometimes in sync with someone for a few moments until the energy moved on. You weren't a good dancer or a bad dancer. You just danced and followed the patterns of sound and light from blinking projectors. I felt the hall's height when I flung my head back at a particularly wild beat of the band. The ceiling was held up by huge vigas made of ponderosa pine.

Rita danced by again and kissed me. I was two years older than Rita, but in high school she had been more popular. She had a lot of friends. None of them did well in school; they were always on the phone with each other or practicing new dance steps in the living room. I was quiet at home and pretended I was above caring about clothes and rock 'n' roll, but secretly it bothered me that I didn't know how to dance. I couldn't ask Rita, though. I was afraid she'd make fun of me, that I wasn't "hip." And besides, you never ask your little sister anything.

In my third year of college, I had a boyfriend who was like a witch. Russell knew things about people. He knew I didn't know how to dance without my telling him, and at the first party we went to he didn't let me hesitate when the music started. He grabbed my hand and pulled me onto the dance floor. "That's it," he kept repeating in my ear when we came close to each other. He led, and I followed. It felt like the first time I'd been on ice skates without holding on to my father's arm. Just out there on the ice all by myself. I was finally out there dancing! First, I felt wonder—it wasn't even that hard. Then I felt awe—why had I been so scared before?

"Good, Nell, good," Russell whispered again. I wanted to dance forever, to make up for all those years I'd hid away in high school. By the end of the night, I'd become a go-go girl or a backup dancer for the Supremes. I loved my body.

When I moved out to Taos four and a half years later, everyone danced like they were electrical strobe lights flashing on and off. I jumped right in and moved my body to totally new dimensions. By then, I'd begun painting, and all I wanted to do was to capture that feeling on paper. A realistic approach would never work—it would be too corny— so I tried abstraction. But I had trouble getting it on paper in the abstract because I wasn't good enough.

Here I go, starting to criticize myself again, I thought. Just then, Lightning bumped into me. I grabbed him and whirled him around. Even as he was turning, he pretended I wasn't there. I was an adult to Lightning, I suddenly realized. I was a teacher at his school, and adults weren't cool. Mostly I felt like a kid inside, maybe twelve, sometimes seven. I felt younger and younger living in Taos.

Too quickly, it was one in the morning and we were standing outside. The heat and sweat of my body met the edge of cold under the heavy sweater that I'd pulled over my head. Neon had parked the jeep up on a dirt patch near the Hall, and it was rattling and chugging in place, his rubber chicken bouncing in time to the motor.

"Cannon has to warm up a bit," Neon said. He wore an ankle-length purple velvet cape, buttoned at the neck.

"Sure, sure," we all said, our breath fogging at our mouths. Most people were still in there dancing or had gone. We were giving Blue and Lightning a ride home.

Suddenly, a long low blue Chevy full of local teenagers drove up and stopped abruptly, nose to nose with the jiggling Cannon. An empty beer bottle sailed out the driver's window and smashed against the foundation of the Hall. I grabbed Rita by the arm as I heard a yell of "Go!" All four car doors flew open, and six kids dashed out, grabbed Neon, and spun him around so his cape floated out in back of him. We all stood frozen. The black sky was broken by stars. The music chopped out of the wooden front doors. The sharp November air cut through my lungs as I screamed, "Leave him alone!"

Neon stumbled and then held out his hands. "Listen, we're all brothers."

Rita crept behind me toward the Hall.

The skinny kid who drove the car—he was no more than sixteen—spat in Neon's face. Then they all ran, jumped in the four open doors of their car, and zoomed down the road, yelling, *"Pendejos!"* out the windows, their back wheels spitting gravel at us.

Blue ran over to Neon and grabbed him by the arm. "You okay? You okay, sugar? Say something so I know you're okay."

"Yeah, yeah, I'm okay." Neon put his hand on Blue's shoulder.

I walked up slowly. I was afraid Neon would feel humiliated.

He didn't, though. He looked down the road. "They don't see we're all one, do they?"

"Maybe it's the cape, Neon. Or the color of your jeep, or your funky chicken," I joked. We all laughed and it seemed to ease things.

"You're not hurt, are you?" I asked.

"No." He shook his head. "Only here," and he put his hand over his heart. I thought he was kidding, but I looked at his face and saw he meant it.

Rita emerged from where she had hidden behind the open door of the hall. "Whew, this is a weird town. I'm glad I'm leaving soon. There's trouble here."

"Let's go home," I said, turning toward the still-chugging jeep, trying to ignore Rita's comment, "before it runs out of gas."

We all sat quietly in the car, passing the night shadows of buildings along the road. A dog appeared at the turn by the Talpa Elementary School and tried to bite the tire and then receded into the darkness.

We let off Blue and Lightning just below the hill to their house. Blue hesitated, as if she wanted to say something. Then I could see she thought better of it and let the door shut.

We drove to the Elephant House farther down the hill. Rita complained about being cold and jumped out of the car as soon as it stopped in front of the commune.

"Good night, Neon." I turned to him and said it quietly. I put my hand on his knee. It was a gesture of gentleness. I felt mixed up about him; he was a fool and a huge human being all at once.

He took my gesture as a come-on and tried to kiss me. I could tell it wasn't one of our usual friendly greeting kisses. It was meant to be more serious, but his eyes closed too quickly and he missed my lips. Instead he kissed the air near my ear as he tried to aim for my face. He didn't see that I'd moved my head.

"Neon," I said. "That's not what's happening between us."

He was good-natured. He nodded and said, "Okay, Banana. I understand."

When I got into bed that night, I reread the single postcard I'd gotten two weeks earlier from Gauguin. The card pictured a donkey wearing a hat. His handwriting was hard to read. He was at a small beach town, practicing music and eating cheap shrimp. "I'm thinking of you," he wrote. And he signed it "Love." I put the card under my pillow and fell asleep.

4

I drove Rita to the bus station the morning after Thanksgiving. It was early and shadows were long. It hadn't snowed yet, but it felt like it would soon. Rita was still groggy. We were late, so there was no time for her to make coffee at the house.

"You should have planned and gotten up earlier," I told her as I gassed it around the curve.

"Oh, Nell, don't start," she whined.

"I'm afraid you'll miss your bus," I said.

"I'm not missing that bus. Maybe there's a coffee machine at the station. Great! I can have leaky brown piss."

"Or you can just go back to sleep on the bus," I suggested.

She groaned. "All the way to New York with no java. Nell, get me some!"

The bus was late. She got her coffee. After a fast hug, I watched her climb the bus steps. My eye caught her leg—she was wearing a short, tight skirt and black tights, and her calf was thick and chunky. It had always been that way. She was a great runner. My sister! A flood of feeling rushed through me. Then the bus pulled away and she waved from the back seat.

I walked across the plaza. No one was around. I felt a little melan-

choly, but I cheered up when I entered Señor Murphy's Candy Shoppe. I
chose a piñon crunch there. If I had gotten an almond crunch it would
have been cheaper, but the piñon ones tasted better. Also, piñon nuts
were local.

"Isn't it awfully early to eat candy?" The old woman behind the
counter smiled at me.

"No, it seems a perfect time and perfect that you're open," I teased
back.

I reached for the square held in tissue paper and walked out the
door. Strips of bells were hung on it for Christmas, and they jingled
uproariously as I left. My sister was gone.

I drove back to Talpa slowly, savoring my candy, looking at Taos
spread out to my right. I felt the relaxation of having the whole weekend
free before me. I'd gotten through my time with her. That's the most I
could say. Rita never did see my paintings, and I don't think she cared. I
doubt I had imparted any wisdom to her either, as my mother would have
liked. Hell, I laughed to myself, I think my wild and crazy sister ended up
being freaked out by the place. I suddenly realized my mother would have
felt the same way. I got a sweet revenge from that thought, and then it
was tinged by an emptiness.

When I got to my house, I pulled out my paints. Yellow, I thought. I
have to make a painting that color and I want the feeling of a rooster in it.
I squeezed lemon yellow onto the palette and then a dab of green, orange,
and for some reason black. Then black led me to squeezing on vermilion,
which led to a very dull olive. I felt suddenly as though something were
pulling me down someplace far away from my original rooster.

"Hey, Banana, come quick! There's someone at the door," Happiness yelled into my room.

Why can't she just go answer it herself? I thought, but I carefully
placed my palette on the nearby table and headed through the kitchen.

It was Gauguin! He was tanned, a pack on his back, his arms
stretched out toward me.

"I missed you, Rose." He grabbed me as he closed his eyes. "I'm so glad to see you."

"Gauguin——" Stunned, I couldn't think of anything else to say.

Then I stepped back, so I could see that it was really him. Yes, there was that wide nose, the red eyebrows, the scar across his chin, and those glasses—I reached for them. "Still didn't get them fixed, huh?"

He became shy. "Yeah, and I'm running out of masking tape."

We laughed.

"I missed you, too." I finally got it out. "Missed you a lot."

We were back in each other's arms. His glasses dangled down his back in my right hand.

Gauguin stepped away and looked at my face. He was nervous. "I missed you the whole time. I got to Machu Picchu and stood on my head, and all I could think was, 'Nell, Nell, Banana Rose, Rose, Nell, Banana.' I had to go all the way to the Andes to realize what I wanted. I wanted you."

I nodded. When we kissed, I saw those stars again, the ones I saw when I stepped on the rake way back when I first met him, and I felt water, all kinds—rivers, streams, oceans—run through me.

5

Three weeks after Gauguin moved back, we drove around the Bosque del Apache, a huge bird sanctuary south of Albuquerque. Gauguin hummed—no, he sang that tune I loved, that spiritual about going to heaven someday. The man in the song doesn't know when it will be, he may be way across the sea. I loved the way Gauguin held the notes. It was like pouring honey out of a green glass jar. From time to time I looked over at him. He wore a crumpled white shirt, stained khaki pants, and a pair of old policeman's black high-top boots he'd found at the Goodwill in Minneapolis before he moved to Taos. We blasted the heat in the truck— that was one good thing about that white truck—old Betsy Boop had a great heater, so we didn't have to wear jackets. We could just mosey around the Bosque all afternoon and be comfortable and look at birds. I had a bird book on my lap and a pair of borrowed binoculars. Gauguin had just bought the fourteen-year-old pickup, and we had come to the Bosque to celebrate his purchase.

We drove at the most twenty miles per hour. All around the reserve the hills and mountains were volcanic rock. I spotted a blue heron. When that dinosaur bird lifted its great wings, I imagined we were back before Christ and all the commotion about religion. Gauguin and I were cave people on our faithful mastodon, the White Nostril. I told Gauguin this.

He paused, then cocked his head in a way that I knew something funny was about to come out. "You know, Banana Rose, I'm Li'l Abner, and you're a little abnormal."

I grew more and more in love with Gauguin, but especially I loved his mind. Out of the blue, I turned to him. "Gauguin, what do you think the difference is between a man and a woman?"

He bit a nail off his pinky that was bothering him. "I don't know. Why'd you ask?"

"I want to know. What's it like to be sitting next to me and be a man?"

"Pass me the water bottle. It's on the floor." He pulled over, and as the motor jiggled in idle, he unscrewed the cap and drank. I knew he was thinking. He handed the bottle back to me. "Banana, I guess I don't feel that much different than you. I know I'm a man and you're a woman"— he shrugged his shoulders—"but sometimes I feel such tenderness for you—for your cheek or your small hand. When I'm kissing your breast, I feel so much wonder, I almost become a woman, like I melt into you."

That was sweet, but I wanted more. "Yeah, but what's the difference?"

"I'm not sure what the difference is—maybe there isn't any deep down. Sometimes I feel uptight that I feel like a woman. My dad's real macho. He always wore the pants in the family, you know, master of the house and all that shit. I never felt like that. Maybe I loved my mother too much."

Gauguin had told me that as a boy he'd played army all the way through age fourteen. His mother worried that he should have grown out of it earlier. He often made the sounds of the different guns for me—he could imitate twenty-one different gun shots. "Here's a bullet that ricochets off a tin roof, goes through a glass window, hits a cookie jar, and then sinks into the buttocks of a cheesecake on the table." He motored up his mouth, puttered, spurted, and ran his tongue along the side of his cheek.

He had also told me that in junior high he'd gotten into a lot of fistfights because he was one of the only white boys in the North Minneapolis school. "Hey, White Paddy, what you up to?" Clarence cuffed him in the head. It was the sixth cuff he'd received that morning, changing classes from algebra to French to woodworking. They were on the long gray stairs heading up to the third floor. The cold light of February beamed through the high windows above the stairwell. First warning bell rang, which meant you'd better be getting to your fourth-period class.

Gauguin had flung down his Latin book, the one with a picture on the cover of Caesar wearing a toga and braided thongs, and turned to face Clarence, who stood on the stair below him. With his bony young freckled hand clenched in a fist, he hit Clarence's small black face with all his might. "I hit him so hard, blood spurted from his nose and flew against the white wall. I was crying so hard I couldn't see straight."

Clarence grabbed the shoulders of Gauguin's shirt and flung him down the stairs, but Clarence kept holding on to Gauguin, so he went with him. They were a ball on the second-floor landing when the principal arrived in his high-shined black shoes.

" 'Young men, what are you doing?' " Gauguin had imitated the principal. "Can you imagine, he called us 'men'?"

When Gauguin's mother arrived to fetch him in the principal's office—he and Clarence had both been suspended for a week—he told her, "I'm not going back. That's it." He'd meant it. His parents knew about Gauguin's stubbornness. In the spring, they moved out to the suburbs.

I remembered that when Gauguin told me this story, I said, "Gee, I've never in my whole life punched anyone."

Maybe that was the difference between a girl and a boy, I mused as Betsy Boop continued in idle. But then I remembered Blue telling me about the mean fight she once had with her husband. She smashed a wooden chair over his head and then dove on top of it. I turned to Gauguin, sitting behind the steering wheel, and told him about Blue. "Can you imagine?" I asked.

"Sure, I can," he replied, "but I guess I didn't realize women did it, too."

So that wasn't the difference. We both could punch. I thought I'd practice punching as soon as I got home.

At that moment I hoped I would spy a golden eagle. "Gauguin, let's get out for a while. It's too early for the evening feeding."

We turned off the motor and put on our jackets. We sat out in the dried grass. I yanked on some tough old dead weeds.

"You know, Banana, sometimes when you come home from work and I've been practicing music all day, I feel like a woman, too. Real soft and receptive." He paused. He was staying with me at the commune. The space was small, but we liked being close. "Maybe you should support me." Then he threw his hand across his mouth as if he had just said something dirty, but his eyes were laughing.

"Gauguin, I'm glad you feel like a woman, because I feel mostly like a man. When we get home, I want you to do the dishes." Then I threw my hand over my mouth.

"How do you feel like a man?" Gauguin asked.

"I don't know. Sometimes I'd like to go to war with everything—fight, punch, throw a bomb in a department store. Sometimes I walk down the street and hope someone will attack me, so I can tear them to smithereens."

"But you've never even hit anyone," Gauguin commented.

"Maybe that's why I want to. I want to be Kung Fu King who fights Godzilla and then eats his legs." I sat straight up, engrossed in a vision in front of me. "I want to be a guerrilla fighter in the Amazon and carry grenades in my mouth. I want to save Jews in Auschwitz and break the head of every Nazi." My fists were clenched. Gauguin stared at me with his mouth hanging open. "I want to ride a great white stallion and go off into the hills like the Lone Ranger. I want to walk into a bar in Manila wearing green army fatigues, sit down and drink six whiskeys straight, then turn around and punch the man next to me. We have a brawl and someone gets thrown through the double plate-glass window, and I swing from the chandelier.''

I flung my head back. "I want to be a matador, a train conductor, head of the FBI, President of the United States, the King of England. Goddamn it, Gauguin''—I turned to him—"I-want-to-be-Ernest-Hemingway. I-want-to-be-Miles-Davis. I-want-to-be-Picasso.'' I said these last words with a staccato clarity that stunned me into reality. "I want to be the greatest writer, musician, and painter in America!''

But I wasn't a writer, and Gauguin was the musician. I was just learning how to paint. Those were men artists anyway. Where did I fit in? I stood up and threw my hands above my head. "I am King Kong on the Empire State Building. I have the American Constitution written by all men in my mouth, and I am about to eat it.''

Suddenly I remembered where I was—the Bosque. I looked around and saw Gauguin walking down by the marsh about a hundred yards away. I called to him. A minute later, he returned.

"Come on,'' Gauguin said as though nothing had happened. "We should head for the feeding grounds.''

I'd almost spoiled a good day. I decided to shut up and get in the pickup.

Betsy Boop started right up. Already we could see the snow geese and the sandhill cranes in the distance. Their great white wings flapped against the red sky at sunset. We pulled over to the side of the road. Gauguin threw himself out of the truck and clapped over his head. "What a symphony!'' he yelled.

I watched as though I were a dreamer. Some of them skidded onto the surface and then settled into the water as if they were sitting down on a couch. There were Canada geese, mallards, and a few rare whooping cranes standing on slender legs and leaning over like young girls in ballet class. Swans swam around the edges like lace. This was winter. Dark blue water, white feathers, and a sky that had gone nuts with color. I could feel the bite of cold.

Gauguin returned to the truck to get his green down jacket, and I

opened my door, got out, and joined him by the shore. All these white
wonderful birds, and my attention was fixed on Gauguin in his green
duckling jacket. I remembered a story he had told me at the top of Talpa
Mountain. Not a story really, because it had no ending. More like some
heat you keep in your mind, the same as if an iron pressed only one place
on your shirt.

It was when Gauguin was a kid, maybe ten years old. He loved to
catch salamanders. Once in late September, he was out in the back yard of
his grandmother's Iowa farm with his head down watching for a salaman-
der to appear. He was in full concentration and wandered out past the
wheat field into an abandoned orchard. Suddenly, when he lifted his eyes
from the ground, he saw a tremendous yellow light at the other end of the
orchard, like the burning bush Moses saw. He thought something was on
fire. Instantly he began running toward it. When he got close, he stopped
short and sucked in his breath.

It was a rabble of monarch butterflies, thousands of them, all feeding
on the rotting pears that hung from the branches or had fallen to the
ground. The monarchs filled the entire tree and all the area around it. He
said his whole boyhood was in that moment. Nothing was before or after.
His body opened, and the frail yellow animals fed on his heart.

D arkness moved in on the Bosque. We became cold and went back to
Betsy Boop, our white bird of flight. The road out of the Bosque was long,
thin, and very flat. It ended at The Crane, a restaurant where everyone
went for hamburgers and to look over their bird books to count how
many different kinds of birds they had seen. Gauguin and I went in The
Crane, too. There was a stuffed owl standing on a ledge over the front
door.

We sat at a booth with spongy red cushions and leaned our elbows
on the wood table carved full of messages. One said, "I'm from Oak-la-
Coma." I nodded at it and said to Gauguin, "This person doesn't like
where he comes from."

Gauguin reached across the table. I felt his hot hands on my cold ones. He brought my hands to his mouth and blew on them.

I smiled at him and said, "I love you."

"Me, too. It was a great day. Wish we didn't have such a long ride home tonight. Are you going to get a hamburger?" he asked jokingly. We were both vegetarians.

I wrinkled up my nose and shook my head. "Let's see a menu." I ordered a grilled cheese, and Gauguin had green chile stew. We weren't much up for talking. A young boy with a crew cut sat next to his father at the next booth. The father had a crew cut, too. I leaned over and whispered across the table to Gauguin, "I think they are from Oak-la-Coma." Gauguin smiled and nodded. The waitress served us. My sandwich was on a white plate with potato chips on the side.

I was halfway through eating when I held up my grilled cheese and said, "Did I ever tell you about how I learned to make one of these?"

Gauguin bit into a flour tortilla and shook his head.

"It was Christmas vacation—I guess I was about fifteen—and my parents flew me down to Miami Beach where my grandparents were spending the winter. They were staying in a one-room efficiency with a roll-out bed and a small gas stove at the Carlyle Hotel on Collins Avenue. Everyone at the hotel was old. In fact, everyone in the whole Collins Avenue area was old. It was my first plane flight and my first time in Miami. The first night I was there, I called my parents long distance and cried, 'I'm taller than everyone here.'

"To cheer me up, my grandmother walked with me the five full blocks to Wolfie's. Wolfie's was a fancy delicatessen with rotating cream cakes on display in glass windows. Grandpa stayed home. He never went out to eat. He drank two-day-old coffee black and ate stale white bread. He used paper napkins that were folded and refolded many times, because he could not waste anything.

"The waitress placed a full bucket of dill pickles and a basket of poppyseed rolls at our table, even before we looked at the menu. Grandma ordered cabbage soup. She bent her small cabbage head over the bowl to bring the spoon to her mouth. I ate flanken in barley soup. Flanken's a meat that gets real soft in soup. The waiter kept filling our water glasses, even if we took only one sip.

"When we returned to the efficiency, I smelled the boiled chicken my grandmother made every day. The smell was in the air all the time. I said, 'Grandma, I don't want to eat chicken.'

"Putting her hand to her mouth, she said, 'But darling, what will you eat?' Hot dogs, hamburgers never entered her mind. She didn't get frantic, though. You'd think she would have, since chicken was the only thing she made in those days, and if I ever refused food, she was afraid I would immediately go into a coma.

"We put sheets on the little cot they had for me and we all went to sleep. The next morning, I was awakened by the rattling of paper. Grandma had walked to the grocery store four blocks away. 'Come,' she said. 'I'll show you what I bought.' There was a loaf of white bread, Kraft American cheese presliced in squares and wrapped individually in cellophane, and a carton of milk. 'I'll teach you to make a grilled cheese sandwich. You can make them whenever you want.' My face lit up. I'd never made one before. We cooked it in her thin tin frying pan and used a white dinner plate for a lid so the cheese would melt. I went mad for those sandwiches. I made at least three a day, and whenever we ran out of cheese and bread, my grandmother and I would walk to the grocer together.

"One night I woke up at midnight—we went to bed about 9:30 every night. I snuck over to the stove in my white cotton nightgown with yellow embroidered daisies, and by the streetlight coming through the window, I made a grilled cheese sandwich. This time I even used two slices of cheese. As I was waiting over the pan for the butter to melt, I heard my grandfather whisper, 'What's she doing?' My grandmother said, 'Shh, let her,' and they turned over and went back to sleep. So there I had full permission to learn a thing and do it whenever I wanted. I waited until the cheese melted out of the sides of the bread, and with a spatula I put it on a plate and sat by the small kitchen table and looked out the window at Collins Avenue. The Carlyle Hotel sign blinked pink over and over again. I didn't cut the sandwich in half. I ate it whole in the humid heat of Miami Beach, with the heaven of my grandparents snoring nearby. It was the most wonderful grilled cheese I ever had.''

"Better than mine? With avocado, tomatoes, and green chile?'' Gauguin teased.

"Yes, the best I ever had.'' I nodded.

6

It was a rainy Saturday in April, and I was acutely aware that Taos was
not Brooklyn. Now, most of the time I was glad of this, but when it
rained on a Saturday, I wanted a matinee movie. There was only one
movie theater in Taos and that theater had a peculiar affinity to only one
movie, *Jaws,* and they only played that at seven and nine in the evening.
You watched the movie eating stale popcorn out of a round cardboard
container. Once in a while, on a Tuesday evening out of the blue, they'd
sneak in a Russ Meyer flick, something like *Faster, Pussycat! Kill! Kill!,* and
Gauguin and I would sit in the audience and eat our stale popcorn faster
and faster.

It didn't rain much in Taos. The Anglos of Taos couldn't handle it.
Most of us were refugees from the outside world, and a slight change in
weather shook our delicate balance with the universe. If it rained, Blue
headed for her fireplace and sat inside it all day, and Big Barney moved his
curtain a quarter of an inch from the window, saw clouds, and went back
to sleep instead of going on a wood run near Tres Piedras.

So what was I, Nell Schwartz, supposed to do with the realization
that I was not in Brooklyn and it was a Saturday and Gauguin was going to
practice his music a good part of the day? We were now living together in

a small three-room adobe near Blue's house. We had no running water, an outhouse, a wood stove for heat, and a gas one for cooking. Our rent was seventy dollars a month. We split it.

I ate breakfast and drove into town. Town was the plaza, stores built around a central square. All the stores were brown stucco like adobe. El Mercado was where you got nails and string, the army surplus was for wool socks, and there was the good old Rexall counter. It was so gray out that the lilacs hanging over the parking lot of the *Taos News* were like wet mops, and there was mud everywhere. You had an inkling it would be a lot sweeter missing and longing for Taos than actually living there just then.

I took my book, *One Flew Over the Cuckoo's Nest,* and plopped myself in a booth at Grandpa George's. Grandpa George was a Pueblo Indian, an elder in the peyote church. He was married to an Italian woman from Baltimore. She had a mole in the shape of a star on her right cheek and four front teeth missing. She was twenty-three years old, and Grandpa George was eighty-two years old. She was five foot eleven, and he was five two. One day I asked her, "How does an Italian girl from Baltimore who majored in physics end up here?"

She was turning over a white flour tortilla on the wood stove. She turned to me, grinning. "I got lucky."

I was on chapter four in the Kesey novel. I ordered chocolate cake. Some things at George's weren't so good, but their chocolate cake was okay. I looked up as Cassandra walked in. Cassandra was a nomad who rode her horse across the mesa in the company of five cats and eleven dogs. I said, "Hi, Cassandra." She said hi back, but I could see she couldn't remember my name. I wasn't insulted, though. Hell, if a person doesn't know night from day, I don't mind that she doesn't know "Banana Rose."

Cassandra used to own a little house in Rinconada, a small town of about eleven buildings below the piñon hills. She was always late for her job at the general store, because she had a terrible time with time. She couldn't understand that if the clock in her house said twelve, the clock in the general store would also say twelve. How could that be? One day she sat at her kitchen table and turned her white Big Ben back to eleven o'clock and then ran down to the post office to see what time that clock said. Lo and behold, it said twelve o'clock. Then she ran home and turned Big Ben to 3:00, 8:00, 6:00. She ran to her neighbor's. The neighbor's clock said 12:05. She ran to Sanistevan's car repair next door. That clock said 12:06.

Cassandra spent the whole afternoon turning the hands of Big Ben. Outside the blue morning glory petals curled in on the heat of the day. Cassandra made 12:30 happen. Then 3:30. Then 8:30. She examined all the half-hours. Then she looked at the quarter-hours. She fine-tuned minutes to 11:23, 4:23, 7:23. She turned midnight to noon, morning to afternoon. The heavens turned faster and the earth spun through stars and sunlight all in her little kitchen in Rinconada.

Cassandra had gone through many winters and springs. By Big Ben time, she was in 1995. Things were spinning in the room. One o'clock, two o'clock. The flowered wallpaper, the pitcher on the refrigerator. Three o'clock, four o'clock, five o'clock, six o'clock. The green linoleum, the vigas on the ceiling, the light switch, the painting of a Cheshire cat sitting next to a mouse with a peace sign above their heads. It was a whole day of spinning. Did her grandmother Beulah die last year, or was she in some future life about to be born? If it were eight in the morning in Rinconada, how could she call Peking, China, in the coin phone down at El Mercado and it not be morning in China, when it would be morning in Taos? And how was it that if all the clocks in Rinconada—she quickly grabbed a pen and paper to calculate exactly how many clocks that was. She figured that if she included Under the Sun Art Gallery, which no one included as part of Rinconada anymore, because they had had a For Sale sign up for the last twelve years saying, "For One Dollar Down You Can Own This Place," Rinconada had twenty-nine clocks. If all of them were precisely correct, so that at 11:01 they all said 11:01, when Cassandra moved her clock to 11:08, how come they didn't all jump ahead? Weren't they all interconnected?

The next day, when she walked into the general store at ten o'clock instead of nine, Jake started to yell at her. She ignored him and pulled out the footstool, reached up to the clock above the cans of ham, turned the little hand back to nine o'clock, and went over to the cash register and began to wait on customers. His mouth fell open. He went over to talk to her. Before he had a chance to say anything, she turned to him and said, "You know the baby I lost last year? She left time, that's all, and spun out into another century." Jake drew his eyebrows together and scratched his left ear.

Cassandra had never seemed so happy and relaxed. At two o'clock she stood on the footstool and changed the clock to five o'clock. She smiled at Jake as she walked out the door waving. "Is it okay if you lock up? I have some things to do."

She went home and put a sign in her big bay window: "If you know what time it really is, you don't need to live here." She hammered three boards across her front door and left. Ever since, Cassandra has traveled the hills of northern New Mexico with all her animals, coming into town only if the dogs have been lazy and haven't caught enough jackrabbits. Then she scavenges food for them. Once in a while she gets lonesome for a clock and sits in the lobby of the New Mexico Federal for a half-hour and studies the second hand moving click click across all the numbers. She sighs, seems to feel at peace again, and leaves on Sugarfoot, her beloved horse, and the whole band of animals follows her.

Jake told me all this one afternoon when I had a flat tire near his store. So now when I see Cassandra, I never mind that she doesn't know my name, since I know she's living in eternity.

I ate the icing between the two layers of my chocolate cake first. It was pretty good. I thought of the icing my mother used to put on my birthday cake. She'd used Baker's chocolate, and the cake shone like a slippery seal. It was still raining out. I finished the cake and paid. I didn't want to sit in George's. I wanted to sit in Ratner's on Delancey Street near the Brooklyn Bridge. I was in a bad mood. I walked down to El Mercado and wandered up and down their aisles. I could get pink moccasins. No, I could get bubble gum in the shape of a toad. I could go outside.

I went outside and sat in the plaza in my yellow slicker. I let the rain fall all over my upturned face, but I wasn't happy. This wasn't romantic. I could go home and start a fight with Gauguin. That could be entertaining. I could tell him I didn't like the way we made love last night. It had been fine last night, but today it could be fighting material. What other fighting material could I think up? He didn't make enough money. I didn't like when he played music the other night and came home at 2 A.M. He forgot to buy me coffee yogurt when he went shopping, and he knows how much I like coffee yogurt. He made fun of the painting I did two days ago, said the circle in the middle looked like a melon, when I'd meant it to look like the world.

I began to smile. I was feeling a little better. I had real things to be unhappy about. I thought, "Gray is gray, and rain is rain. Rain is a plural word. If only one raindrop fell from the sky, would it be rain? If that raindrop fell only on me, would I be the only one who knew rain?" I decided to go to Rexall and get some chewing gum. The gum was twenty-seven cents.

I took a walk down Morada Lane, east of the plaza. It was a long dirt road, edged by Russian olives. The ruts in the road were filled with puddles. I stood in front of one and watched the rain hit the water's surface. The puddle only reflected gray sky and a vague brown image of my face. I walked to the end of Morada Lane, but I wasn't finished walking, so I went up past the Mabel Dodge house and kept going. Mabel Dodge Luhan was a rich woman from the east who'd moved to Taos and married an Indian from the pueblo. Out behind her house was pueblo land —miles of sagebrush, and to the left a little cemetery with a morada. Way in the distance I could see a cottonwood, the only standing tree. I headed for that cottonwood; when I got there, I was going to hug it. The earth was very muddy and sucked each of my footsteps, but it was the smell of the sage I remember most. Sage is the color of a blue line in your notebook. Don't think blue. Actually look at the line, then water it down a bit. Make the color run over the whole page. Let it become diluted turquoise, let it mix with a touch of yellow, and let it stand against a red brown. Now let that color become smell. Fill the gray air full of rain. Let your ears go dead. There is no sound. That's what it was like back there behind the Luhan house.

The cottonwood had just sprouted new green leaves. I wrapped my arms around its trunk. In the distance on the ridge, I saw Cassandra on Sugarfoot, her five cats and eleven dogs following her into eternity. I liked Taos again. Brooklyn was another world.

Then it dawned on me—of course I knew what to do today. I didn't need to start trouble with Gauguin. I could paint! Why had it taken me so long to figure that out? I suddenly felt sure and confident. The cottonwood gave me courage—I felt it in my body—and the sage and the mud and the rain breaking open the sky all told me I could paint. Paint something good and finish it.

I ran almost all the way back to my car through Kit Carson Park, down Bent Street. I was breathless, gulping for air, my open jacket flying behind me. I passed Blue's truck in the parking lot, and I saw Happiness across the street in front of the Taos Inn. She waved—at least I think it was her—and I waved back, but I couldn't stop to talk. I wanted to hold what I was feeling inside. I wanted to pour it all out into a painting.

When I got home, I could hear Gauguin in the other room, practicing scales. I didn't poke my head in because I didn't want to bother him and I didn't want him to bother me. I pulled out my acrylics, but before I used them I took a piece of charcoal and drew a fat mountain, an upside-down V, just like a kid would do, right in the center of the thick paper. Then I drew a star on the left and a quarter moon, low so it looked like it was receding in the distance, on the right side of the mountain. I sketched a few crooked rocks down below the moon but nearer to the mountain, and I drew a few birds in the sky. The birds were V's, too, but right-side up, also like kids do. And as I worked, I felt things. Drawing first let me get ready for painting. I felt space inside me and the majesty of space beyond—almost as though space were time and the painting would be ancient, would have distance, going all the way back to the dinosaurs. I drew some ridges, jagged and irregular, back between the moon and the mountain and then on the other side, too, below the star. Then I added more stars.

I wet my brush and worked quickly, squeezing paint onto the palette and sometimes directly from the tube right onto the paper and then spreading the paint with the brush.

Gray on the mountain. Then purple. Then some blue. And green tinged at the base. A yellow sky the color of ripe pears. Then I made the yellow a bit brighter. The moon was gold and the stars were silver. There was a rich blue-black at the top of the ridges and a gray-black wash in the center of them. I painted the flight of the birds, the space around them, almost eggshell blue with a darker blue for the actual V's. And at the edge where the ridges touched the yellow sky there was a thin line of flaming orange.

I hesitated with the rocks, closed my eyes, and my hand found pure shocking pink. I splashed that color on the rocks.

The painting was happening! It was alive—I was alive. I stepped back and I almost loved it. It needed a title. I grabbed a thin black pen and in tiny letters in the corner wrote, "After Rain," and then I loved it all the way. It was complete. I was so excited I wanted to run and get Gauguin. No. I wanted to wait. I flopped on the bed. I gripped my hands behind my head and lay on my back looking at it leaning up against the back of a chair.

I heard Gauguin open his door. "Nell?" he called. "You home?" He appeared at the bedroom door.

"Look." I pointed with glee.

He turned his head. "Hey." He paused and stepped over in front of it. "Hey." He reached for it.

"Don't touch it!" I jerked up. "It's still wet."

Gauguin pulled his hand back and made a low whistle sound of admiration. He turned to me with a slow smile. "It's nice, real nice."

My heart felt like it was going to break out of my body. " 'Nice'? That's too Midwestern. In New York we'd say 'gorgeous.' "

"How did you do it?" he asked.

"Fast," I said.

He grabbed me and hoisted me onto a chair, then pointed up at me. "Banana Rose Schwartz, ladies and gentlemen. Look out, world, here she comes!"

I bowed like a prima donna from my elevated position, then stood there on the chair, smiling.

The next day, I woke up early. I wanted to start painting right away, but as I walked through the kitchen, I thought of making huevos rancheros to surprise Gauguin. I checked the refrigerator. We had blue corn tortillas. I was glad. I loved that color against the yellow of the fried egg and the red of the chile. Then I thought of adding fried potatoes—they'd be good— and baking corn muffins. Pretty soon it was ten in the morning, and Neon was at the door.

"Do you want to eat with us?" Gauguin offered.

"What a question." Neon smiled and slipped into the chair at the side of the table.

I placed the hot muffin tin on the wooden table, and Gauguin whistled. "Wow, this, too, Nell?"

Neon shook his head. "You're sure lucky to be with her."

Gauguin split open a muffin and its steam rose up. He smoothed apricot jam over it. I could tell he was thinking. "Neon, why don't you go out with Blue?"

"She wouldn't have me," he said, biting into a potato.

"Maybe if you'd wash more often," I said bluntly, sniffing exaggeratedly at the air.

We all laughed. Neon hit my knee. "C'mon, Banana."

After breakfast the three of us went out to the river and didn't return until almost dark. It was too late to paint then, and besides, I was too tired anyway.

7

"Hey, Nell, where are you going?" Gauguin yelled after me.
"Never mind!" I screamed, and slammed the screen door
and dove into my car.

It was the middle of May. I looked out the sideview mirror and saw
Gauguin standing at our front door, trumpet in hand, wearing a pair of
old khaki cutoffs, naked from the waist up.

There was orange still on my hands and it smeared on the steering
wheel. I'd left the palette out with chunks of paint on it. They could dry,
and I'd take them off with a razor later. What a waste of materials, I
thought. What a waste of time, too. I hadn't been able to get anything
right since that one Saturday a month and a half ago. Now I hated painting
again. All my pictures were either ugly or I didn't finish them.

I gunned the car faster, spewing up a cloud of dust behind me on the
winding dirt road. I was heading to town and then north past town. This
was the third time I'd gone there this week, each time after trying to
paint.

I made a right at the blinking light and then took the first left. I
got out near the canyon rim and began to walk the ridge line. Down
below I could see the town of Valdez. I had the feeling that with the
right wind my feet would leave the ground, that I would float in cur-

rents with the ravens, who drifted above the small adobe houses hud-
dled below in fields. I wanted to fly. I visualized magpies and hawks,
but I couldn't feel the essential motion of a bird. My heart wanted to
soar, but I couldn't lift my body. How do I feel as free as I did that
one day out behind the Luhan house? I couldn't go back to the cottonwood. It had already given me its gift. I told Gauguin to fuck off
when he said I wasn't disciplined about painting. I told him it was
none of his business, it wasn't my style to practice scales like he did.
But what was my style?

I was concentrating on how to fly. The sky was an intense blue—
deeper than blue—it was heaven and it was calling me. My legs were
hanging out my red shorts, and in my mind they were lifting.

Just then I saw someone walking in the opposite direction on the
ridge. We came upon each other face to face. She was the tallest human
being I had ever met. I arched my head, like a finch to a stork, and the
first words I said to her were, "How tall are you?"

"I am six foot one in my bare feet." She stared back at me hard. She
had deep gray eyes, short blond hair that seemed to be chopped instead of
cut, and an almost perfectly heart-shaped face. Her eyebrows were so
light, they seemed not to be there at all, and I noticed she held one
shoulder higher than the other. On that Thursday she was wearing a red,
black, and white plaid button-down, short-sleeve shirt and blue jeans. She
was barefoot. The next thing she said to me was, "You're not big enough
to be a raven. Maybe a sparrow." Then she walked around me and kept
going along the ridge.

First my head twisted and then my whole body, so I could follow her
with my eyes. She had a book stuffed in her back pocket. I squinted. I
could see *The Ballad of the Sad . . .*

"Hey—" I ran after her. "Are you reading Carson McCullers?"
She turned, pulled the book out of her pocket, and flashed me the cover.
"I read it in tenth grade. I loved it," I said.

"I've read it about eight times. Have you read it since tenth grade?"
she asked.

"No." I looked down. "Do you live around here?" I asked, changing the subject.

She nodded and pointed to a small adobe on the other side of the road.

"How did you know I was pretending to be a bird?" I asked.

"Because I do that, and I could tell."

"I'm Nell." I held out my hand.

"I'm Anna." She had big hands, too.

"Do you live alone?"

"Yes." She paused. "Do you want to come in for tea?"

"Sure, I'm a little tired from flying right now, anyway." I was trying to be charming, but it came out sounding corny.

We walked through a wooden gate and down a narrow dirt path. The back door was open, and the screen slammed behind me. There was only one big room with a blue sofa bed—a white sheet hung out below the cushion—in the corner, a hot plate on the red kitchen table in front of the window that faced the ridge. The desk was actually a door on some cinder blocks. There were books everywhere. Anna cleared three from the kitchen table when she brought over the green teapot.

"Flannery O'Connor, Tennessee Williams." I read the book spines. "You like Southern authors?"

"Yes. They have so much of America in them," she answered.

"I loved *Gone with the Wind.*" I could see this didn't impress her. She pursed her lips. I wanted to impress her. There was a wine-red overstuffed chair with carved feet by the wood stove. "Where do you come from?" I asked, changing the subject again.

"I was brought up in Nebraska, but I went to school in Colorado." She poured mint tea into two purple cups, using a strainer to catch the leaves. She had long fingers.

"Hey, did you ever read Willa Cather? I just read a book by her. Let's see, what was it called?" I snapped my fingers. "*My Ántonia,* that's it, all about Nebraska."

"Yeah, we read her in high school."

"Well, did you like her?"

"I dunno." Anna pushed a piece of hair from her face.

Hmmm. Willa Cather didn't impress her either. "How old are you?" I asked. I was curious about her. "Do you like living alone?"

"Yes, I like it a lot. I've always lived alone. I'm writing a novel."

"What about?" I asked.

"Oh, I'm not sure. It takes place on a Nebraska farm. The woman on the farm is so lonely, she communes with the cows, and when the cows are sold for meat, she goes crazy," she answered.

"Gee." I scratched my ear.

"It takes place in the 1800s," Anna said.

"How long have you been in Taos?" I was asking so many questions, I felt like Agatha Christie, searching out facts for a new mystery.

"Nine months. What about you? What do you do?" The tables were turned. She asked the questions now.

"I fly." I smiled. Maybe she would like me.

"What else?" she asked.

I wanted to tell her I tap-dance, I sail, I drive semis, I'm a short-order cook, I live in a cave, my mother is an antelope, I eat kosher salami, I have no willpower, I get lost on the subway, I have eleven aunts, my cousin is a rocket scientist, a horse once kicked me in the teeth.

"I teach part time in the winter at Red Willow." I told her the truth instead. "And I'm trying to paint."

She wasn't listening. She looked out the window. When she turned back to me, her left eye was turned in toward her nose.

"Anna, are you okay? Your eye's in." This was all spooky, and I was nervous.

"I know. I'm okay. It does that sometimes. I'm supposed to do eye exercises to keep the muscle strong. I forgot the last week," she explained.

"Can you make it go back?" I asked, alarmed.

"Yeah, just give me ten minutes. I guess I can't cheat on the exercises." She stood up and went over to the window. Suspended on a string in the middle of the window was a rubber ball. She reached out and swung it. She slowly swayed her body, keeping her eye on the ball. When the ball finally came to a standstill, she did it again.

I watched one and a half swings and then walked over to the bookcase. All of the Beats were there. Jack Kerouac, Gary Snyder, Diane DiPrima. A whole row of Hemingway, and then Anaïs Nin, Colette, Ken Kesey, Alan Watts, Lorca, Pablo Neruda. Then an author named Jane Rule, Djuna Barnes, Jean Rhys. I turned back to look at Anna. She had long arms. I looked beyond her to the kitchen counter and the refrigerator, which shifted into a loud hum. She had electricity. There were three red five-gallon plastic containers on the floor. She hauled water. Gauguin and I had one of those containers. I filled it at the school. Two white dishcloths were hanging over the wood counter.

"Anna?" I broke the silence. "Can I talk while you're doing these exercises?" I asked.

"Yes, but not fast, because another part of me is concentrating."

"How old are you?" I asked again.

"I'm twenty-seven," she answered.

"Who are you friends with around here?"

"Not too many people."

"Does it get lonely around here?"

"Yeah, some." She reached out and stopped the ball. "I'm done." She turned and smiled. Her eyes weren't cockeyed anymore.

"I ought to be going." I felt nervous.

"So soon?"

We ended up sitting on an old green torn car seat in the back of her house. We both stretched our legs out long in front of us and leaned back with our faces in the sun.

"If only we had some lemonade with lots of sugar." She laughed. "My mother used to set me up in the driveway with a Kool-Aid stand. I'd sit and read Freddie the Pig books." Anna sat up and turned to me. "Have you ever read those books? By Walter R. Brooks. I can't remember much about them, but I loved them. About a pig."

"No, never heard of them." I sure wished I had. I squinted up at her. She looked like rain, that fresh.

"Well, anyway," Anna continued, "I'd wait for someone to come. I thought I was going to get rich with that little lemonade outfit. No one ever came. We lived on a farm, miles from anything. The horses in the field across the way hung their heads over the fence, only the horses had no money. After what seemed like hours, my mother came out, plopped down a quarter, and bought some."

I opened my eyes again. My face had been in the sun for a long while. Anna looked yellow. Everything was golden, the tall weeds, the hard, dry dirt. I felt dizzy. "Anna, didn't you have any brothers or sisters to buy lemonade?"

"Yeah, I have an older brother, Daniel. But we didn't get along too well when we were young." A long pause. She was thinking of something. "I once caught him jerking off in the woods near our house. I was eleven. Daniel was thirteen. It was fall. He cracked open a milkweed pod. You ever see one of those?" she asked.

"I think so." I nodded. I was getting nervous again.

"Well, the seeds are white and real silky. Daniel filled his hands with them and jerked off into them. Must've felt good. I was in the shadow of an elm. I was scared, and I made a sound. He caught me before I even had a chance to move and smeared his hand all over my face. It was sticky and the seeds stuck. He hissed at me, 'Don't you ever tell anyone.' He squeezed my arm real tight. I got the message. Hell, there was no one to tell anyway." Anna scratched her leg. "What about you? Do you have any brothers or sisters?"

I put my hands behind my head and leaned back. "I have a younger sister. She wants to be a rock star. Lives in New York. She's twenty-four and worked for a while as a bartender in a fancy club. She wears silver sneakers and auditions for bands. We don't see each other much. She was out visiting at Thanksgiving. She thought it was boring here, kept wanting to go to clubs." I laughed. "I told her the only club here is the Boys' Club. She went to Safeway at midnight and walked up and down the aisles because it was the only thing open. They were restocking the shelves. Oh, yeah, and that sheepskin place. They stretch skins all night. She even went there. Anything with lights on.'' I flicked an ant off my knee. It was getting cooler out, and the shadows were growing longer. "Y'know, I should get going."

"So soon?" Anna yawned.

I hesitated. "Do you want to come for dinner tomorrow night? You could meet Gauguin," I said.

"I don't have a car."

"If you can hitch there, I'll drive you back or you can stay overnight. We have an extra sleeping bag. Do you have something to write on? I'll give you directions."

She went in the house and brought out a green spiral notebook and opened it to the back cover. "Here, draw a map." She handed me a yellow pencil.

I drew the long dirt road, past the cemetery and Barela's candy store. I drew a square with a pitched roof and a door for the candy store. I turned to Anna. "Don't get carried away when you pass the candy store. I think it's a front for the mafia. The mafia sneaks three sheep from Eloy's barn down the road, finds no one in Taos wants them, and then sneaks them back under the cover of the candy store. Big operation. Last year the store had four pieces of licorice for sale. This year they have two. Someone from Truchas bought one, thinking it was a cheap way to repair the soles of his shoes. He's dead in a ditch now. He got hungry and ate it. Once I saw someone come out with a soda."

"Soda?" Anna questioned.

"Oh, pop. I always forget that out here you say 'pop.' In New York we say 'soda.' Not baking soda—the kind you sip through a straw." I turned and smiled at her. There I was again, trying to be charming.

I drew plum trees by the ditch as part of the map. I made the ditch a wavy line. I drew the trees laden with plums. I even drew Mel's totem pole near Blue's house and Arturo's lambs on his front lot. Seven of them. The scrawniest things you'd ever seen.

"Okay, okay. I'll find it." Anna laughed and pulled the notebook from me.

"Come around six. Bring some of your novel, if you want. I'd love to hear it," I said.

Anna looked down and then over at a tree. "I haven't shown it to anyone."

"Well, it's up to you. I'm sure Gauguin would like to hear it, too. How long have you been working on it?" I asked.

"A year and a half."

I left Anna, and on the way to Talpa, I stopped in Safeway and bought jack cheese, corn tortillas, sour cream, green chiles. When I got home, the coolness of the adobe rose up to greet me. The house was dark with small thick windows. Gauguin and I had stapled up screening to the outside frames so the windows could be opened. I looked around our small kitchen.

I put the brown bag from Safeway on the table and went into the bedroom and lay on the bed. We had a flower-patterned blue and white rug to cover the hard, unfinished adobe floor. I wasn't tired. I just wanted to lie down. I liked Anna, especially her eyes, even if they were cockeyed.

Gauguin was whistling outside. He passed by the bedroom window. "Gauguin," I called when he entered the kitchen. "Where were you?"

"Out practicing."

"Gauguin, I met a writer today. I asked her for dinner tomorrow night."

He stuck his head in the bedroom and smiled. "Is that why you left the groceries on the kitchen table?"

8

Anna came for dinner at the time of rose sunset. She entered the house through that soft light and sat down at the kitchen table. I served enchiladas with sour cream and chopped green onions spooned on top after the tortillas, onions, chiles, and cheese had bubbled together in the oven. They were my specialty. I wanted to make a good impression on Anna.

She picked at them and asked for a beer. We didn't have any beer in the house. Gauguin and Anna seemed to like each other, but it was clear that she was going to be my friend. Gauguin excused himself after dinner and went in the back room to practice. We could hear him chopping out a song on his guitar, the instrument he used whenever he tried out something new. Ping. Ping. Long pause. Ping. Ping. Ping. Short pause. A full strum. After a while we didn't hear him, though he continued to play.

"Did you bring your novel?" I asked.

"Yeah," she answered, and brushed a chunk of hair from her face.

"Read me some," I said.

"Do you have any wine?" Anna asked.

"Yeah, I think we might have some leftover stuff in the fridge." I got up, cleared the dishes, and put two glasses down on the table. I poured white wine out of a green bottle and settled back in my seat. "Okay, go ahead." I nodded.

"I'm nervous. I don't know what to read to you." Anna looked into her glass of wine and then up at me.

"Were you born in Nebraska?" I asked, changing the subject.

"No, my parents met in Connecticut. My father was from Nebraska, and when I was in the third grade, he wanted to move back. Have you ever been to Nebraska?" she asked.

"I've driven through. My sister was busted in Kearney. She spent two weeks in jail there," I replied.

"What'd she do?" Anna asked.

"She was driving along with a bunch of friends at 3 A.M., and they were all high on Quaaludes. They were headed for California, and they stopped in a café. The owner took one look at them and called the cops. Rita's hair was out like Jimi Hendrix, and she was wearing her silver sneakers. You could just see it. Five stoned freaks from New York stop in Kearney for juice." I laughed. I tried to imitate the way Rita said it.

"She's lucky she got out," Anna said, and took another sip of wine.

"Yeah, I think the judge made fun of her last name. Schwartz." I took a sip of my wine, too.

"It's amazing he even knew it was Jewish. Most people out there don't know what a Jew is." Anna brushed some more hair out of her eye.

"Are you going to read?" I asked, getting back to her novel.

Anna sat with her back to the stove. Over her left shoulder was the window and beyond that the night. "I'll read you the part about Louise and the cows on Christmas," Anna replied.

"Okay, shoot." I leaned back with my arm stretched in front of me on the table. I held the wineglass.

Anna took another gulp of wine and began to read in a shaky voice.

I tilted my head to the right as though to listen better. I really didn't know much about Anna. She had finished her glass of wine, and I filled it again. She read without pausing and without looking up.

. . . White and brown, bronze, black. Cows of every color came. They knocked down the barbed wire fences, as though they did not exist. Those boundaries that kept them in their place most days, this night nothing contained them.

And the wolves too. The wolves were bad that winter and everyone knew it. Yet when Louise heard the first wolf-cry, she was not alarmed. The first howls were taken up and echoed with quickening repetitions. A black drove came up over the hill, but Louise and the cows were unafraid. The wolves looked no bigger than dogs, and they ran like streaks of shadows. There might have been one hundred of them. They came to the center with the cattle.

Birds too. Sparrows, looking smaller on the backs of cows, flew down from tree branches. Louise thought the moon had risen, because at the center of the animals golden light emanated. She looked up. There were only stars. She got up, and like the prairie dogs, who were coming now too, she moved toward the center. A warm breeze blew gently across the winter night. As though responding to some silent signal, all the animals at once kneeled, bending their front legs.

At this point Anna looked up. "Should I go on? Is it beginning to sound corny?" She rubbed her cheek with her hand.

"No, keep going. I'm into it." I smiled and nodded.

The sparrows bowed their heads. In unison, all the animals began to moo and howl and bark and screech. It sounded like a holy choir. It began low and it ended high. It was broken by a sudden, complete silence for about two minutes.

Louise looked around. She wanted to be nearer to the cows, but she didn't dare move. Then it was over. The cows at the center turned slowly, causing all the other animals to break the circle. The wolves shot back, dark and swift, across the fields. Then the prairie dogs. The sparrows lifted off the cows' backs. Louise backed herself against another oak tree with her hands behind her and watched. Her heart was very open as though it had taken in the golden light at the center. She wondered what that golden light had been.

Anna looked up. She licked her bottom lip. I could see her left eye was moving in a bit.

"Well?" she asked.

"Are you Louise?" I took a leap.

"Some. And some not. What'd you think? Did you like it?" Anna asked nervously.

"You know, I swear it sounds like Willa Cather a little bit," I said, and then paused. "I can't believe you don't like her."

"Are you selling Willa Cather books?" She laughed, but I could tell she was annoyed. "I never read my writing aloud to anyone." Our eyes met. I noticed her right front tooth was crooked. I knew she wanted more from me, but I didn't know what else to say.

Just then Gauguin walked in from the other room. He had his shirt off. You could see a little of his small belly, because his belt was low. His whole chest was covered with red freckles, and he had about five red burly hairs at each nipple. Anna seemed to get uncomfortable.

"Gauguin"—I didn't move from my seat—"Anna just read to me from her novel."

"Hey." He smiled and put on his glasses. "Great, I'd like to hear it sometime."

Anna bent over her folder. I could tell Gauguin understood she was reticent about her writing. He turned his head. "Can I have some wine?" he asked, seeing the bottle on the table.

"What's left of it." I pushed the bottle toward him.

He went across the room to get a glass from the cabinet. "I think there's more down below." He pulled up another half-finished bottle and uncorked it.

Anna was relaxed now. "Nell tells me you write songs."

"Yeah, love songs about Nell. 'Nell has a belly. She doesn't let me near her when my feet are smelly,' " he sang.

"Gauguin, why don't you sing us a real one?" I asked enthusiastically.

"Maybe later. I thought we could go for a walk," he said.

"Okay." I nodded. I looked at Anna. "Do you want to go? Then I'll drive you home."

"You can stay the night if you want." Gauguin looked at Anna.

We left the wine on the counter and walked out into the cool night. There was no moon, but the stars gave enough light for us to see where we walked.

We followed the narrow footpath up by the reservoir, past two rusted junk cars, and stood under some Russian olives, watching the lights of Taos in the distance. Gauguin took my hand. He wasn't wearing his glasses and I wondered how much he could see. Both Gauguin and Anna began yawning. I told them they had both drunk too much wine and that's why they were sleepy.

Later, I was too tired to drive Anna home. She stayed overnight. She slept in my green sleeping bag, the one with the red flannel lining. The next morning I was pleased that she was there. Gauguin made us toast and fried potatoes with green chiles. I sat at the breakfast table grunting and making wolf sounds, trying to get them to join in. They wouldn't. I looked from Gauguin, pouring hot water into the one-cup coffee filter, to Anna, sitting in her T-shirt at the other end of the table. There was something similar about them, but I couldn't put my finger on it. Something about them both being from the Midwest, which meant they were both dumb as crickets and slow as tractors. They weren't going to become wolves, magpies, or hyenas at the breakfast table with me. I howled alone, and they chewed at their toast.

9

Because Gauguin and I didn't have a phone, if we thought of some-one, we just thought of them. We didn't call them, make a date, and put it on our calendar. Then when that Wednesday rolled around, we weren't obliged to stay home, waiting for them at noon, rather than doing what we really wanted, like going to the river for the whole day. Instead, people came wholly and physically into our lives. They appeared at our door, knocked, and we let them in. We had some tortillas with them, took a walk, played music, or just sat together on the front bench, watching the mountains that looked like two elephants kissing. And then our visitors left.

But after the night that Anna came for dinner, I wanted to see her a lot. She didn't have a phone either, so I had to drive out there and take my chances. She wrote most of the day. I'd stand on the rim, practice my flying, and then drop in on her. We'd sit on her old car seat out back, drink lemonade, and tell stories. I'd talk about my painting a little, though not much. I didn't quite know what to say. Sometimes she told me about what she was writing. I think I was the only one she talked to about it. Sometimes we went for a short walk on the rim and imagined flying together.

We'd call out birds that we wanted to be and then see how they got

along. Once I was a chicken and she was a hawk; another time she was a
sparrow and I was a finch. We tried to make the birds' sounds, too, and
sometimes the wind lifted enough that we were sure we were about to
take flight.

One time when I popped in, Anna seemed more dreamy than usual.
She said she had had a good day of writing. I told her she was lucky. My
latest painting had ended in blobs of brown and unclear figures.

"Maybe those figures are bugging you," she said offhandedly, reaching for a pink shirt to go over her tank top.

"Huh? What do you mean?" I asked.

"I don't know. Nell, this is just a guess, but maybe it's something to
do with your parents. They don't seem to accept your painting. Maybe
you're busy fighting them instead of doing it."

"Huh?" I said that brilliant word again.

"It's a hunch, that's all."

Anna didn't usually talk like this. I really didn't understand what she
was saying, but then tears sprang to my eyes. I followed her out the door.
We were heading for the rim to practice flying. We crossed the road.
"Hey, Anna, since when are you Sigmund Freud's old aunt?"

She snorted and lightly pushed me away. I'd never noticed before
how beautiful her back was. Broad shoulders coming down like a V at her
waist. I wanted to reach out and touch her. Did I love Anna or hate my
parents? If Gauguin had said what Anna just had, I would have despised
him.

"What do you want to be today?" Anna turned to me.

"A pelican."

"A pelican? Nell, you can't be that. This isn't the ocean."

"I can be what I want." I curled my bottom lip.

Anna looked at my face. She nodded. "Okay, you can be what you
want."

I held open my arms, but instead of using them for wings, I wrapped
them around Anna and began to cry.

We stood there, and she stroked my head.

The sun began to set along the ridge line.

Another day in early July when I came to visit, she wasn't home. I knocked. "Anna?" I knocked again. "Anna?" I lifted the black latch, and the door swung open—she never locked up. No one was there. The bed wasn't made. I stepped in and went over to her desk, thinking I'd leave a note. There was a list on her table. "Do the laundry. Bring paper clips, paper, writing pens, emery board, and enough rice for ten days." So she went someplace for ten days. Probably to write.

She probably likes writing better than me, I thought belligerently.

Sometimes I felt that she'd rather be writing than be spending time with me. Once at Steven's Kitchen I was telling her about a dream, talking with my mouth full of pecan pancakes, too excited to swallow. Suddenly, I noticed she was drumming the fingers of her right hand on the tabletop.

"Hey, Anna," I asked. "Are you listening?"

"Yeah, Nell. It's just that I think I'd better get back to my novel. I missed a whole day yesterday when we went hiking, and then I slept over."

"Didn't you have a good time?" I asked.

"I had a great time. It's just that I've got to work. There's no one out there that's going to make me do it, but myself. You should understand from your painting."

"Okay, let me finish these pancakes and I'll drive you home." I took a big swig from the tea that was already cooled to lukewarm. The truth was, I didn't understand. I thought it was more fun any day being with Anna than painting.

I was used to Gauguin wanting to practice music, but that didn't bother me as much. He was in love with me, and besides we lived together. I got to see him as much as I wanted to, and if I really acted miserable and fainted all over the place, he wouldn't practice that day. We'd go to the river or down to Santa Fe.

"I wonder where she went? She never mentioned it to me," I thought out loud. I squatted down to watch the birds fly below me and above the town.

I'd left Anna's house and had gone back to the rim. I looked over the town of Valdez, thirteen crooked adobe houses sighing back into the earth. I counted eight horses in different corrals and seven goats lost among chicken coops, outhouses, and pickup truck graveyards.

Two magpies swept by. A raven. I closed my eyes and imagined myself sailing through air. I lifted my right outspread arm so I could veer to the left. I almost completed the turn, when I stopped. "Oh, hell, I can't fly today. I'm going home to get Gauguin."

When I arrived home, there was a note on the table. "Rose, Jet stopped by and we went to the river. Be back by dinner. I'm madly in love with you, Gauguin."

Shit. No one was around. I started up to Blue's and then remembered she was out camping in the Pecos. I could read, I thought. We had just taken *Nine Stories* by Salinger out of the library. We had read "Laughing Man" aloud the other night. I could reread it. I went out on the front bench. It was too hot. I jumped up and went back in the house, slamming the door behind me. Shit! I sat at the kitchen table.

Salinger was on the table. I strummed my fingers on the book, bit the inside of my lip. I glanced down at Salinger and a space appeared in my mind. I filled it in: Salinger was from New York, I surmised. I'm from New York. I put the two together: Therefore, if Salinger can write, so can I! A smile spread over my whole face. I quickly got out four pieces of loose-leaf paper and a pencil from a drawer in the back room and began to write.

Nell walked into Rexall Drugs to buy some cashews. As she passed the counter, she saw some Donald Duck sunglasses. They were red.

She reached out and took a pair off the cardboard display rack and put them on. "Is there a mirror?" Nell asked coquettishly in her new glasses, turning to the counter clerk. He pointed to a small square mirror by the cosmetic counter. She walked over and peered at herself. The glasses were too small. They made her nose look big. She didn't care. They were perfect, she thought stubbornly. She paid the exact amount for them: sixty-nine cents. She counted out the four pennies after the two quarters, the dime, and the nickel.

Then she went out into the plaza. Lo and behold, along came Anna from across the street. She walked right over to Nell and told Nell that she looked beautiful. Nell crossed her arms and turned away. Anna got on her knees and begged Nell, "Please, be my friend."

Nell refused and replied, "You only want me for my sunglasses."

Anna begged some more, "Please, Nell, it's not your glasses. It's you. I won't write anymore if you don't want me to. I'll just play with you."

I stopped writing. I realized that Anna never called me Banana. I began writing again:

"Nell, I love your name Banana Rose. Where did you get such a name? Banana, dear, if you would be so kind, I'd like to take you across the street for a malted." Anna would do anything for Nell. Nell saw this and conceded because of the goodness of her heart. Nell was very compassionate and forgiving and was full of Buddha nature.

I stopped writing and leaned my head on my left hand. It was getting cold in the room. I tucked my feet under my legs.

I went to the top of the page and titled my work of art *The Malted Afternoon,* a novel by Rose Schwartz. I kept out the names Nell and Banana from the author's name, because they were already in the novel. I didn't want my public to know the story was about me, the author.

"It's not such a big deal to write a novel." I smirked. "Anna can go fuck herself."

I wished Gauguin would get home. In my next novel, I would write about him. In the novel his name would be Clem. " 'Oh, Clem,' said Columbine as she fainted in his arms."

10

The next day, I sat in an idling Betsy Boop outside the Plaza Bar above the movie theater while Gauguin ran in to see if he had a gig there next month. We had just been to the post office and I managed to get our mail right before they locked the door.

A thick envelope from my mother was on my lap. I hesitated and then put my index finger below the flap and ripped it open. There was a clipped *Daily News* article about Charles Manson and another one about Isaac Bashevis Singer and why he wrote in Yiddish. Then a two-page handwritten letter fell out.

"Dearest Nell darling," it began. "We're worried about you. We haven't heard from you in 8¹/₂ days"—so who's counting?—

and then it was only a postcard, and every time I call the school, they say it's summer vacation and you are not there. What kind of school is that, anyway? When I called two weeks ago, they said the students were on camping trips. Can't they afford to put those children in bungalows? Please, Nell, call us. Why don't you get a phone where you live? Your father is worried sick, as am I, and if you don't care about your parents, think of poor Grandma. Every day she asks me, so have you heard from her yet? Imagine my shame in having to say no. You know how much we love you.

Rita is home for the summer. She ran out of money. You know how expensive Manhattan is. She is auditioning as a singer and the music that comes out of her room—such noise! Bless her heart, Grandma walks around with her hands over her ears. But it's a pleasure to have her around.

Your father says if you won't visit us, he'll send me to see what you're up to. Your poor father, he works day and night. Business is good, but it's hard to find honest help. Johnny quit last week to try his hand at the pickle business.

I have a nice brisket defrosting. I wish you were here to eat it. Please, Nell, write soon.

Lots of love,
Mom and Dad

I stuffed the letter back in the envelope and blanked out. I couldn't think. I just sat in the truck. I noticed that the S on the Plaza movie marquee was hung backward. A woman with rhinestone sunglasses walked by. She wore skin-tight white pants and walked a poodle on a chain. I hadn't seen a poodle in years. Wait a minute—she looked just like Aunt Ruth. I moved my head closer to the windshield. Could it be? Then I sat back in my seat. Cool it, Nell, I said to myself. What do you think, your relatives are invading Taos plaza? I imagined Uncle Morris from the Bronx, Uncle Al from the yeshiva, Aunt Mildred and Cousin Sarah all marching around the plaza, looking for a kosher deli. Good luck. I started to laugh.

Just then, Gauguin stuck his head in the open window. "What's up? I'm sorry I took so long." He got in the driver's seat. "Want to read me your mother's letter?"

"Naa, she sends her regards." I started to laugh.

"Yeah, I bet. She's some writer. She seems to write you every other day." Gauguin started the ignition. In all the months I was with him, he'd gotten one card from his mother.

"Jealous?" I asked.

As we drove down Placitas, I told Gauguin about *The Malted Afternoon*. We pulled in front of the House of Taos. Gauguin was quiet. I could tell by the way he took off his glasses and put them on the dashboard that he was thinking about something he wanted to say.

"Banana, I think you're a little bit in love with Anna."

"No, I'm not a little in love with her. It's all the way, but she's obsessed with her damn novel. She left for ten days without letting me know. I stopped by there, and she was gone." I got out of the car and headed for the restaurant.

Gauguin followed. We sat down at a table by the window. "She's not married to you, you know." He paused. "Banana, I think you need something to do this summer. If you're not working, you get antsy." He had his glasses back on.

We ordered a mushroom and onion pizza. I gulped down some ice water. They served us salads. We were silent, our heads bent over the lettuce. Suddenly, I looked up.

"Yeah, like what?" I snapped at Gauguin and hailed the passing waitress. "Excuse me, please. Can I have a small Coke? No, make it big." I turned and glared at Gauguin. He didn't dare say anything, even though we had sworn off sugar for the whole summer. "I could read a novel every day. I could sit under a tree until I get enlightened." They brought the pizza. Gauguin pulled out a piece, then turned the plate around.

"How about doing a painting every day," Gauguin cautiously suggested.

I glared at him again. I had told him clearly a while ago never to discuss painting with me, that his ideas weren't helpful.

"It was just a suggestion." He took another bite from his pizza.

I switched the topic. "The problem with Anna is, she's writing a book about the wrong subject. Who cares about cows? I say leave them for India. She should write a novel about me!'' I stretched my neck and tilted my head toward the ceiling.

Gauguin had just taken a gulp of water, and he sprayed it all over the pizza. I started to laugh, too.

Gauguin said, ''Why, Rose, it probably never occurred to her. You should mention it. 'Oh, Anna, by the way, have you thought of me as the main protagonist of your novel? I know you've already written three hundred pages, but you can just toss them away.' '' Gauguin shook his head. ''Banana, you are too much.''

''Well, what else should I do with my life if I can't make it as a heroine? 'Oh, Banana, wherefore art thou?' '' I paused and changed my tone. ''You know, I've been thinking about going backpacking alone in the Pecos. What do you think?''

''Sounds great.''

''Gauguin''—I waited until he put down his water glass—''I get scared. You have music, and Anna has writing, and sometimes I feel left out. Like who am I? And then I put all this pressure on painting, like that will define my life.''

''Just do it if you want,'' Gauguin said. ''I think you're great either way.''

I decided not to say anything else about it. He didn't get it. It wasn't his fault.

I was quiet the rest of the meal, just chewing pizza, gulping Coke. Gauguin was looking at a pamphlet about horseback riding on the pueblo that he found on the window ledge at the restaurant. I noticed the shape of his ear, and suddenly I felt a rush of love for him.

The night before Gauguin had told me to sit perfectly still on the kitchen chair. He came over and began kissing me, but he said I couldn't kiss back. Down my neck he went. Small, thick kisses and along my collarbone. He undid one button of my pale yellow blouse at a time and every once in a while he commanded in a soft voice, ''Don't move.''

''Pleeese,'' I moaned.

"No," he said.

My breasts were aching, the nipples hard below the cotton. I had no bra on, just the thin fabric of my top. My blouse now was all unbuttoned, and he pushed the left side over and licked at my erect nipple with his wide tongue.

"Oh, Gauguin," I said, my hands pressing the wooden chair seat on either side of my buttocks.

"No," he said. "No talking."

He put the blouse back over my breast, slowly so I felt the cotton run along my nipple.

Then he knelt in front of me and separated my legs, kissed my inner thighs. I was wearing my red short shorts. He kissed up to the brim of my underpants. He ran his finger inside the elastic, all along until his finger ran thump over my hardened clitoris.

I groaned. "Shh," he whispered. And he put his fingers inside me. My eyes rolled back.

"You want me, don't you?" he said.

I nodded, now silent, still, and obedient.

"I don't know if you can have me." He smiled, considering. He stood up. "Come with me," and he took my hand and led me into the bedroom.

I was all wanting. I lay down on the bed and he pulled off my shorts, leaving my blouse on, unbuttoned.

He took off his pants, and his penis sprang out from the side of his undershorts. I reached up for him and he had no hesitation. He came down to me on the bed.

I rolled an ice cube around in my mouth and smiled, remembering this. Gauguin was checking the bill. I rubbed my foot along his calf.

He looked up, a hundred miles away, and took his wallet out of his back pocket. I watched his hands, long, freckled, delicate fingers, wrinkled around the knuckles. Those hands had touched me—I felt awe and desire. My breath became smoky. I ran my hand along the edge of the table and crossed my legs.

He counted out two fives. "You owe me one," he said.

"I know," I said, but I didn't mean a five-dollar bill.

As we walked outside, I was aware of my thighs touching each other under my long skirt. I wanted Gauguin.

When he got behind the wheel of Betsy Boop, I slid over to him. I said, "Okay, now it's my turn."

He turned to me. He didn't know what I was talking about. I pulled his T-shirt out from his pants and put my hand on his belly. It was tender like I knew it would be. He caught on. "Not here," he said. We were in the parking lot behind the plaza.

"Yes, here," I said. "You just listen to me now." I bit his shoulder. Then his earlobe. He took his hands off the steering wheel in an act of surrender.

I unzipped his pants, put my hand in them and whispered in his ear, "I'm going to take you." I felt him harden and his breath thicken. Then I bent my head down to his lap.

"Oh, Nell," he groaned.

I stopped a moment. "Shh," and then I kept going.

Suddenly he grabbed me. "Get up." We were parked near a rented car. "Here come some Texans."

"Who cares," I said. I sat up and began to pull off my shirt.

"I care," Gauguin said, and yanked down my shirt, switched on the ignition, put the clutch in reverse, and peeled out of the lot backward.

"Oh, Gauguin." I pouted.

He put his hand on my knee. "I'm sorry, Nell. I got scared."

I was quiet for a while, feeling myself land back into an ordinary body again. "It's okay. I'm just disappointed."

"I hear you," he said. "We can make love when we get home." He made the turn to Talpa.

It was 8:30, but it was still semilight and there was that smell of summer, different from Brooklyn but summer just the same.

Gauguin pulled up to the house. "Ready for bed?" He kissed my cheek, his hand on the nape of my neck.

"Naa." I shook my head. "I'm not interested now."

Gauguin stood still in the kitchen for a few moments. I knew he was thinking, C'mon, Nell, you wanted me just a little while ago.

I got out a candle and put it on the kitchen table. "I think I'll stay up awhile," I said.

"I'm going to go to bed. You sure you don't want to come?" He bent down and licked my ear. He knew I loved that.

I shook my head. "Nope, not now."

He hesitated, then turned and stormed into the back room.

I lit the candle, turned off the overhead light, and sat at the kitchen table. Two moths were soon circling the wick. The white one's wing began to burn and crackle in the flame. I blew the candle out and walked outside. I sat on the bench in front of the house. The sky was so big. I leaned back against the stucco, my legs straight out in front of me. The black horse whinnied in the corral around the bend.

I heard the screen door snap open. It was Gauguin. "I couldn't sleep without you."

"Come here beside me." I patted the bench. "I was just sitting here and smelling."

"What were you smelling?" he asked.

"Summer, the way it is in Talpa," I said. "And then I was thinking how I'd like to get that smell down in a painting, how the smell feels in my lungs and muscles."

"I'd like to feel your lungs and muscles, too."

I chuckled and pushed his hand away. "You can only sit with me if you behave."

"Okay, I'll behave," and Gauguin, too, settled into the night and its quiet.

The black horse whinnied again. Gauguin yawned and looked up at the sky. "You know, the first horse I loved was Dixie Sue. I was eight, on my grandmother Mary Ellen's Iowa farm—the same place I saw those monarch butterflies. Remember?"

I nodded.

"Yeah, Dixie Sue had white stockings and a star in the middle of her face. Her eyes were deep brown and the size of golf balls. Together me and Dixie heard the sound of summer when we rode through the fields. The hills were filled with oak, scrub brush, and sumac. We commiserated over the heat as we sweated and swatted mosquitoes. We were best friends.

"My grandmother worried that I was too in love with that horse. She said only young girls loved horses that way. Sometimes in the middle of the night, I'd sneak out barefoot. I knew by instinct where in the large pasture Dixie Sue would be feeding. I'd climb on her and lean back, so my head rested on her rump. I'd just lie there and look up at the stars, a lot like tonight. They spread over Iowa like a great dark American flag." He sighed. We both were leaning back, our eyes glued to the sky. "Dixie Sue'd just continue to eat the sweet grass, hardly moving. She knew it was me on her back.

"Sometimes we'd take off in the moonlight. I'd hold tight to her bronze mane. The bluffs along the Blackhawk River and the narrow paths between shrubs and trees were lit with a shimmering silver, and there was a guiding light.

"Once we came to the top of a ridge farther than we'd ever been before. Nell, I never told anyone this." He hesitated. "Nell, we saw angels. Three of them. They were having a cookout below the ridge." When he said "cookout," I started to laugh. "No, I'm serious. They were sitting around a fire and their bodies shimmered like rippled water that you can put your hand through. Two of the angels were yellow, but the middle one, she was the color of salmon meat. She was beautiful. Dixie Sue and I just kept gazing at her. Then the angels got to realizing we were there. We could tell, because they began twinkling faster. We didn't want to bother them, so I yanked Dixie Sue's mane. She turned her long neck and head and we started home. The whole way back I hummed 'Angels Watching Over Me, My Lord.'"

Now I was sitting erect, looking at Gauguin. "Wow," I said. "Was that true?"

He nodded. I took his hand and tried to imagine seeing angels.

"Gauguin, I don't think there were angels in Brooklyn. At least not when I was growing up."

"Sure, there were," he said. "You just weren't looking in the right places."

We got up and went to bed. Just as I was falling asleep, Gauguin began to talk as though finishing the conversation we were having out on the bench. "Nell, sometimes I think I am a horse. I used to watch the horse in front of me when I rode with someone, how long and graceful its back legs were. Their legs move right into their hips in a magnificent motion—"

I fell asleep just then and in my dream I was an iguana on a beach. I turned over and woke up. It was a short dream. Gauguin was still awake; his arms were up on the pillow behind his head. "Hey, Gauguin," I said. "You might be a horse, but I'm an iguana."

"Oh, Nell, you are bananas," he said.

"No, really. I dreamed I was an iguana, just now. I'm an iguana!" Gauguin laughed and I hit him.

Gauguin began to make whinnying noises like a horse. I felt his hot breath on my neck. This horse began to make love to his iguana. His iguana lifted her short green iridescent front legs over the horse's shoulder. We turned over each other as I closed my eyes. Horse and iguana. Horse of ribs and hanging flesh, old horse rolling in bed with the sharp fast body of iguana. Above us was a waterfall. Egrets hung from trees like white gardenias. Bougainvillaea were draped over the branches of a magnolia tree. What country were we in? Horse and iguana didn't care about country. We felt the sun on our backs, and we slithered over rocks as we joined our juices together near a shallow wide river, flowing over sand embankments.

11

"I'm thinking of going backpacking alone in the Pecos," I told Blue to her back. She was bent over, picking spinach from our garden.

She stood up. "Look at this, will ya?" She held up green leaves. "Right here on our own little ol' dry land. Come, I'll make you something fancy—eggs Florentine. Got them fresh from Henry." She took my hand.

I sat in the window seat of her small adobe while she cooked the eggs over her fireplace. "So you're going to the woods all by your lonesome."

I nodded, but she couldn't see me nodding.

"Banana, go to Heart Lake. Not the Pecos. The Pecos is too rough. This is a journey you're going on. Go to the heart." She turned her head from stirring the eggs.

"How do you know?" I asked.

"I know." She put the eggs in two bowls and handed me one. The yellow of the yolk stared up at me from the bed of sautéed spinach, sprinkled with orange cheese. This was Blue's style of being gourmet. It was good, but I knew it wasn't eggs Florentine.

"You want something, Nell Rose. It's written all over you. You have to go find it, sugar." She rubbed my knee. "But you have to go to the right place to find it."

"What do I want?" I asked her.

"You tell me." She smiled.

"I want to be a painter, Blue," I confessed.

She nodded. "And you're afraid. No one in your family ever did anything like that. All your mother ever told you was to get married."

"How did you know that?" I asked.

"And you're afraid you'll be no good." She paused. "I don't sit in the fireplace all day for nothin', honey lamb." She tickled my arm. "My family is rich and respectable and Southern. When I was five, Elsie, the cook, smeared black soot across my forehead and said, 'Chile, you not made fur this here world. You get out someday.' I thought she meant I'd have to shoot myself with my granddaddy's pistol. Then much later I heard her tell Sonny, her boyfriend, one night when he picked her up after dinner, 'That chile's a mystic. Mark my words.' I didn't know what that meant except my mother wore Mystic Blue perfume. So all that spring I walked around smelling the magnolias and the azaleas, everything that bloomed, so I could figure out how I was like perfume. Old Elsie knew a thing or two, and she gave it to me."

I nodded. "Blue, do you think I could really become a painter?"

"If you want to," she said, taking a spoonful of her eggs Florentine.

I went to Heart Lake near Questa, as Blue instructed. It was an eight-mile hike. I carried a red frame pack on my back and walked through sunlight and shade on a narrow dirt path. Along the way, wild strawberries grew close to the ground. I bent and picked the bittersweet red dots that hung from the dark green plants. A stream rippled nearby. I stopped several times to sit on the white flat rocks that bordered it. About halfway to the lake I took off my shoes and socks, and while the stream ran over my bare feet, I broke open an eight-ounce Nestlé's bar. It had almonds.

The sugar pact that I'd made with Gauguin had gone to hell over and over again. It was a lot like meditation, I surmised. No matter how many times your mind wandered, you brought it back to the breath. No matter how many times I bit into chocolate, I remade the nonsugar vow between bites.

As I neared Heart Lake, the trail became steep and I walked almost on my toes, placing one foot directly in front of the other to go up the incline. When I reached the top, I saw a perfectly still green lake with rock cliffs at the far end, just as Blue had described. No one else was there.

I leaned my backpack against a birch by the lake's edge and began to collect firewood. Blue had told me it rained a lot this high up, and I wanted to find dry wood before it became dark. I collected a pile of twigs and dead branches. Some were wet and green, but I figured if I got the fire going strong enough, it would dry out the damp ones. I unzipped the back pocket of the pack, took out some folded newspaper, and balled it up to start the fire. I placed small twigs and bigger pieces of wood over the paper. The wind picked up. The ground itself was wet. It probably had rained up here earlier in the day. The paper burned some, but the fire went out when it touched the twigs. The twigs were wetter than I wanted to believe. I lit ten matches and still the fire didn't catch. I crumbled more paper. Eventually, the twigs dried out just from the heat of burning paper.

The sun was setting and night began to crawl down my back. It was cold. The twigs and then the branches finally caught with the last match of the book. I stood up and looked around. I hadn't had one thought in my head the whole time I'd worked to light the fire.

I tied a tarp to the low tree branches and rolled my sleeping bag out under the tarp. I sat back on a rock and pulled some garlic, a small bottle of oil, an onion, a pot, some wheat bulgur, and cheese out of my pack. I peeled the onion with the jackknife I had borrowed from Blue. I threw the brown onion skins into the fire. They burned slowly. They too were wet inside. I'd always been afraid to be alone in the woods. Now that I was here, there was nothing to be afraid of.

After I ate and stared into the fire for a long time, I got into my bag and let the fire die by itself. All night the wind blew hard and the tarp rippled and jerked against its ropes. I slept intermittently, dreaming of my grandmother. She came to the woods to visit me. She had on her plaid apron, and her hands were brushed with flour. She was making a cake. "Come, mamala, don't sleep in these woods. It's not nice. You should sleep in a bed."

I said, "Please, Grandma, I'm okay."

She shook her head. "Jewish children are never safe." She turned around and carved a heart out of the tree bark and handed it to me. "We all suffer," she said, and nodded. Her face was kind, and I knew she meant no harm. I woke abruptly. "Grandma," I called out. I wanted to ask her my question. She was gone. There were only the woods and me in my bag.

I was glad when the sky turned gray. I'd been alone now for twenty-four hours. As it grew paler, I sat up in my bag. I thought I'd meditate with my eyes closed.

After a few moments I opened my eyes and saw an ant crawl over a pebble. I breathed out slow. No enlightenment. The air smelled good. I breathed in. Last night making the fire I had had no thoughts. There had only been the match rubbed across rough paper, the twigs, the dirt, the newsprint. Where had Nell gone or Banana Rose? I leaned against a tree and began to cry. I didn't know why I cried. I wanted to run home and see Gauguin. I blew my nose in my hand.

After I made breakfast I walked around the lake. Then I came back to my campsite and made a lunch of peanut butter and crackers. Then I finished my Nestlé's bar. Then I didn't know what to do. I took off all my clothes and sunbathed, reading *Man Who Killed a Deer* by Frank Waters. It was a good book and I read for a long time. The shadows crossed me and I was chilly. I put on my long underwear. My clothes, hands, hair all smelled of fire smoke. It was still too early for dinner. I wandered into the woods, looking for more wood and keeping my eyes out for good rocks. I wanted to bring one back to Blue. Not a big one, just one that would fit real well in her hand. I imagined her hand. It was a worn hand with a small gold antique ring on her middle finger. A mystic? It figured. Blue didn't seem to have any ambition, but she wasn't lazy. Of course, you couldn't be a mystic and be ambitious. A mystic's job was to sit around and do nothing. I scratched my head. I'd better watch out for wood ticks. Blue, a mystic. I repeated it over and over to myself, as though I were rolling a rough stone around in my mouth. Yeah, it fit. I wanted to be something, too.

I threw an armful of small branches and a dead limb down by the campsite. Then I saw a small piece of pink quartz, the shape of a heart. I put it in my pocket for Blue and went to look for more wood.

I remembered the question I'd wanted to ask my grandmother in my dream. So, Grandma, how do you become a painter? I picked my nose. I really got into it. There was no one around to stop me.

It's beautiful around here, I thought. I saw a grove of aspens. To be a painter—I got that far, and then my mind wandered to dinner. I could make brown rice, fry it in oil, and add an onion, a carrot, and two eggs I had brought. A little tamari. Hmmm. I wish I'd brought more chocolate. I planned to stay until noon tomorrow.

I sat down below a tree I liked, leaning my back against it. I didn't want to read anymore. I was quiet. I didn't fiddle around, and I wasn't trying to meditate. So here I am, I thought. A chipmunk dodged in and out of the tree's shadow. Then a second one joined the first.

The next morning, I woke early. The sky was lightening, and I could see soft pink above me. This was my second morning alone at Heart Lake. I took in a deep breath, pulled my arms out of the sleeping bag, and put them behind my head. The pink above me became a darker pink, then the sky turned steel blue and felt far away, way above the treetops.

Suddenly, a bird called across the forest and its sharp sound made me jerk up in my bag. I sat up so quickly—meeting the cold in only my T-shirt, still clinging to my sleep-hot body—that something snapped in me. Out of nowhere, in that moment, I understood how to fly! It wasn't my arms that were my wings—it was my heart. Of course! The two halves of your heart break open through your chest and carry the whole human body up! The sun cracked through the trees, and I was carried up through those branches, like a human raven, heart first. I landed on the top of an aspen and chirped "Amazing Grace" for the whole forest.

That afternoon I flew down the hill. The pack was light on my back. It didn't all make sense, and I didn't want to try and figure it out, but now I knew I could paint. Yes, and I wanted to make pictures, beautiful real pictures. I didn't have to fight my parents for permission anymore. Trees didn't ask the sky to be trees. I understood this now. I could be a painter.

12

"Hi, Nell." I turned around. It was Anna. I was taking *Paul Cézanne's Letters* off the shelf at the Taos Book Store.

"Hi, Anna. I haven't seen you in a while." I felt casual about it now, but also happy to see her.

"I was away. I got back three days ago." She brushed her hair out of her eyes. "Hey, do you want to get a malt at Rexall's?"

"Okay," I said. I paid for the book at the counter.

We sat on the swirling blue seats at the drugstore within arm's reach of the Pepto-Bismol and Ex-Lax. "It's my treat," Anna said, and smiled.

"Where've you been?" I asked.

"I got your note when I got back. Sorry I missed you. Steve Cordon gave me his cabin near Truchas for ten days. He went east and I thought I'd take advantage of it. I needed to get down on the novel. I ran into Jake at the co-op and he offered to drive me over." She again brushed some hair out of her eyes. "It's getting real hard. I'm not sure anymore who Louise is. She's running away from me."

I curled the corner of my white paper napkin. "Like you're running away from me?" I bit my lip. It just came out. I couldn't help it. I'd felt perfectly happy since my solo journey in the woods and here I was starting trouble.

Anna turned and looked at me. "Nell, did I hurt your feelings? I'm sorry. It was a last-minute thing."

I continued to curl the napkin. I pressed my lips together. "It's okay." I felt completely foolish. That wasn't what I wanted to talk about. I wanted to tell her I was painting.

The waitress placed two glasses in front of us. Then she brought over two silver containers from the lime green malt machine. With one in each hand, she poured half of the frothy liquid into each glass and left the other half in the containers. Anna got vanilla. I had chocolate. The waitress, who was smacking gum and wore a hair net, gave us each other's flavors accidentally. Anna and I switched them, tapped our glasses together, and drank. The malt was thick and I asked for a spoon.

"I just remembered! Didn't you and Gauguin say you weren't going to eat sugar this summer?" Anna exclaimed as though she had discovered something.

"Yeah. I cheat. He probably doesn't. He's very honorable." I smiled with true satisfaction. The malt was good. "This is a special occasion. He'll understand."

We sipped and spooned and didn't say much. There was a long mirror on the back wall behind the counter. Anna's and my images were blocked by utensils and milk cartons that were on the cutting board, but we could see a bit of each other. Anna sure looked pretty. When she looked into her malt, you could see her lashes against her cheeks in the mirror's reflection. I wore a coffee-colored tank top. At one point our eyes caught in the mirror, and we smiled at each other.

I poured the second half of my malt into my glass. It had melted, but I still ate it with the long soda spoon. Anna only finished half of hers and then pushed it away.

"How come you're not finishing?" I asked, eagerly bent over mine.

"I don't know. I lost my appetite," she said.

"I would too if I ordered vanilla." I shook my head.

She waited for me to finish and then paid for both of us. "Want to walk over to Kit Carson?" Anna asked.

We strolled through a green playing field, past a baseball diamond, and under huge cottonwoods that must have been planted when Kit Carson was alive. We walked over to the small park cemetery where Carson was buried. The grass grew high around the gravestones. It was too much trouble to hand-clip that close, so if the mower didn't get it, the grass just grew. We sat on the ground, leaning against a tombstone. Neither of us talked. I thought, Uh-oh, we've run out of things to say. Then I said, "Anna, I went backpacking by myself while you were gone."

"Yeah?" She was twirling the end of a long weed in her mouth. The golden tassels hung down.

"I meditated up at Heart Lake—ever been there?" She shook her head. I continued. "It's a good place. During the meditation at one point it came to me that you suffered. You know, over your book and all." I was nervous. Maybe I shouldn't have brought this up. Why wasn't I telling her about painting instead, and how I learned to fly? I felt stupid. I decided not to say anymore, better to wait and see her response.

She was quiet for what seemed a long time, but in truth, I think it might only have been a moment.

"Nell, I'm into women." She broke the silence abruptly.

I was confused. I thought we were going to discuss my backpacking trip. "So? So am I. I love women."

"Nell, you don't get it. I love them instead of men." Anna relaxed.

"Oh." I tried to understand what she was saying. I turned to her, my eyebrows knit together. "Does that mean we can't be friends?" There was still something I wasn't getting.

"No. It's just that there is a whole part of me I was keeping from you. That's why I might have seemed so distant." She paused. "Nell, I'm a lesbian." She said that word. Nothing was blurred now. I wanted to say something, but she had more she wanted to share. "And another thing—I went crazy a while back. Before I moved to Taos."

I was still digesting the word *lesbian* and the fact that Anna was one, but instead I asked, "You went crazy? What happened?"

"I was living in a small town in Nebraska. Elgin, Nebraska." Her voice got higher when she said the name of the town. "After I graduated college in Colorado, I didn't know what to do with myself. I knew I wanted to write, but what else? I stayed in Fort Collins for a year and worked as a pizza cook. Then my uncle offered to teach me bookkeeping so that I could take over as the bookkeeper for his company. They manufactured fire engines in Elgin, Nebraska. It's flat there and cold in the winter—I mean real cold. There's a one-room library, open from 1 to 4 P.M., Tuesdays and Thursdays. A housewife ran the library and filled the place with Betty Crocker cookbooks. So there I was, the only queer in town, trying to write and learning to fill numbers into squares in black books, while my uncle drank Wild Turkey and had an affair with his secretary."

"God, how long did you stay?" I asked.

"Well, I'm slow. I stayed for three and a half years. I practically ended up running the business. I know more about engines and public sales than the whole Taos Council did last year when they voted to buy three trucks," Anna said.

"Didn't you get lonesome?" I asked.

"You bet." She paused, twisted her mouth to the left. "Even me, a loner who likes her solitude, I couldn't take it. There was no one to talk to. I drove down to Omaha on the weekends. There was a dyke bar there. I didn't know anyone and I'm shy." Anna brushed hair again from her eyes. "I finally met someone, Clarion." Anna smiled. "She had red hair and lived on a farm. We went together for six months. She had a husband who beat her, but he got so drunk on weekends, he didn't realize she was gone."

"Did you like her? Did you have much in common?" I felt dumb.

"Yeah, we were both lonely, and we wanted each other. Anyway, her husband caught us one night. He shoved her aside—she just cowered —and he beat me up. I had a broken nose, a black eye, and couldn't raise my arm all the way for weeks. I think some ribs were busted." Anna was animated telling this story. I could tell she was glad to get it all out. "When I got back to Elgin, I told everyone I'd been in a car wreck.

When they said, 'But your car's okay,' I told them it was my boyfriend's car that got wrecked. I told 'em he had a Cadillac.'' She shook her head and laughed. "What a coward I was!''

She turned to me. "Are you with me?'' she asked. I nodded. "Well, to make short of it, I couldn't take it anymore. About a month later, I quit my job, but I didn't have the courage to leave town. I didn't know where I'd go, and I'd bought the house I was living in. Two stories. White clapboard. I even fixed the roof myself one summer.''

"Yeah, so?'' I wanted to know what happened.

"I just hung on. I kept saying I was going to write, but I didn't, and I started doing speed. Can you imagine? Speed, in that slow town? I got prescriptions from the doc. It was supposed to be for my period cramps. Then I got downers from the pharmacist in the next town. There was no drugstore in Elgin, only a grocery that sold liquor, hardware, and some canned and frozen foods. We all had big gardens. It saved you from constipation.'' She laughed.

"After a while I didn't leave the house. My eye went totally in. I stopped doing the eye exercises, and I used to hang my head out of the attic window. I think I was even drooling at the mouth when my mom came to get me.''

"Wow.'' I looked at my hands. I picked two blades of grass and tore them into tiny pieces. "You don't seem crazy now.''

"I'm not. It was the circumstances. Plus in Taos you can be anyone, and it's okay. Eventually I cooled out. Of course, my folks helped. They liked having me around. Out of the blue a while back, Daniel had enlisted in the army and was sent to Vietnam. My parents were worried about him all the time. He returned soon after I left for Taos.

"I stayed with my mom and dad for a few months. I started writing again, and it kept me sane. Maybe that's why I'm so uptight. I don't want writing to get away from me—it's all I have.'' She looked at the back of her hands.

I put my hand on her arm. "Did you think I was coming on to you, because I wanted so much of your attention?''

"I wasn't sure, but I also realized you were real tight with Gauguin." She had her legs stretched out in front of her. She picked up a stick and hit the toes of her high-top black sneakers with it.

I looked at her sneakers. "You know, Anna, you have big feet." We both laughed. I loved the way Anna laughed. It sounded like Russian olive leaves rustling in a summer breeze. "We're still friends?"

"Sure. Better now, because I told you everything," she said.

"Tell me more about your novel. How's it really going?"

"Oh, okay. Not so good. I don't know." She shrugged and frowned.

"You know, Anna, I told Gauguin that you should write a novel about me. I was only kidding, but now that I think of it—" I smiled and put my index finger on my chin. Anna rolled her eyes. "But seriously," I said, "it must be hard to have Louise in the eighteenth century. Why not write a novel about yourself or about Taos or what it's like to be a lesbian?"

"Aw, no one's interested in that. What's interesting about my life?" she scoffed.

"Hey, Willa Cather became famous writing about Nebraska—you should read her some more. Forget about those Southern writers—just be yourself. Besides, I think you're wonderful. I'd love to read about your life," I said.

She was embarrassed. "There you go again about Cather. We'd better get up," she said.

It was almost seven o'clock, and when the sun goes down in Taos, even if it's summer, it starts to get chilly. We walked back across the park to the gate. The trees were dark green now, with long shadows. I knew the sun was setting off on the mesa somewhere, the place Anna loved best, where she had lived when she first came here. I reached over and took her hand. She was at least a head taller than me. She was the tallest person I'd ever met.

13

Eventually we cleaned out the chicken house by the garden and used it for a place to meditate. We'd sit in there like hens waiting for something to hatch. Mostly what hatched were thoughts.

"Hey, Gauguin, I was thinking we should go backpacking," I said.

Gauguin turned his head slowly. "Is that what you come up with after a half-hour of meditating?"

"Yes, and let's go for a whole week," I said.

We went to the back country of Bandelier, a national monument of ancient pueblo ruins. The dirt road leading to the unexcavated ruins in the back country was rocky, the muffler on Betsy Boop fell off, and we spent a lot of time trying to wire it back. Neither Gauguin nor I was a mechanical genius. We finally threw it in the back seat and chugged loudly to the trail head, arriving in the late afternoon. We hiked in three miles until it became too dark to see, then laid out our sleeping bags, crawled in them, and skipped dinner. I must have been asleep for about an hour when I woke to the heavy breathing of an animal. I jerked up and saw two eyes staring at me in the moonlight. I could tell it was huge.

"Gauguin," I whispered urgently. He was deep in sleep. "Gauguin." I reached out my arm and shook him.

"What?" he said, his breath smoky with dreams.

"Gauguin, there's an animal out there!"

His body jerked in his sleeping bag. "Where?" He squinted and felt the ground next to him for his glasses.

"Right there." I pointed.

The animal shifted its weight. "Yeah, I just heard him. You're right. I think he's watching us," Gauguin said in a hoarse whisper. "And I think he's big."

"What should we do?" I asked.

"What can we do?" he answered. "Let's just lie here awhile."

I was sure it was a dinosaur or the ghost of a medicine man. We should never have come to a place full of ancient ruins, I thought. Gauguin fell back asleep. I stayed up alone, guardian of the great animal, mostly hoping to guard myself. The animal didn't leave, but it stayed where it was and didn't come closer.

The sky finally turned blue gray. I dared to look in the animal's direction. I lifted my head off the rolled-up towel I used as a pillow and squinted to see better. Staring back at me was a red cow! Not the kind you milk, the kind you eventually eat. It must have gotten lost and, lonesome, wanted to stay near us for company.

With my feet still in the bag, I kicked Gauguin to wake him. "Let's go. The sun is coming up." When I spoke aloud, the cow wandered off.

We hiked through fields of wild flowers, dark boulders, and forest, finally moving into more desert land. We turned toward a stream.

"Let's rest," I said, flinging off my pack and sitting down by the stream, taking off my shoes and socks. I cracked open a chocolate bar.

"Rose, now remember," Gauguin cautioned. "We each have one chocolate bar and it has to last the full week we're here. It's our only sugar treat this summer."

Uh-huh, I nodded.

The sun settled on my bare knees and I warmed my hands in patches of light that fell between leaves. Then I turned to Gauguin. "You know, I don't care, Gauguin. I'm gonna eat the whole thing," I said. I tore off the wrapper and bit off a chunk. It was good. The bite had a whole almond in it. "Want some?" I asked, offering it up in a magnanimous gesture.

"No. Now remember, I'm not sharing mine with you on the fifth night out here. We each have our own," he repeated.

I laid back on the edge of the stream and looked up through the oak leaves. "Gauguin, you couldn't be so cruel. What if I promise to make love to you eight hundred times this week?"

"Cute, Nell, real cute. But no. You'll have to live without chocolate if you finish yours." I grimaced. I already had finished it.

Oh, who cared. I smiled. No brontosaurus had eaten me last night. That was all that mattered.

"Let's go." Gauguin put on his shoes.

We followed the stream, which cut a swath of green through land that was mostly rock, arroyo, and cactus. After hiking five miles, we found a good spot to camp under a cottonwood, near a place where the water formed a pool. This would be our base camp and we could hike out to the ruins for a few hours at a time. There was no water near the ruins.

Each morning, Gauguin worked on a song about a waterbug. It was not going well. If he asked me, I would have told him a waterbug was nothing to write a song about, but he never asked me and I kept my mouth shut. I had other things to do. I was drawing airplanes and coloring them in with a box of pastels I had brought. I drew houses the way kids do, with smoke coming out the chimney, and colored tall buildings with many windows. No nature drawings. Nature was too hard to draw. I was just having fun, not caring if what I drew expressed anything deep. I read *Tortilla Flat* while Gauguin sat by the stream and watched waterbugs for inspiration. He watched them real hard and then wrote fast for three pages, hoping something brilliant would flow from his pen. Nothing brilliant came, and he ripped the used pages out of his notebook and balled them up. We used that paper to start campfires.

Near the end of the week, I filled a plastic bag full of water, clasped it with a rubber band, and ventured out by myself into the desert and the unexcavated ruins. The sun was hot, and there was no shade. In the daytime, Gauguin and I wore no clothes, so I was very brown. I put on only my sneakers to go out to the ruins.

The ruins in the back country looked like sand mounds. Cacti grew through the doors and windows of the timeless structures. As I climbed over a fallen wall toward the doorway to a small room, there was the eerie feeling that the ancient Indians were with me, and I wasn't sure they approved of what a human being had become. I felt self-conscious and wished I had worn clothes. Decades of pale dirt had filled in any square corners. My utter aloneness in the small room scared me and I climbed out quickly.

On top of a buried mound, I found a red anthill. It was the only action in this ghost town, so I squatted down to watch, feeling the sun on my back. Two ants dragged a dead fly up the hill. One lost its half of the fly and ran behind to push. Ants crawled in and out of a hole in the center of the hill. My attention was riveted.

Suddenly, I sucked in my breath. A bit of blue emerged from the center hole, balanced on the back of an ant. I looked closer. It was a turquoise bead—very small with a hole in it, a sky pearl you could string on a necklace. My fingers moved fast. I grabbed it, toppling two red ants. I stood up and stepped away from the hill, holding it in my open palm. It was so small. I groped for a pocket to put it in, but I had no pockets. I was naked. I stuck the bead in my mouth, under my tongue for safekeeping.

I ran most of the way back. I was so excited—I couldn't believe my find. The ancient people had given something to me. I wanted to show Gauguin. Leaping over a dirt mound, both legs spread in the air like scissors, I swallowed it. It wasn't big enough to feel go down, but I knew it. I stopped dead. The last of the American Indians, and I had been stupid enough to swallow it. I took a deep breath and walked steadily back to camp, half angry, half foolish, and another half wild—I had ancient turquoise inside me.

Gauguin was by the stream, still watching waterbugs, and his shoulders were burning in the sun. I leaned down over him and pushed him back on the soft dirt, held him by the arms, and stared at him hard. "Forget the waterbugs," I said. Gauguin was below me, watching. My face elongated into a beak. I had the force of an eagle. I lifted him in my talons, and together we flew over the trees by the stream, then past that, over the ruins, then higher into the blue sky until sunlight obliterated everything. We flew in that light, in circles and half circles, rolling over each other. I could have traveled for a long time, but I lost Gauguin.

He fell to earth, suddenly sat up, and went over to the campfire to make dinner. He stirred the brown rice with a fork, slowly dropping in salt granules from between two fingers. I walked over.

"Banana, I'm sorry, but I feel frustrated about that song. You're in a different space." He paused. I was quiet. "Besides, this is it. We have nothing left to eat. I told you we should have carried in more."

"I'm hungry," I said. It was my only response.

"Tomorrow, if you want to stay—"

"I want to stay," I cut him off.

"We have to fast," he finished his sentence.

"Okay by me." I was determined.

He turned his back to me. I didn't bother telling him about the turquoise. I went down by the stream and hunched at its edge, watching the water's moving light. His disappointment wasn't going to taint me. It was too good here to let anything bother me for long. Gauguin would get over his snit. I let the air comfort me. It was the best time of day, right before the sun goes down. Cool but not cold, long shadows and a soft quiet in the trees.

"Nell," Gauguin called. "The rice is almost ready. Want some?"

I hesitated. I walked over to the fire. "Okay." I nodded and picked up a bowl.

"Of course," he said slowly, "*I*'ve been saving my chocolate." He was in a completely different mood.

My face lit up. I forgave him everything. "Gimme!" I reached out my hand and fell from a squat onto my butt.

He shook his head and laughed.

"Gauguin, I will do anything." Then I tried a new tactic: I looked demure.

"Sorry, there's nothing I will want after dinner more than chocolate." He grinned.

"Me either," I said.

After we ate the very last rice kernel in our bowls, Gauguin pulled out his Kit Kat. I forgot he hadn't gotten a Cadbury, like I had.

I pleaded with my eyes.

"No, and quit looking at me like that," he said.

He opened the aluminum foil. Four wafers. He broke off one and ate it slowly. I watched and then I grabbed. He blocked me. "Now, now, Rose." He was cruel.

I knew what a dog felt like. He finished his second wafer, first holding it up in front of me. I sat still. He looked down, paused. "Here, you can have the last two." He reached out his hand.

I jumped, then stopped. "Let's share the last two."

Gauguin was startled. "Okay, thanks," and we both smiled. He handed me one and we ate them at the same time. "Why, Rose, sometimes I think you're growing up." I knew I wasn't, but I let him think whatever he wanted.

We fasted the next day. "Banana, let's leave half a day early and have chile rellenos at Sophie's." Gauguin was never good on a fast.

"No." I was resolute.

"Well, well, Miss—excuse me—Ms. Determination," he said, and we stayed.

The next day, high from fasting and a week of living in the woods, we ran down along the narrow footpaths at the edge of stone cliffs, my lightened red knapsack streaming through the green needles of ponderosa pine, and Gauguin's white sneakers flopping against the beige and then red earth. The smell of the outdoors went straight into our bodies and stayed there as we hit the old car and dashed out through rutted roads to civilization, to Santa Fe, to Sophie's.

We sat in the pale blue-green wooden booths, and both ordered chile rellenos with green chile. After the woods, humanity seemed extraordinary. There were forks, napkins, water in glasses, a table to lean our elbows on, and signs spelling out, MOCHA CAKE, PEACH COBBLER, DUTCH APPLE PIE, CHEESECAKE, HOT FUDGE SUNDAE. What an amazing thing a human being was! Not only could we bake cakes, we could have posters saying what we baked, and the mere reading of the poster made my eyes water, my mouth go slack.

I thumped my fingers on the blue tabletop and watched plates of food go by. "Maybe I should have gotten enchiladas," I told Gauguin.

"Naa, Sophie's rellenos are the best." He waved his hand. We were both hungry.

I nodded. He was right.

The waitress brought us our plates. "These are hot. Careful." She held them with potholders and placed them before us.

The green chile poured to the edge of the plate was still bubbling. On the side were pinto beans and Spanish rice.

I reached for a flour tortilla. I put a pat of butter on it, which slid off, leaving a trail of yellow liquid.

"Hey, these are hot," I exclaimed admiringly.

"Banana, your hands look like monkey paws." Gauguin watched me tear the tortilla in half.

The white cheese oozed out of the relleno as I cut it with my fork. I used the tortilla to collect it and I also smeared it in the sauce. "Ummm, good." It was finally in my mouth.

"I wonder how they stuff these?" Gauguin called over the waitress and ordered a cup of coffee.

"Who cares?" I said with another bite in my mouth. "I'm going to get peach cobbler for dessert." I gulped some water. "This was the best trip I've ever had. What was your favorite part?"

"Well, it wasn't trying to write that damn song about the waterbug. What was yours?" He looked up at me.

"Everything," I said, feeling the turquoise inside of me.

14

"Gauguin, you're not going to believe this." I'd just returned to the house from a teachers' meeting at Red Willow. We always had them in late August.

"What?" Gauguin looked up from a magazine he was reading at the kitchen table.

"My mother is flying in this Friday. She arrives on American at 11:35 in the morning. She left a message for me to phone her."

"Wow!" Gauguin said, and I looked at him expectantly. He smiled. "Hey, I'd love to meet old Edith."

"Oh, yeah?" I said, raising my eyebrows. "Don't be too sure."

"Is she going to stay with us?"

"Are you kidding? Where? No, I'd better make reservations at the Kachina."

"How long is she coming for?"

"I don't know. I just got the message. I have to call her. Not too long, I hope. Rosh Hashanah is early this year, so she'll have to get back."

"What's that?" Gauguin asked.

"The Jewish New Year." I was half out the door and called back, "I'm going to see Blue for a minute." I had just heard her pickup drive past our house.

"Hey, Blue!" I ran up the hill, waving my hand with the note in it.

She slammed the truck door. "Hey, sugar, help me carry these groceries in." She handed me a brown bag.

"What's this?" I asked, as I unpacked her bag on the kitchen table. "Christmas lights—and tinsel? It's August."

"Yeah." Blue was beaming. "I found it in Safeway on sale. I'm going to decorate the whole house."

"Now?" I almost forgot my mother was coming.

"Sure, and then I'll take it down before Christmas and give it away." Blue was very pleased with herself. She hummed as she opened the refrigerator. Blue was always so logical.

"My mother's coming this Friday," I said.

Blue held the fridge door open. "What good news! I always wanted to meet her. Does she have pretty eyes like you? Let's have a party for her."

"A party?" I asked in disbelief.

"We can ask Neon, Happiness, Tiny—"

"Blue, please. I'm nervous enough. I haven't seen her in more than a year." I sat down.

Blue stopped putting cans of dog food away. She blinked her eyes several times and then came and sat down beside me on the couch. "Oh, I get it. Your mother. Well, what's she like?"

My mother's plane was two hours late. There had been a thunderstorm in Chicago, and they'd had to circle a long time before they could land. "Nell"—my mother began weeping in my arms—"I thought the plane would crash and I'd never see you again!"

I smiled weakly. "Of course you would." I patted her back and then took a bag she was carrying. "What's this?"

"Oh, I brought some things for you. A kosher chicken, Barton's truffles, Ebinger's cookies, dill pickles, stuffed cabbage, a challah Grandma made. Some things from the freezer. You'll see." Talking about

what she brought pleased her. She looked around the Albuquerque airport. "My, this is"—she dug around for the right word—"primitive."

I smiled. "Well, it's not Kennedy."

After we got the rest of her bags off the carousel, we walked out to
the parking lot. She squinted, not used to such bright sun. She took hold
of my arm and looked out at the Sandias. "My," she said, "that looks like
Israel, in the Negev desert." She grew quiet.

We stopped for a bite to eat in Santa Fe and continued on through
Española and Velarde and then entered the gorge. "My," she said.
"My." She said that word over and over. New Mexico was a strange place
to her. Sage, chamisa, dirt roads, treeless hills, and such open space. She
was out of her element. She had no words for what she saw.

"Those houses"—she pointed to an adobe—"they're made of dirt.
And that"—she pointed to the Rio Grande—"it's not that big. I thought
it would be like the Hudson River. And look at that." There was a white
cross leaning off a steep cliff. She bent her head near the windshield to see
it better.

We stopped for peaches at the Russian woman's stand in Rinconada.
She touched the red chile ristras hanging above her head and insisted on
paying for the peaches. "My," she said when we were back in the car and
she bit into one. "They're so juicy and ripe." I realized I'd almost never
seen her outside of Brooklyn.

"My, everything's so big," she said, swiveling her head around.

"Yeah," I said. "I love all the space."

"Well, we have the ocean back east," she said defensively. "There's
Coney Island, Jones Beach." Now she was on a roll. "We have some
things. There's the subways, the *Daily News,* the synagogue, your father
and mother, your grandmother and sister. Nell, why don't you consider
coming home?"

Just then, we completed the horseshoe turn below Taos, and Taos
Mountain became visible. The plain swept out from it, revealing the
distant gorge that looked like a crack in the earth.

"Look," I said, and nodded my head out at the scenery.

She caught her breath. "I've never seen anything like it."

Now we drove straight north, Taos Mountain in front of us. That friend, that majestic teacher, that god, I thought. It could even shut my mother up.

But not for long. "Nell, I hope the hotel is clean and has air conditioning. I need a good hard bed."

"Don't worry, Mom. It will be perfect. Besides, it's seven thousand feet up. The nights are cool. And there's no humidity."

"No humidity?" That amazed her.

We pulled into the Kachina. After we got her room key, I told her, "I'll pick you up in an hour. I have some errands to run. We're going to the house. Gauguin's making dinner."

I bent to kiss her good-bye and she grabbed me. "Oh, Nell, I'm so happy to see you."

"Sure—me too, Mom." I peeled her arms from around me.

I ran to the post office to pick up our mail and stopped in at Dori's for a cookie.

"Hey!" Neon called from a back table.

"I can't stay long. My mother's here." I sat down at the edge of my chair. I wore white shorts and a red cotton top. My mother said you can never have too much summer white.

"Oh, so that's it." Neon took a sip of tea. "You seemed nervous, the same way you were with Rita. Both my parents have high blood pressure so they can't come to such a high altitude." Neon shined a big toothy grin. "I'd like to meet her."

"Not today," I said, looking at Neon's beaded moccasins and the leather pouch dangling from his belt. "I have to go."

My mother had changed into white polyester pants and a hot pink blouse. "How do I look?" She turned around so I could see her from all angles. She wore gold earrings and three gold dangle bracelets. People said we looked alike. I couldn't see it. She had short, very curly black hair with a few streaks of gray and black eyes with blue eye shadow smeared on her eyelids. She was shorter than me, and stouter. When she was fifteen she weighed 160 pounds, and though she lost all that a long time ago, she couldn't forget it.

"You look fine," I said.

"Not pretty?" she asked.

"Yes, pretty." I held the door open for her. My whole childhood I had had to assure her of her beauty. My father thought she was gorgeous.

We pulled up to our house in Talpa. I could see she was stunned, but she said instead, "My, it's so simple."

I looked at it. "I guess so."

Gauguin came out to greet us. He was almost dressed up in new jeans and a red Guatemalan shirt.

He took my mother off guard when he hugged her after I introduced them and called her by her first name. "Welcome, Edith," he said. All my friends back home called her Mrs. Schwartz.

We walked into the house. "I didn't know that people lived like this anymore," she said, looking around at the wood stove and bucket of water. "My," she said, "it's primitive."

We sat down to eat. "Nell, don't forget to put the food I brought in the refrigerator," she said. "The meat is defrosting."

I got up and put the food away and then sat back down on the bench.

Gauguin had set the table with fresh daisies and our best plates from the flea market in Santa Fe. He held out his arms. "Let's hold hands," he said.

My mother reluctantly took his hand and then reached for mine across the table. We closed our eyes. She closed her eyes, too. There was silence except for the incessant buzz of a fly on our ceiling and the sound of a chain saw in the distance.

"Thank you," Gauguin said. "Thanks for bringing Edith here."

I squeezed my mother's hand gently, then we let go and opened our eyes.

Gauguin had made vegetarian enchiladas with blue corn tortillas. He took my mother's plate and served her some. I tossed the salad.

She was very quiet and then blurted out, "Just who were we thanking?"

"When?" I lifted the lettuce onto her plate.

"When we held hands."

"Oh," Gauguin stepped in. "I guess the earth and heavens. Maybe the airline you flew on."

"Don't worry, Mom. It wasn't Jesus."

She picked at her food. I thought the enchiladas were delicious and told Gauguin. My mother agreed, though I knew she didn't like them. She'd never eaten Mexican food before.

Gauguin told my mother about his father's architecture business and how he used to visit his grandmother in Iowa every summer.

"Only in the summers?" my mother asked.

"Yes, but we talked on the phone every week in the winter." I knew this was a lie. He'd never even spoken to his mother the whole time I lived with him.

"And did you go to church?" she asked.

"Certainly," he said. This, too, wasn't true and it was the wrong thing to say.

"Catholic?" she asked.

"No, Protestant," he said.

"My, hmm." She grew quiet. "How nice."

"We have ice cream for dessert," I chimed in before my mother began talking about the shame of Christians for not speaking out against anti-Semitism. My mother loved ice cream. "What flavor did you get?" I asked Gauguin.

"Cherry vanilla," he said proudly.

Even I grimaced at that. "No coffee or chocolate?"

My mother said she was on a diet anyway and then asked where the bathroom was.

"It's out back," I said. "Come, I'll show you."

"Out back?" Her mouth fell open.

"Mom, I told you months ago that we had an outhouse," I said.

"Yes, but I thought you were just kidding or you said it to aggravate me." She was flabbergasted.

We walked outside. "Nell, I just can't."

"Oh, come on, Mom. What else are you going to do?"

"I'll hold it in," she said.

We got to the outhouse door and I opened it.

"Oh, my god! I can't. The smell!" she shrieked.

"Hold your nose and go in," I demanded in a no-nonsense voice. Here we go again, I thought. Now my mother is my little sister, too.

She held her nose with one hand and struggled to pull down her girdle with the other. I didn't want to watch. I shut the door and told her I'd stand guard outside.

"Nell, I can't see," she called through the door in a weak voice. I opened it a crack to let in the dim evening light. "Oh, Nell," she whined.

She sounded so helpless, I weakened. "Mom, do you want me to drive you back to town to go to the bathroom?"

"Please, Nell, my pants are half up and half down. Help me."

I opened the door. Blue's goats bleated up the hill.

"What's that?" She was startled, but still she did not take her fingers off her nose, so everything she said sounded nasal.

"Nothing," I said. "Nothing. Step out so you can take your fingers off your nose and pull up your pants."

"Nell, I can't. Someone will see me." She stood with the flesh of her hips and stomach—the belly I came out of—hanging over the elastic of the girdle. The polyester white of her pants seemed to glow in the dark. She was wearing white patent leather shoes.

"No one will see. There's no one around." Of course, just then we heard a pickup fly by on the road in front of our house. Then I had another suggestion. "Hold your breath, and then pull up your pants with both hands." I looked in at my mother. She looked so pitiable. "What do you want me to do?" I asked.

"Pull up my pants for me. Please," she begged in a nasal voice.

I reached in and jerked them up over her hips. She stepped out of the outhouse.

"Okay, let me run in and get the car keys, and I'll drive you to the hotel."

I ran into the house. "Where's your mother?" Gauguin sounded alarmed.

"Don't worry. She didn't fall in. We're going back to the hotel to the bathroom. Forget making coffee," I called as I ran out the door.

My mother was already in the car. I started it up.

"Please, tell Gauguin for me, 'Thank you for dinner,' " she said meekly.

"Oh, sure. No problem." I took it easy on the dirt roads. I didn't want to shake her up anymore.

We parked in front of the Kachina. She reached out her arm and put her hand on mine.

"Nell, come in with me."

"Okay," I said.

I sat on the bed and read a copy of *New Mexico* magazine I found on the nightstand while my mother was in the bathroom. The toilet flushed and she emerged.

"Nell, let's call Daddy. It's not too late in Brooklyn. They'd love to talk with you."

She dialed the number.

"Irving? Hello, Irving, it's me. Yes. She looks beautiful. Tell me. What? Your voice doesn't sound good. What's wrong?"

My father was telling her something. My mother uttered, "No, no" and "My god" every few moments. Then she hung up.

I was sitting on the bed. It had a big flowered black-and-white cover. "Hey, wait. I thought I was going to talk. What happened?"

"Nell," she said, her hand still on the phone. "I have to go home as soon as possible."

I sat up. "Is it Grandma?" Tears sprang to my eyes.

"No." She waved her hand. "It's Rita, again." And then she told me what happened.

Rita had been playing music so loud in the afternoon that the neighbors called the police. When there was a knock on the apartment door, Rita, who had been taking a bath, answered it naked. There was no one else home and the policeman had to scream to be heard over the record player. A small group gathered in the hall and it never dawned on Rita to put her clothes on. Lugging two bags of groceries, my grandmother had reached the top of the stairs and almost had a heart attack when she saw Rita with the police.

"I'm so worried. I don't know what she'll do next!" My mother had her hand to her mouth.

"Oh, Mom, come on. That's Rita. You've come to visit *me*. Stay. They can all take care of themselves."

"No, I have to go." My mother's eyes were faraway. I'd been through this before. There was no changing her mind. She had to save my sister. "I'll leave early tomorrow morning. You'll drive me to Albuquerque?"

"Sure." I rolled my eyes to the ceiling. Just what I wanted to do— drive six hours round-trip the same route I'd done today.

"I've seen enough of this area already. I just wanted to make sure you were okay," she said.

I rallied for a moment. "But, Mom, you've never been out west before—"

"Never mind. I have to go home."

I nodded slowly. She would never meet Blue or Happiness or Neon or eat at the House of Taos or visit Red Willow or see my paintings.

15

Sometime in late November, Anna and I had lunch together. She wore a gray crewneck with a white T-shirt underneath. I could see the white sticking out around the collar of the sweater. Anna's clothes always looked like Anna. They were simple, long and baggy, always gray, brown, or black. She wore a braided leather band around her left wrist and was the only person I knew who didn't have pierced ears.

"Anna? Do you think I'm pretty?" I asked. She looked up from her sandwich. She was surprised.

"Doesn't Gauguin tell you?"

"What does he have to do with it? I want to know if *you* think I am." We were at Steven's Kitchen, and the lunch crowd had emptied out. I took a swig of my water.

"Nell, what do you want to know that for?"

"I guess I never know what you think of me. I figure you like me, but I like to hear it," I answered.

"You mean, am I attracted to you? Yeah, you're attractive, but you're straight, which means I'm out. I just don't think about it much. We're friends." She took another bite of her sandwich.

"How come I never hear about anyone you go out with?" I asked. She smiled. "Because I never go out."

"Why not? Aren't there lesbians around? Aren't you attracted to anyone?"

"Nell, I like being alone. I haven't made love with anyone in a year and a half. It just happens when it's right. I can be patient," Anna said.

"You're too passive." I frowned.

"We're just different. I hardly saw any folks when I was growing up. I'm used to being alone."

"Are you still planning to go home for Christmas?" I asked.

"Yes."

"Why, if it's so lonely there?"

"Well, I miss my ma." She hesitated. "Nell?"

"Yeah?"

"I'm thinking of moving back there."

I stopped my grilled cheese sandwich midway to my mouth. "What!"

"I said I'm thinking of moving home." She said it tentatively, but I felt certainty underneath. "I'm broke. I'm sick of my novel. It doesn't feel right. I miss the cornfields, how they're plowed in March, dark and wet. The smell of manure. I don't know. I love Taos, but it's not my home. Nebraska's my home, and I want to see if I can be there again."

"Are you forgetting the slaughterhouses and that there are no lesbians?" I was incredulous.

"Well, not in Elgin, but I know there are some in Omaha and Lincoln. I thought I might move to Lincoln. There's a university there." She was almost finished with her club sandwich. An old fly that should have died at the end of the summer walked across my bread. I waved it off.

"How serious are you? When did you get this idea?"

"It's been cooking slow in me, and yesterday I found out there are no more extensions on unemployment," Anna said, and pushed some hair out of her eye.

"When will you go?" I listened carefully now.

"I thought I'd go for Christmas and stay." She looked straight at me.

"But we've only been friends such a short time." I looked down at my hands.

"We'll always be friends." She reached out and touched my wrist. "And, yes, I think you're pretty. I love your dark eyes and your curly hair." One thing about Anna, she always came around. I smiled, and there was a moment of silence. I couldn't imagine Taos without her. Already I felt a rising sense of dread at the thought of her leaving.

The waitress brought over the bill, and Anna grabbed it. "I'll treat you." She paid at the cash register. Then she held the swinging door open for me in a gallant gesture and bowed from the waist.

"Ma-dame," she said, smiling.

We walked down Bent Street and looked at the Christmas decorations. Already there were the traditional farolitos lined up along the adobe rooftops. It was such a simple decoration—a brown bag with sand in the bottom to hold a lit candle that reflected golden through the paper—and one that I loved. We smelled cedar smoke and piñon coming from chimneys.

"You're going to leave all this?" I asked Anna, gesturing widely. I couldn't believe it.

"Yes," she nodded.

When I went home, Gauguin was playing the accordion in the back room. He had found the accordion at a garage sale the week before and figured out how to play a few simple songs on it. He liked trying out different instruments.

"Nell, is that you?" he called out.

"Yeah," I called back, and sat down on a wooden chair by the kitchen table.

"C'mon back."

"No," I yelled out to him. I traced the blue checks on the table-cloth.

Gauguin walked in and put his hand on my shoulder. "What's up?"

"Anna's leaving." I looked up from the tablecloth.

"Where to?" He ran his hand through my hair.

"She's leaving. That's all." I pushed his hand from my hair, walked over to the window, and breathed on the pane so it became foggy. I drew a heart in the center of the fog with my finger. Gauguin waited by the table. "She's moving back to Nebraska. Says it's her home." I turned around to look at him. "Doesn't anyone love it here like I do?"

"I can understand her wanting to go," he said softly.

"Everyone seems to leave. They come and go in Taos. No one stays forever like I want to." I hated everyone.

"Well, you know how I feel. There's no way to make a living here." He stepped behind me. "Nell?" He ran his finger along the collar of my sweater.

"Oh, you! You wanted to go six months after you moved here," I spat back, and stepped away.

"I like it, but there's nothing happening. It's pretty, but pretty gets old." Gauguin was angry now too. Then he paused and softened. "I've stayed here because of you."

"I'm going for a walk," I said, and slammed the door behind me.

I didn't walk far; mostly I stood out on the dirt road and looked up at the sky, turning my head at the sound of Blue's goats. There was a bite in the air that carried me down the dark river of winter.

16

In the middle of December, Anna left. I drove her to the Lamy train station, and on the way we stopped in Santa Fe.

"Hey, let's go for lunch. We have plenty of time," I said, trying to be cheerful but feeling like I might burst into tears at any moment.

"Okay, but I don't want to miss the train." Anna sat in the passenger seat, opening and closing her hands.

"Hey, Anna, would you cut it out? These are our last moments together. I'd like them to be meaningful. Could you at least act as if they were?" We pulled up at a sandwich shop in Tesuque.

"Sorry, Nell. I'm just nervous."

"Would you quit calling me Nell? I'm Banana!" I got out and slammed the car door. I didn't want her to leave.

"Hey, wait! We have to lock the car." Anna went to my side, opened the door, pushed down the button, and then slammed the door closed.

I didn't wait for her. I went into the restaurant and stood by the blackboard menu. Anna came up behind me and put her arm around my shoulders.

The waitress showed us to a table by the window and took our order. I asked for potato chowder. Anna had a sprout salad and lentil

soup. It had snowed that morning and the blacktop was slick and wet. It
stood out against the snow and the crystallized tree branches. A red Chevy
pickup turned the corner onto a long dirt drive full of mud and slush.

"Hey, Anna, there's a trailer park." I pointed. "I remember hearing about a palm reader who lives there. Want to go? You should know
your future before you leave."

"Naw, Nell—I mean, Banana." She was really trying. "I just want
to be with you. No palm reader. I want just to pay attention." A broad
smile spread over her face. "Maybe I'll write about us sometime." She
pretended her finger was a pencil and she wrote on the green tablecloth.
" 'Nell, who liked to be called Banana, sat in the simple sandwich shoppe.
She feared her friend leaving, but her friend knew they would always be
together.' "

I grabbed the pencil from her, which was her finger, and began
writing, too. " 'Nell had a sorrow in her, not only because Anna was
leaving, but because Gauguin wanted Nell to leave, too. Once leaving
began, it continued until there was nothing left.' " I liked my last line. It
made me feel like a poet.

Anna looked at me. "So *that's* it. What's going on?"

"Gauguin's sick of Taos." I ate a potato chip that came with the
soup.

"Will you go with him?" Anna asked.

"I don't know. There's only one thing I love more than Taos, and
that's Gauguin. He's been wanting to go for a long time, but I haven't
given him much space to talk about it." I shrugged. I wanted to change
the subject. Anna nodded.

I studied Anna closely. I was determined to remember everything
about her. Her knuckles were bigger than her fingers; her wrists were
thin. Her hair, which was mostly straight, had a curl behind her left ear.
She sometimes chewed at the ends of her hair and she clipped her finger-
nails short. She seemed calm, but I knew her to be nervous underneath,
never sure that she was really sane.

She was telling me about a mare her mother still had. "Ginny is so

old now, you look at her and she doesn't look like a horse anymore."
Anna liked animals. They matched her silence. I think what I liked most
about her was that she knew something about herself that no one could
take away. Something nameless.

Just before the waitress came over to ask if everything was all right,
Anna put a strand of hair behind her ear. I made that gesture bind me to
her. "You're not eating, Nell," she said to me.

"No, I'm not hungry." I turned the spoon around in the soup.

"Do you remember when we walked down to the Rio Chiquita after
you'd eaten peyote buttons?" Anna asked. "You didn't say one word the
whole walk, and then when we got to the river—" I started laughing and
nodding, knowing the end. "I thought you were into something really
deep, like the oneness of nature. I was waiting for you to say something
profound. Just when we got to the river's edge, you stopped, looked at
me intently, and said, in the most serious voice, 'The frogs in Pittsburgh
are as big as cocker spaniels.' "

When she said that part about cocker spaniels, I laughed so hard, I
choked on my potato chowder. "Here, drink this." Anna handed me a
glass of water. I took a big gulp. A tear rolled down my cheek and I shook
my head from side to side.

When we reached the station, there was only one other woman waiting for the train. She wore a net on her gray hair. At her feet was a
shopping bag. We could see a box of tissues in it and what looked like
crusts of sandwich bread in a plastic container. She wore a yellow cardigan
and a heavy white shawl. Though it was December, it was hot in the sun.
She sat on a bench, leaning against the station wall.

I leaned over and whispered in Anna's ear. "Maybe she'll give you a
Kraft American cheese sandwich on the train, if you're good."

Anna crinkled her nose. We heard the train coming, and we stood
up. Anna had two big gold suitcases and a box. I was going to ship the rest
of her stuff. The front of the train passed and stopped ahead of us.

Anna grabbed me. "Nell, I'm gonna miss you."

I helped her lift her bags up the three steps. Then she jumped down again. "Hey, Nell." She bent to my ear, and in a whisper loud enough to be heard above the engines, she said, "If you didn't have Gauguin, I'd be in love with you." My head jerked around. She let out an enormous happy scream and jumped on the train. She smiled so big, I was sure her crooked front tooth would fall out.

I yelled above the train, "Are you serious?" She nodded vigorously, laughing so much I wasn't sure whether to believe her. I gave her the finger. Under the big sky, the train pulled away, past the red cliffs. She waved.

I stood on the platform, watching the train disappear and listening as its sound became faint.

Now Anna was gone. No more malts at Rexall's. Maybe that was a good thing, since she ordered vanilla anyway. I told her it was disgusting. She didn't listen. I liked that about Anna. She had her own mind. What else didn't she listen to? She didn't listen when I told her about the way Gauguin made love. Now that I thought of it, I ought to be mad at Anna for not listening, but how could I be? I loved her and she had just now left on this train headed somehow for Nebraska and away from New Mexico.

17

A week after Anna left, Blue came over to our house and said she wanted us to meet her new boyfriend. I was surprised when she first told me about him a month ago. I didn't know she even went out with men. It happened suddenly. He was riding a motorcycle through the blinking light north of town and he almost smashed Blue's dog into smithereens.

She screamed after him, "You jerk! Watch where you're going!" She grabbed Bonnie's collar and dragged him whimpering across the road, back to the Texaco station. Then she shoved the nozzle from the gas pump into her pickup. When the register recorded $8.11, the man on the bike sped up beside her.

He took off his leather glove and held out his hand. "Sorry about your dog, ma'am."

Blue didn't look up. She snarled at him. "Think you're a big shot on a motorcycle, don't you?" She climbed in her truck and slammed the door.

That was it. He fell in love with her and followed her home. She ignored him, told him to get his trashy bike off her land. He must have had some kind of mystical connection with Blue, however, because though it was late September, he sent her Christmas tree ornaments, silver balls that had Day of the Dead paintings on them. They fit perfectly with the way she was decorating her house that fall. After that, she was willing to meet him in town a few times for malts at Rexall's. He loved to eat and would order two for himself. Blue barely finished hers. Things happened gradually, she told me.

I said sure, we'd come to dinner.

She was pleased.

Sam stood up from the table when we walked in.

Oh, my god, I thought. He looks like a madman. Blue may have been a tinge mad, but this was all-out crazy. His hair was matted, his skin rutty. He wore a T-shirt ripped wide open at the neck. He had thick hands. He didn't say a word of greeting, just stared at us.

I could tell Gauguin was stunned, too. He tried to make a joke. "Hey, I like your hair. Did it with an egg beater?" Blue laughed behind her hand.

Sam simply responded, "No." He didn't register that it was a tease.

When we sat down, Blue asked, "Want a beer?"

I didn't. Gauguin did. Sam was already drinking.

Blue had made delicious posole with green chile and onions. The natural accompaniment would have been tortillas, but Blue made french fries to go with it. She put a big plate of them, still greasy from the frying pan, on the table. They turned out to be delicious together.

"Hey, Blue." I closed my eyes and made believe I was touching a crystal ball. "I can see it now. A restaurant: Blue's Babies. And the food will be unusual combinations: sardines with refried beans, cornflakes in ginger ale, fried liver and raw apples."

We all laughed, except Sam, who bent over his plate and kept eating. Blue, Gauguin, and I talked about goats and chickens, Sylvester, her rooster, our garden, about Lightning, who was visiting his father for the holidays. Gauguin even sang a new song he was writing, and I told Blue about two pictures of shadows I had drawn.

"Shadows?" Blue asked.

"Yes, I'm experimenting with pastels. I'm trying whatever comes into my head." I glanced over at Sam. No reaction. I wanted to kick him under the table. Hey, you! I wanted to scream. Wake up!

Blue said, "That's good," and she put her arm over Sam's shoulder, scrunching him near her. "Do you like the posole, honey?"

Even then he didn't say anything. He nodded like a hairy sheep with a heavy head.

"Maybe we should leave," I suggested nervously when dinner was over.

"Not yet. I have something to tell you." Blue looked over at us while she cleared some dishes. Our motion to get up from the table stopped. I was afraid she was going to tell us she was getting married. "Sam is a carpenter. He's building a house for us up on the mesa, and when he's done, I'm moving in with him."

Sam still stared straight ahead.

"You're moving! Not you, too?" I cried in disbelief.

"It's only eight miles away." Blue looked at me.

Gauguin asked, "What kind of house?"

Blue answered Gauguin. "Oh, it's a very unusual house. Sam's making it up as he goes along."

Gauguin looked at Sam. "I bet," Gauguin said.

My hands were sweating. I felt emotional. The mesa? That was where Anna had lived when she first came to Taos. All that space, she said, healed her. My heart started to ache, remembering Anna. I didn't say another word.

Blue walked us out the door while Sam moved to the couch. The night was cold and snappy. She took my arm. "Banana, I'm not leaving. Don't worry, I'll still be around—I'll always be here. Good or bad, Taos is my home." She understood how I was feeling.

"Promise?" I grabbed her. "I miss Anna so much," I breathed into her shoulder.

"Come with me one day to the mesa and see where I'll be living. It won't be for a while. Probably not until next September. Sam's doing it all by hand.''

"Okay," I said, and let her go.

Then Gauguin hugged Blue and thanked her for the delicious and unusual dinner.

Gauguin and I walked down to our house. We could hear Blue shutting her door tight behind us.

"Banana, he's a weirdo," said Gauguin, and we both started to laugh.

18

In February, it snowed so hard that we had to order an extra cord of wood. The wood we had collected in the fall on wood runs in Gauguin's pickup was not enough to keep us warm through that much cold. The cord we bought had half birch, some piñon, and some cedar. The piñon burned hot, because of its dense sap. The cedar smelled good and was the best to split open, because it was so beautiful.

The morning after the cord was delivered, I went out to chop wood, the way Gauguin had taught me. My breath thickened as it hit the air. The sky was a frozen blue, a color so clear no one yet has been able to name it.

I put a log of cedar on an old tree stump that was near the woodpile. The log split the long way and exposed the red heart of cedar. I opened that red heart over and over again in the stiff morning light.

By the time I was finished and had gathered an armful of wood to carry inside, clouds had formed, and it had begun snowing all over again. I stomped my boots at the doorstep to get the snow off them and then I swung into the kitchen. Gauguin was at the table, finishing his breakfast of fried potatoes, green chiles, and biscuits.

"Let's go for a walk," I said.

"Okay," he said. I went back to the front door.

"Oh, Banana," Gauguin sang, like the words to an opera, "why does an elephant paint his toenails all different colors? I'll tell you the answer on the way.''

We walked up the hill behind Blue's house. Gauguin was ahead of me. He moved in and out of sight between piñon and falling snow.

''Well, why does he?'' I yelled. ''Why does the elephant paint his toenails?''

''All different colors,'' Gauguin added. ''Get to the top and you'll get the answer!'' he yelled back.

By the time we reached the top, my heart was beating fast and I was sweating. I pulled off my brown wool cap and stuck it in my pocket. I took off my mittens. Gauguin turned and kissed me. His lips felt cold against my hot ones.

''Well, why does he?'' I asked. I closed my eyes and stuck out my tongue so I could feel the snow fall on it.

''What?'' Gauguin had a quizzical look on his face.

I tugged at the sleeve of his green army jacket. ''Tell me now. Why does the elephant paint his toenails different colors?''

''I'm not telling until you give me ten kisses,'' he said, remembering the joke. Our breath was a fog between us. I kissed him only once and stood back.

''I know,'' I said. ''To leave his footprints in the cheesecake.''

''No,'' he said, laughing. ''That's how you can tell the elephant was in the refrigerator.''

''How?'' I was confused.

''His footprint was on the cheesecake,'' he answered.

''Oh.'' I still didn't get it. ''And what about the toenails? All different colors?''

''Let's start from the beginning.'' Gauguin didn't want his joke to get lost. ''Why did the elephant paint his toenails all different colors?''

''Because he was going to the junior prom?'' I no longer cared.

''No, be serious,'' Gauguin demanded.

''Okay, serious. So he could get his social security number and pay taxes like a responsible citizen." Finally I got to tease him. We stood face to face. I liked this. I was getting interested again.

"I'm not telling the joke. It's ruined." Gauguin became stubborn.

"I'd like to ruin you. Let's go home." I took one step down the hill.

"No, wait." Gauguin touched me on the shoulder. "Look." He nodded his head out toward the view.

I looked out at the two mountains that came together like two elephants kissing. "Where can you find two mountains that look like two elephants kissing?" I asked.

Gauguin pointed out across the landscape.

"See, I give you easy jokes," I said.

"That wasn't a joke," he answered as we both gazed ahead.

The whole Rio Grande plain spread out in front of us. To the right was Taos Mountain, like a great thunder god, covered in storm white. I sighed. This was the most beautiful place in America.

"Nell," Gauguin whispered.

"Yeah?" I reached out to hold his hand. A jackrabbit flashed by between two piñons. I turned my head fast to watch it disappear. I heard Bonnie barking far below.

"You love it here, don't you?" Gauguin asked.

"Yes." I nodded and then I turned suspiciously. I suddenly realized he was building up to something, and I knew what was coming next.

"Nell, I've got to move. I want to play music, and I don't want to do it for the Friday night ski crowd anymore."

"I just can't go. I never felt like I do here," I said.

"C'mon, you've got to see my point." Gauguin let go of my hand. He'd been trying to get me to listen for weeks now.

"Please, later," I said, and began running in the soft snow.

He came after me and clutched my arm. "You've got to let me talk, Nell!" He was screaming now. "I'm not staying here forever."

I put my hands over my ears. "I don't want to hear it. Don't scream at me!" I yelled. "First Anna, now you. I don't know what to do. I love you. I hate you. I'm all mixed up. I don't want to go away." I started to sob.

Gauguin grabbed me. Tears were streaming down his face. His glasses fogged, and he pulled them off. "Please, Nell, please," he wailed.

"I can't. I don't know what to do." I felt like a caged animal. I bolted and began racing down the hill.

Gauguin ran after me. I dodged in and out of piñons. I was moving so fast, I felt like a jackrabbit. I gulped for air. He was close. I could hear his loud breathing but not his footsteps in the snow.

"I'm going to get you!" he called from behind. Suddenly, it became a game. He caught up, and then as he passed me, he yelled, "Last one to the house is an elephant!"

I grabbed his jacket. "No, you don't!" I yelled back. He tripped me and I rolled three feet. The snow was dry, and I quickly brushed it off. I could hear his laughter as I saw his jacket flash between two piñons.

"Stop, stop!" I screamed. I scrambled up and dashed after him. I hated being beaten in a race.

By the time my wet face hit the heat of the kitchen, he was already undressed and in bed under the covers. My boots squished on the floor. I bent and flung one boot off. "Wait until I get you," I called into the bedroom.

I climbed into bed and grabbed for him. "Ouch, Nell, warm up first." He dodged my hands, but he couldn't get far. "Ouch, ouch," he squealed.

Then I began to kiss him. He moved his face away. "Nell, I can't make love just yet. Can we talk first? I really need to."

"Okay, let's talk." My heart was much softer after the race. I turned on my back and traced the vigas on the ceiling with my eyes. "What do you want to say? I'll listen," I said. The third viga from the wall had a long crack in it.

Gauguin paused awhile. I counted the wood boards that lay on top of the vigas. "Look, I can't stay here forever. I've got to go, Nell. Come August first, I'm leaving, with or without you."

I finished counting the boards. There were twelve. "Where do you think you'll go?" I asked.

"I don't know. New Orleans? Denver? Anyplace?" he reasoned.

I took in a deep breath, turned, and put my arm over his shoulder. "Gauguin, I love you. You've been really patient, haven't you?"

"Well, I love you, Nell. I wish it felt right to stay."

I could see how relieved he was that we were finally talking. "I'll think about it," I said.

"What?" he asked.

"Whether I could come with you or not."

"Nell," he said.

He kissed me long and slow. We didn't say another word. With my eyes closed, I saw rock gardens, bare cottonwood branches by the river. I made love out of something old and broken. We knew now that this would not last forever, this room, these windows, that sky outside. Our lovemaking was tender, the way pears lean on each other in a round bowl, and the whole time I heard the bells on Blue's goats tinkling in the distance. The snow fell and I fell with it.

Later, I sat at the table as Gauguin heated up black bean soup, his back toward me.

"Gauguin, remember when we went to Israel and Kita's wedding up in that meadow near El Salto? When we brought that blue bowl full of cut pineapple and cantaloupe?"

"Yeah? How come you're bringing that up?"

"I don't know. I'm reminiscing. I want to remember everything as it was before I go," I said.

When he turned around, a big smile was spread over his face. He placed a bowl of soup in front of me. "You mean you're going to come with me?"

"What else can I do? You're the only thing I love better than Taos. I can't imagine life here without you. Maybe if we went to Denver, I could find a painting teacher."

"How about Boulder?" he asked.

"Yeah, we could go there." I started to cry. Gauguin came around the table and held me. "What will you do?" I asked.

"I could paint houses again, like I did before I left for Peru. I got real good."

"And then you'd play at night?" I asked. He nodded.

After dinner, I sat at the table. I could hear Gauguin in the next room practicing scales.

I remembered the Thanksgiving just past, when we had stayed up all night at the Luhan house. Gauguin and Neon drummed. Anna didn't like parties, but I'd talked her into coming and she had a great time. Happiness was there, too, and Blue, Lightning, Cucumber, Tiny, and Fine Point. I brought my feet down one at a time to a slow sway in tune with the beat. When the sun finally rose and Gauguin and Neon quit drumming, I still stepped, one foot after the other. My feet were stepping with an internal drummer, my heart, and it felt as though I would never stop. I did stop, though, when Cedar brought out the sour cream chocolate cake I had baked the day before. She held it high. "Hey, let's have this for breakfast. We never got around to eating it last night."

With my first bite, I said a spontaneous poem. "The title of my poem is 'Chocolate Cake.' " I paused. I said the title again. " 'Chocolate Cake: I made it and I ate it.' " I liked it, it sort of rhymed.

Cucumber, who was a totally pure macrobiotic, said, "I got one: 'Chocolate Cake: I didn't make it and I hate it.' " She squatted in the corner, eating a whole-wheat cracker.

Sitting at the kitchen table, thinking of that Thanksgiving, I began to cry all over again.

19

U h-oh, there's Sam, I said to myself as I turned the corner, heading
out of Rexall's. I wanted to avoid him. It was March, three
months after that dinner at Blue's. Whenever I visited her now, she was
alone. I had begun to think Sam was a mirage. I wanted it that way.

"Hey, Banana!" he yelled. I couldn't believe it. He could speak.

"Oh, hi." I hesitated and made like I didn't recognize him for a
moment. "Oh, Sam," I said, haltingly.

"Yeah." He smiled such a sweet smile, I was taken off guard. His
hair was still matted. "It's nice to see you." He was friendly, too. "Have
time for something at the counter?"

I was so stunned, I nodded yes and followed him back into Rexall's.
We sat on two swivel stools.

"You should come up sometime and see the house I'm building for
Blue."

I nodded. I was still speechless. We both turned away from each
other when the waitress placed our drinks on the counter. We leaned over
our straws. I had a lemonade, Sam had a root beer. We said nothing for
half the drink.

Then Sam raised his head, turned to face me, and blurted, "I'm so

in love with Blue and Blue loves you so much that I got scared. I wanted
to make a good impression and instead I froze.''

"Oh," I said. "That's okay." Was it okay? I didn't know. I was
embarrassed that he was saying this stuff.

"Really, you should come up to the mesa. Blue told me you're
leaving in August. Come before you go. It will almost be finished and I'm
making a chicken coop out of bottles and beer cans as a surprise for her.''

"Sure, I'd like that." I nodded. We finished our sodas, left Rexall's,
and waved good-bye on the sidewalk.

I hadn't wanted to like Sam, but suddenly I found myself liking him.
I wondered how much I had disliked him because I thought he was taking
Blue away from me. I guess I had wanted things to stay the same, even
after I left. I wanted to imagine Blue forever on Talpa hill and the mesa to
be someplace that only existed before Anna met me.

20

A month later, Gauguin received a Western Union telegram delivered right to our door. It was early morning. Gauguin stood barefoot, holding it in the kitchen.

"Open it," I said, excitedly.

" 'Pick me up in Las Vegas. I arrive April twenty-ninth, at 4 P.M. TWA.' " Gauguin read it aloud. It was from his father.

Gauguin looked at me. "That's today."

"Gee, your father gives even less notice than my mother. I'll go with you." Then I changed my mind. "Maybe I'd better stay and clean up. I can make dinner. Las Vegas is only a two-hour drive away. You should be back in time."

"Are you sure Las Vegas has an airport?" Gauguin asked.

"I'm pretty sure. I've heard they do. Call TWA from the post office and find out," I suggested.

"Naa. If he got a flight there, they must be landing." Gauguin paused. "Holy shit! Rip's coming! It's just like him to do something spontaneous like that."

"Let's put him up at La Fonda on the plaza. He'll like it. They have D. H. Lawrence's erotic paintings," I said.

"What do you mean by that?" Gauguin got defensive.

"What's wrong? I thought he was artistic, being an architect," I said.

"Oh." He started to laugh. "I thought you meant he was a horny bastard."

We both laughed. I hadn't thought of that, even though Gauguin had told me that Rip slept around. It was what finally broke up his parents' marriage.

"I'd better leave around one to have plenty of time. Nell, I wonder how long he's staying. I have a gig in Albuquerque tomorrow. He'll be too wiped from traveling to drive three hours down with me, and then I'm staying overnight."

"Cancel it," I told him.

"I can't do that. I worked too hard to get it. Rip will understand," he said.

"Well, I guess you know your father better than me. If it were my family, they'd freak if I didn't drop everything to be with them."

"Yeah, they're not like that, and besides, he gave us such short notice."

I headed back toward the bedroom and then turned. "So, I'm finally going to get to meet someone from your family." I came back and hugged him. "I was beginning to think they were a mirage."

At eight in the evening, the front door opened. Gauguin stepped through and dropped his car keys on the floor.

"Nell, I waited. The air traffic control man said that no commercial plane had landed in Las Vegas in eight years!" Gauguin crumpled into a chair.

"We got another telegram from Rip fifteen minutes ago." I handed it to Gauguin.

He read it: " 'Where are you? I thought Las Vegas was right nearby. Can't get a flight to Albuquerque until tomorrow. I'll take a limo up. See you then. Rip.' "

"Oh, no!" Gauguin put his head on the kitchen table. "He flew to Las Vegas, *Nevada*."

I wanted to burst out laughing, but I saw how upset Gauguin was. "Let's skip the dinner I made. I'll save it for tomorrow. We can just have dessert. Apricot cobbler." I knew it was his favorite.

"No, let's eat dinner. While Rip is coming up here, I'll be going down there—for that gig!" His face was so broken up, it looked like a jigsaw puzzle.

"Well, you have to admit it's kind of funny," I offered.

Gauguin didn't think it was. "Very funny, Nell, very funny. You wouldn't be laughing so much if it were your family."

Gauguin left for Albuquerque at two the next afternoon and Rip arrived at four on the one limo a day that stopped in Taos. When I picked him up, I recognized him immediately by his hair—red, though graying at the edges—and his spray of freckles. He was taller than Gauguin, maybe six foot, and he had a slight limp. Gauguin had told me he'd been in a bad car accident six years ago.

"Rip!" I called out, and waved.

"Ah, so you must be Nell." His face lit up. He came over to me and bent down and kissed me.

"Gauguin had to go to Albuquerque—" I began to explain.

"When will he be back?" His face fell as he cut me off.

"Tomorrow afternoon," I said.

"And I leave the day after that." Then he brightened. "Well, I always wanted to see Taos."

I took him and his brown leather suitcase to the La Fonda.

"Why don't you come for dinner tonight?" I offered. I hadn't planned to entertain, but I couldn't just leave him alone. "I'll pick you up at seven."

He seemed pleased.

I dashed over to Safeway. They had a sale on mushrooms that had

become a little old. I could get a whole bunch for half price. I thought I'd
make mushroom Stroganoff, one of my specialties.

I drove home and began to cook. On a sudden impulse, I walked up
to Blue's.

"Come to dinner tonight. Gauguin's father will be there."

"Sure, sugar, I'd love to. Want me to bring anything?"

"Just yourself."

"Me, too?" Lightning stuck his head out of his room.

"Perfect," I said. "But *you* have to bring something—your hat!"

He giggled. He was wearing his wool cap, as usual.

I felt relieved as I walked back down the hill. I didn't want to be
alone with Rip. It felt awkward—I hardly knew him—and besides, I
remembered Gauguin told me once that Rip had tried to make one of
Gauguin's old girlfriends.

I had to drive back into town to pick Rip up before I finished
cooking. When we arrived back at the house, he offered to help.

"Here, could you finish slicing these mushrooms?" I handed him the
bowl, a cutting board, and a knife, and he settled down at the kitchen
table.

"They seem a little old," he said, holding one up.

"Oh, they're fine. I got them cheap, so I could get a lot more." I
turned from the salad dressing I was making and smiled.

"You're sure?" he asked, cutting them gingerly.

Just then, Blue walked in with Lightning ahead of her. I could see by
the way his face lit up that Rip thought she was gorgeous. I looked over at
her. She was wearing a red velvet jacket she had sewn by hand.

I introduced them. Rip popped right up into a standing position and
took her hand. "My pleasure," he said.

"I just adore your son, Gauguin, and he looks just like his daddy."
Blue tweaked Rip's nose.

This undid Rip. "Please, please, let me get you a chair."

"I'm fine. Just get back to what you were doing." Blue nodded
toward the cutting board on the table.

"Oh, yes, yes. I love to help around the kitchen." Rip sat back down.

I wished Gauguin were there. I wanted Rip to stop gawking at Blue. But Blue seemed oblivious to it.

"So you're an architect?" Blue asked when we finally sat down to the meal. "I just love dirt architecture. There are anthills all over the place, and sometimes I squat in front of one for a whole hour. Ever do that? I've been dying to see inside, but I don't want to hurt the little bitty ants, so I just watch them come in and out, in and out of that top hole."

"Why, yes, yes. I never thought about that. Maybe you could show me one." He turned to me. "Nell, do you have anything to drink? I'm awfully thirsty."

I jumped up. "Oh, I'm sorry. We have water. You should drink a lot, especially because it's so dry and you're new here."

I handed him a glass and filled a pitcher.

"Honey, this dinner is delicious," Blue chimed in. She'd almost emptied her plate.

"Oh, yes, yes," Rip conceded. I could see, though, that he was nervous about eating the mushrooms. He thought they were rotten, but he wanted to impress Blue, so he suddenly chugged down whole mouthfuls, followed by big gulps of water. "Yes, sir, this is delicious!" By the time he was finished, he had drunk three glasses of water. He went to the outhouse.

While he was gone, Lightning looked up from his comic book. "He's weird, Banana. I like Gauguin a lot better."

Blue placed her hand on Lightning's arm. "He just comes from a different place, sweetie." Then she turned, and with her hand cupped to the side of her mouth so Lightning couldn't see, she whispered to me, "He *is* weird," and scrunched up her face.

I nodded. I started to say something, but just then Rip stepped back in the house. "Wow, is it beautiful out there! Worth the trip. Worth the trip."

I served up the leftover apricot cobbler.

"I don't get to see sky like that in the city," Rip continued, "but sometimes I visit Camille, my mother, in Indiana, and we sit out on her porch and it feels good." I placed a dish of cobbler before him. He looked down. "Oh, sweetheart, this looks delicious."

Rip snapped his fingers. "That's it! Blue, you look just like Camille when she was young."

I burst out laughing.

"What's so funny?" Rip turned to me. "I'm serious."

Blue stepped in. "Oh, Nell, honey, I just love this cobbler." She leaned right into Rip's face and asked, "Did your mother make dessert this good? I bet she did, didn't she? You love your mother, don't you, sugar."

Rip was in heaven. "Yes, I love Camille." I thought he might begin to cry.

At this point, I excused myself to the outhouse. I also wanted to see what the night sky looked like. As I passed the Russian olive, I looked up in supplication. "Heaven help me." I couldn't make Rip out. One minute he seemed like a lech or a con artist and the next he was just a grown-up little boy.

I drove Rip home that night and told him Gauguin would come by as soon as he returned the next afternoon.

"Oh, sure. I'll just walk around Taos until he gets here." He thanked me for dinner and told me what "a fine gal" I was, also how much he enjoyed meeting Blue.

The next morning I was setting up a still life on a low table. As I bent down to put a pear on the table, I glanced out the window. No! I stood up quickly. I couldn't believe what I had just seen. I shook my head. I bent down and looked again. Sure enough, there was Rip, coming down the road on a big black horse, trying to hold on to a ten-gallon cowboy hat with his left hand while his right was gripping the horn of the saddle. The horse was trotting, and Rip was bouncing hard, his spanking new red cowboy boots wedged into the stirrups, his buttocks slamming down over and over on the leather saddle. He made a right before our house and went up the dirt drive. A guitar was slung over his shoulder. Was he going to serenade Blue? This couldn't be true. Gauguin's father had some screws loose. I stood up.

Suddenly I had a terrifying thought. He's going to kill himself on that horse! Calm down, I said to myself. I'm sure he can ride. This is none of your business, Nell. Just sit down and do your still life. I bolted for the door.

"Holy shit!" I said out loud as I ran up the hill.

Bonnie's barking had frightened the horse. He was stumbling and bolting every which way and was about to head for our vegetable garden. The chickens had dispersed in a flurry, and Sylvester had flown to the roof of a truck. Rip, scared to death, had dropped the reins, and they were dragging on the ground. Blue was trying to grab them.

"Oh, my god! Oh, my god!" yelled Rip from atop the horse. The horse's hoof smashed through the fallen guitar. Rip's hat dangled down his back, the string choking him around the neck.

"Grab the reins, and get off!" Blue screamed. Her goats had scattered and were heading up the hill behind her house.

"I can't! I can't! Please get me off!" Rip yelled back.

Henry Sandoval, the neighbor across the ditch, came running over. He swooped down on the horse, grabbed its reins, yelled for Blue to take Bonnie into the house, and began leading the horse around in circles while stroking its mane. "Climb off," he commanded.

Rip gladly swung his right leg over and touched ground.

"Well, thank you, sir. Thank you." He held out his hand.

"Later," Henry said, and concentrated on the horse.

I crossed the ditch and came over. Blue walked back out of the house. "Thanks, Henry," she called out.

Henry walked the calmed horse over to the fence and tied its reins to the post.

"No problem," he said. "I've got to get home to my chickens," and he crossed back over the ditch.

Blue turned to me. "Henry always thought Anglos were jerks. Now we've proven it to him."

I looked over at Rip.

"I need to sit down for a minute," he said. He looked very pale. "I thought it would be easier to ride a horse." He turned toward Blue. "I thought I'd come and sing you some songs we sang down in Indiana."

"Your guitar's busted." I bent down to pick it up.

"Oh, no! I borrowed it from the hotel clerk. Where's a music store down here? I'll go get him another." Rip reached out his hand as I passed the broken guitar to him.

"Music store's in Santa Fe," Blue said, looking at the splintered instrument.

Suddenly, it felt as though we were all moving in slow motion.

"Your boots? New, huh?" I asked. "Comfortable?" I could tell they weren't.

Rip grimaced and changed the subject. "What should I do about the horse?"

"Can't you ride?" I asked. "Gauguin's so good."

"He learned from Alice's side of the family. No one on my side ever came near a horse."

"So why'd you ride up here?" asked Blue.

"Well, it's the West. I just got a hankering to," Rip explained meekly.

I nodded. "Uh-huh. We didn't ride much in Brooklyn, either."

"You mean you can't help me with the horse?" he asked.

I shook my head.

"I hurt my back years ago—thrown off one. I can't help either," Blue added.

The midmorning sun was intense. "Let's move into the shade," I said.

"I've got to drive to town in a minute to pick up Lightning." Blue headed for the house.

I could see it was going to be me and Rip and the horse. "What's his name?" I asked, and looked over at the big animal munching some weeds.

"I think they called him Flash at the stables," Rip told me.

I nodded. "Well, how are you going to bring him back?"

"Nell, do you have an old pair of my son's sneakers? These boots are killing me."

"No." I shook my head. "Gauguin took his two pairs of shoes with him."

"He only has two pair? Why, I ought to buy that boy some." Rip tried to muster some authority, but it quickly faded. "Well, I guess I'll have to walk Flash back. I'm certainly not getting on him again."

"It's five miles. Take you about two hours." I had this strange feeling I was in a play, but none of the actors belonged except the horse and the land.

Rip walked over to the horse. He put his big hat back on his head and reached for the reins.

I walked him down the long driveway to the road in front of our house. "Sure you'll be okay?"

"Oh, sure, don't worry about me." He waved.

I watched him hobble past Joe's in his new red boots. The horse walked obediently behind him, happy now that it had no weight on its back. My hand reached for the doorknob as my eyes remained fixed down the road.

What about other barking dogs? I thought. Talpa was full of them. And cars? Trucks?

"Rip!" I yelled, waving my hand and running after him. "I'll walk you to the pavement." I wasn't sure what I could do to help, but he seemed so helpless.

He smiled weakly. He was defeated, but I could see he was glad for the company. "How far's the pavement?" he asked.

"Half-mile."

"Boy, do I have blisters." He shook his head. "I can't wait to get back to the hotel. Blue probably thinks I'm a damn fool."

"I'd forget her. She has a boyfriend." I eyed him conspiratorially. "Should have asked me."

"Oh, I never think about those things. Alice was engaged to someone else when I met her."

I nodded.

"When will Gauguin be here?"

"Late afternoon."

"You know, Nell, you're the best-looking girl Gauguin's ever been with," he said, turning and looking at me.

I ignored his comment. "Here's the pavement. Got to head back." I stepped away from him and waved.

In the late afternoon, I was sitting at the kitchen table when Gauguin burst in.

"Nell, I went direct to the hotel when I pulled into town, and I couldn't find Rip. When I called up to his room, he didn't answer. It turned out he was in the bathroom the whole time. He has the runs and he's nauseous, and when he's not on the toilet, he's soaking his feet in the tub. What a mess."

"I'll say," and I told Gauguin what happened that morning. He said he'd heard some version of it from Rip.

"What's wrong with your father, anyway?"

"He's crazy when it comes to women. He busted up the family when I was ten over a woman house painter—she came to wallpaper the living room—but Alice kept taking him back. He thinks all women are goddesses like his mother."

"Jesus, is he that foolish?" I asked, incredulous.

"No, he's actually pretty smooth, I'm afraid to say. He's just out of his element, has some romantic idea about cowboys. You should see him back home, where it's his turf."

"I'd rather not." I was sitting in front of the still life I had intended to paint that morning. It was of a melon, three pears, and a blue teapot. I picked up my brush.

"Rip says he was poisoned by the mushrooms you made last night," Gauguin told me.

"Come on, you don't believe that, do you? I ate them and I'm fine, and so did Blue and Lightning." I looked up from the arrangement of fruit. "He's probably got the glitch. He drank a lot of water last night. You know, everyone gets sick when they first come to Taos until they get used to the water."

I was suddenly tired of Gauguin's father. I hadn't seen Gauguin since yesterday, and that was how he greeted me? I began to paint the melon yellow.

"Well, I'm going to try to get him something to make him feel better and see if I can hang out with him some more. He leaves early tomorrow." He stepped toward the door.

As he reached for the knob, I said, "You know, I didn't poison your father."

"I know." He ran back and kissed me. "Got to go!" he called, and ran out the door.

I sneered in his direction and then went back to my picture. What a family, I thought. Then I thought of my family and decided I should shut up.

The yellow looked good on the melon. I added some orange.

21

It was in May that I dreamed of Isaac Bashevis Singer. I was living in the town of Taos, which in the dream was a broad avenue of cars, taxis, and flashing neon lights. I wrote Singer a letter, and he came to visit me. He rode a white horse that changed into a burgundy-colored Morris Minor. He parked in front of Grandpa George's. I waited inside to meet him at a table with a red linen tablecloth. The room was dimly lit. As Isaac passed under the front door, a sign blinked: "Steaks as Smooth as Butter." He sat down next to me and said, "I have a cold."

My mouth fell open. I was afraid he'd die.

The waitress came over and he ordered chicken soup. He asked, "Could you make sure there's a lot of breast in it?"

I said, "But Isaac, you've never eaten meat in your life!" Then I woke up.

Two nights later I had another dream, this time set in North Dakota. I was in a small café in a town named Upton. My grandfather drove up in a white jeep, entered the café, and sat across from me. I was eating a cucumber. I was nervous, so I talked a lot. I couldn't control my mouth. I told him about a math test I had just taken. He turned to me and asked, "What's four times four?" Then he looked at the menu and I understood that he was about to order a hamburger.

I yelled, "No!" and woke up, my heart beating hard. I looked around. It was morning and Gauguin was not lying next to me. I got out of bed and went outside. Gauguin was sitting on the bench out front with a plate on his lap. The plate was blue and there were two fried eggs on it with toast.

I sat down next to him and told him the whole dream and how I felt in the café. He nodded. I told him the whole dream again, this time describing more of how it had felt to be in North Dakota. Then I told him the dream I had had two nights before, the one where Singer met me in Taos. Then I just sat on the bench, looking out at the mountains like two elephants kissing.

Gauguin didn't say a word. After a moment, he held up a forkful of egg yolk, my favorite part. He put it to my mouth and I ate it.

A week later, I told Gauguin I had to have chicken, that I had to buy a chicken at Safeway and cook it and eat it. Until that moment, I had been a vegetarian for seven years. I would eat turkey on Thanksgiving if someone else cooked it, but mostly I ate no meat. The meat department in the grocery store was essentially nonexistent to me.

Gauguin asked me if I was sure I wanted to do this.

Yes, I said.

He drove me over to Safeway in Betsy Boop and waited outside while I went in. I leaned over the cool refrigerated air and stared at cellophane packages. Yup, they still sold chickens and chicken livers and wings and thighs. I felt dizzy. The chicken was fifty-three cents a pound. I saw a row of packages in which the chickens were cut up in eighths. The chicken skins were pale yellow. I could see the raw meat underneath. My hand reached out and picked up a package. I felt its soft coldness. I dropped the package back and ran down the aisle and turned the corner. I stood in front of the saltine crackers and wept, but a voice in me urged, "Do it. Go ahead. Buy it," and I knew the voice was not the devil. It was me. I wanted to eat meat again.

I went around the corner, picked up the package of chicken that was cut up in eighths, and stood in line to pay for it. As I waited, I chewed a stick of spearmint gum and tears rolled down my cheeks. The cashier rang up the price, put the chicken in a brown paper bag, and handed it to me after she counted out my change. I took the bag in my left hand and marched out the automatic exit door as if I were accompanied by Beethoven's Ninth.

Gauguin started up Betsy Boop, and it jiggled loudly in idle as I settled myself into the seat with the chicken on my lap. I felt the truck's accusation, also the magpies' and the cottonwoods', as we chugged along the road back to Talpa. I was Abraham bringing Isaac to the sacrificial rock. Gauguin said nothing and then he turned on the radio. It was full of static and a country singer's voice droning on about a yellow moon. He turned it off.

When we got home, I made chicken with wine and onions. Gauguin said it smelled good, but he was going out to practice with a new band. I sat alone at the kitchen table with a thigh in wine sauce in front of me. I took a bite. I put it down. I felt slightly nauseous even before the chicken hit my stomach. There was something about cooking meat myself and eating it after seven years that really made it meat, really drove home "animal" in my mouth.

But I wanted it, and I knew it. The two dreams I had told me that. I wanted to eat meat from now on, but there was no mistake about it. An animal had died and I was biting into its flesh. I finished eating the thigh and slurped up the onions in wine sauce.

From that moment on, in a hundred ways I tried to say good-bye to Taos. "Look, Nell," I'd say as I rode down to the Red Willow School. "See the turn, the broken fence, the fallen adobe. Take it in," but it didn't work. I never really believed I would leave New Mexico.

22

"Jesus, Nell, what the hell are you doing?" Gauguin ran across the yard and grabbed my arm. I sat in the driveway, my mouth covered with dirt.

"I'm eating it," I said.

"What is the matter with you?" I looked up. It was August first.

"You're eating the land?" He was incredulous. I lifted another handful to my mouth. He shoved my hand away and lifted me to my feet.

"I don't want to leave!" I screamed.

"Cut it out already, will you?" Gauguin said.

"No!" I pulled my arm away from him and stomped up to the vegetable garden at Blue's. She was visiting her mother in Baton Rouge. We'd said good-bye so many times before she left that it became unbearable.

It was the best vegetable garden we ever had. I sat down and pulled out small tender pigweed that grew near the heads of Bibb lettuce. We could make salade niçoise. I'd ask Gauguin to go into town for a can of tuna. There were some potatoes back in the kitchen we could boil.

"Nell." I heard him coming up to the garden.

"Do you want to have a salad?" I yelled without turning around.

"Nell, the truck's packed. Everything, including our dishes. We're

149

leaving. Now." I looked up at him. I didn't say a word. I began to pull weeds again. Gauguin squatted beside me. "Please, Nell," he said softly.

I started to cry. "I can't." I shook my head. "I want to make a salad."

"C'mon, the house is empty." Gauguin pulled gently at my sleeve.

Hearing the word *empty*, I stopped, pigweed still in my hand. Something shifted in me, and I knew it was all over. I stood up and followed Gauguin to the truck. I settled into the passenger's side and stared at my hands in my lap.

"Aren't you even going to say a final farewell?" Gauguin asked as we pulled away from the house.

"No, I'm carrying it all with me. I've got it all in my head," I said quietly. I pictured the orange-flowered curtain that hung from thumbtacks at the windowpane, the braided brown rug in the kitchen, the black wood stove, the bumpy adobe walls that we'd painted fresh white, the turquoise windowsills, the Russian olive by the porch, the shadow from the marijuana plant that grew so high last summer, it took up all the light by the back door. I started to chew at my hair, the way Anna used to do.

We hit the blacktop, and at the turn the truck skidded a bit.

We drove past the terrible Mexican restaurant where Blue had gotten food poisoning so fast, she started vomiting immediately after the last bite of her taco, past the courthouse with the farmer's market in front. Red chile ristras hung from posts. Past the one stoplight in town, past JCPenney's where I had bought orange plaid flannel sheets, past Kit Carson Park and the post office on the left. Box 1206. I suddenly remembered I'd forgotten to return the key. "Gauguin, we've got to stop at the post office. I have to return the key."

"They're closed, Nell. It's Sunday. You can mail it to them," he said.

Box 1206. I was sure the mailbox was filling with letters for Nell Schwartz that I would never get.

"We've got to stop. I've got to get my mail," I said in a last-ditch attempt never to leave Taos.

"Jesus, didn't you have them forward it on Friday?" Gauguin was exasperated.

"Yes, but you know how they are." Then I took a deep breath and just gave in. "Okay, keep going." I looked out the window, defeated.

Past the entrance to the pueblo, past Taos Mountain, though you couldn't ever pass it. It followed you wherever you went for a hundred miles. Past cows and the nodding wild sunflowers that grew all along the edge of the road like a thin yellow highway line. I started to cry. Gauguin reached out his hand and touched my leg.

"Are you mad at me?" he asked.

I turned in disbelief. "Gauguin, we're leaving . . ." I paused. "I hate you," I said under my breath.

"Yeah, should be in Boulder by nine tonight," he replied. We slowed down at the blinking light and then continued at top speed.

Past the chamisa, past the bar in the valley at Arroyo Hondo, past the sign for San Cristobal. The road ascended and then evened off into Questa. Past Questa and the café that sold thick shakes, past the grocery store with the public phone outside.

"I can't believe this is happening," I said aloud.

"It's only six hours north. You can come back and visit," Gauguin said.

"You're an asshole. I hate you," I repeated.

Gauguin began to whistle. I looked out the window again. The land was full of sagebrush and stretched for miles. Back, way back behind me, I felt water rising. It was in an adobe house and the water washed away the whole house and the fields behind the house. Something was drowning as we headed north into another world.

PART
II

23

Houses were hard to find in Boulder, and they were expensive. We slept on an old friend's living-room floor for a week and a half and finally, out of desperation, rented a room in a house with two biology students, Dell and Eddie, who were in their junior year at the University of Colorado. We slept in the back room, which was originally the den and had a door that opened onto the back yard.

At 6:30 our first morning there, Dell ran through our room with his spotted police dog, Dilbert. He wanted to let him out in the yard.

Gauguin, half asleep, raised himself on his elbow. "Uh, Dell, couldn't you use the front door? We're sleeping."

Dell turned to Gauguin as he held the screen door open for Dilbert. "Oh, sorry, guys. Dilbert had to go real bad. I didn't know you were sleeping."

"We were," Gauguin confirmed it.

"I'll be quieter next time," Dell assured us.

"Next time don't come through. Use the front door, and go around," Gauguin said. This time his voice was just below the level of a threat.

It didn't matter. Dell ran through every morning, and it was always early, between 6:30 and 7 A.M. Each time we screamed at him. Then I laid my head back on the pillow. At that moment each morning, I experienced memory: I'd left Taos. I was living with two college students. I was in a town without adobe, without the pueblo. Suddenly Taos Pueblo mattered. While I was in Taos, it had just been a part of everything. Now that I was away, I realized it was the essential sacred gem of the place. There was no core like that in Boulder.

Five days after we moved in, I was sitting at the kitchen table when Dell and Eddie brought in three brown bags full of groceries. They unloaded sugarless Graham crackers, brown rice in a box, whole-wheat spaghetti, kidney beans, cold-pressed safflower oil and sesame oil, peach kefir, orange-sweetened buckwheat cookies, sprouted wheat bread, raw peanuts and cashews, organic carrots, avocadoes, lemons, tea with fourteen herbal flavors, and soy milk.

"Hey, guys"—I had picked up the salutation from Dell—"did you go shopping at the co-op?"

"Nope. At Safeway," Eddie explained as he threw the carrots into the vegetable bin of the refrigerator.

"Huh? You're kidding. They sell this stuff at the supermarket?" I held up the soy milk.

"Sure," Dell chimed in, and nodded.

I scratched my cheek and read the label on the tea: "Jubilation." Then under the tea's name the box read, "Bless you, you are good." The tea was blessing me. I scrunched up my face. There was so much talk about the New Age up in Boulder. This must be part of it, I thought. It was then that I promised never to drink anything but Lipton's. Lipton's didn't ask anything of me. With Jubilation, I had to consider the state of my soul.

As I sat at the kitchen table, Dell and Eddie went to their rooms and changed into shorts and running shoes. They were going to jog down the street, but before they left they tore open the cellophane on the buckwheat cookies and each took two. "For energy," Eddie said, holding up his cookies. He saluted, then he and Dell dribbled out the door.

I leaned my elbow on the gray Formica tabletop and stared at the package of cookies. I reached out and took one. I bit into it. It tasted like cardboard. No, worse—like eating a windowsill, and it was as tough as an old Buster Brown leather shoe. I spat it out into my hand and grimaced.

That night, to be hospitable, Dell and Eddie invited Gauguin and me to have soup with them. They made it themselves. Gauguin said he had to go to the library. I told him that was a pathetic excuse. I walked into the kitchen alone to face what America had come to.

"Hey, guys," I said. "What's for dinner?"

"We made seven-bean soup and a side dish of brown rice." Dell flashed me a big smile. The refrigerator hummed loudly, the fluorescent light above the sink was on the blink, and their two ten-speed bikes were jammed against the wall next to the kitchen table.

The three of us held hands before we ate. I waited for them to say something. They didn't. Their eyes were closed. I waited a little longer. Then even longer. Our hands began to sweat. I said, "Thanks," and we let go of each other's hands. They stood grinning. I sat down. Eddie placed a bowl of soup in front of me and a huge white plate of brown rice.

I picked up my spoon and noticed the soup had no aroma. I scooped some soup into my mouth, and my teeth almost stopped dead on the surface of the kidney, pinto, and aduki beans. They were hard.

"Hey, guys," I said casually, "how long did you cook these beans?"

"Oh, for a while," Dell said as he crunched into his and swallowed.

I grimaced. It was supposed to be a smile. "I suppose you cooked the brown rice that long, too?"

Yes, they both nodded, their mouths full.

After they finished eating, they cleared their dishes. "Hey, Nell, you're a slow eater," Dell remarked. No one in Boulder knew me as Banana Rose.

Yes, I nodded, and added, "I like to digest my food."

I watched them wash their dishes. "Where are you going now, guys?"

Eddie paused in front of me. "We thought we'd go see *Rocky*." They waved and half-jogged out the door.

"Have a good time," I called after them. As soon as they were gone, I dumped my soup and brown rice down the garbage disposal. Then I walked out into the twilight of our front yard. The streetlights had just come on. I lay down on the dried lawn. Dell and Eddie thought it was unecological to waste water on such things. The lawn had burned, and the landlord had charged them their security deposit.

Lying there on the bleached Boulder lawn, I thought of New Mexico. I turned over and buried my face in the burnt grass.

Gauguin found a job house painting. He climbed ladders and turned walls from green to decorator white. He came home each night with his jeans and face speckled with paint. I found a job in a halfway house helping troubled kids with their schoolwork. The counselors at the house confiscated the kids' dope and then smoked it themselves in an upstairs bedroom.

At night, Gauguin and I walked down to the local jazz club on Pearl Street, sipped white wine, and listened to musicians draw out notes that came directly from their bodies. Gauguin took to smoking bedes, narrow cigarettes from India. I watched him watch every move the clarinet player made one night in early October, and as he listened, he smashed bede after smoked bede into the glass ashtray. As we walked home he stepped hard on the dried fallen leaves that covered the sidewalk.

"Nell, what have I been doing all these years? All that time I blew the trumpet in the Talpa hills, I was wasting my life. I can't even earn a living. I've got to grow up," he said as we passed a streetlight.

I spun around. "You're wasting *your life*? I fucking moved here because of you! Why don't you become a rock star already, so leaving Taos will make sense?" I stormed down the street. I turned my head and yelled back at him, "And I haven't painted a picture since we've been here!"

Gauguin caught up to me and grabbed my shoulder. "Nell! What about me? You think I'm happy?"

We were both breathing heavily. I shoved his hand away. "I hate you," I said. I was crying now. "I can't stand living with Dell and Eddie and their damn dog Dilbert." My face was in my hands. "This place is making me crazy—I can't take it anymore!"

I lay in bed awake that whole night. The next morning, I told Gauguin I was moving out, and that afternoon I found a small room to rent in an old woman's house, far away from the university. It took only two hours to pack up my stuff. Before we left Taos, we had thinned our possessions. Gauguin was stunned. He helped me load up Betsy Boop and drove me to the other side of town.

The first night I was there, I couldn't believe what I had done. On the second night Gauguin slept over. On the third night we talked about living together again when we saved some money, so we could get a better place. I began to make my little white room livable. After a month, Gauguin also found a room in someone's house. It was a block away from mine. When we saw each other, we either made love and cried or we fought.

One Sunday, he spoke to his father long-distance in Minneapolis. Rip offered to train him as an architectural draftsman for seven dollars an hour. He got off the phone and didn't say anything. I had slept over at his place that night. He mused all afternoon. We took a long hike in the hills.

"Nell, I have to go," he finally said. "You think I'm a failure anyway, and you hate me for pulling you out of Taos. I'll make money, and you'll come visit. Maybe you could move there." He paused. "I can't ask you now. Not after moving you once."

I was numb. I just listened. Gauguin was moving to Minneapolis; he was going to leave in a month.

It was at 5 A.M. on a Monday in November that Gauguin loaded the final carton into the back of Betsy Boop. We stood by the curb to say good-bye.

"Nell, I love you so much—I can't believe all this is happening."

Gauguin wiped his nose with the sleeve of his flannel shirt. "You'll come
visit soon, won't you?" He half-asked and half-begged.

I nodded. "Good luck." I held him by the collar. "Drive carefully." I felt too choked up to say anything else.

He positioned himself behind the wheel and slammed the door shut.
He leaned out the open window and we kissed. I watched the red tail-
lights of Betsy Boop disappear into the predawn fog that engulfed the
residential street.

I walked back down the block to my place. Since it was so early, I
went back to bed and fell asleep. I dreamed I was back at Dell and
Eddie's. I was alone. It was early morning. I was sitting up in bed,
remembering that Gauguin had moved. In the dream, he had moved to
New York City. Suddenly, Dell came bounding in with Dilbert. But
Dilbert was a cocker spaniel.

Dell said, "Hi, sorry I woke you."

"Oh, you didn't wake me," I replied. It was the first time in six
years that I hadn't yelled, "Dammit, Dell, use the front door!" Without
that, he didn't know what to do next, so he did the most surprising thing:
He called Dilbert back into the house and walked him through the front
door and out into the yard. Then the phone rang. It was a black phone. I
picked it up. I didn't know who it was, but I told the person the story
about Dell and Dilbert. As I spoke, a rosebush full of thorns began to
grow across the window. Then I heard Gauguin's voice in the phone.
"See? It was worth me leaving."

24

With Gauguin gone, I went to work and then came home. I sat in my back bedroom and just stared at the walls. The old woman sat in her rocker in the living room all day with her three cats. She was hard of hearing. In exchange for cheap rent all I had to do was shop for groceries once a week, vacuum the carpets, and change the kitty litter. The cats never went outside. They were old and as still as doorknobs. The woman's name was Clara. Her cats' names were Crackers, Cheese, and Wine. They were yellow, white, and black. Sometimes I would come out of my room at night and sit with them.

"You're sad," the old woman screamed one evening.

I nodded.

"Well, what do you do?" she asked.

I screamed back and was surprised at what came out. "I paint," I said.

"Well, go and get 'em." She used her hand to shoo me away.

"Get what?" I asked.

"Your coloring stuff," she said.

I obeyed. I found my pastels and a white drawing pad at the bottom of a box in the closet. I never even unpacked them. I walked back into the living room, sat on a cushion on the floor, my legs splayed out on either side of the paper, and began to draw the old woman and her cats. Clara seemed pleased by the attention, and the cats purred wildly, hunched in balls around her feet.

I did three sketches in a row. Clara didn't ask to see them. She just sat with her eyes closed, rocking softly, her head leaning on a plaid blanket folded over the back of the chair. I didn't offer to show them to her either. This gave me a tremendous sense of freedom. I could draw what I wanted, almost in secret, in a place far away from all the painful things in my life.

I drew the next night and the next. By Thursday, I had moved my pad from the living room into the kitchen. I got out my watercolors. I did a painting of the cupboards, the high ceiling, the red-and-white-enamel kitchen table. My sadness brought me down to the level of concrete things. How could I explain my life? One day in love with Taos and Gauguin, another day busted up in an old woman's house in Boulder. I studied what was in front of me: the black linoleum floor with ticks of yellow, the philodendron plant on the counter in a brown clay pot, the yellowing venetian blinds, always drawn tight across the window.

I was surprised how much I was enjoying painting. I was surprised I could do it while my whole world collapsed. The phone never rang in Clara's house, and I knew it was too early to expect a letter from Minnesota.

Then on a Friday after work, two weeks after Gauguin had left, I ran into Neon at the Manhattan Deli on the Boulder mall. We didn't quite recognize each other. As he reached across the white counter to get his plate of strawberry strudel and cup of steaming coffee, I tentatively asked, "Neon?" His hair was short. He wore a button-down shirt and new jeans.

He turned, smiling, and said, "No, Eugene," and a whole window opened around his face. I knew Eugene in that moment better than I had ever known Neon and we smiled at each other.

"I'm Nell now," I said. I ordered some chocolate bobka and a cream soda. We sat together in a booth.

Eugene told me he had taken up Buddhism. "My teacher said it's a very generous act to honor my heritage, my father and mother. So I reclaimed my old name, Eugene. It took a while to get used to it. Actually, it was a relief. Neon? I was a clown in Taos.'' Eugene finished his coffee and ordered a ginger ale.

"I didn't think you were a clown. I liked you," I said.

Eugene now worked as a carpenter and took waltzing lessons. "I love swirling around ballrooms," he said. "You couldn't do that in Taos."

"Why not?" I asked, always quick to defend Taos.

"Because there wasn't any room big enough." He smiled at me.

"There was old Martinez Hall," I interjected.

"Yeah, but it wasn't exactly waxed," he said, and we both laughed.

"Come to think of it," I said, "I don't think I ever saw the floor. The lights were dim and it was always full of people dancing their asses off to loud electric music."

After that meeting at the Manhattan Deli, Eugene and I spent time together. It was as natural as sap rising in maple trees. If I didn't hear from him for a week after a date, I never worried. There was a trust between us from knowing each other in Taos. He even helped me pick out a great secondhand Plymouth. And when he tried to kiss me now, his lips didn't miss mine the way they had in his pink jeep long ago.

Often I met him at the Record Shoppe on the mall, where he was working building shelves. He sang as he worked and sometimes banged his foot on the linoleum floor in rhythm with his voice. We didn't talk about Gauguin much, but each night Eugene and I slept together, Gauguin slept with us. We could feel his presence, a largeness about everything we did. As though we weren't just embracing each other but a third person, too.

One morning he woke and turned to me. "Nell, last night a whale visited me. I sat on the plains of North Dakota in a small hut, and the whale—like a great gray god—came out of the plains, as though it were the ocean." He lifted his right hand to show me the rising motion of the whale. "The whale bared his belly to me and handed me a spear. He said, 'Use this spear, eat me, and you will be nourished.' ''

Eugene lifted his big head off the pillow. "Have you ever been to North Dakota?" he asked me.

I shook my head.

"Me either," said Eugene. His head fell back on the pillow and he looked up at the ceiling.

Then I remembered my dream about meeting my grandfather in North Dakota. I told it to him. We decided that North Dakota had some kind of magic.

A week later, Eugene dreamed that an eagle came to him in the same place in North Dakota. Holding out his great talon as if it were a hand, the eagle demanded, "Give me your heart." Eugene didn't hesitate. Eugene handed over his heart. The next day, in dream time, the eagle returned.

"You have given me your heart. Now I will give you my heart and I'll travel on your left branch for as far as North Dakota reaches to Wyoming." In the dream Eugene then became a beautiful tree, "the kind they have in Africa."

"Acacia?" I asked.

"Acacia," he said, and nodded.

I was happy to be with Eugene. Even though he wasn't Neon anymore, he still had magic. I could go to bed with him, close my eyes, and feel open land, sage, the edge of Taos Mountain where it touched the sky.

Sometimes he came home with me in the evening and we'd sit with the old lady. I'd draw; he'd play with the cats.

"Her name's Clara," he said, after he first met her. "Why do you call her 'the old lady'?"

"I don't know. I think it's affectionate, like Neon or Banana Rose. I want her to be a hippie," I explained.

He nodded. He understood, but he always called her Clara.

He talked to me a lot about Buddhism, and soon I began sitting with him at the meditation hall.

"Life is suffering," he'd repeat to me when I had a faraway look in my eye, and we both knew what I was thinking about.

In that first month, I did twenty paintings and I liked eight of them. After a while I stopped painting interiors of Clara's house. I could sit in front of her and paint something far away. I did one of Minnesota. I'd never been there, but I tried to imagine what it was like. Gauguin had told me Minneapolis had twenty-five lakes—I couldn't fit in twenty-five—I drew an aerial view, with eighteen lakes separated by clumps of trees and tulips. There were tall brick buildings and a river running through the center. I tried to do an aerial view of Taos, too, but my hand shook when I drew the mountain. I put the painting away for another time.

That night I wrote Anna a postcard. "I miss you. I love Gauguin. I'm painting. It's good to have that even here in the middle of dark canyons. I'm dating Neon. Don't ask. What's Nebraska like? Maybe I'll visit sometime. Love, your best friend, Nell."

I slipped it into the mailbox early next morning, while there were few cars yet out on the streets and tree shadows were long. I tried to imagine that little slip of my life traveling to Anna, and I wondered what her mailbox looked like.

25

On a Saturday in late January, when the days were the shortest, I decided to treat myself to matzo ball soup at the Manhattan Deli. The sky was a dark blue and the air was bitter. The mountains surrounding Boulder looked cruel to me.

I sat down in a black vinyl booth, and when the soup came, I spooned the soft matzo ball into my mouth. The warm chicken broth felt comforting; I was lonely.

After I finished the soup, I paid the bill at the counter, popped a white mint into my mouth, and headed home. Halfway there, I turned around suddenly and walked straight to the meditation hall Eugene had brought me to, climbed the long stairs, and picked up the application to take refuge vows. As I wrote "Nell Schwartz" across the top lines, "Banana Rose" blinked in hot pink lights in front of my eyes. "How long have you been meditating?" the application asked. I wrote, "Forever." The form completed, I slipped it into the top slot of a wooden box, then walked downstairs and out into the glaring sunlight.

Eugene became excited when, that night, I told him what I had done. "Why don't I do it, too?" he said, and the next day he signed up. We both were officially becoming Buddhists.

The ceremony was set for the following Wednesday night. I was to meet Eugene at eight o'clock and he would save me a sitting cushion.

That Wednesday at lunch I knew I couldn't go through with it. I took a half day off from work and drove out to Gold Hill and through the woods.

Abraham, Isaac, Jacob. Rachel, Esther, Sara, Rebekah. The trees were empty of leaves. I looked up and saw Stars of David twinkling from the branches. King Saul, King Solomon, Grandpa Samuel, Uncle Morris, Cousin Sarah. I wasn't a Buddhist. I was lonely.

I arrived back at the old lady's at 7:30 in the evening. Changing slowly, I knew I'd be late. I wanted to miss the ceremony.

As the last bells were being rung, I slipped into a back seat in the audience.

At the reception that followed, I found Eugene and tapped him on the shoulder. He was wearing a navy suit from the Salvation Army.

He swirled around. "Where were you? I saved a place and everything."

"Congratulations." I paused. I looked down at my hands. "Neon— I mean, Eugene—I couldn't do it." I looked up. "I'm a Jew. I'm not sure what that means, but that's what I am."

He was quiet for a moment. I could see he was thinking, So what? I am too. Then his face changed and he smiled. "Look at my new name." He unrolled a small scroll. "Great Heart Bird," it read.

I was delighted. "Your dream told you this."

"Yeah." It dawned on him. He had forgotten his dream.

That night, I walked home alone. Eugene went out with other initiates to celebrate. I lay in bed for a long time. Then I turned over and reached for the phone. I dialed 612-555-4063 and waited for someone to answer. It was past midnight.

"Hello?" I heard after the fifth ring.

"Hi, did I wake you?" I wondered if anyone was sleeping next to him.

"Nell?" Gauguin was surprised. I had woken him from a deep sleep. I started to cry. "Nell! I miss you. Come. Come and lie next to me."

26

In late March, Eugene drove me to the airport in Denver. It had taken two months for Gauguin and me to save enough money for me to fly north. In Colorado it was spring, and I had already gotten tanned lying out in the hills. For Minnesota, Gauguin said I should bring my winter coat, "just in case."

When he met me at the Delta terminal, I felt water all over again, like I had the first time I glimpsed him at that Shabbos in Taos. It reminded me of what I'd seen on the runway when the plane was taking off. It looked like water, but it wasn't water at all—it was radiating heat. We kissed a nervous hello and I felt my knees tremble. He took my hand and we walked down the long airport corridor.

As we drove through Minneapolis, I looked out at sturdy homes, proper square blocks, shrubs, and curbs. There were no buds yet on the trees. Branches seemed relieved just to be alive. I could feel a bitterness in the Minnesota air, unlike anything I had experienced before. I understood then that I was in the deep north.

We arrived at Gauguin's place. He lived in the bottom half of a green clapboard two-story house. The front door opened directly into the living room. Gauguin had made the adjoining dining room into his bedroom so the back bedroom could be his music studio.

"Well, here we are," he said, putting my suitcase down on the wood floor.

The living room was empty except for a red Salvation Army couch and a flowered rug. I stepped onto the carpet. "My mom gave me that as a welcome home present."

I could see a mattress with a quilt thrown over it on the floor in the next room. That was it. No curtains, no chair, no bureau.

The rooms were large, the walls were white, and the floors were wood. "I like it here," I said. "Things seem so crowded in Boulder. I like the feeling of space this place has." I was nervous. Under the polite conversation, my body screamed for Gauguin.

We stood at opposite ends of his mother's rug. Neither dared take a step toward the other. We could both feel the electricity between us. My spine was undulating.

"Banana Rose." Gauguin broke the trance.

We ran to each other. We were together again. The world felt golden.

I couldn't get enough of his lips. My tongue ran along his teeth, his face grasped in my two hands. "Sweetheart, sweetheart," I whispered urgently.

"Yes, yes," Gauguin repeated over and over. He took my hand and put it on his pants. I knelt down and unzipped his fly.

Dusk became darkness. A velvet night surrounded us. We rolled around on the flowered rug, half dressed, half naked. My eyes lost sight. My body raced across three and a half months of wanting him. My finger was in his mouth, my tongue in his ear.

"Gauguin, I love you so." I ran my palm across his face. He was crying. I bit his shoulder, his neck.

"I want you, I want you." Gauguin pounded his body inside me.

Now my body could admit how much I had missed him. I split open and screamed in ecstasy.

He clamped his hand over my mouth. "Nell, there are neighbors upstairs!"

"So what?" I grabbed his wrist and kissed him.

"Nell, we're not in Taos."

I moved my face away from his. "So?" I was confused. "What do you mean? Do you know them?"

He nodded. "They're straight. Nice, but real middle class."

The headlights of a passing car moved across the back wall.

Just then I noticed that his hair was real short. My mind reeled back to the airport. He'd had on a white button-down shirt. I touched his head.

"Do you like it?" he asked.

"It's kind of straight looking. I have to get used to it," I said. "You know, I must have been so nervous, I didn't see it at the airport. You got new glasses, too?" I reached across the rug for them. They had round lenses.

"My father got them for me. He said I couldn't come to work with taped ones." We both started to laugh.

The next morning I woke early. Gauguin was sleeping next to me in bed. It was good to see him in the morning. There were his arms, his long thin legs, those thick lips in the dim early light of the apartment. With a wild flood of warmth, I wanted him all over again. Maybe some things did last, I thought.

Gauguin awoke and kissed me on the lips. "Wait until you see what I have," he said, reaching behind the mattress.

He pulled out a jar from against the wall. "Let's eat some psychedelic mushrooms as a celebration."

I agreed. We hadn't eaten the night before, so our stomachs were empty. Gauguin unfolded the aluminum foil in which he kept the mushrooms and placed a small dried one in my mouth. I hardly had to chew. It crumbled on my tongue and I swallowed. Gauguin did the same.

"Let's go out," he said.

I wanted to stay in bed with him but said, "Okay."

We put on some clothes, zipped up our jackets, and walked across the bare living room to the front door. The morning was brisk and the sky was gray. As we crossed the street at Riverside and Eighth, I began to feel the effect of the mushroom. It was as though all the blood in my body had become a river and the water were rushing downstream. I clutched Gauguin's hand.

"Nell, are you okay? Could you not grip my hand so tightly?" He turned to me. "Put one foot after the other, and we'll get to the curb." He blinked a lot. His eyes looked like two Ferris wheels.

We got away from the traffic and neared Riverside Park. Gauguin steered us toward the Mississippi. My body settled into the trip. My eyes were windmills. I turned to Gauguin.

"We are by the Mississippi together, Gauguin. You and me. The river of Huck Finn," I exclaimed. I stood on a rock and opened my arms to the gray sky and told America how I loved it. The Midwest made me very patriotic. I enumerated what I loved about my country. "I love the stars on your flag, your rock 'n' roll music, your fuzzy TV stations that I never watch. I love the freckles on Gauguin's arms."

I smiled and looked tenderly out at that great, dirty, wide, and lovely river. My head bent toward my right shoulder, and I sighed. Gauguin looked up from where he was digging with a stick in the dirt.

"What?" he asked.

Then he said, "Come here, Nell." I got down from my rock and crouched next to him. "Look at what I drew." He'd drawn an elephant. "This elephant is purple," he said.

"I can see that," I said, and we smiled tremendous smiles at each other. It was miraculous. Gauguin and Banana Rose had survived and were together again. Gauguin's hand was trembling as he touched my cheek. His veins stood out and his arm looked deathly pale after a Minnesota winter.

We got up and walked along the riverbank for a while. I was thinking hard, but because of the mushrooms, no thought held. I tried to make sense of love and Taos and this river.

We neared the Franklin Avenue bridge. Gauguin took my hand, and we walked a little farther toward a tree that hung out over the river. He stopped me. "Nell?" I turned to him. His face looked screwed up. "Nell, I love you and I don't know what happened. I've missed you like crazy. Let's get married."

For a long time I stared at his mouth and noticed how many wrinkles it had. Then I looked at his eyes for one moment only. We both became very shy. He'd asked me to marry him. Had I heard that right?

We walked side by side for a while longer. I stooped down by the bank and picked up a stick. I drew hearts in the wet dirt, but I couldn't say anything. I watched two brown ducks swim in circles around each other under the bridge. I thought to myself, I could marry Gauguin. Our children would be real Americans, half-breeds, and they would walk with their sunflower hearts by the Mississippi.

Gauguin touched my shoulder. I stood up, smiling, but still I felt shy. "Let's walk over to the Riverside Café. I'm getting cold." Gauguin bent his head in the direction we should go.

The café's windows were steamed, and there were university and underground newspapers strewn about on wooden chairs and empty tables. I sat down in a red vinyl booth while Gauguin went to the counter and got us some winterberry tea. They gave him the tea in a stainless steel teapot. I poured the yellow liquid through the strainer and into one of the thick white cups. The tea leaves caught in the strainer. The trip was wearing off. We had only eaten one mushroom each. I handed Gauguin his cup of tea, then looked him in the face. "Did you mean what you asked before by the river?"

"Yes," he nodded.

"I'd love to marry you," I said.

I poured myself some tea and we clicked cups together. I could leave Boulder. I could reclaim a part of my life, the part with Gauguin. The tea felt good after the bitterness outside and the cups warmed our hands.

When we got back to Gauguin's apartment, I called my parents in

Brooklyn to tell them about our plans. My mother shrieked, "There's not our kind out there! What will you do?"

Gauguin sat on the opposite side of the kitchen table. I wrinkled up my nose, put my hand over the mouthpiece, and whispered to him, "She's in shock. She's delighted."

"I bet." He laughed.

The four months Gauguin had been in Minnesota, he had worked for his father in downtown Minneapolis. He played music two nights a week with a couple of old friends from high school and had dated a woman named Sherry, who worked down the hall from him. She was Irish with green eyes and auburn hair and very white skin with a spray of freckles.

He went to his mother's for breakfast every Sunday and then spent Sunday afternoons writing songs. He was writing beautiful songs, all sad, about waitresses, brick buildings, 1940s radio shows, and Chippewa Indians in housing projects in downtown Minneapolis. He played them for me on the fourth night I was there. I sat next to him on the bench in front of the old black upright piano.

After he sang "Black April," a song about a nuclear holocaust, Gauguin turned to me. "You know, Nell, I feel as though I threw my life away those years in Taos. What was I doing then? I came back here so broke, my father had to lend me money for boots and wool socks. I was the prodigal son returning home a failure."

My eyes burned. "Gauguin"—I looked at him—"those were the most important years of my life. It was home. I felt lost in Boulder."

"You sure you want to move up here, then?" he asked.

"Yes, I want to be with you," I answered. We grabbed each other and kissed for a long time. A flood of feelings washed over me. "You know, every time I smell rain, it brings me back to the smell of sage. Sometimes I feel bewitched by New Mexico. I've felt so torn living alone in Boulder, stranded in the middle between the two of you."

"You talk as if New Mexico is a person."

"It almost is. It calls me——" I paused. "The way you do."

Gauguin studied the backs of his hands. "I guess Taos was never like that for me. I don't miss it much; I've just missed you. Now that I'm back in the city, I can't believe that we lived that way for so long—dirt floors, no running water. Meanwhile, everyone else was growing up, learning how to make a living. Here I am now, working for my father. It feels weird."

That Sunday we went to breakfast at Gauguin's mother's. Alice lived in a brick apartment house on the north side of town. The elevator was broken, so we had to walk up two long flights of stairs.

When we got to the third floor, Alice was standing in the hall with the apartment door wide open. "Honey!" she cried as she took Gauguin's face in her hands and gave him a big kiss on the lips.

Surprised by such a blatant show of affection, I awkwardly moved from one foot to the other.

"Oh, Mom, I want you to meet Nell." Gauguin stepped back and presented me.

"Hello, Nell." Alice reached out her hand.

Now I could see her close up. She had high cheekbones and dyed black hair in a short permanent. Her skin was pale, her lips were thick like Gauguin's, and she wore bright red lipstick. Her eyes were dark blue and sparkled when she looked at Gauguin. The spark went out when she turned to me.

The living room was dominated by a flowered couch and matching flowered curtains that hung on either side of a big window. A white wicker end table held a pile of *National Geographic* magazines, and there was an afghan thrown over a red chair. Above a wooden bureau hung a group of framed photos. I stepped over to see them better. "Is this you, Gauguin?"

"No, that's his uncle, my brother, when he was a boy," Alice explained while lighting a cigarette.

"How about this?" I pointed to a young boy by a boat, holding up a fish.

"No, that's not him either." Alice blew out a puff of smoke.

"Hey, girl, why don't you help her?" Gauguin flirted with his mother. "Here I am." He stepped over and pointed to a young boy on a horse, wearing shorts, a white T-shirt, and a bandanna tied around his neck.

"Oh, is that Dixie Sue?" I asked.

Alice snickered. "You told her about that?"

I watched Gauguin turn slowly and face his mother. "Yeah, you know I loved that horse."

Alice waved her hand. "Let's have some food. Gauguin, you must be starving." She walked into the kitchen.

Gauguin and I continued to look at photos. "There I am," he pointed. I felt the weight of his hand on my shoulder. "That's me and Alice's dad at Christmas one year. There's none of Rip," he whispered.

"Food's on," Alice called from the dining room.

We turned and joined her. From across the room, I noticed how skinny she was in her royal blue slacks. My mother would be jealous.

We sat down and she handed me a plate of scrambled eggs.

"These are delicious," I said after tasting them. "There's fresh basil in them, isn't there?"

She nodded and turned to Gauguin. "Want some coffee, sweetheart?"

He reached out his cup.

"Where can you get fresh herbs around here?" I asked.

"We have Lund's. They sell everything, from all over the country," she snapped at me.

I was confused. I thought I had asked a reasonable question. Why was she so defensive?

Gauguin quickly held up one of her biscuits. "You can't get these in Lund's. Only Alice makes them like this."

"Mmm." I nodded and slabbed on some more honey and butter. "They *are* good."

"Don't they have them in New York?" she asked. She was half

curious this time, but cautious. Now I got it. She was afraid I was a New York snob, that I would think Midwesterners were hicks.

"No, not like these." I smiled. "Mostly as kids we ate rye bread, pumpernickel, and bagels. My father owns a luncheonette."

Her eyes narrowed. "Didn't your mother bake?"

"No." I shook my head. "My grandparents lived with us. My grandmother baked cookies, pies, and—" I was about to say challah, but suddenly I felt shy about the braided bread we ate on the Shabbos.

"Well, when Gauguin was young, I baked every day. Right, honey?" She patted Gauguin's hand and seemed to soften.

Gauguin nodded and took a big bite out of his biscuit.

"Then"—she looked down at her hands—"when I got divorced fourteen years ago, I didn't have time. I went back to school and trained as a dental hygienist."

"Oh, do you like doing that?" I tried to brighten things. "I always appreciate going to get my teeth cleaned." I smiled at her broadly.

"You do?" she asked, amazed. "Most people dread the dentist's office."

"Not me." This seemed to please her. "I like keeping my teeth healthy."

"Well, you do have a nice smile," Alice offered.

"Thank you," I said. "I even thought at one time of becoming a dentist."

Gauguin burst out laughing. "Nell, you?" He pointed at me. "Come on."

Alice took my side. All of a sudden she was a feminist. "Why can't a woman become a dentist?" She turned on Gauguin.

"I didn't mean that." He held up his hand. "It's just that Nell's a teacher. I can't imagine it."

"Oh, it has always been a secret wish of mine." I turned to Alice. "Did you know that Doc Holliday and Zane Grey were dentists? Also Thomas Welch was one. He was the founder of Welch's grape juice."

"My, I didn't. Let me write that down." She got up to get a pad and pencil.

When her back was turned, I made a face at Gauguin and whispered under my breath, "I'm not just a teacher. I'm a painter."

He was taken aback, as though he'd forgotten all about that.

When Alice returned to the table, Gauguin announced, "Nell and I are getting married."

Alice's mouth fell open, but she quickly recovered. "Well, my, well, well, congratulations." She bent over to kiss the top of Gauguin's head and stroked his cheek. "My boy, I'm so proud of you."

Suddenly she turned to me. "I thought they wouldn't let you marry out of your religion."

I felt my face flush. "Oh, my parents are very liberal," I explained.

When Gauguin and I got back in the car, he leaned against the seat. "Whew, that was hard."

"What was going on? After you announced our engagement, she ignored me the rest of the breakfast, except for that one jab at me being Jewish."

"She's never gotten over her divorce. It killed her. And she doesn't want to lose me." He started the car. "My dad had been cheating on her for years, but the final straw was when he went out with my old second-grade teacher. Maybe she thinks I'm cheating on her, too."

"But if she feels so possessive of you, how come she never called and hardly wrote all the time you were in Taos?" It didn't make sense.

"That's the way she is."

"Oh." I nodded. Some explanation.

There was something in the way Alice sucked in the smoke on a Camel that I couldn't forget. I thought about it the whole while we weaved through the streets of Minneapolis. Then I realized what it was: It accentuated her cheekbones. Gauguin seemed awkward with her. I sensed something yellow and sexual between them.

This will be hard, I thought to myself. I had no experience playing the other woman.

27

I flew back to Boulder, gave notice at my job at the halfway house, and began to pack. On the long afternoon walks Eugene and I took, he would stick his face in the blooming lilac bushes. "So you're going to be married?"

I slept with him my last night in Boulder. The next day he shook my hand before I stepped into the car, then touched my cheek. "Take care of yourself, Nell. I forgot to tell you, I love you. You are a great being." I threw my eyes down to his chest. I couldn't bear looking into his dark crow's gaze. I took his hand in both of mine. "I will write," I said.

Eugene leaned into the car and wrapped a red wool scarf around my neck. "I think it will be getting cold." I nodded, not sure what he meant. I pulled away from the curb and headed toward Fort Collins.

A half-hour into my drive north, it began to snow. The snow fell hard. The full spring leaves caught the flakes and were weighed down by them. I could no longer see out my car window, so I pulled to the side of the road and walked two miles in my sneakers to a motel. The wind blew steadily, and above me I heard cawing. I looked up and saw a crow. It circled twice over my head and then disappeared, swallowed up in this great spring snowstorm. I knew the crow was Eugene.

The next morning, the hills outside the window of my rented room glistened. I read magazines in the motel lobby all morning until the roads were cleared, wrapped in Eugene's red scarf. As I ate my lunch of scrambled eggs and English muffins, I felt the gaze of his crow eyes. "You are a great being." What had Eugene meant by that?

At about two in the afternoon, I was able to get back on the road. The sun felt good as I walked to the car. The car was cold, but it started right up. I had trouble getting the clutch in second and had to let it warm up before I took off into the white spring.

I drove across the northern part of Colorado and was in Ogallala, Nebraska, when I stopped in a Howard Johnson's for the night. I'd rarely stayed in a motel—mostly I slept on friends' floors. Now I was staying in one two nights in a row. They gave me room 211. My eyes were red from driving, and I called Gauguin for the first time in two weeks.

"Gauguin, I'm tired. I'm scared. You should have flown in and driven back to Minneapolis with me," I cried.

"Nell, don't start," he said.

We were on the edge of an argument. Instead we hung up quickly. When I got off the phone, I went down to the cocktail lounge.

"Can I have a scoop—no, make it two scoops of coffee ice cream with bittersweet hot fudge?" I asked.

"Ma'am, we don't serve ice cream in the cocktail lounge," the waiter explained to me.

"Well, is the luncheon counter open?" I asked.

"No, ma'am, not at this hour," he said.

"Well, then, how am I going to get my coffee ice cream?" I asked.

"I'm sorry. We serve drinks here." He began to get rigid. I paid it no mind.

"Could you sneak into the fountain area and get me some ice cream? Please—I'll pay extra," I cajoled.

The waiter, who looked eleven but, I was sure, had already studied geometry in high school, sighed. I looked at his large Adam's apple. I waited.

He did it! He proudly brought me two scoops in a silver dish. The hot fudge was cold, but it was the best sundae I ever had. I ate it slowly with a silver spoon. I wanted to make it last.

28

The next morning, it occurred to me: Should I stop at Anna's? After all, I was in Nebraska! I took out the map. Why hadn't I thought of this before? I knew she lived in Omaha, in a small apartment over a hardware store. I could follow Highway 80 and stay with her overnight. At first I had thought I would drive straight through to Minnesota, but now I was in no hurry to hit Minneapolis. I was getting scared. It would be good to see Anna.

I stopped at a Texaco station and asked the attendant where I could find a pay phone. He pointed to the cashier's room.

I dropped a lot of coins in the slot and dialed Anna in Omaha. How come I had never thought of calling her long distance before? I asked myself. We only wrote. The phone rang twice.

A man answered. "No, Anna moved."

"Who are you?"

"I took the apartment over from her a month ago. Just a minute. I think I have her new address," he said.

I wrote down the phone number he dictated, but just as he began to recite her address I spied a cooler full of Tab, Dr Pepper, Fresca, Coke, and bottles of orange juice. I stretched the phone cord to get at the OJ.

"Just a minute. Just a minute. What's the address?" I asked again.

"Eight twelve Columbine," he repeated. "It's in Dansville. She moved there."

I hesitated. "Where's that?"

"North," he explained.

"What'd she do that for?"

"Money. She was offered a part-time teaching job there for next fall."

I unscrewed the lid from the OJ bottle. "Thanks." I hung up and stuck my hand in my pocket for more coins.

Her phone rang. It rang and rang. No answer. I hung up and headed for the car to look at my map.

"Hey, you! Aren't you going to pay for that?" I had the distinct impression that someone was addressing me.

I stopped, turned around, looked at the attendant in the doorway, then looked down at the OJ in my hand. "Oh, sure. Sorry. Is Dansville far from here?"

My plan was to drive to Dansville and find 812 Columbine. It wouldn't be hard. I'd surprise Anna. She'd love it. If she wasn't home, she couldn't have gone far. The town looked small on the map.

I got off the freeway at Grand Island and headed north on 281. The road followed the railroad tracks for a while. Most of the towns I passed had only a bar, a gas station, and a tall granary. Then the land spread out around it. This was the lonesomeness Anna had talked about. I stopped in a relatively large town that had a strip of stores and walked along the sidewalk looking in the windows. People eyed me suspiciously. Emerson, pop. 127, knew who belonged. I didn't. I went into a secondhand store and browsed through the boxes of clothes, mirrors, and plastic dinnerware. I found a pair of very used boys' brown cowboy boots. I tried them on. They fit perfectly. Well, no, they didn't fit perfectly. They were a half-size too small, but they were perfect anyway and I bought them for fifty cents. The woman behind the counter was luxuriously large and wore a beautiful full-length nylon dress with green flowers on a black background. She had bought it in the store just the other day, she told me.

"Oh, you'll like these. Just oil 'em a little when you get home."

I continued on to Dansville. When I got there, the bank clock blinked 8:02. I could see it from blocks away. As I waited for the streetlight to change, I had this strange feeling that it was always 8:02 in Dansville; 8:03 never came up. A sign on the road said the town's population was 20,000. I stopped at the Sunoco.

"Where's Columbine?" I asked the attendant.

"Not sure. Hey, Bert, where's Columbine?" The attendant turned to Bert.

Bert took the cigar out of his mouth and grinned as though he had just been asked something sexual. "Columbine, huh? What do you want with that?" I was too tired and too eager to see Anna to be bothered with Bert. I didn't say anything. He pointed north. "Take this road up to the next light, turn left, go five blocks. There's a stop sign. Make a left, and there she is. What number do you want?"

"Eight twelve."

"Should be four blocks down."

I repeated the directions to make sure I'd got them straight. It was a watery gray dusk and the flatness of the land gave it a big feeling. I parked in front of 812, a big white clapboard house. I rang the bell. A man with a big belly answered.

"Is Anna here?" I could hear the television in the background. There was a commercial on about Pepto-Bismol.

"No," he answered through the screen door.

"Well, do you know where she is?"

"She lives up there." He opened the screen and pointed to a door on the second floor.

"Thanks." I ran up the outside stairs and rang the doorbell four times in a row. No answer. I sat down on the top step and rested my head in my hand. What had I done? What if she had gone away for a few days? I decided to check out the neighborhood and then come back.

I walked to the corner and turned left onto Spitz Avenue. It was dark out now. "Where could Anna be?" I was feeling foolish for arriving

without contacting her first. I passed a bar on the corner called the First
Avenue. Its storefront had that art deco kind of glass brick. I turned
around, opened the door, and walked in. It was the type of place where I
imagined Anna went. In the dim light I could see a long wooden bar with
black booths opposite and a jukebox lit up emerald green. I sat in the first
booth. No one else was in there.

"Can I help you?" The old waiter wore a white apron.

"Yes. Can I have a glass of sherry?"

"You mean cherry? We have cherry-flavored brandy. Blackberry and
strawberry, too."

"No, sherry. You know," I said.

"How do you spell it?"

"S-h-e-r-r-y."

"Nope, never heard of it."

"Okay, can I have a glass of Chablis?" I paused. "I mean, white
wine."

The waiter scratched his head. "I'll see if I can find you some." He
came back with a beer glass filled to the brim with white wine. "Seventy-
five cents, please." He held out his hand. I gave him a dollar and told him
to keep the change.

What a bargain, I thought, until I tasted the wine. It tasted like
squirrel piss. The lonesomeness of Nebraska entered the bar as a smoky
mermaid. She made me thirsty and I drank the terrible wine too fast.
Lonesomeness left me. I began to miss her because in her place came the
ocean. The barstools and the jukebox lights were swimming. I got up and
backstroked out the door. The night was humid.

I made a left instead of a right down Spitz Avenue and became
slightly lost. A car of teenage boys in a convertible zoomed by and yelled,
"Orange ade tonight!" I thought I'd like to Orange-ade with them and
watched the car disappear in the distance down the great boulevard of
Dansville, Nebraska. The truth was, I was suddenly happy and at ease. I'd
always fantasized about small towns. Now this Jewish girl from Brooklyn
was finally getting to be part of small-town America. On this night I

walked casually down a small-town street in khaki shorts looking like everyone else. Well, not quite. I was dark and I had a heart tattoo on my left shoulder blade. I had dropped acid about fifteen times, and that alone made me a stranger to this town in the middle of America.

On my first acid trip I'd watched a red rose in a vase tremble, opening its petals. I watched it for ten minutes, and in those ten minutes it had opened completely and with it my heart. By the end, I was screaming in glee and my friends ran in from the next room, afraid I was freaking out and about to jump out the window. I tried to tell them that the rose and I were one, that my insides were the same red as the petals on the flower. They looked at each other and worried about me. In that moment, I understood lonesomeness and knew that behind it was the rose, that without the rose there was no lonesomeness. You can only be lonesome if you once had a connection.

If there was so much lonesomeness in Nebraska, I thought, there must have once been some great connection. I felt I understood this place as I walked back toward Anna's. The trees seemed particularly inviting. The house lights swam in my eyes as though I were squinting. I had gotten the heart tattoo after that first acid trip. Where was Anna anyway? This time as I walked down Columbine, I knew she was home.

Anna didn't seem that surprised to see me at first, not that excited either, but she warmed up. That was the way she was. As though she'd put her emotions out on the laundry line to dry and then left them there. I had to yell at her, "Hey, Anna, don't forget that love T-shirt you left out on the line. It's gonna fade in the Nebraska sun." She turned her face to me, smiling, and she remembered. E-motion. She seemed to be more beautiful than she'd been nearly a year and a half ago. She was wearing a pink shirt, and her hair was long. I'd forgotten about her cheekbones. She sure had them. Her face was like a valentine that came to a point at her chin.

"So, you're going to marry Gauguin," she said, looking up from her mason jar filled with lemonade. It was 2 A.M. We were sitting cross-legged on her brown couch, facing each other. As usual, Anna had a small place, one room. The bed was near the couch. We'd been sipping her homemade drink slowly for the last two hours.

"Yes, I'm going to marry Gauguin."

"How come?" Anna asked.

"Because I can't be without him, and I'm going to be thirty."

"What does that have to do with it?" She was good at asking questions.

"I don't know. When I hit thirty, I just want to be married. I never did before in all the years in Taos."

Anna looked at me suspiciously. I wasn't feeling too sure. I shrugged my shoulders. "It's something I have to live out. I'm still in love with him. He's my golden boy." I put my finger on a slat of the venetian blind and pressed it so it bent and I could see out the window. It was quiet outside and there was a Chevy pickup parked across the street.

I glanced back at Anna. She was really looking at me, in a way I'd never seen before. It made me nervous. I caught her gray eyes. They held me like a dash in the middle of a sentence. My nerves disappeared. I heard twigs snapping. She bent toward me and placed her lips on mine. I suppose someone would call this a kiss. I wasn't sure, because she was a woman and I was a woman, but, yes, it was one pair of lips against another. I closed my eyes. She kissed me again. I walked through doors, down long gray corridors with windows high up opening onto a blue sky. I kept walking.

After my mouth had been kissed to the color of plums and the shape of Italian tomatoes and my body was a pregnant fruit, Anna stood up. She led me over to the nearby bed, and she lay down. I lay down really close to her, as if I were a paper clip and she a horseshoe magnet. Anna slowly unbuttoned my cotton blouse. This was a woman's hand that now put its face over my right breast. I felt the awe of a child flying down a water slide in summer. I dove down, down into dark water.

We became hips, legs, small tender creases, lips between our legs, mounds of rough hair and sucking sounds, licking saliva and salt. Anna wasn't Anna. Nell wasn't Nell. We were woman, one woman, and I took woman into my arms for the first time. I wasn't sure if I was hugging Anna or Anna was hugging me or I was hugging myself. But it was the delicacy of her face that astonished me the most. Could this be what a woman's face is like? This cheek, these lashes, this shadow around the nostrils? I ate Anna whole that night as though she were a watermelon and my face dripped with pink juice.

The next morning, I wasn't quite sure what had happened. Between Anna's plaid sheets, I turned and asked her, "Anna, did we make love last night?"

She yawned and stretched her long body out until it seemed to fill the small room. She looked at me as though I were crazy. "Nell, you weren't *that* drunk from the First Avenue. Yeah, we made love." Then she smiled, remembering I was a neophyte. "Some would call it that." She rolled onto her side. "Are you okay? You're not freaked out?" She bent to kiss me again. The sun filtered through the blinds and made stripes across the bed. I didn't want to kiss Anna anymore. I felt nervous again. What was I doing? Did I have to marry her, too? "I'm going to take a shower." I jumped up from the bed.

In the shower, I let the water pour over my face and hair for a long time. I couldn't think straight, feeling I was supposed to do something. I didn't know what it was, but I didn't want to do it. I used the big blue towel hanging on the rack to dry myself, bending and rubbing it over my calf. My leg stretched out in front of me, heel on top of the pink toilet seat cover. Suddenly I remembered a rainstorm I had once seen when I lived in Ann Arbor, Michigan, before Taos. I was standing by the screen door watching the rain hit the street and bounce an inch or two. The green lawns were soggy. The smell was as fresh as steel. I remembered that I had thought of that storm when Anna and I went to bed in the middle of the night. Anna was thunder cracking open clouds. She touched my breast and it poured and poured.

I finished drying and stepped out in Anna's red robe. She was sitting at the kitchen table in a white T-shirt. I went over and sat across from her.

"What's up?" I asked.

"You tell me."

"Oh, Anna." I ran my finger along the crack in the wooden table, avoiding her eyes. She was in pain, scared. I'd better get talking, I thought.

"Anna, I've never made love to a woman before. I liked it"—I hesitated—"but I'm getting married. I thought I'd spend the day with you, leave tomorrow morning. I don't think I want to make love again. I could sleep on the couch." I was an idiot. She wouldn't look at me.

"Shit." I got up and stood by her, stroking her hair. "Please, Anna, I love you." I told her about the rainstorm and the doors I walked through when she kissed me. "Look, it was great. I'm fucked up. I don't think I can handle anymore, and besides, I have to see Gauguin tomorrow." I knelt down next to her. "Anna, help me."

She was stiff for a moment. Then she reached out her hand and touched my cheek. She asked, "You don't hate me, do you? You know, for making love with you. You're not disgusted, are you?"

"No, no, never!" I looked at her so straight and clear that cantaloupes could have broken open. It felt good. I was sure of us again.

She smiled. "Let's go down to the Uptown for breakfast. I'll read you something I wrote."

"Is it okay?" I asked.

"What?"

"That I don't want to make love anymore?"

"Yeah. It was something we've had to do for a long time but didn't get around to until now."

I beamed. "You mean you always wanted to make love to me?" I felt proud. My friend wanted me.

She turned to me. "Sure. The thought crossed my mind. Didn't it occur to you?"

"No," I replied. "I didn't think about it, because I didn't know how. I'd never made love to a woman. But I've always been crazy about you."

"Me, too."

The Uptown was eight blocks from Anna's house, and you had to enter through an old hotel lobby. "C'mon, I want you to meet Jackson, the cook. He's a friend." We piloted between black round tables to the kitchen door in the back. "Hey, Jackson, come over here a minute. This is my friend, Nell."

I could hear him whisper to her, "One of your sweethearts?"

"Naa, just a friend." She looked at me.

I felt weird. Now everyone thought I was a lesbian. Anna and I sat at a back table. There was a deer's head mounted on the wall opposite us.

"What's up?" Anna asked.

"Nothing," I answered.

"C'mon, Nell, something's wrong."

I couldn't hide. She knew. It was easier to lie to Gauguin. If I said "Nothing," he let it pass whether he believed it or not. Anna was going to push. In truth, I liked it. She cared. "Well, to tell the truth, I'm feeling like a lesbian."

"Don't worry, you're not." She said it fast and nasty.

"Fuck you." I looked down at my napkin.

We sat quietly for a while. I ordered pecan pancakes, fresh-squeezed orange juice, and tea. She wanted fried eggs and potatoes. We both relaxed.

"I'm sorry," she said.

"Me, too. Why don't you read to me?"

Anna had put the novel aside for a while and was writing short stories. She pulled a notebook from her jacket pocket and read me one. It was about a kid on a bicycle. He fell into an anthill. The ants covered him and he went crazy. "Did you like it?" she asked.

"Yeah." I wasn't sure what to say. It was pretty gruesome. Then I thought of something. "Anna, do you remember when Gauguin and I went backpacking at Bandelier? You were still in Taos then."

"Yes." She wasn't sure what I was getting at. She wanted me to talk about her story.

Instead I told her about how I'd swallowed the turquoise pearl that the ants carried out of their hill on top of the ruins.

"Yeah, uh, Nell, what's the point?" I think Anna wanted to punch me.

"Wait, I'm getting to it. Ants are deep. My story shows it. They are messengers from the old world. I think your short story is deeper than you think." I was smiling, proud of my conclusion.

"Nell, I haven't read this to anyone. Can't you say something else?"

"I said it was deep, what else do you want?" I couldn't help it—I started laughing. Old Anna and her writing. This time she did punch me, but she was laughing, too. Actually, I thought Anna was doing really well with her writing, because she could laugh about it. She was more relaxed.

"From your cards, it sounded as if you did a lot of painting in Boulder." Anna pushed some hair from her eyes.

"Yeah, I did." I nodded. "I was so happy in Taos, you'd think I'd have painted more there. In some odd way I thought my painting was tied up with Gauguin's music. And then I was also sustained by you; knowing you were across the valley writing helped me to paint. I felt supported. But in Boulder I was all alone."

"What about Neon?" Anna asked.

"He kissed like a fish." We both burst out laughing.

"I knew he would," Anna choked out through guffaws.

"Actually," I said when we'd calmed down, "Eugene was fine. It's just that Gauguin is the deepest love of my life."

"Deeper than your painting?" I thought it was an odd question.

I nodded. "I guess. Why?"

"Just a thought." She shrugged her shoulders. "Nell, it's just that you love things really deep."

I smiled. "Well, don't you?"

"Not with the same intensity. I get more lost. My lonesomeness sometimes takes over. I lose my purpose. I put off writing. Your suffering made you paint. It drove you deeper into what you love," Anna said. She was curling her napkin.

I forked a bit of pancake into my mouth. What was she saying? "Anna, I'm no better than you. You've been working at your writing a long time."

"I know." Now she was looking out the window. "Sometimes I think I shouldn't have left Taos." She shrugged. "But I'm here now, and the best part is, Daniel and I have really become close. Vietnam broke him. All the killing he saw turned him against war. He's much more accepting of me. When I moved back, he said, 'Sis, you mean a lot to me. I didn't realize that before.' I was shocked. At first I didn't believe him, but he meant it. He's come to visit me a few times."

"That's great, Anna."

Just then the waitress came with the bill, and we fought over who was going to treat whom.

I left Anna the next morning. She sure looked pretty, standing by my car. She wore a white button-down shirt and jean cutoffs. There was something about the gray in her eyes and her hair that looked beautiful against the clouds. It was a white sky, not as good as New Mexico, but as I drove farther north along Highway 281, I almost forgot that. Rich earth soon to be planted with corn rolled into hills. It was a big place. No wonder Anna was so tall.

I pulled over by some trees and squatted to pee. The windshield was full of dead bugs. It smelled so sweet outside. I wasn't sure why I should go on. I could stop in Pierce, Nebraska, pop. 67, and disappear.

I got back in the car. Something Anna had said the day before kept coming back to me. We had been walking in the cornfields. She was ahead of me. She stopped to pass me the joint we were smoking. As I took it from her, I said, out of the blue, "Anna, I thought the hippie years would last forever."

We kept walking. I breathed in the smoke and she turned to take the joint back. Our hands reached toward each other. "We have to go on, Nell. That's the message. We have to go on." We walked all the way to the end of the corn row, turned around, and came back again.

PART
III

29

The road was straight, up 281. I passed Julie's Hilltop Café, went west at O'Neill to 81, and then north again over the Missouri River and into Yankton.

Anna had once said she wanted to have her ashes thrown into the Missouri when she died, so when I got to the bridge, I pulled over. I could see Anna in the Missouri. It would be good to throw the ashes right off this bridge. It was a creaky bridge with wooden planks, and at the other end was Yankton, a yellow city. Not a city really. Brick buildings lined up to stop your eye against the plains. I could see the Conoco station and a rock shop from where I stood on the bridge. A warm breeze touched my face.

Anna was a big person and would have a lot of ashes. It would probably make a little island when I dropped them in the Missouri. I'd be Vasco da Gama and discover it. I'd call it Anna Island and leave an enchilada on it in case Anna got hungry. I'd miss Anna, I mused, and the way she kisses. Kisses! Oh, my god, I'd kissed Anna!

I got back in the car and drove through Yankton. What had I been doing kissing a girl? It was the most naked thing I'd ever done. Even though I was alone in the car, I felt shy. I had enjoyed kissing Anna, but right now it was too much. Someday I'd let Anna know how it really felt.

I'd tell her I couldn't remember, so we'd have to do it again. While we were doing it, I'd try hard to concentrate, so I could describe the feeling, that place where lips meet. I'd run to a piece of paper and write it down, but I'd forget by the time I got to the paper, so I'd have to run back and kiss her again. Over and over. Touch lips, close eyes, put a little pressure, feel the tongue along my teeth, pull away, and run to the notebook. It would be exhausting, but I'd get it. To kiss Anna was to roll a very round raspberry in my hand and not crush it, and then pop it in my mouth. I smiled. That was it. I reached Interstate 90 in South Dakota and turned east. Only one more turn north on 35 after I hit Minnesota. I'd be in Minneapolis before I knew it.

Suddenly I had a sinking feeling. I remembered it was Gauguin who'd told me about kisses being like raspberries. I'd never eaten a fresh raspberry in my life. Maybe raspberries were a Midwestern thing. I'd stolen Gauguin's line to think about kissing someone else. It was gray out, and the gray stretched a long way across the flat land. I was passing Adrian, Minnesota. I couldn't see the town from the freeway. Gauguin had driven this route when he left Boulder last November. He'd written a song about the Christmas lights giving a chill up over the hill of the highway. It was a good song. He sang it to me over the phone. Thinking about Gauguin I felt really sad and I couldn't say why. Not angry or scared, just that kind of bottom sadness that you know is the truth. Gauguin and I would be living now in a city that was a stranger to me.

Past Worthington, Jackson, Fairmont. There was a Stuckey's off in the distance. The sky was pale yellow where the gray met the horizon. Past the exit for Blue Earth. I liked that name. Maybe we should live there. Naa—right then, even small American towns with exquisite names couldn't hold me. I would have given anything to see a kosher salami sign. Instead, looming up was a large green sign for Albert Lea and another one for Highway 35 north. Ninety miles to the Twin Cities. I wrapped around the cloverleaf and the sun that did not come out was at my back.

I stopped in Clarks Grove for gas. The tank was half full, enough to reach Minneapolis, but I wanted to stop. I bought some Wrigley's, standing at the candy machine for what seemed like ten minutes. My right hand sat on the silver knob you pull for your selection to drop down the chute. Let me stay here and pump gas, I thought to myself. Maybe I should paint a picture of the candy in this machine. I didn't want to drive the next ninety miles. Paralysis set in. The attendant asked me if I needed change. His question thrust me forward.

I got back in the car, pulled out of Clarks Grove, and entered the ramp to the big highway. It was 5:30 in the afternoon, rush hour, but down by Clarks Grove there was no one rushing anywhere. See, I should have stayed, I thought to myself. Clarks Grove was heaven.

I was so nervous about arriving in Minneapolis, I suddenly remembered Stuart Rosen, a guy I'd dated back in Ann Arbor. It must have been because I was back in the Midwest. Stuart couldn't get an erection. It had to do with Russell, Kansas. He had been brought up there by his grandparents. They didn't talk to him much and went to bed early. He was left alone each night to pedal his blue Schwinn around the streets in moonlight. It was something about the treelined streets and his grandmother pouring out cold cereal in the morning that kept him soft. I just knew it. Hard to say a man stayed soft because of a town, but I did know there was something back there that he brought to bed with him.

Stuart couldn't get desire straight. Instead, as we lay out on the windowsill eight stories up, he whispered to me about the Vietnam War. He had ended up in Cambodia, before there was trouble there. "Women masseuses massaged me until I came." I turned from him, slightly nauseous. It'd been only in the steaming forests of war—the other side of the world from Russell, Kansas—that he could pour his white cells into a stranger's hands. I remembered his lips. I liked his lips, they were fleshy. I even liked him. It was a long time ago.

Highway 35 North was a straight arrow. The flat green land grew out around me. The clouds had cleared, and to my left the sun began to set. It was a wild sunset. As I hit the sprawling suburbs that began at least forty miles away from the city's center, the sun turned deep pink. The clouds were an ice blue where they weren't streaming with gold and fuchsia light. The whole western sky was suddenly enormous. Could this be as good as New Mexico? I asked myself. Probably not, but still it was pretty good.

The suburbs—Burnsville, Bloomington, Richfield—skimmed through the wheels of my car. Suddenly, a thin, flat, navy blue building, like a wafer, shot straight up in the sky. King Kong could never climb it, I thought—there was nothing to hold on to.

It dawned on me that I was lost. Gauguin had never given me directions to his place. I knew it was in the Cedar Riverside area, but I didn't know how to get there. I turned off at the Seventh Street exit and was immediately swallowed by the red-light district. Nell, I said to myself, here's your last chance. Become a topless gogo dancer. "Banana Rose, the girl with the yellow heart and rose red lips." I knew my hippie name would eventually come in handy.

White neon flashed "Girls, Girls, Girls." I wanted to roll down my window and yell, "What's all the fuss about girls? I just had one in Nebraska! It's not such a big deal. They talk to you afterward."

I wanted to see Gauguin. I didn't want to see him. I stopped at the curb and asked a man holding a lighted cigarette where Cedar Riverside was. He leaned in a little too close to the car. I was about to yell "Rape!" but he pointed to Fourth Street. "Make a right and follow it over the bridge. You'll be right there."

"Thanks." I rolled up my window. The car stalled and then bounced into first. The streets began to look familiar from when I'd been there in late March, except the trees were now full of leaves. I parked in front of Gauguin's house. I sat down on the cement stoop. Two steps up, and I would be knocking at Gauguin's door. I could feel the rough concrete through the seat of my pants. This would be the last time I would see Gauguin, because this time would last all our lives, and there wouldn't be any more separation. We would be married.

Mr. Steak and a Mobil station were across the street. I imagined making love to the three-flash-pause-two-flash rhythm of Mr. Steak's red neon sign. The white walls would take on the color of the neon and we would be just like every other married couple in their bedroom.

I got up from the stoop, knocked on the black wooden door, and heard the double locks quickly being undone. Gauguin flung open the door, grabbed me, and pulled me inside. Each moment welled into the next like a chameleon changing colors. I was the wall, the ceiling, the windowsill, Gauguin's lower lip, the bark of the elm on the curb. Then I was none of that, only my tender fear, trembling in Gauguin's arms.

"What took you so long? I was worried." He held me closer. "I thought you'd be here yesterday." He slammed the door shut with the top of his foot. We held each other for a long time, my face pressed to the side of his face, my arms around his neck. Soon we fell into his unmade bed, which was across the living room into the dining room.

I don't remember a thing about that lovemaking except that it was fast, hungry, almost desperate. Our hands, mouths, and bellies were blind, and we groped to climb all the way back into the plums and wild roses of Talpa. I don't think we made it. I don't think it was possible.

Afterward Gauguin asked, "Do you want dinner? I'll cook for you."

We ate brown rice with green peppers, red onion, and tofu in a tangy brown sauce.

"Let's go for a walk down Riverside." Gauguin handed me a checkered flannel shirt. It wasn't evening anymore. It had become dark. Everything was cement and humid and a slight chill permeated the air. At Twelfth Street, Gauguin motioned. "C'mon. Here's a bar I want to show you," and we stepped through the doors.

Gauguin ordered a St. Pauli Girl. When I hesitated, Gauguin nodded. "Get a beer too."

"What kind?"

"How about Löwenbräu?"

"Okay."

I looked around. Mostly men stood at the bar with us. In the back, more men with big biceps leaned over a pool table. Peanut shells littered the black-and-white-tiled floor. Gauguin drank straight from the bottle, so I did, too. Actually, the bartender never offered us glasses. We finished the beers and walked the same route home.

When I pulled down the sheets to get into bed, I noticed bloodstains. I called to Gauguin, who was in the bathroom. He came out with a toothbrush in his mouth.

"What's this?" I pointed.

"Oh." His brushing slowed down. "I didn't get a chance to change the sheets before you came. Sorry." He paused. I looked away, into the living room. We had made no promises before I moved here, but suddenly I felt trapped. I'd never slept with anyone else in the whole state of Minnesota. Gauguin was my only connection.

"Banana"—he put his hand on my shoulder—"I stopped sleeping with Sherry over a week ago. I'm sorry."

I shrugged. "It's okay." Then I flung the blankets off the bed. "Change 'em now!"

30

Five days after I arrived in Minneapolis, I lay down on the couch in the living room, looked out the window, and counted how many times the Mr. Steak sign flashed across the street. I thought this would prepare me to get back into painting. I planned to watch that flashing sign for fifteen minutes and then get up, unpack my paints, and begin. Suddenly an idea came to me—I'd do a painting postcard to Anna and then another one to Blue. This idea excited me. I wouldn't actually send them the paintings. Instead, I'd talk in my head as I painted, trying to express to them what my life was like now. In Anna's, there would be the Mobil gas station across the street where I walked just yesterday to buy some gum. Spearmint gum. Anna liked to know details like that. To Blue, I'd want to express what it was like to live in humidity. Take a blue Buick. For an inch above its hood the metal seemed to mix with the air, as though the air here pulled a thing out beyond itself. Blue would like to hear about something mystical like that.

And then I'd do a painting postcard just for myself. It would have the clear definition of New Mexico, one piñon standing on a vast mesa where the dry air let the piñon be a piñon and not get mixed up with anything else. Then one more painting for Gauguin of the petunias and zinnias that grew along the edge of the house, telling him how yesterday I sat on the cement stoop under the tremendous maples and watched leaf shadows move across my lap.

Just as I was about to get up off the couch to begin, the phone rang.

It was Gauguin. He was at work. "Nell, my dad wants to see you. He wants to go shopping with you, buy you a dress as a wedding present."

"Huh?" I replied. "Gauguin, I don't want a dress."

"Just come down. We can meet for lunch at noon. Take bus twenty-one on the corner."

"But it's 10:30 now—I was planning to paint," I said.

"Paint later. You haven't seen my father since Taos."

"Okay, okay," I said, and we hung up.

Just then, I heard a plunk. The mailman had dropped the mail through the slot in the front door. I went over to collect it. Discount coupons from Applebaum's, a gas bill, a postcard of a monkey in a bib with a banana in his paw. I turned over the postcard slowly. I knew who it was from.

Dear Nell and Gauguin,

Best wishes on your wedding and congratulations. I wish I could be there. I'm happy for you.

All my best,
Eugene

I held the card in my hand, leaned against the cool wall, and then slid down it to a crouch at the bottom. Neon. My finger ran across his thick handwriting. Neon. I felt a terrible ache in my stomach. I could hear the trees rustle outside through the screens. "Neon," I said it aloud this time, "I miss you." And I bowed my head over my knees and just stayed there. No tears. I didn't have time. I had to dress to meet my father-in-law.

We ate lunch in a dark green leather booth at the Silver Slipper with dim lights above us. Gauguin and I sat on one side, Rip on the other.

"Do you mind?" he asked, and held up a long thin cigar wrapped in cellophane.

"No, of course not." I shook my head, and he unwrapped it.

"Gauguin tells me you applied to teach at Central High School. That's very commendable. It's a rough neighborhood." He nodded toward me and lit his cigar.

"Yes, I like working with inner-city kids. I feel at home with them." I wanted to say, It will be a relief to see someone who isn't white. I was amazed how Scandinavian the city felt.

We ordered from the menu. I had a club sandwich, but I asked them to hold the bacon. Rip and Gauguin had hamburgers and fries. Gauguin had mentioned that he'd started to eat meat, but I hadn't actually witnessed it yet. He was going to eat a burger in front of me! I wanted to say something, but I didn't feel comfortable in front of Rip.

Rip also ordered a gin and tonic and encouraged us to do the same. We both declined.

"So, Nell, what can I get you for the wedding?" he asked, taking a sip of his drink.

"How about getting something for the two of us?" I asked.

"Well, I wanted to make up for blaming you for those mushrooms. Gauguin explained about the—what did you call it?—the gluck?" He turned to Gauguin and flicked his cigar in the ashtray.

"The glitch," I said. "Yeah, everyone gets it the first time they visit. Don't worry. It's forgotten."

"Well, how about a nice sundress? I bet you'd look pretty in one." He smiled.

Just then the waiter served us our meal. Rip ordered another gin and tonic, and I bit into a potato chip from my plate.

"How's business?" I asked. I wanted to change the subject, and

Gauguin had told me they were designing some big complex. I took a sip of my water after I took a bite of sandwich. I didn't like my sandwich. They put slices of pickle on it.

"Oh, great, great." He nodded.

I could tell we weren't going to get into a lively conversation about architecture. I decided to tell him about my painting; after all, Gauguin had told me Rip loved art. I explained the postcard idea. "I'll think of an individual as I paint." He ordered a third drink and nodded. Gauguin excused himself and went to the bathroom.

Just then, Rip leaned across the table and took my hand. His breath stank from alcohol. "You know, Nell, Gauguin doesn't realize what he has," he whispered in a heavy voice.

I pulled my hand away. "Yes, he does. He knows he has a lecherous father."

Gauguin reappeared. "Gauguin, we were just talking about you." His father beamed.

I looked from one to the other. No, they were not the same. If I weren't sure of that right then, I'd have to walk out and leave this city.

"Nell, you'll excuse us. We're late." Rip stood up, threw his linen napkin on his plate, and took the check to the cashier.

"Banana," Gauguin whispered, "I'll see you at home," and he kissed me.

I sat in the dim light for a while after they left and wondered whether I should tell Gauguin about his father. I decided not to.

31

I'd been in Minneapolis now for three weeks. An easel was set up in our living room and paints and thick paper were spread out on the floor. After working hard for four hours straight, I took a break one afternoon and walked the three blocks to Shur's market to purchase some chocolate chips. I thought I'd bake cookies. When the owner rang up $1.95 on the cash register, I said, "These were on sale for $1.69."

"Oh, you're right! Thought I was trying to jew you, didn't you?" He laughed.

He put the yellow bag of chips in a brown paper sack and placed one quarter, one nickel with a buffalo's head, and one penny in my open palm. I closed my hand quickly around the change, picked up the bag, and pushed open the screen door. It slammed behind me as I walked out into the June heat.

Standing on the sidewalk, I thought, What did he mean by that? Does he know I'm a Jew? I blinked, waiting for the light to change. I was about to cry.

That evening, Gauguin and I walked to the local pizza parlor for a late dinner. We ordered a mushroom pizza with extra cheese. Gauguin drank a Löwenbräu from the bottle, and I sucked on ice from my Coke while we waited for our order.

"You know, Gauguin, I don't know why people don't get smart and sell chicken pizza. They could drop whole legs, wings, and breasts on top of the sauce and pour cheese over it. They could call it Italian Chicken. Someone could make a fortune." I was only half joking.

Then I changed the subject. "Gauguin, you know in the grocery today the owner said, 'Did you think I was trying to jew you?' when I pointed out he was about to overcharge me for a bag of chocolate chips. What did he mean? How did he know I was Jewish?"

"Oh, Nell, haven't you ever heard that expression? It doesn't mean anything—he probably doesn't even know that it has anything to do with Jews. It just means 'cheating.' You know, 'jew me down.' " Gauguin tossed his head as though to brush it off.

My right hand went into a fist around my paper napkin. They served us the pizza. The air conditioning was too cold, and I didn't want to eat.

Suddenly I wished Minneapolis were Brooklyn, full of Jewish neighborhoods, brick buildings, and garbage cans with their lids chained to spindly trees so they wouldn't be stolen. I wanted to be able to drop in at my father's luncheonette, the Empress Deli, and see his thick hands reaching for the green canisters of cole slaw, his face reflected in the mirror behind the blinking "Kosher" sign. He'd be wearing a long white apron, his white shirt sleeves rolled up to his elbows, and every once in a while he would shift the cigar in his mouth from the right side to the left.

The Empress was down the avenue from my junior high school. Sometimes on the way home I'd stop in to see my father and to sit on the high red stools and do my geometry homework. I'd glance up at him every once in a while when I stopped to sip the ginger ale he had poured into a tall glass and decorated with a maraschino cherry.

He'd yell at me, "Nell, you're a silly girl. Quit looking at me and get back to your homework. Do you want me to turn on the TV? But we can't watch *The Mickey Mouse Show*. This isn't a kids' store." He then flicked a white linen towel around the water glass he held, giving it a shine.

"Dad, can I have a pastrami sandwich? And don't make it so thick that I can't put my mouth around it all." He got rye bread from the kosher baker down the block.

"Well, the parts you can't eat"—my father took the cigar from his mouth and placed it in a glass ashtray—"you can hang from your hair."

I became convulsed with laughter and almost fell off the stool. "You're a silly girl, Nell," he repeated for the hundredth time.

I loved my father. I didn't want to feel weird about being Jewish. I longed for a pastrami sandwich and asked Gauguin where we could get a good one in Minneapolis.

He took a bite from his slice of pizza and said he didn't know but that he'd ask around.

The next week, he took me to The Sandwich, the only deli in the Twin Cities. I watched a woman in the next booth eat corned beef with mayonnaise on white bread, and I could tell by the way she was eating it that she thought it was actually good. I grimaced when I saw a young man in another booth pick the lox off his bagel before he ate it. Gauguin saw the grimace and asked what was wrong. He was poised to bite into a pickle. His mouth was full of cole slaw.

"They're eating corned beef with mayonnaise! They're picking the lox off their bagels!"

"Who's they?" he asked.

"Everyone," I said. I looked around. Suddenly, the Nazi army occupied The Sandwich. There were six Nazis crammed into each booth. They were throwing the lox and pastrami at their snapping German shepherds and Dobermans. "Please, let's get out of here," I said. "This isn't a real deli. I'm not hungry."

"Wait, let me finish eating." Gauguin held up his hand. "Nell, don't you want your chopped liver sandwich?"

"No, I don't want any of it. I'll meet you in the car." I was sure my sandwich was ground pork hemorrhoids passing as chopped chicken liver. I dashed out of The Sandwich. Though it was hot and humid out, I rolled up the car windows and waited for Gauguin with the doors locked.

32

The day before the wedding, my parents flew in from New York. This
was the first time my father had met Gauguin, and he was determined to like him. After all, he would be family soon, and family was
everything to my father. He had animal blood loyalty.

He gave Gauguin a strong handshake in the airport and then pulled
him close and engulfed him in a big hug. "My son-in-law," he said
emotionally. "Now there will be another man in the family."

When Gauguin was released, he said, "Why, hello, sir," and his
clothes fell back in place on his body.

"Nell, I'm starving." My father turned to me. "Where's a great
restaurant?"

We went to the Lilac Room, the restaurant in my parent's hotel in
downtown Minneapolis.

"This is real fiddledeedee," my mother said when the waiter served
her a very small portion of salmon on a large white plate surrounded by
eight peas and two small roasted potatoes. *Fiddledeedee* was a term my
grandmother used. It meant acting fancy but serving so little food, you
walked out starving. The walls of the Lilac Room were wood-paneled,
and crystal water glasses sparkled on the table.

"Boy, does he fonfer," my father said when the waiter walked away.

This was another one of my grandmother's expressions. It meant talking through your nose or putting on the dog.

My father looked down at his roast beef, shaved so thin you could see through it. "Nell, after we leave here, let's stop someplace to eat."

After we dropped my parents off, Gauguin said, "What was your parents' problem? My family has always gone to the Lilac Room for birthdays and special occasions. I love that place."

"Well, they're used to Brooklyn. They like a lot of food. They like to eat," I explained.

"We ate. I still don't understand."

"I think it's cultural, that's all." I opened my window and breathed in the summer air. We stopped at the light. "Gauguin, tomorrow we'll be married." It felt like some completely unknown adventure. I could easily have said, "Tomorrow we're going deep-sea diving."

"Yeah," Gauguin said, and reached across the car seat to take my hand.

The wedding was on a Sunday afternoon in Gauguin's father's back yard. Rita arrived that morning. I hardly knew anyone at it except my parents and my sister. Anna couldn't make it. Neither could Blue. My friends from the Elephant House sent us a photo of everyone standing in front of the house. The old lady from Boulder sent us a vase with a painting of a cat on it.

There were about thirty-five of us, including Gauguin's parents and friends of Gauguin and his family. Camille, Rip's mother, sent a telegram. We all stood in a circle outside in front of the judge.

I didn't change my name. I figured I was born Nell Schwartz and should die Nell Schwartz. I ignored the fact that I had once been Banana Rose. Gauguin said it was fine with him that I didn't take his last name. Gauguin planned to stay Gauguin, though it wasn't his legal name.

He'd gotten the name Gauguin when he took an acid trip in the woods in northern Minnesota. For three hours he could not remember who he was. He'd stumbled past hundreds of birches. All of them were the same. He finally found the cabin where he was staying and bent down in the rearview mirror of his red truck. He thought he'd know his name if he saw his reflection, but there was no one in the mirror. He touched his face. He could feel it. He looked in the mirror again. There was no image; it was as though he didn't exist. He jerked up frightened, and in the moment his head snapped back he realized he was everything. He looked around him: "I'm the pines, the bark, the needles, the sun on the needles. I'm this truck, this wheel—" He put his hand on the black rubber tread. Then he walked to the cabin porch and lifted his right foot to put it on the bottom step. He was the foot, the step, the screen door, the hand that pushed the screen door open. He felt the coolness of the cabin air inside; he was that, too, and he began to cry. He went to the sink and ran the cold water. He noticed, as though for the first time, that water was transparent. "I put my hand under it and opened my fingers and just looked at how my fingers moved." He stared out the window over the sink, turned off the water, walked into the living room, and flopped on the big red chair in front of the fireplace. "There was nothing I wasn't, and everything was magnificent." He picked up a book of twentieth-century art on the coffee table and flipped the pages. The book fell open on page 212. There was a picture of a painting of Tahitian women. He took the leap from the artist to himself and spoke the words, "I-am-Gauguin." It resonated. He said it again. "I am Gauguin." That day he found his name.

My mother wore a violet silk dress to my wedding and was afraid she was too high-style for the Midwest. A thin strip of woods separated Rip's back yard from the highway. Every once in a while you could hear a semi rumble by. I wore a peach dress. In front of us on the grass were placed three white vases of carnations and tiger lilies. A breeze picked up just as the judge was about to speak, and a vase blew over. My parents took it as a signal for them to begin crying uncontrollably. My father, who is six feet tall and weighs 220 pounds, leaned on my tiny mother and wept inconsolably into her shoulder as though no one else were there.

"Edith," he gasped, "our Nell is leaving us."

"Wait, I have a tissue." My mother opened the gold clasp of her small beaded purse and pulled out a white linen hanky, embroidered with a purple pansy. Mascara ran down her face. My father blew his nose as we all watched. They broke down into another spasm. Gauguin looked at me. I shrugged and turned my palms heavenward in supplication. My sister, Rita, bit the side of her lip. Gauguin's parents had never seen anything like this.

"Hey, judge, you're marrying the wrong couple," Rip cracked out of the side of his mouth. "The show's over here!" He nodded at my parents, who forced themselves to laugh and tried to control their hysterics for the next ten minutes.

It was a simple ceremony. We didn't mention God. Mostly we weren't sure who God was. Was He Jewish or Episcopalian? I actually believed "He" was a She. And what about Buddha? Our parents wouldn't like Buddha. The day before the wedding, Gauguin and I had quickly written up what the judge would say. It was about love. That was firm ground. We were sure we loved each other.

As the judge spoke, a bluejay alighted on a branch of a poplar behind his head. My eye caught it and I missed some of what the judge was saying. I came back when I heard, "Nell, do you take this man to be your beloved husband?"

I snapped to. "Yes," I said.

The judge turned to Gauguin. "Do you take this woman to be your cherished wife?"

"I do," Gauguin said clearly.

Secretly, I wanted the marriage certificate to say, "Banana Rose and Gauguin were married on a July day." Instead, it read, "Nell Schwartz and George Howard." That startled me. Even Alice and Rip called him Gauguin. I'd known somewhere vaguely that Gauguin's given name was George Howard. I had asked him once what it was when we were in a hammock in Talpa, but seeing it written I couldn't connect it with the man I knew. Gauguin was always Gauguin, first and last. If you had wanted him to have a last name, it would have been Gauguin-Gauguin, as if to repeat the same name intensified his existence.

As soon as the ceremony was over, my parents fell into each other's arms, crying again. When my father grabbed me for congratulations, he knocked out the fresh white gardenia I'd carefully pinned in my hair that morning.

In a photo of Rip and Gauguin taken the morning of the wedding, they are both facing the mirror and Rip's arms are around his son's neck. He is showing Gauguin how to knot a tie. You can see Rip's freckled wrist reaching out of his blazer. Gauguin is concentrating very hard and Rip is smiling.

At the reception we ate fried chicken and potato salad that Alice had prepared. We had a three-tier chocolate wedding cake in my honor. There is a photo of Gauguin's face close to the cake, licking the pinky that he'd just stuck in the chocolate icing. I am standing behind him, wanting my share.

In the middle of the reception, Gauguin and I snuck away for a short walk down the suburban street.

"You know your mother is really kind. She looks around to make sure everyone is comfortable," he said to me. It felt as though we were both glittering. After all, this was our wedding day.

"Naa. She's just nervous. She's never been with so many non-Jews." We laughed and put our arms around each other.

When we returned, there was a commotion on the patio. Rita had disappeared with the drummer from the four-piece band. My father found them behind the garage, passing a joint back and forth.

"How could you do such a thing? And at your sister's wedding!" My father was beside himself. My mother was wringing her hands behind him.

Rita sauntered back onto the dance floor and began snapping her fingers, doing a wild, provocative dance to a Rolling Stones song the band played. All the wedding guests gathered around her to watch.

First my father was bug-eyed and furious, but then he relaxed when he saw that everyone was admiring her. "She sure can dance," he said, proudly.

In the early evening, my parents asked me to call a cab. I went to the phone in Rip's bedroom, and my mother followed.

"Now, Nell, please remember to eat well. Make him matzo ball soup. He'll learn to like it. A capon is good. Go to a butcher." She spoke to me as I sat on the bed and talked to the Yellow Cab dispatcher.

"Ma, I don't know how to make matzo balls." I hung up the phone receiver.

My mother gasped just as my father walked in. "Edith, what's wrong?"

"How could we have let her marry? She can't cook!" She turned to her husband and began to weep. "She's just a little girl."

They were in each other's arms again.

My father broke down, too. "Do you remember when she was born? Our little Nell."

"Mom, Dad, please." I was wringing my hands.

Rip was at the door. "Hey, they're at it again."

Gauguin, Alice, and several of the guests crowded the doorway.

My father looked up, let out a chuckle, and said to my mother, "Edith, we're being watched," as he wiped tears from his cheeks.

My mother fluttered her hanky in the direction of the door. "Well, you caught us again. We tried to wait till we got back to the hotel."

Everyone spilled into the bedroom. "Someone here must know how to make good matzo ball soup? Please teach Nell." My mother looked beseechingly around the room. "I can't believe her grandmother let her go away to college without knowing."

Alice stepped forward. "Don't worry. If it's in a cookbook, I'll figure it out."

"Oh, thank you, Alice." My mother hugged her. "Now I know I'm leaving Nell in good hands."

The doorbell rang. Someone in the hall called, "Cab's here!"

There was a flurry of activity as my mother's shawl and purse, my father's pipe and jacket were gathered up.

We all stood at the front door. "Take care of each other," my father called out the open window of the departing taxi.

We all waved wildly.

I went back into the house and over to the food table. I nibbled at Alice's chicken. I had been too nervous earlier in the day to eat anything. "Alice, you are a wonderful cook." She was standing nearby, and I hugged her.

She stiffened. She hadn't seemed to when my mother hugged her.

"Your parents are adorable. How long have they been together? They seem so compatible."

"Oh, forever," I said, licking my fingers and then reaching for a green grape. "No one in my family ever divorces." Then I realized what I'd said. I looked at Alice. Her head was bent over, counting forks. "Alice." I took her arm. "I'm sorry."

She looked up and bit her lip.

"It's okay," she said, and just then I could see the lines under her eyes. I looked past her shoulder out to the patio where Rip was dancing with Caroline, one of Gauguin's friends, who wore a low red dress.

"Thank you for all the wonderful food you made." I attempted to hug her again, but she reached for the bread basket across the table.

33

Ten days after the wedding, Gauguin and I drove to New York for a reception at my parents' home. We didn't leave Minneapolis until nine in the evening and drove singing at 2 A.M. through Chicago. At four in the morning we rented a hotel room in Indiana. This was the first time we'd ever been in a hotel together. Once while we were in Taos, we'd driven to New Orleans to hear jazz, but we slept outside at truck stops, in sleeping bags, in the shade of vast semis, and in the smell of oil and gas. The hotel off the expressway in Indiana cost thirty-five dollars a night. We couldn't believe it was so expensive.

We were tired, but I insisted that we make love. I didn't want to waste the hotel room. After a little effort, lovemaking broke open in us. The anonymity of the hotel room gave us a new freedom. Our bodies felt like bronze bells, and we sang out together over the grain elevators, slaughterhouses, and steel mills we had seen as we drove through the Midwest. We climaxed at the same time and were loud about it. Then we leaned back into the long hotel pillows and fell into a hard sleep as the gray light of dawn crept across the sky.

The next morning we drove on through the hills of Pennsylvania to the northern tip of New Jersey, land of beefsteak tomatoes. We were exhausted when we reached Brooklyn late at night and collapsed in my childhood bedroom at the back of the apartment.

We woke late the next day. I lay in bed, looking at the blue-and-yellow-print wallpaper and the hearts I had drawn on it above my head in pencil when I was sixteen. I heard a lot of activity down the hall. I looked at the Big Ben windup clock on my old bureau and jerked up to a sitting position.

I shook Gauguin. "It's one o'clock! Get up—the reception's in an hour."

My grandmother knocked at the door. "Nell, Nell, do you want breakfast? I'm sure your husband is starving."

Gauguin and I looked at each other and giggled at the reference to "husband."

"Grandma, come in," I called. Gauguin looked at me in shock and dove under the covers. Only his head was sticking out.

"Mamala." My grandmother swept across the bedroom and took my face in her hands. She kissed me. Then she turned to Gauguin. "Hello, young man. Get dressed, and I'll make you something to eat. I'll give you real food before the caterers come in and try to poison you. What does he want?" She turned to me. "Does your husband want a chopped liver sandwich? Bagels and lox?" She saw the expression on my face. "Oh, he doesn't like that?" She clucked. "Don't worry. I'll make you a nice chopped egg sandwich. On rye. You'll like it." She smiled at Gauguin and left the room.

"Nell, was that your famous grandmother? The one who taught you to make grilled cheese sandwiches?" Gauguin was amazed.

"Yup." I nodded.

We got dressed. I wore the peach dress I had worn for the wedding in Minneapolis, but this time I didn't have a fresh gardenia in my hair. Gauguin wore his tie and jacket, and he was able to tie the knot at his throat now without his father's help.

As we sat in the kitchen eating my grandmother's food, we watched the caterers stream by. The kitchen was attached to a large screened-in back porch, and out the window we could see the trays being placed on tables.

"Good?" my grandmother asked as she opened the refrigerator.

Yes, we agreed, our mouths full, nodding our heads.

Then she scowled at a caterer who accidentally walked in the kitchen. "In my day, we served food at weddings, not cardboard and doilies," she said to no one in particular. "Your grandfather would turn over in his grave to see what we're eating at your wedding. He loved you so, Nell."

"I wish he were here, Grandma," I told her. A bite of chopped egg sandwich stuck in my throat.

The guests swarmed in promptly at two o'clock. There were Uncle Morris, Aunt Ruth, Cousin Sarah, Cousin Saul, Aunt Ann, Aunt Helen, Uncle Harold, Uncle Carl from Miami, Cousin Judy from Asbury Park, and my mother's old high school friend Pearl from Boston. They all headed down the long hallway to the back porch and the food.

"Nell, it's so good to see you!" My aunt Helen let out a whooping yell when she spied me on the porch and ran over. She had a streak of red lipstick across her mouth and dyed orange hair. "I am so happy for you. Marriage is wonderful." Her husband, Uncle Ted, had died two years earlier of a heart attack.

My father took moving pictures of the reception with the old eight-millimeter camera that had been used in our family for years. Only twice did he focus the camera on me: One time I was eating chopped liver; the other time I stood with Gauguin, and we held vodka and orange juice in clear tall glasses. Most of the footage at the reception was of my mother. He followed her into the kitchen where she sampled a cheese puff, then he followed her in her violet dress through my aunts and uncles on the porch and paused as she stood, her feet close together, her head arched at an angle, like a sparrow, listening. Someone was telling a joke. You could tell, because everyone was laughing. Then she nodded her head, sipped her scotch on the rocks, and turned to the camera, full faced.

Gauguin and I stood on the porch most of the time and smiled. We clicked glasses of vodka together and got drunker and drunker. Eventually, we stood tongue-kissing in the middle of the reception.

My mother walked by and kicked me in the ankle. "Cut it out, Nell," she stage-whispered from the side of her mouth.

My sister, Rita, stood with her old high school buddy, Mimi, in a corner of the back yard, eating little kosher hot dog hors d'oeuvres. She had just been in the alley and was stoned on grass.

The next day, I took Gauguin to Jones Beach. We picked our way through the browning bodies and laid our checkered blanket near a couple eating cheese sandwiches on dark bread and blaring Beethoven on their portable radio. On the other side of us were three high school girls who poured Coppertone on each other every half hour and resembled capons on a rotisserie grill. Their radio blared a rock station.

Gauguin had never been to New York before. I told him to wait while I stood in line at the concession stand for potato knishes and perfect round scoops of ice cream that you unrolled from cardboard containers into your cone.

"What's a knish?" he asked.

"You'll see. Only in New York do they serve them on the beach," I explained.

Gauguin burned easily and had to wear a T-shirt most of the afternoon to protect his shoulders. Looking at the field of people on the beach, he said over and over, "I've never seen anything like this."

The next day we rode the subway from Brooklyn to Manhattan. I immediately took him to a kosher delicatessen on the Lower East Side. Our waiter was bald and had a heavy New York accent. He took one look at Gauguin and knew he wasn't a native.

Gauguin pointed to an item on the menu and asked, "What's this?"

The waiter slapped his hand on Gauguin's shoulder and said, "This all is real gen-u-ine flanken." He said it in a Texas accent, thinking he was imitating Gauguin. Naturally, Gauguin wasn't from Texas, but in New York anything that isn't New York is a slow drawl.

"You-all might like some chitlins in your chicken soup." The waiter pronounced this with lots of space between the letters of the words, as though the sound of the language echoed the flat open plains outside of Dallas, Houston, and San Antonio.

Gauguin was defensive. "I'm not from the South. I'm from Minnesota."

"Oh, yeah? Where's that?" The waiter had a big smile on his face and he slapped Gauguin again on the shoulder. This time he wanted to help. "Have the brisket," he said in his regular voice. "It's good. You'll like it."

I looked over at Gauguin. Confusion swam across his face.

"Hey, try the pastrami here. You'll see what I've been talking about," I suggested to help him. He ordered it on rye.

When the waiter left, Gauguin said, "What the fuck was all that about?" I shrugged and didn't say anything.

The waiter returned, this time gallantly. He proudly placed the pastrami sandwich in front of Gauguin. The meat was stacked so high that it fell over.

"Now there's a sandwich!" The waiter nodded at it, turned on his heel like El Capitaine, and marched off to the table across the room by the window.

Gauguin was impressed. "I can't get my mouth around it!" he exclaimed.

I loved New York in that moment.

"Nell, it's amazing that every Jew in the street doesn't drop dead from hardening of the arteries. Just like that!" He snapped his fingers. "Right in front of the subway cars and garbage trucks. Help! Pastrami clogged my heart!" Then he pretended he was collapsing from a heart attack.

When he recovered, he reached for a whole pickle in the metal tub that was placed on the table, bit down hard, and smiled.

We ate apple strudel for dessert and afterward took the subway uptown to the Museum of Modern Art. A blind beggar singing "Swing Low, Sweet Chariot" reached out his hand as we passed him in the station. Gauguin dug in his pocket for change and then said, "Hell," took out a dollar bill, and placed it in the man's cup.

"Thank you. May God be with you." The beggar's voice rang out in the airless underground.

We came out into daylight and fumbled a bit while our eyes adjusted. Gauguin stretched his neck back as he looked up at the tall Midtown buildings. He was fascinated by the falafel vendors. "They even sell that on the streets!"

I nodded and laughed. I enjoyed New York with Gauguin. Everything was fresh for him.

We entered the lobby of the museum. The air conditioning felt good. The city streets were steaming.

We went upstairs to the permanent collection. A Klee, a Picasso, a Monet, a Bonnard. One after the other.

Gauguin was stunned. "I can't believe we're seeing the real things, not just posters or postcards."

Gauguin joined me in front of a painting, then leaned toward the wall to read the card. " 'Intérieur à la boîte à violon,' " he pronounced in his silliest French. "By Henri Matisse." He stood back with me again.

"What does it mean?" I asked. I had taken Spanish in high school.

" 'The inside of a violin box,' I think." He scratched his head.

A black violin case lay open on a pale yellow upholstered chair in the lower left-hand corner of the painting. The inside of the violin case was blue. The chair was by an open door that led out to a balcony overlooking the sea. On the other side of the room was a dressing table with a round mirror. The walls of the room were pale yellow, like the chair but with a swirling pattern.

"I want to paint like that someday," I said, mesmerized. "I want that freedom. How he thinks it's okay to make art out of something that ordinary—I've been trying that since Boulder, but look how sure of himself Matisse is.'' I pointed to the black strokes that indicated birds out the window. Then I pointed to the sea.

The museum guard in the corner took a step forward and coughed. I retracted my hand.

''Yeah, and look at the people below the balcony,'' Gauguin added.

''Amazing—he made each one with just a gesture of black paint.'' My body was sucking in the painting. I felt how Matisse felt, saw what he saw—and what couldn't be seen with the eyes, things that were not in the room he was painting but that the canvas demanded be there.

Gauguin grabbed my hand. ''C'mon, let's go find some paintings done by my namesake.''

I moved differently after that Matisse painting. Every step I took was a block of color. Every breath was a shadow. Every movement of my head or hands was a shape, and every painting I saw was a banquet of language. The painters were talking to me. I never knew before how much paintings spoke without words and told me in form and color about the natural unity of the world.

This visit with Gauguin felt like my first real trip to the museum, as well as his. I was meeting these painters now with hunger and friendship. They could teach me something. And it felt good to have the man I loved and had married standing beside me.

When we got to the third floor, Gauguin grabbed me right in the middle of one of the galleries. He was excited by everything he was seeing. All he'd expected was a hug in this public place, but I turned my head and kissed him so full on the lips, my tongue so deep in his mouth, right under an Alexander Calder mobile, that it felt as though we were flying through space, like two people in a painting by Chagall.

As we neared Ohio, on our drive back to Minnesota through Pennsylvania, we thought of stopping at Gauguin's Aunt June's, only thirty miles south of the highway. But when we approached the turn, we stopped at Stuckey's instead and walked up and down the aisles of pecan chews and

Ohio T-shirts in the kind of daze that driving across flat country induces. We ordered one hamburger to share and stood at the counter watching the thin blond man throw a ball of ground meat on the grill so hard that the meat flattened out, but just in case, the cook also pressed the spatula over it. In front of us was a glass case with a light that kept warm the precooked french fries in individual white bags. I ordered some. We paid, took our food to the orange booth by the window, and ate quickly. The hamburger was good. We ordered another one. Outside the sky was pale blue and stretched out forever. I asked if they had coffee ice cream.

"You must be from New York. Only New Yorkers driving on to California ask for coffee. Nope. We got chocolate, vanilla, and butter pecan."

After dawdling for too long, we decided to skip Gauguin's aunt and head for Rip's mother, who lived in a small town in Indiana. It was out of our way, but we didn't care. We got back in the car and continued west. When we got to Logansport in late afternoon, we passed a Dunkin' Donuts, made a right, drove down half a block, and parked in front of a small stone house with a large white porch. We knocked at the front door. No answer. We went around back.

There she was, in a white apron, squatting barefoot by the peas. She was eighty-two years old and had warm patches of pale red freckles all over her arms and face. She was tying clear plastic bags to a thin white string she had strung across the garden.

"Camille." Gauguin called his grandmother by her first name.

She looked up. We hadn't told her ahead of time that we were coming. "This is to fool the birds. I devised it myself," she explained, half to herself. Then she paused. "George?" She squinted as a big smile blossomed in her face. "My word! Help me up, honey. It's so good to see you." She looked past him at me. "This must be your bride." We hugged. Her body felt generously soft and full. "Come in the house." She looked back at me. "My, George, she's pretty. I like her dark skin and her hair's real nice."

She wiped her hands on her apron, climbed up the three concrete steps, and held open the back screen door as she ushered us in. The kitchen was cool and pale green against the humidity that clamped down among the dogwood and spruce trees outside.

Immediately Camille began to make her famous chicken and dumplings. As she cooked, she rattled on about how beautiful she'd heard the wedding was, how cute my parents were, how tired we must be from our long trip, and how she had once visited New York City when she was thirteen.

"Camille, you know you don't have to do this. We can take you out." Gauguin held up his hand.

"How often do I have you? Don't you miss my dumplings? Here, you just sit still and sip at your pink lemonade. Nell, do you want some cookies? I've got some Oreos in that jar there, the one with the fat belly. I figure the jar's been eating too much and wants you to have a cookie. Ah, wait." She brushed some hair out of her face. "I'll scoop you up some vanilla ice cream. George, hand me that big silver spoon over there on the drain board. I'll pour some of my peach preserves over it. Right from the tree out back."

"Camille, are those old trees still making peaches?" Gauguin asked.

"Well, yes, if the frost don't get them first. This year I think I'll be lucky if I get two peaches from all four trees together."

She ran back and forth from the refrigerator to the stove to the gray Formica table. Her small fists were powdered with white flour. When she rolled out the dough, she pressed her full weight into it and stood on her toes for leverage.

I stirred the ice cream as it melted in my dish. Gauguin motioned to me with his eyes to eat it. I didn't want to.

"Camille, tell me about George when he was a young boy," I asked. It felt funny to call Gauguin George.

"He was the sweetest thing. Remember, George, how you used to catch salamanders, kiss them, and let them go? You learned to do that in Iowa with your grandmother Mary Ellen. I was afraid you'd get warts. Then remember when you were twenty-one and came to visit here in that black limousine you drove, painted pink and silver? Your red hair was down to your shoulders. I thought, *'Now* what's he up to?' But you still ate my dumplings and peach preserves and I said to myself, 'Don't worry, Camille, the boy's just fine.' Honey, hand me that Mazola oil.'' She pointed to the bottle above the sink. ''How's your dad? Tell me, George'' —she turned her blue eyes away from the dough and toward him—''does he ever go to church? I worry about him and pray each Sunday for him to find his way. You know, he can't get into heaven if he doesn't go to church.''

''Now, Camille, Rip will find his own way,'' Gauguin assured her.

''Well, I know he's independent, but you can't fight God. You'll lose. He's got all the big atomic weapons wrapped into one.''

''Where'd you hear that?'' Gauguin asked.

''The preacher said it last month.'' She paused in her kneading to look at Gauguin. ''He says, 'The president thinks he's mighty, but let you tell me, one sweep of God's hand, and the whole world will be blown up.' '' She nodded emphatically and in wonder at God's power.

''You mean, 'Let me tell you,' '' Gauguin corrected her.

''That's what I said.'' She turned to me. ''Honey, you don't have to eat it, if you don't like.'' The vanilla ice cream was soup in my dish.

I smiled weakly. I'd never understood why someone would eat vanilla ice cream.

After Camille fell asleep in front of the TV, Gauguin and I took a walk in the cool evening. We held hands and strolled under the bright lights of the Dunkin' Donuts parking lot.

''Does your grandmother like me?'' I asked.

''When you went in the bathroom, she whispered to me, 'She's real sweet. I like her shiny dark hair,' but I think it helped that you liked her dumplings.''

We slept that night under a pink satin coverlet on a bed that was soft and full of lumps. It was the one Camille and her husband had slept in. He was a coal miner, and when the mines closed, he left. They never heard from him again until he died fifteen years later. His brother sent Camille a telegram. "Robert died. We buried him in Greeley, Colorado. Send money for the tombstone." Camille read the note, sat down in the kitchen, put her face on the table, and cried, her hands tucked into the pockets of her white apron. She sent money for the gravestone from what she'd made baking bread in her big oven and selling it still hot to her neighbors.

The next morning, we ate cornflakes and more peach preserves. I cried when we left Camille. I cried because I loved her and I loved my own grandmother, and I cried because the wedding and the honeymoon were over and now we were headed straight through the Midwest to Minneapolis, for good.

34

"Hey, Gauguin, where's your wedding ring?" We had just passed the exit for Eau Claire, Wisconsin.

"I took it off," he said.

My eyes moved from his left hand on the steering wheel to his face, which was looking out at the blue slate highway with its broken yellow line. We had been driving for a long time.

"You took it off? How come?" We had bought them at a hock shop on First Avenue for thirty dollars apiece. I liked wearing mine.

"Because you didn't change your last name," he said, still staring ahead.

"What? Before we were married, you said you didn't care. You've got to be kidding."

"I'm not. I felt weird telling my grandmother you were Nell Schwartz. Even at work right after the wedding, my dad made fun of it, says I married a women's libber."

I stared at his ringless finger. I was filled with a sudden rage that flashed like a bright quarter. This couldn't be possible. Who was this man sitting next to me? It wasn't Gauguin. I stared straight ahead, trying to compute. I looked at him again. I was right. It wasn't Gauguin. It was George Howard. I'd married the wrong person. Right then and there, I let out a terrible scream. Then I gave it words. "What does the fucking ring have to do with my name? You're nuts!"

I grabbed his right arm below the elbow with my two hands and squeezed as tight as I could. "I'm not changing my name," I yelled. "You said it didn't matter to you." I wanted to get out of that car before we reached the Minnesota border.

"Nell, let go of my arm," Gauguin said in a low, measured tone. "I'm trying to drive. I've been thinking about it, and I've changed my mind. Changing your name *is* important to me."

"Why the fuck didn't you tell me instead of taking off your ring? What does one thing have to do with the other?" Suddenly, I was a mathematician, trying to make the equation compute. It didn't. I went back to my old profession, a madwoman.

"Fuck you, George Howard!" I screamed.

35

Tears ran down my cheeks and across my lips. I licked them. I was trying to paint. A brush was in my right hand and a cloth in my left. That morning, Gauguin and I had had another fight.

As he left for work, I'd yelled, "I'm not doing all the dishes. I don't care if you work for your father. I'm not doing all the housework."

I was having a hard time being married. Gauguin told me one night that he wanted to be boss. It was the second Tuesday in August at eight in the evening. It was still light out, and I could see the bathroom from where I sat at the kitchen table. The bathroom was white, but in the light of dusk, white took on the shadows of gray and blue.

We were eating an avocado salad that Gauguin had made. I was on my second bite. I crunched into a lettuce leaf.

"Gauguin, this is good," I said cheerily.

"Nell—" He hesitated. "I don't want to be cooking. I want to be boss in this house."

When I heard that again in my head as I stood in front of the painting, the words shot down to the muscle of my heart and squeezed it. The blood rushed to my throat, and I had the urge to vomit. I heard it over and over, *"I want to be boss. I want to be boss . . ."* It was impossible for me to paint. I wanted to bolt out the door and go downtown, get Gauguin, and belt him.

I wiped my face with the sleeve of my painting shirt, put down my brush, and decided to go for a walk. I meandered down Riverside. It was still summer, but I could smell fall in the air and almost see it at the edge of tree leaves. Soon it would be Rosh Hashanah and Yom Kippur. Being back in a city reminded me of the Jewish holidays. I'd fled all that when I went away to college. Judaism had seemed oppressive in Brooklyn, old-fashioned, something my parents did, but now I kind of missed it. I wondered where there was a synagogue.

I didn't mind doing a little bit more than Gauguin, I mused. After all, he did go to work, but then again, I wasn't just sitting around. I was setting up a studio in the living room. I'd begun a series of paintings: pears in the corners of rooms. I'd already painted yellow pears sitting in the four corners of the bathroom. One was of two in the corner under the toilet, another showed three together in the bathtub corner. I added a green one there.

Suddenly the sun peeked out from behind a cloud and struck the maple tree above my head in an extraordinary way. Gauguin couldn't possibly be serious about being boss. That was George Howard, a million miles away in downtown Minneapolis at his father's office. I was in love with another man. I was in love with Gauguin.

A warm feeling suddenly filled my belly. My knees got weak. Yes, I was in love with him. I thought back just a few nights ago. We'd been lying in bed with only a thin sheet over us. The air had been humid, but a cool breeze blew in through the screens. Just as I was drifting off to sleep, Gauguin had touched me between my legs.

"I want to tell you a story," he whispered in my ear. "When I was at work today, I thought of you. I got up to go to the water cooler. I bent over and took a white paper cup"—I began to moan. "I took the white cup and put it under the nozzle." He paused and put his tongue in my ear. "I pressed the nozzle. I wanted you." The heat of his breath in my ear made me wet. "A bubble came up in the water cooler. My cock hardened behind my fly." He moved on top of me. I spread my legs. "My cock wanted to spring out of my pants." He entered me.

"Ohhh." I felt like a thousand fireflies were feeding on the walls of my vagina.

"Gauguin." I blew out his name with my breath.

"Yes, yes." He kept his mouth at my ear. "Nell, Nell, I love you."

I looked up at the sizzling maple. Now *that* was Gauguin, the man I had married. I shook my head. This George stuff—I was just imagining it.

The phone rang when I entered the house. It was Gauguin. "Nell, my mom wants to come over tonight. She baked us a peach pie. I invited her for dinner."

"Great. What are you going to make?" I asked nonchalantly.

There was a long pause. "I guess I could pick up a pizza." Pause again. "Alice doesn't like pizza." Another pause. "Nell, could you make something?"

A sparrow was singing on our window ledge near the petunias I had planted in the flower box. "Okay," I said casually. And then I had a thought. "It's Friday night. Why don't I make roast chicken? We can do a Shabbos."

"Great." Gauguin was relieved that I'd cook. He hung up.

The phone rang again right away. "Uh, Nell, I don't know about Shabbos. Alice doesn't know much about Jews. You know, an Iowa farm and all. Maybe we shouldn't do it?"

"We'll just light candles. It'll be okay." We hung up. Well, it's time she learned, I thought.

I rummaged through an old jewelry bag and found the Star of David my father's mother had left for me in her will. I put it on and looked in the mirror. "Banana Rose, you are still magic."

The table was all set when Gauguin came home. "Hey," he said. He was pleased.

I smiled primly. With an apron covering my tight jeans and white T-shirt that read, "Georgia O'Keeffe lives in New Mexico," I was the perfect little wife.

Alice came soon after. Her pie was covered with a blue-checked cotton cloth. We placed it between the two unlit candles.

She surveyed the kitchen. She could smell food cooking. A suspicious look crossed her face.

"Oh, Nell made this whole meal," Gauguin said cheerily.

I understood. She thought her poor son had had to cook after being at work all day.

I turned from the sink. "I made a traditional Shabbos meal." Then I explained to her what Shabbos was.

"My," she said, "my." She sounded like my mother.

I lit the candles and said the prayers.

"My, I never heard Hebrew spoken before," Alice said as we sat down at the kitchen table. "I guess that's what Jesus spoke."

"Jesus doesn't have much to do with this." I cut a leg off the chicken and put it on her plate. "Dark meat?"

"Yes." She smiled weakly. "Gauguin told me how your grandfather used to play school with you, and you played the teacher."

I nodded. "Yes, we had a great time."

"Is that Jewish?" she asked. "I mean, it sounded so indulgent. No adult played with me when I was growing up."

What was she getting at? "That's too bad," I said. "It was a lot of fun." I forked some green beans into my mouth.

Alice looked around the kitchen and into the bedroom. "Gauguin, this place looks a little messy. Maybe Nell should buy a vacuum cleaner."

Reaching into the refrigerator for some ginger ale, I said, "Oh, Gauguin, you can pick one up tomorrow." The kitchen was a combat zone.

"This is good, Nell," Gauguin said as he bit into a buttered potato. He saw his comment wasn't going to amend things. He tried another

angle. "Alice, after we finish, Nell should show you some of her paintings."

Bingo! I lit up. "I'd love to show you my work."

Gauguin's face relaxed.

Alice's didn't, though. "What work? I thought you were a schoolteacher."

"Oh, we Jews do a lot of things," I said gaily, screwing the top back
on the ginger ale.

H er peach pie was delicious. I made tea to go with it. The Shabbos
candles were half burned down now. We had no electric lights on except
the bathroom one in the hall.

"I love summer, don't you, Nell?" Alice asked.

I nodded, holding my cup of Lapsang souchong in both hands.

"Especially after a winter here, it is such a relief," Alice continued.

I nodded again. I was content that she was addressing me.

"Two winters ago it didn't go above twenty below for four months
straight," Alice said.

I sat up in my seat. "Really," I said, amazed. "I knew it was bad but
not that bad."

She nodded emphatically. "Oh, yes." She was pleased she was
impressing me. "But it doesn't matter what the weather is, my Volks
always works."

"That's good news," I said.

Gauguin coughed and got up and headed for the bathroom.

"You know, they were designed for the Third Reich. Every time it
started that winter, I'd say to myself, 'Thank God for Hitler!' ''

Just then, the space in that summer kitchen became twenty below.
Outside the window I could see the lilac branches freeze, standing stiff
against the white picket fence.

I never heard *thankfulness* and *Hitler* used in the same sentence.

Hitler had invented the Volkswagen, and life in Minneapolis, Minnesota, some thirty years later was easier because of it.

I said nothing, but my whole body was an ice brick.

Alice knew something terrible had happened. She didn't know quite what, but she could sense it.

Then I reached my hand across the table for a jar. I asked her in an unfamiliar voice if she wanted wild honey for her tea.

Her hands flew to her face. "I must be hurrying home. The ham I took out of the freezer this morning must already be defrosted." She got up suddenly and blew out the front door. "Oh, say good night to Gauguin."

I was stiff as a cadaver. I heard her pull away in her Volkswagen.

The toilet flushed. Gauguin walked into the kitchen. "Hey, where's—" He looked around. "What happened?"

I turned my head and looked at him blankly. All emotion was flushed out of me. "How do I get to your mother's house? She left her pie plate. I know she'll want it. She told me she plans to bake some more."

"Nell—"

"Just give me the directions," I demanded.

I got in the car and put the key in the ignition. How could she say that about Hitler in front of me? I pulled out of the parking space and turned left at the corner. Six million Jews were murdered because of that monster. Those are my people! Turning onto the freeway, I started to sob. I was crying so hard, I could hardly see the exit signs, but I kept driving. I pulled off at Cretin Vandalia in St. Paul. I had driven in the wrong direction, farther away from Alice's, but I didn't care.

At the light I made a left and drove down an unfamiliar residential street. "Ashland Avenue," the sign read. I pulled over in front of a row of duplexes and fumbled in the glove compartment for a tissue. Snot was running out my nose. Glancing in the rearview mirror, I could see by the

light of a passing car that my eyes were swollen. I'd been crying a full
twenty minutes. I found a tissue, blew my nose into it, and crumpled it in
my tight fist.

And what she said about my grandfather! I'm not spoiled—he *liked*
to play with me. He liked the *kindala*. The thought of my grandfather
made me collapse over the steering wheel and sob anew. I loved him and I
loved being a Jew.

At home my family had talked about the Holocaust so much, I was
sick of it. When I came back from college, I used to say to my mother,
"Yeah, but the U.S. is doing it now in Vietnam, and the Turks did it to
the Armenians."

"It's different," my mother cried.

I didn't believe it was different; I didn't understand that it was
different because the Nazis had done it to my people. At the time, I was
afraid to identify as a Jew. But now, sitting in this car in St. Paul, I was all
Jew, every cell in me, all the way back in an unbroken line to Moses. No
one could take my Jewishness away from me. And no one around me was
going to slur my people. I felt my body grow as big and as deep-rooted as
a tree. I had to get out of that car before I burst through it.

It began to rain. A few drops fell through the open window, damp-
ening my left arm. Suddenly I wanted nothing in the world more than to
be in that beautiful rain, beating on the black street, with the streetlights
glittering in the puddles and on the slick asphalt. I shoved open the car
door and flung myself out. I thundered down the sidewalk, past stoops
and garbage cans lined neatly along the curb for the next morning's
pickup. The rain fed me, and I gobbled it up.

My T-shirt was soaked by the time I got back to the car. I slammed
the door shut, then began to laugh. At first it was more like a hiccough,
but then it grew and grew until I was gasping and wiping my eyes. Eight
full years of Hebrew school had left me a devout rebel. It took an ignorant
comment by an Iowa-bred farm girl to bring me back to my roots.

Sitting behind the wheel, I breathed deeply until I regained my
composure. Alice's pie plate sat on the passenger seat. I took an old

envelope out of my purse and wrote a note: "Alice, here's your plate. I thought you might want it. I think you and I should get together in the next week and talk. I'll call you. Nell."

I turned the car around and headed toward Minneapolis. Alice's street was quiet. I climbed the stairs—the elevator was on the blink again —and left the pie plate with the note at her door.

I got in the car and hugged the steering wheel. I started the motor and flipped on the radio. John Lennon was singing "Imagine." I sang along with him as I drove home through the empty streets.

Alice called me the next week during her lunch hour. We met that Wednesday at Tommy's Grill. Alice said it was one of her favorite places. I didn't pay attention to the place and only ordered a bowl of split pea soup. I was nervous, and I wanted to get to the point right away.

"Alice, you know I get the feeling you don't understand that I'm Jewish. What it means." I began shredding the paper napkin in my lap. "Sometimes you make comments that are offensive to me, and I don't think you realize it."

Alice gazed at me intently, and as I spoke, she nodded her head. "I know you're Jewish." She stopped nodding. "Of course, I didn't know any Jews growing up in Iowa, and even here, I've rarely met one. There's Dr. Eisenberg, the dentist down the hall, but he doesn't look Jewish. I mean, he's blond."

"There are blond Jews, even redheads with freckles, like Gauguin," I said. I wasn't going to let her get away with anything. "That's a stereotype that we're all dark."

"You do seem different to me, though," she confessed.

"How?"

"There's just something about you—I don't know," she said.

"You mean, that my parents got emotional at the wedding? That my grandfather played with me?" My voice was rising. I took a breath. I had every right to say what I was saying.

"You don't seem to want to do the housework. My son—"

"That's not Judaism. That's feminism," I cut her off.

"Nell, I'm sorry. I get mixed up." She put her hands at the edge of the table. "I've been so nervous around you. I don't know, I wanted to be a good mother-in-law to you, the way Camille was to me. I guess I botched everything up, especially my marriage."

I couldn't believe what I was hearing. "No, you didn't! He was a terrible husband. He slept around."

"Oh, you know? I guess Gauguin told you?" She looked at me beseechingly. She wore a thick layer of face powder, and I noticed how some of it had congealed in the lines at either side of her mouth.

"Yes." I hesitated. "He mentioned it." I could see she was starving for affirmation. "You were very strong to leave."

"You know, women of my day stayed married no matter what."

"Times are changing." I nodded my head. "Maybe now you can understand why I don't want to do all the housework. I'm not a maid."

"It's so hard, Nell. When I see him with another woman—" She looked down.

"Who? Gauguin?"

"No, Rip." She gave a little laugh of recognition. "Well, maybe Gauguin, too. I've been awful, haven't I?" She reached her hand across the table and laid it on mine. "Please forgive me? All I know is the kind of marriage where the wife cooks and cleans and the husband is the boss."

Hearing that last word I cringed. "Do you understand it's different now?"

Just then, the waiter brought over the check.

"Please, let me get it." Alice grabbed it off the tray.

I had barely touched my soup.

As we walked out, Alice took my arm. "Please, Nell, give me another chance."

I remembered last Friday night and my walk in the rain down

Ashland. Alice still didn't have a clue who I was, but she was Gauguin's mother and she was trying now.

"Okay," I said, "but on one condition."

"Of course," Alice replied. "What is it?"

"Please don't thank God for Hitler."

36

"So what do you do all day?" my mother asked.

"Mom, I found a job, but it doesn't start for three weeks," I replied, the telephone receiver cupped between my ear and left shoulder. I was standing in front of my eleventh pear painting. This one was of a corner of the ceiling in the living room, and I had the pears suspended in a hanging planter.

"Nell, what kind of teaching job starts at the beginning of November?"

"This one," I said impatiently. It had been hard to land a job in Minneapolis. Finally, federal funds had come through for a remedial reading teacher in a junior high school.

"Do you see Alice and Rip—what kind of name is Rip, anyway? Do you see them often? Oh, how I wish you lived in Brooklyn. Any chance of you moving here?"

"Mom, you ask me that every time I talk to you." I reached for lemon yellow with my paintbrush.

"Well, is there a chance?" she tried again.

"No," I said emphatically.

"You should have Gauguin's parents over every Friday night for dinner," she insisted.

"Mom, they're divorced, get it? They aren't a couple anymore. Besides, they don't want to come over so much. And they're not Jews. Friday is Shabbos."

"Why don't they want to come over?" she asked suspiciously. "Aren't you keeping a clean house?"

"Ma, please, I have to go. Send my love to Dad, Grandma, and Riteey. Okay?"

We hung up.

I cleaned my brushes and ambled down to the bus stop. It would take two to get out to the Jewish Community Center, but I didn't care. I liked taking city buses; they made me feel ecological.

I had joined the health club at the JCC a month ago and was on an intramural volleyball team. It was comforting to be around other Jews, even if they were Midwestern Jews. Of course, I didn't tell my mother that I had joined the club. It would please her too much.

In late afternoon, when the bus let me off on the corner, I could see Marian, our upstairs neighbor, sitting on the stoop. I waved, and when I got to our place, I sat down next to her.

"What's up?" I asked.

"Matthew's not coming home tonight till late. I don't have to make dinner." She smiled, pleased.

"Hey, want to walk over to the Riverside Café for an early dinner?" I ventured. "Gauguin won't be home till seven." I was proud that I knew some places now in the city.

"You know, this is where Gauguin asked me to marry him," I explained after we sat down, our plates piled high with cheese enchiladas. I took a forkful. "This isn't bad. Almost as good as New Mexico."

"What's it like there? I've never been. My family liked to stay close to home. They played it safe." She took a swig of water.

"My family hardly left Brooklyn," I told her. "I discovered New Mexico later on my own."

"You seem different from other people here."

"How so?" I asked her.

"You know, looser. We're all kind of conservative. No one from my family ever left Minnesota."

"You're kidding." I took a bite of salad. "Not me. Once I hit New Mexico, I knew I was home."

"How come you're not there now?" she asked.

"I dunno." I looked down at my plate and stabbed at my food. I didn't want to talk about this. "I left, that's all." What a dumb answer, I thought to myself.

I glanced up at Marian. She looked down. I didn't want to be unfriendly. I just didn't want to tell her about who I used to be. I wasn't sure Marian would understand my past life.

"Hey, look at those dog paintings." My mouth was full of cornbread. "There, on the brick wall."

Marian turned her head around. "Oh, they have monthly shows here, I think."

"They do, huh? For anybody?" I asked.

"I dunno. You could ask," she said.

"Just a minute." I got up and walked over to the cashier. "How do you get to show here?"

She didn't know what I was talking about. "On the wall"—I pointed—"the pictures?"

"Oh, that. Ask Margaret, the manager. She's behind, in the kitchen. I saw her a minute ago." She turned her head and yelled, "Hey, Margaret, someone here wants to talk with you."

A minute later, a blond woman about my age appeared. "Can I help you?"

"I'm a painter"—as I spoke those words for the first time, my blood raced through me—"and I'd like to have a show here."

"We have an opening in February. You frame it, you hang it, if you sell anything, you keep the money," she told me.

"For the whole month?" I asked. She nodded.

"Can I just mat them?" I asked.

"Sure," she said.

"Okay, sign me up."

I floated back to the table. "I'm having a show here in February. It's my first." I was stunned how quickly it had happened.

"That's great," said Marian. "Let's toast." She held up her water glass. "To Nell's one-woman show, the first of many." We clicked glasses.

"I've got to get working." I looked at the walls of the café, figuring out how many paintings it would take. "Twenty. I need to have twenty ready. I've got about eight that I like well enough so far." My mind was buzzing. "And I probably should type up a personal statement." I paused. "I should sell them cheap since it's my first." I looked around. There was a very scruffy clientele, mostly university students. "Otherwise, no one could afford them."

Marian looked around. "Do you think these people buy art?"

"Probably not, but I'll only charge fifty dollars a painting, just in case." I popped a cherry tomato into my mouth.

37

By the second week in December, the weather hit a constant twenty-five below. Gauguin didn't have to leave for work until later, and it was agony to leave the heat of his sleeping body as I crawled out of bed in the dark. I had to be at school by eight o'clock, and I gave myself at least a half-hour to drive there, especially since there might be ice. When the cold hit my face as I went out to the car each morning, I was thoroughly stunned. I couldn't get used to it. Never had I experienced weather like this.

The flu was going around the school and had a strong hold by the middle of December. When I walked into class on the Wednesday before Christmas, not only were the students absent, but Jean, my aide, was too. I usually taught five or six kids at a time, but today only Maurice, an eighth grader, showed up for the fourth-period class. He was chunky and had the sleeves of his gray sweater pushed up to the elbows.

"Hey, it's only you and me." He looked around and smiled.

"Yes. Why don't we read a story aloud?" I said enthusiastically, showing him that I thought reading was a treat. Elm Street Junior High was in the northeast section of Minneapolis. Locals called the place Nordeast, and it was like a separate country of Norwegian immigrants.

Black kids were bused in from the yellow cinderblock tenements on the other side of town.

"You'll sit next to me?" he asked. "And help me with words I don't know? You know, there might be a few I don't know."

"Fine. You pick out a story." I watched him go over to the rack of books that were easy reading and high interest. He selected a thin volume, then came and sat beside me at a long wooden table.

The third floor of the school hadn't been used in five years, but when I arrived to teach in this special program, they'd put me there. It was the only classroom used on that floor, and the janitor, a bulky man in green trousers with a hundred keys hanging from a ring on his belt, quickly informed me, "The third-floor ladies' room isn't in our contract. We don't clean it. You have to use the one on the second floor." And he pointed to the stairwell.

The cover of the book Maurice had selected had a photo of a group of boys his age standing around a motorcycle. "I'd like to get me a motorcycle. My mama says I can when I'm fifteen and if I lose weight. A doctor put me on a diet. Mama boils my meat so all the fat goes in the water."

"You look thinner, Maurice. I was going to ask you if you were on a diet," I said.

"Yeah, for three weeks now. I eat boiled potatoes and no eggs and no cookies, no ice cream, no butter, no french fries, no malts, no Milk Duds, no Jujubes, no cake or pie or Oreo cookies or Twinkies." His eyes grew large as he counted the different foods off on his fingers.

"Hmmm, why don't we open the book and start reading? First the title." With Maurice, it was easy to get off the subject. I liked teaching reading, especially with such small groups. I got to know kids individually, which was unusual in a public school.

" 'The Boy Who Wanted a Bike.' " He pointed to each word with his index finger as he read it. He turned to me. "They don't mean a bike you pedal. They mean a motor bike."

"You're probably right. Can you tell me who the book is dedicated to?"

"This book is dedicated to the one I love," he sang, and laughed. I smiled. "Do you know what *dedicated* is?"

"Yeah, you're dedicated to someone. My sister's thirteen. She lost her last baby, so this time my mom is taking real good care of her. My mom's dedicated to her. She makes her lie down a lot and not work, and my mom cooks for her."

"She's thirteen and she's having a baby?" I asked. Now I was off the subject.

"Yeah, her boyfriend is seventeen. He leaves every morning to go home to his mama's and work out. He's got barbells over there."

"Does he work?" I asked.

"No, he stays with my sister," Maurice explained to me.

"Does your mom work?" I was caught.

"No, she's taking care of my sister."

"Here, let's start reading." I pressed the book open to page one.

"Why don't you read it to me?" Maurice suggested.

"I'll tell you what—you read one paragraph, and I'll read the next," I said.

"Let's see how long this chapter is." He counted four pages and shook his head. "I don't know if we can finish it by the bell."

"Let's try. At this rate we haven't read one word." I pointed to the book.

" 'Joe was standing on the street when a boy went by on a motorcycle . . .' " Maurice read the first paragraph. He stumbled over two words. One was *alley*. I told him the word. I didn't make him sound it out. I did not want to explain that *all* in *alley* didn't sound like the word *all*. The other word was *mechanic*. When he finished the paragraph, he smiled and pushed the book toward me. "It's your turn."

I read my paragraph slowly, giving Maurice a chance to rest after his turn. When I finished, I looked at him. He was staring out the window.

He had a sweet round face. "What's it like in those houses? And what's those little houses?" he asked.

"You mean the garages?" I asked.

"Those are garages? For cars?" He digested the information.

"Yes," I answered.

"I always look out the window of the bus at the streets. There's so much space here."

"You've never walked down those streets?" I asked him.

"No, I only see them from the classroom and from the bus," he said.

"When it gets warm out, we'll take a walk. Now let's see if we can keep reading until the bell rings."

The bell rang. Maurice stood up. "I gotta go. I'll see you tomorrow." He waved as he walked out the door. We had only gotten through two paragraphs.

After lunch I had a prep period and then one more class to teach. I looked at the school absentee list for the day. Only Randall wasn't absent from seventh period, and if I knew Randall, by seventh period he would have skipped out. It began to snow again. I watched the flakes fall on the frozen rooftops. As I looked out the window, I wondered where Gauguin was eating lunch in downtown Minneapolis.

I locked my classroom door and went down to the teachers' lounge on the first floor. The lounge was painted a pale yellow, and the only daily newspaper was being read by the French teacher. I went over to the Coke machine and dropped a quarter and a dime in the coin slot. The PE teacher, the hall monitor, the math teacher, and the science teacher were all sitting around a small table in the corner playing poker. Smoke curled from two cigarettes in a red plastic ashtray at the gym teacher's elbow. They were playing for money and she was winning. They didn't worry that the principal might walk in.

The principal was a man in his early sixties who in the cold weather went out to the local bar down the street every Monday, Wednesday, and

Friday for lunch. When it was warm, he sat in his car at noon and chugged down Johnnie Walker Red. If I met him in the hall, I could smell the liquor, even though his mouth was full of mints. He had been in the navy and would salute the teachers whenever he saw them.

The teachers' lounge was crowded and there was no place to sit. I left with my Coke in my hand and climbed the broad stairs to the third floor. Standing at the top of the stairwell, opposite the third-floor women's bathroom, I wondered whether my classroom key would unlock the door. I tried it. Yes, it unlocked. I walked in. There were squares of unused toilet paper strewn on the floor. The window at the far end was opaque, but one pane was clear. Through it I could see the snow falling all over the empty trees and streets of Nordeast.

I brushed ten dead flies off the windowsill that had been lying on their backs with their legs in the air, and in the small cleared space I leaned my head down on my arms and sighed. Where had life brought Nell Schwartz? No answer came to me, but in that hollow space I had an idea.

I lifted my head up, smiled, and walked back to the bathroom door to check that it was locked. I returned to the windowsill and brushed off the rest of the flies. Pulling down my tights and panties under my skirt, I hopped up on the windowsill and raised my hand in salute: "To Banana Rose." And then I masturbated, my eyes closed, my head leaned back against the cold windowpane.

As I was about to climax, I heard a plow in the street pushing aside the thick snow. Back in the bathroom, the dead flies joined me in my ecstasy and hovered for a moment above the floor tiles before they dropped dead again to the ground.

Gauguin and I cooked dinner together that night. He complained about how he wasn't playing much music and hated going to work each day. I knew he was jealous of my upcoming art show. When I first told him about it two months ago, he had acted excited, but I could tell from his

eyes that he felt panicked—I was getting ahead of him, and in his home-
town.

He should talk about hating work, I thought to myself and didn't say
anything. In the building where he worked, I knew he often saw Sherry,
the woman he had dated before I moved to Minneapolis, but I never
questioned him about it. I suspected he still wanted her.

"So what happened today?" I asked as we sat down opposite each
other.

"Nothing much. What about you?" Gauguin asked, his head bent
over the steaming brown rice on his plate.

"Well, I think the gym teacher is having an affair with the hall
monitor," I said conspiratorially.

"Yeah?" Gauguin held his fork in his hand, his elbow on the table.

"Yeah. The school brings the monitor in with the bused kids. He has
nothing to do all day but yell at the kids who don't have passes. I saw them
touching each other by the pool."

"Did any kids see it?" Gauguin asked.

"No," I said.

"Are they married?" he asked.

"No, both are single."

"So what's the big deal?" Gauguin served himself some more
salad.

"Gauguin, it's public school. The kids go wild over anything like
that. You should have seen when I said, 'Armand, if you're late for class
one more time, I'm going to kiss you when you come through the door.'
It took me five minutes to quiet the class down from making kissing
sounds."

"That's what you do all day?" Gauguin asked. I ignored his conde-
scending tone.

"Yeah, and Armand said, 'What will your husband say? Does he kiss
girls too?'

" 'No,' I said. 'Everyone at his job stays in their seats.' " I looked
sideways at Gauguin as I tilted the water glass toward my face.

"I'm gonna go and practice." He finished eating quickly and got up from the table.

"Gauguin," I called after him. "Do you still love me?"

He stopped at the kitchen door. "Sure I do, Nell. I'm just unhappy. I'm not any closer to making music than I was in Taos." He turned and went into the back room. I cleared the dinner dishes, washed them, and left them to dry in the rack.

38

"Nell, do you want this one here?" Gauguin held up a blue abstract.

I removed a nail from my mouth. "Yeah, a little lower."

"And this one here?" He reached for a painting of a red truck.

"Uhh, okay." I stood back. "Yeah, I like it." Gauguin was being really helpful. It made me happy. Maybe the jealousy had gone.

"Oh, and I got you something. They're behind the counter," he called over his shoulder as he hammered.

I went to look. "Oh, Gauguin!" There were eight purple irises with one red rose in a green vase. I carried them over to where we were hanging and thanked him.

We were almost finished. Three of Gauguin's musician friends walked in carrying their instrument cases. "Where should we set up?"

"Over there," Gauguin said, and left to work with them.

I hung the last painting, another abstract of deep blue, purple, and a hard pink all swirling with a red star in the middle. The upper third of the paper was almost all left white.

I stood back. I was pleased. Six of the sixteen pear corner paintings were up and two paintings I'd done at the old lady's in Boulder. There were five postcard paintings, including one to Henri Matisse of a pink lawn chair, one I'd done from memory of my father sleeping in his big chair after coming home late from work, and one of the Mississippi with the Minneapolis skyline in the background. I even included the first real painting I ever did, the one after I'd walked out on Indian land and met that cottonwood.

It wasn't officially an opening—after all, it was a funky student café —but I didn't care. I rearranged the flowers in their vase.

Lunch customers began to trickle in around eleven in the morning. Well, this is the beginning, I thought to myself, and took a deep breath. A young girl with stir fry and rice and a wedge of thick chocolate cake carried her tray to a table. Her friend followed. I stared at them. Look, I said under my breath, look at my paintings! They didn't look up. Two young boys with their mother pointed to my painting of a truck, but I couldn't hear what they said.

I guess I should just be glad people are around, I thought. It was a bitter cold Saturday. When I drove over that morning, it'd been zero degrees and had begun to snow. Each time someone opened the front door, a terrifying gust of wind flew in and made everyone shiver. I'd made a few friends since I'd been in the Twin Cities, but I didn't know if any of them would come in this weather.

Just as Gauguin and his group began a Duke Ellington song, Marian and Matthew entered and went over to my work.

I watched them from across the room. Marian stood in front of one of the pear paintings and pointed. Matthew nodded. I'd begun painting them because I wanted to feel grounded where I lived. Painting something made me intimate with it. At first, Minneapolis had felt alien: square lawns, square blocks, square corners, no modulated adobe. But then the squares had become an object for my painting and I grew to like them. I became friends with all the corners in our apartment.

And the pears? I reached for a glass of water. The café said I could have anything I wanted to drink free, but I was nervous and wanted only water. The pears? Once Gauguin and I made love, and it had felt like two pears touching each other. It was a long time ago, but when I began my first corner painting, the flesh of that fruit rose inside me.

Maybe it was a dumb idea, I thought, maybe everyone will hate my work. I bit the side of my fingernail and spat it out. I suddenly wanted everyone to go home. I wanted my paintings back. I didn't want anyone to look at them. Matthew stepped up close to one of my abstracts. I had framed that one, and he was breathing on the glass. Nell, let go, I whispered to myself.

Marian and Matthew drifted over to the food counter. I just sat on top of a table, as if it were my dog house, and guarded my bones across the room.

A few more people stopped, trays in hand, to look at my work. I heard one older woman say to her husband, "Those are unusual. I kind of like them."

Gauguin came over to me at 2:00 when his friends left. He seemed happy to be alone with me. "Nell, be patient. It will be up for a month. People didn't all think they had to come today."

"Do you think they'll like them? Are they too expensive?" I asked.

"Art isn't people's first purchase. Groceries are more like it. That's why your father makes a good living and Van Gogh starved." Gauguin put his arm around me.

Just then Alice walked in. She came directly over to us. "My, it's cold out there." She pulled off her gloves. "So where are they?"

I pointed across the room and walked over with her. Gauguin went to get us tea. "My, that's a truck. And aren't those pears? Under a toilet seat."

I nodded.

"I was afraid I wouldn't be able to make anything out in them. You know how modern art is. Rip always wanted me to go with him to art museums, but I never wanted to." She stepped to the next picture. "Nell, those pears are hanging from the ceiling! And those—they're in the cupboard! The cupboard in your kitchen." She turned to me. "You paint such ordinary things."

I was enjoying myself thoroughly. Gauguin came over with some spearmint tea and poppyseed cake. "Alice, this restaurant is where I proposed to Nell," Gauguin said.

Alice didn't answer. She was engaged in a painting. "Nell, this one I like best of all." She turned to me. "I don't know what it is, but it makes me feel something."

Both Gauguin and I looked over at the wall. It was one of the three abstracts in the show. "I don't know what it is either," I said. "I had a dream I couldn't remember, and as soon as I woke up, I went right over to the easel and began to paint."

Alice nodded.

I continued. "I painted three in a row. That's the second one."

"Tea is getting cold," Gauguin chimed in. We went over to the table. "Alice, you should have come earlier. I was playing music with old Doug Rolletter."

"Oh, that's nice, dear. Your friend from high school?" She turned to me. "Nell, it feels like a mystery. What was the dream about? I love mysteries. I've read all the Agatha Christie books."

"I don't know." I shook my head. Then a smile broke over my face. "I know. I'll call it *Foreshadowing*."

"Of what?" Gauguin asked, and there was a tinge of impatience in his voice.

"Of things to come!" Alice offered.

Just then Rip walked in with a striking blond woman on his arm. She was almost as tall as he was.

Alice grabbed her coat. "Gauguin, dear, Nell, I have to go," she mumbled, and bolted for the door. I don't think Rip even saw her, he was so engrossed in the woman at his side.

They rambled over. "Hey, here's the artist. Where's your beret and smock?"

I smiled weakly. Boy, was he corny.

"Oh, this is Saundra, not *Sandra* but *Saundra*." He almost whistled her name. "This is Nell, the artist, my daughter-in-law. You already know my son."

"Oh, yes," Saundra said. "We went out for lunch with—what was her name?"

I stiffened and turned to Gauguin.

"Sherry," Gauguin said quietly.

"Well, where are they?" Rip managed to take his hands off Saundra and clap them together.

"Over there." I pointed. Sherry? All four went out to lunch?

"Nell, let's go over with them." Gauguin took my arm. "It was nothing, Nell," he whispered in my ear.

"Yeah, sure," I said. I felt sick.

I didn't hear a word Rip said. I just nodded and agreed, and finally he and Saundra left. It was late afternoon and they were going to a cocktail party.

"Let's go," I said to Gauguin. "I'm exhausted."

Gauguin gathered up the nails and hammer. I put my arms around the vase of irises and we carried them out to the car. It was still snowing. The white streets and drifts made the single rose even redder.

The car was cold. Our breath fogged in front of our faces. Luckily, we only had a few blocks to drive home.

"Well, that was great." Gauguin started up the engine.

I nodded, looking straight ahead.

"Nell, what are you thinking?" Gauguin asked as the car warmed up.

"How I can paint live roses in winter," I said, still not looking at him.

"And underneath that? What are you thinking?" he asked.

"Sherry."

"Oh, come on, Nell. You're still friends with Neon."

"Yeah, but I don't go out to lunch with him." I turned to face him.

"Yeah, but you'd like to," Gauguin retorted.

"I feel trapped. This is all your world."

"Yeah, and you have an art show in my world, and I go to work for my father." He steered the car out of the parking lot.

"Let's drop it," I said. "I'm tired."

Three days later, Marian phoned. "Nell, there's a review of your show in the student newspaper."

"What?" I said.

"The *Minnesota Daily*. It comes out at the U every day. Someone saw your show and wrote about it. Here, you want me to read it?" she asked.

"Yes, please." I sat down on a kitchen chair.

Nell Schwartz, who recently moved here from New Mexico, paints so you laugh. This artist has a sense of humor: Pears all over the house, a Pillsbury sign over the Mississippi, a pink lawn chair for Matisse. These are her urbane paintings, but when she's serious she goes back to where she came from. Three abstracts of blues, purples, and pinks recall the source of the New Mexico landscape and hold the haunted quality of beauty that permeates the land there.

Schwartz is traveling in two directions: one of wit, the other of nameless beauty. This reviewer puts his bets on the second. There's already enough lighthearted work around here. Show ends the end of February.

"Wow!" I said. "Wow. Would you mind reading it again?" I paused. "Never mind. I'll run out and get a copy—five copies. Where do I pick it up?" I was thinking in my head: one for Anna, one for Blue, my parents—who else?

That night, I showed it to Gauguin. I had decided to drop the whole thing about Sherry. I wanted to believe him, and besides I was too happy about my art show.

"Congratulations," he said, and hugged me. He seemed to be honestly making an effort.

While I was in his arms, I thought: New Mexico. I have to visit there and paint.

Gauguin and I let go of each other. The light of the kitchen was between us. This summer, I thought, this summer I'll go.

39

Dear Anna,

    I'm sitting in a small café in Gothenburg, Neb., on my way back from N.M. Went there by myself for 2 wks. No, I can't stop to see you—there isn't time—but I feel you, so I'm writing this. I'm painting a lot in Minn. The funny thing is I went down to Taos on purpose to paint + I didn't do even one while I was there. Instead I hung out on the mesa—your favorite place—with Blue + Sam (I like him a lot now, but he's still weird). Lightning's away at camp in Colorado, but wouldn't you know it, while I was there he ran away and came home. B. + I hiked up Wheeler + almost made it to the top + then quit; we said we didn't want to be too ambitious. I missed you while I was there. Maybe we should have a homecoming + meet on the rim or in Talpa or at Steven's Kitchen.

    The thing is: Who cd paint that place? It's so gorgeous, more than my imagination could hold. It was more beautiful than anything I remembered. It is *the* place on earth—and we lived there! Do you miss it? Me, too.

    Anyway, it's been kind of hard being married. G. + I decided that while we were away from each other if it felt right we

cd sleep with someone, just as long as we quit after the 2 wks.
Then driving out it felt funny. Like, hey, I'm married now. I
don't want to do that. I thought of checking out Neon in Boulder
but I heard he's on a six-month meditation retreat—yikes! But I
slept with Tiny for old time's sake. Just once. I kind of hated it.
It made me feel crazy, but I was afraid G. was going to do it + I
wanted to be even with him.

    I start teaching again at the end of Aug. + it'll probably start
snowing in Minn. on Sept. 1st.

    How's yr writing going? I haven't heard from you lately.
What's up? Yr still my best friend.

Love,

Nell

P.S. The salad bar in this place is full of marshmallows and
canned pineapple. Yum.

40

I stood in our living room, my arms full of bags I had carried in from the car. I flopped on the couch. "Whew, is that a long trip from New Mexico. I thought I'd never make it. Hey, the apartment looks real clean." I looked around. "Well, what'd you do while I was gone?" We'd only talked once on the phone in the two weeks.

"I slept with Sherry," Gauguin blurted out.

"You what? When?" I sat up.

"I can't remember." He paced the floor in front of the couch. "Monday night was the first time. I just thought we should tell each other right away."

It felt as though my stomach had just fallen down to my knees.

"Oh, so you slept with Sherry!" I barked.

"What about you?" Gauguin was alarmed. He hadn't expected such a strong reaction from me. I got up, ran to the bathroom, and slammed the door. I sat on the toilet, trying to figure out what I was feeling.

Gauguin yelled through the door. "Hey, Nell, I thought we had a pact."

He said something else, but I couldn't hear him. I was imagining the open windows in Sherry's apartment near Powderhorn Park, yellow curtains blowing in and out, scraping against the dirt on the sills, how the voices of kids riding their bikes around the lake wafted into Sherry's bedroom. But Gauguin didn't hear them, because he was busy feeling her soft white thighs against his back. I knew the way unattached lovemaking could be. He could be free to feel only her body. But it wasn't so unattached—Sherry and he had a history, and they saw each other every day at work.

When I came out of the bathroom, I punched Gauguin in the chest as hard as I could with my fist. Then I started to laugh loud and crazily. Gauguin was so pale, I think his freckles disappeared.

I stormed into the kitchen like a raging bull and began hammering nails into the white wall above the kitchen table. Gauguin stood in the doorway and said quietly, "Nell, what are you doing?"

"I thought I'd hang up some pictures of New Mexico." There were now six large black nails in the plaster with no apparent pictures.

"Nell, can't you wait?" he asked nervously. "We haven't even taken all your stuff from the trip out of the car."

Just then I broke. I threw myself into a chair and cried with my head on the red table. Gauguin came quickly over to me and stroked my hair. He bent close. "Nell, what's wrong? We said we could sleep with other people, if we wanted, when one of us was away."

I just sat there crying. We were both so naive, so stupid.

When I finally lifted my head, I said, "I can't handle it. We're married."

"C'mon, let's unpack your car," he whispered.

I looked at him. "You don't get it, do you?"

His face looked like a prune. All the life was drained out of it. "C'mon," he said.

"You're crazy. You just told me you fucked someone else—not anyone, but Sherry—and you want me to unpack the car?" I wanted to claw his face with my nails.

"Well, I'll unpack it," he said.

Suddenly, I didn't know what else to do, and I followed him out the front door.

After I carried in one box and a bag full of sage I'd picked on the mesa, I turned on Gauguin, who was walking in the front door with my backpack, and began to scream, "I hate you, you fucking bastard! I'm going to fuck the first person I see on the streets. I'm just going to grab him and fuck him!"

"Nell! Shhh, the whole neighborhood will hear you." He slammed the door behind him. "Please—"

"That's all you have to say?" My eyes were popping out of my head. *This* was the man I married? The more controlled he got, the wilder I felt.

He laid the pack down on the sofa, turned to me to say something, and then melted. "Nell, I didn't know," he sobbed. "I thought it would be okay."

"You're an idiot!" I screeched. "You're just like your dad."

"Don't you ever say that!" He surged forward.

"Why not? It's true."

Gauguin narrowed his eyes and gritted his teeth. His right hand was clenched in a fist and he came up real close to me. I wanted to say how Rip two-timed his mother, just as he'd done to me, but I got scared. I'd never seen Gauguin look like that before.

But as I stepped back, rage overtook fear. I screamed, "I hate you!" turned on my heel, and headed for the bedroom.

I flopped on the mattress and burrowed my face in the quilt. A crystal hung from the window and I could feel the sun's reflection on my bare legs.

I heard Gauguin's voice behind me in the room. "Nell, please, let's talk." I suddenly realized that he was frightened.

I sat up. I felt like I had crossed over the River Jordan into a realm of Hell. I looked at him. Yes, he'd lost all his freckles.

"Can we talk?" he asked again.

"Yes." I sighed. "You might as well tell me the whole thing."

"Sure you want to hear it?" He sat down on the bed.

"Might as well." I looked straight ahead at a poster of a rose on the wall and traced the flower with my eyes.

He spoke quickly and nervously. He'd gone out with her four times and slept with her three. I felt like a priest at confession. I didn't look at him once while he spoke.

He told me how they had talked about not wanting to hurt me; Gauguin assured Sherry that he was in love with me and nothing could come of it. He said Rip knew nothing about it.

I kept staring straight ahead.

He had finished. "Nell?" He didn't dare reach out and touch me. "Nell."

I thought maybe I would kill myself. At least my mother would miss me. I'd have my ashes thrown off Taos Mountain.

"Nell," he said my name again.

Maybe I should kill him. Maybe Sherry.

He stood up. "If you're not going to talk"—he hesitated—"I'm going in the back room."

I turned to him with cold eyes. "I hate you."

His lips twitched. He started to say something else and then stopped himself. He got up and left.

I felt frozen. I cried for a while, then couldn't anymore. I stood up and went back to where Gauguin was.

He was pounding out boogie-woogie on the piano.

"Gauguin?" I opened the door. "Do you still love me?"

He stopped playing. "Of course I do. You're talking to me again?" He turned on the piano bench and opened his arms. I entered them.

"Do you promise you do?" I softened.

"Yes, Nell. I had no idea it would hurt you so much." He kissed my neck. We hadn't seen each other in fourteen days.

Suddenly I snapped shut again. I couldn't help it. I pushed him arm's length away. "I can't believe you did it. How could you do that to me? We're married!" I got up, went out of the room, and slammed the door behind me. Gauguin pounded on his piano again, screaming something about the pines where the sun never shines as I ran out the front door.

The afternoon light shocked my eyes and I was momentarily

stunned. There were Mr. Steak and the Mobil gas station, but they were different now. Everything was. This street we lived on, that tree on the curb—they were all unfamiliar. I ran into the back alley. As I passed the side of the house, I could hear Gauguin still banging on the piano.

I threw up the garage door and grabbed my bike from against the wall. I pedaled hard, streaming down Riverside Avenue on the wrong side of the street. I looked at my wrists. They were tanned from the New Mexico sun. I pedaled harder and harder, shifting the bike into tenth speed. I turned onto Cedar. I pedaled all the way to Thirty-sixth and made a right. I wanted to get on Highway 35 and pedal back to New Mexico. Instead, I rode over to Thirty-fifth near Hennepin and stopped in front of Polson's Poultry Supplies. A big orange sign hung outside. In bold black letters it read, "Sale Today on Capons. Two for the Price of One." I took out the five-dollar bill I always kept rolled in my shorts' pocket and entered Polson's.

The black-and-white-checkered linoleum floor was covered with sawdust. The man behind the counter must have had cancer of the nose. It was big and red, and you could see all his pores as if it had been blown up.

"Can I help you?" he asked.

"Yes, I'd like a chicken. Cut in eighths, please." I sounded like a normal person.

He weighed my chicken on the scale, then stretched the wing from the pale yellow body so he could cut it off. He wrapped my eight pieces in white paper and wrote $2.98 with a black wax pen on the wrapping. I handed over my five-dollar bill. He gave me my change, which I put in my shorts' pocket, and I picked up the package. I walked through the sawdust to the front door, opened it, and walked outside. There was a garbage pail on the corner two stores away. I walked over to the corner, flung the chicken in the garbage, got back on my bike, and rode madly down Thirty-sixth toward home.

In the kitchen, Gauguin was making a tuna sandwich. "Do you want one?" he asked. I could see his eyes were swollen. He'd been crying. "Where'd you go so long? I was worried about you."

"No." I stood by the stove. I was a mad dog. "I don't want tuna. I want chicken."

"We don't have any," he said logically.

"Well, get me some." I wanted him to prove he cared.

"No!" He was indignant.

"Fuck you!" I yelled. "I bought some chicken and threw it out!"

Gauguin seemed exhausted. He sighed deeply. He didn't ask why I threw the chicken out. If he had, I wouldn't have known why either. I bought a chicken and threw it out? I felt crazier in that moment about the chicken than the fact that Gauguin had slept with Sherry. He'd slept with Sherry! I looked over at him. He had the second half of his tuna sandwich left to eat. I wanted to sit at the table and say, "Help me," but I couldn't. I grabbed the half of the tuna sandwich off Gauguin's plate and threw it against the wall.

That night, Gauguin and I lay on our backs in bed next to each other like two cadavers. Gauguin addressed the ceiling.

"Nell, I promise never to sleep with anyone again. Sherry doesn't come close to how I feel about you." Then he began to turn toward me.

"Don't you dare touch me," I commanded.

He settled back on his back. "Nell, we can work this out. Didn't we work out moving from Taos?"

"No," I said sharply. "We didn't work out anything." I was debating whether I should tell him I had slept with Tiny. It wasn't the same thing, but Gauguin probably wouldn't understand. I didn't enjoy it with Tiny. "It doesn't matter anymore. Nothing does. I'll never be able to open to you again. And don't tell me Rip doesn't know. That man could find sex in a paper bag. I feel humiliated." I turned toward him, not out of affection but for emphasis. "How could you do this? You've ruined everything."

I decided not to tell him about Tiny. He could just use it to justify himself. Tiny was a thousand miles away. Sherry was in my face.

Neither of us could sleep. It felt as though we were lying on an iceberg in the Arctic Ocean. We both tossed and turned but were careful not to touch each other.

Finally, Gauguin bolted up. "I'm sleeping on the couch."

"Good riddance," I said.

He got a sleeping bag out of the closet and grabbed a pillow off the bed.

The next morning, Gauguin left for work. I heard the front door shut and I turned over. I had all day alone. I was sure his father knew. Everyone knew. My heart physically hurt. All those years before with other men, I didn't care if any of them had slept with other women. But I cared about Gauguin. We had said we could sleep around, but I had no idea how much it would hurt. I wanted to get back at him for all this pain.

I looked out the window. Just then, in my mind's eye I saw the cottonwood leaves next to the bare rock of the Rio Grande gorge. I put my head in the pillow and started to sob.

For four days, Gauguin and I hardly spoke to each other. He left for work; he came home; he slept on the couch at night. I walked around the house in a daze. I took things out of my suitcases as I needed them—a toothbrush, underpants, a pair of shorts—but I couldn't unpack. I left the bags exactly where they were on the first day. Sometimes I felt like a wound slashed open with a butcher knife; at others, like a razor blade ready to cut at Gauguin's heart.

On the second day I thought of ringing up Marian. The phone rang twice and then I hung up. I didn't want to talk to her. Besides, she'd probably heard us arguing through the floor. I wanted to talk to Anna or Blue. But I didn't call them; I was too ashamed to tell anyone what Gauguin had done. I tried painting, but my arm felt listless and all the colors looked the same.

On the third morning my mother phoned. "Nell, how are you?

Why haven't you called? You know you should after a trip—what if you got in an accident?"

"Fine," I said.

"Well, it's not fine. Tell me, how was it?"

"Fine," I said.

"Was Gauguin okay while you were gone? Personally, I wouldn't have left. How could he possibly manage without you?"

"Fine," I said again. I knew no other word.

She went on to tell me about the new way she'd read to make pot roast. "You add onions, *not* at the beginning, but in the middle of the cooking. Isn't that clever? It saves the flavor."

"Fine," I said for the fourth time.

I stared across the living room out the window at the green siding of the duplex next door. I just wanted to get off the phone.

"Nell, is something wrong? Don't tell me you and Gauguin had a fight."

"Fine."

"For heaven's sake, what's fine?" she shrieked.

"Everything, Mom. I have to go. The water's boiling." I hung up the phone.

I certainly didn't want her to know what happened. She would die.

On the fourth night, when Gauguin came home from work he left a note on the kitchen table and then went into the bathroom.

I stepped up to the table and read it: "Nell, can I take you out for dinner tonight? How about that Italian place on Riverside? We could try it."

He stepped out of the bathroom.

"Okay," I said.

"Great. Let's go in ten minutes. I'm starving."

Caruso's had wrought-iron chairs and tables with glass tops. It was still early and only three other tables were filled.

"You want wine?" Gauguin asked.

Yes, I nodded.

"Red or white?"

"I'm not sure." I looked at the menu. "Red. I'll have eggplant parmigiana."

"Good choice. I'll have that, too," Gauguin said.

It felt like I was on a blind date with someone I hated. Neither of us could think of anything real to say.

"This seems like a nice place," Gauguin offered, looking around.

I nodded. "Yeah."

They served us our salads. There was too much dressing. My lettuce sat in a pool of vinaigrette. I speared a tomato with my fork and held it over the plate. The oil dripped off. "Umm," I said, and put it in my mouth.

The whole meal was like that. The eggplant was lost in the dish of tomato sauce. The garlic bread left my hands greasy.

Gauguin and I hardly said a word to each other, but we kept drinking wine.

By the time the dessert menu came, I was tipsy. "I bet they fry the ice cream in Mazola."

We both began to laugh. "This is awful, isn't it?" Gauguin said.

Finally we had something to talk about. "Yeah, they mistook a rock for eggplant and then drowned it in sauce," I said.

I downed the wine in my glass and poured some more. I leaned forward, putting my elbows on the table.

"You're cute," I said as though I had just met him.

"So are you." Gauguin reached out his hand and stroked my arm.

I flinched for a moment and then settled into letting it feel good.

"Wanna go back to my place?" he joked.

"Maybe, but first I want to try some chocolate ice cream."

Gauguin called the waiter over. "Let's order two."

We finished the bottle of wine as our ice cream melted in silver dishes.

"Nell, have we ever gotten drunk together?" He laughed.

"I don't thank soo," my words slurred.

He caught me by the elbow as we walked out the door and swung me around at the curb. "Nell, I love you."

We kissed passionately, leaning against a parked car.

I looked around. People were staring at us. "Let's go home."

As soon as the front door shut behind us, we ripped off our clothes and slipped under the bed sheets. We groaned at the sensation of skin on skin, my breasts against his chest, his arms across my back, our legs stretched out long next to each other.

Then I froze. "I can't," I said, remembering Sherry.

Gauguin swallowed. "Oh, Nell, I'm sorry."

I let him hold me for a while, then pulled back and looked at his face. "I really hurt. I don't know if I'll ever get over it."

He nodded and was silent.

We lay naked, next to each other, for a long time. My mind was blank and felt dry, like uncooked oatmeal.

Suddenly I noticed the neon light of Mr. Steak blinking through the window into our apartment. I remembered sitting on the stoop that first evening I drove up here, how I imagined making love to the rhythm of that light. The whole place had been new to me then, with the delicacy of twilight filtering through spring leaves. Just before I arrived, I'd made love to Anna and before that Neon. The whole Southwest had been at my back as I drove, and I'd carried it with me up to Gauguin's stoop. A surge of energy crackled in me as I lay in bed.

I turned to Gauguin. "I want you," I said, my voice full of a new authority.

I began kissing his mouth as though I owned it, as though every inch of his body were my possession.

"Nell!" he said, first from surprise, then delight. "Nell."

I climbed on top of him. "That's right," I said, "you're mine."

Everything's mine, the whole world is mine, whistled through my body like a mantra. I glistened with sweat.

Gauguin was trembling. "Nell, I love you so much."

I took him out of an ancient power and he came into my body. "I bet you do," I snarled into his ear. "Now you remember this."

"Yes, I will, I will."

And then I rolled off of him and climbed through the night into a dark sleep.

41

Two weeks later I received a call from my mother in the middle of the afternoon.

"Darling, guess what? Your father and I just got off the New Jersey Turnpike. We're heading for Minnesota. We plan to be there in three days. Your father can't take the heat anymore in the city—it's been the worst summer. We know it will be cool in Minnesota—what with all those lakes and so far north. We'll stay for two weeks."

"Mom—" I started to say how humid and hot it was in Minneapolis, but she had hung up.

They're coming, I said to myself, and felt a sour taste on my tongue. I was afraid the heat was a pretense, that my mother suspected something was wrong because I had continued my monosyllabic conversation with her the other two times we spoke.

I immediately began cleaning the house. As I was vacuuming, Gauguin came home. "Well, well, Nell, what's come over you?" His face lit up. "The little housekeeper."

"Shut up," I said, turning off the power. "My parents are coming. For two weeks."

"Two weeks?" Gauguin sat down on the couch. "Why so long?"

"You know how they are," I said by way of explanation. He nodded but had no idea what I meant.

Marian and Matthew were going camping in Wyoming and offered to let my parents stay in their apartment upstairs.

As soon as they arrived, I showed them upstairs and my father declared that he was boiling. He wiped the sweat off his forehead with the back of his hand and declared, "Don't you people believe in air conditioning?" He immediately found a little standing electric fan that Matthew had bought at a garage sale, carried it with him into the toilet, placed it in front of him, and turned the switch to high. When he was finished, he went back outside to unload the car.

"Edith, three? Three." He turned to me, holding up three fingers. "She thinks she's the Queen of England. One suitcase for her jewels, one for her coronation, and the third is just filled with shoes. Nell, do you know how many pairs of shoes your mother has? This whole block"—he made a sweeping motion with his arm—"couldn't hold all her shoes."

"Please, Irving, a woman—she *needs* things. C'mon, bring them to the second floor." She turned to me. "Nell, it's so good to see you." She gave me a big hug and kiss.

"That's why she has me around. Nell, tell me, do I look like a valet?" My father lifted the third suitcase to the curb.

"C'mon, I'll help you." I lugged one up the stairs. "Jesus, Mom, what do you have in here?"

"Dear, not you, too. There are things in there," she said mysteriously. "Female things. Lingerie, jewelry, cosmetics."

When we'd finished with the luggage, I made us coffee in our apartment.

"Where's Gauguin?" my mother asked. She looked around her. "Hmm, things look in order."

I stiffened. "Everything's fine," I said.

"Yes, that's what you said on the phone. 'Fine!' " she mimicked.

"Gauguin will be home after work," I explained, and clenched my mug.

My mother came down that evening wearing a particularly good-looking white linen skirt with three buttons down the left side, ending in a slit by her knee.

"Was that the white skirt you wore to Aunt Helen's last summer? I don't remember noticing how nice it was," I said.

"No, it's a different one," she answered.

"You mean you have two white skirts?" I asked in astonishment, emphasizing the *two*.

"No"—she smiled—"I have many, but I only brought three." I stood there aghast. "Nell, let's walk down to a food store and fill the refrigerator," she suggested.

"Why? I bought forty dollars' worth before you came," I said.

"Well, I saw some space in your fridge, and I thought we should fill it." She got up from the couch. "You look a little thin. Are you eating?"

"Of course I'm eating."

"C'mon, please your mother just this once," she pleaded.

"Okay, okay. Maybe we should take the car," I said.

"No, I've been in a car too long today, and besides, in Brooklyn we walk everywhere." She was looking toward the door.

"This isn't Brooklyn." I got up. "We could walk to the Northtown Co-op."

"Fine, fine." She was out the door.

While squeezing every cantaloupe in the pile of eighty, my mother asked, "So, Nell, how is it?"

"What? I got a bag of cherries," I said.

"No, marriage. Good? Yes? You like it?" Bingo! Edith found the perfect melon and held it up like a prize.

"Yes," I said, and reached for the round fruit in my mother's hand. "Hmmm, it smells good. Mom, you're an expert," I said, and hoped she didn't notice my avoidance.

She looked at me hard. "Nell, you must give a hundred percent. Your father, he's a baby. I give and give. That's the way."

"Not mine." I pushed the cart to the check-out line.

When we got back, Gauguin was sitting in the living room with my father.

"Hi, Nell," he said, and then kissed me on the cheek. He hugged my mother and welcomed her.

We all went into the kitchen and cut the melon into eighths. We ate down through the salmon-colored meat to the green, flipping the rinds in the wastebasket and then replacing the lid to keep the flies away.

"Boy, this is a hot summer," Gauguin said.

We turned on the news. The announcer said that all over the country it was hot. "Chickens and old people in Texas are dying on the spot because their blood is literally boiling. Stay out of the sun!"

"Oy," my father said. "Chickens dying in Texas. I am so hot! Edith, I'm exhausted. Let's go to bed. I'm even too hot to eat dinner. Please, let's go upstairs."

My mother's mouth hung open. "No dinner, Irving? Are you okay?"

"I drove all day." He headed for the stairs and my mother reluctantly followed.

Gauguin and I went to bed early, too. That night it was so hot, I didn't even have the energy to think about Sherry. That was a relief.

My parents had been with us a week when I drove with them out to Stillwater, a town built on the bluffs of the St. Croix River. The town was considered very quaint with its cobblestone streets. Within a half-hour, my father was panting and sweating from walking up the steep hills.

"Let's stop here and have something to drink." It was a sidewalk café called The Parsley. White wrought-iron tables with large red-and-green umbrellas were set up on the sidewalk all the way to the curb. We chose a table near the street, because it was in the shade of a maple.

"Would you like to see a menu?" the waitress asked.

"Yes, please," my mother responded.

"Edith," my father growled under his breath, "we only stopped for a drink; some ginger ale or a Coke."

My mother paid him no mind. She looked at the list of selections. The waitress went to serve a table near the door.

"Just as I suspected. They serve fiddledeedee here too," my mother announced.

The waitress returned. "I'll have a scoop of peach ice cream." My mother nodded, closing the menu.

"I'll have a Perrier," I said.

"Nell," my father groaned, "don't order a Perrier. I'm begging you. It's a rip-off. They put water from the Hudson River in green bottles and call it French. Then they add bubbles and people like you order it for two dollars a glass."

I turned to the waitress. "I'll have ice and lime with my Perrier, thank you."

My father looked up at the waitress with a martyred expression. "No one listens to me. I guess all I can afford to order now is a coffee. Black."

My mother was about to place the first spoonful of ice cream in her mouth when we heard a tremendous roar around the corner. We all looked up. Suddenly the street was filled with motorcycles. Harley-Davidsons, Sportsters, and 1200s pulled up at the curb right in front of us. Men and women in black leather, snapping gum and sucking on unlit cigarettes, dismounted from their equine machines. One man had a scar from his forehead down his nose to his chin. In sleeveless jean jackets, other men exposed swollen biceps, tattooed with American eagles, skulls and crossbones, Nazi swastikas, and "Joan loves me or else." One woman in skin-tight silver pants and purple high-heeled leather boots stepped away from her man as they left their bike and crossed the street. He shot out his arm, grabbed her long black hair, and jerked her to him. "Where do you think you're going?" he sneered.

My mother's ice cream melted on the spoon, poised before her open mouth. None of us moved. The bikers all piled into the bar across the street. We watched until thirty-one motorcycles gleamed black and still like beetles. The last red-bearded man disappeared into the bar with a chain hanging out the back pocket of his jeans.

I took a deep breath and a sip from my Perrier. I looked at my parents. They were in shock, but my father still managed a comment. ''And every one of them''—he nodded—''has a mother.''

The waitress came over. ''They're headed for the big bikers' convention in South Dakota. We see a group of them about once a day.''

''Can we have the check?'' my father asked, and then, under his breath, he said, ''Let's get out of here.''

When we were settled in the car, headed back to the Twin Cities, he said, ''Boy, this is some place. Hot and humid as the devil, and they accost you with Hell's Angels when you stop for a cup of coffee. Nell, you can't be too cautious around here. It looks nice, but they've got something up their sleeve.'' He lit up a Bering Plaza cigar, and I had to open a window, even though their car was air conditioned.

As we pulled up to the curb in front of our house, Gauguin waved to us from the stoop. He had come home from work early to surprise us. All of a sudden, I realized how hard he was trying to connect. In fact, he had been trying for the last three weeks, but it had been so tense between us, I hadn't noticed. Out of the blue, I felt an opening in me as I sat in the back seat of my parents' car. It wasn't *all* his fault. I *had* been with Tiny, and we *both* had made that stupid agreement about sleeping with other people. We could work it out. After all, weren't we married? A small voice in me said, ''Go ahead, love him again.'' And like pressing the shift key on a typewriter, so the carriage raises a quarter inch to make capital letters, I made that small shift, too, and it mattered. Something in me relaxed.

By the time I opened the car door and stepped out, I was different.

''Hi, Gauguin.'' I waved cheerily.

When we got up the porch steps, Gauguin said, ''Alice just called to apologize. She can't make it tonight. She's not feeling too well.''

"What's the matter?" my mother asked.

"Didn't say. Alice is real stalwart. No matter how sick she is, she usually ignores it. So I think it's a good sign. She's being kinder to herself."

My mother nodded. I could see what Gauguin said made no sense to her. "Can't we do anything?"

"Naa." Gauguin waved his hand.

That night when we went to bed, I told him I appreciated his effort while my parents were here. I touched his shoulder in a tender way and we began to make love. I felt the zinnias blooming orange and red under the lilac bushes and all the plum branches fruiting in our yard as I took him into my body. All of summer woke up in me. Basil leaves shone even in the humidity, Bibb lettuce grew full in a row next to the tomatoes all within the length of my torso. My legs hummed and a bird warbled in my head.

The next morning, Gauguin and I sang songs together outside, like in the old days, leaning against the house's foundation, as the shadow of the duplex next door crossed our outstretched legs.

My father must have heard us singing. He came dancing out the back door, a newspaper on his head. " 'When the red, red robin comes bob, bob, bobbin' along.' "

We laughed.

"Let's go out for bagels. An air-conditioned place. Oh, last night your mother accidentally kicked Matthew's kitten. What's its name? Red Dog? Peculiar name for a cat. But it's fine. You know your mother and animals. I'll go and get ready. Be down in ten minutes. Your mother's sleeping late."

After he left, I turned to Gauguin to explain. "My mother doesn't like dogs—or any animals. She bunches them all together. She has no particular reason. Her parents didn't like them either. I think it's a throwback to the ghettos. The Cossacks used dogs when they attacked the Jews."

Gauguin nodded. "Wow."

When we returned from breakfast, my mother was up, dressed, and packed.

"What's this?" I asked. "You're not leaving for three days."

"Nell, we have to get home," my mother said.

"How come?" I asked.

"It's just time. We're hot—"

"And we're worried about Grandma and Rita," my father added. "It's a long time for them to be without us."

I rolled my eyes. Here we go again. I didn't even make an effort to stop them or ask why they hadn't told me earlier.

My mother hugged me hard on the top step of the stoop. She whispered in my ear, "Nell, give a hundred percent. If he doesn't do the dishes, you do them. Why, your father hasn't done anything for thirty-five years. If I waited for him, the house would fall down around our ears." Then she let go of me. My smile looked like the letter Z turned on its side.

At the end of August, I was invited to exhibit in an eight-woman painting show in downtown Minneapolis. The opening was in December, only three months away, so I frantically rushed to produce some new work before my teaching job started again at the beginning of September.

One late afternoon as I was busily applying red to the surface, it dawned on me: Hey, I never even mentioned painting to my parents the whole time they were here, and they didn't see any of my work. I shrugged. I'll send them photos after the show. I can't think about that now.

I was engaged in the picture before me. I was using canvas now. The paint spread well. After my show at the Riverside, I decided I could splurge more on my materials. I didn't know where the picture was going. Dusk set in outside, and I turned on the ceiling light.

Just then Gauguin came in. "Nell, I joined a band."

"You're kidding!"

"No, I'm not. The other musicians are nineteen years old, but I don't care. I want to play."

"Where are you going to play?" I asked, brush still in hand.

"Oh, they're kids. They'll take anything. They have gigs on weekends in small towns in Wisconsin. We'll even play in high school gyms. When I'm home, I'll still free-lance for my father."

I was stunned. "What? You're quitting your job? You didn't even discuss it with me."

"Hey, you got your show. I have to do something." His face grew tense.

"Oh, so that's it." My eyes narrowed.

"What's it? I want to play." He slammed the bathroom door.

Five nights later, he came home from his first gig at four in the morning, and I punched him in the arm as hard as I could. He slept on the couch. I hated him as much as I had after the Sherry business. I thought of moving out, but a week later we found out that Alice had cancer.

42

Alice had grown up on Sand Hill Farm outside of Cedar Falls, Iowa. She once told me, "Oh, Lord, it was so lonely there as a young kid, I'd eat dried husks of corn in October, just to hear the sound in my teeth." Then she gave off a cynical laugh that showed her nicotine-stained teeth. "My own mother had an affair with the hired hand, and my father, who was tired, didn't bother to notice."

Now she had to face that loneliness all over again, holed up in her one-bedroom apartment. When I'd visit her, I'd sit at the end of the white couch where she lay. She slowly sipped cherry-flavored morphine from a cut crystal glass, her inheritance from her mother who had died of cancer. Wrapped in a white sheet, Alice continued to suck cigarettes, all the while holding the elegant glass of pink liquid. Friends came in and out, bringing flowers and fruit, layer cakes and donuts. But Alice couldn't eat any of it. She grew thinner and thinner until the only thing she could digest was a bit of rice cream slowly spooned into her mouth. But her blue eyes stayed the color of cornflowers that grew wild in summer at the edges of country roads.

Gauguin quit the band to be home more and help his mother. He went back to work for his father full time and visited Alice's apartment every day after work. He read aloud to her from *Time* magazine.

One night he came home late. "Nell, I carried my mother to the bathroom and placed her on the toilet. I held her thin body as she sat there. When she was finished, I wiped her and carried her back to the couch. She can hardly even hold down the morphine now. She needs shots." Then he folded over on our maroon couch and wept until it seemed the earth poured out of him and into his hands.

Later that night, he yelled, "Nell, goddamn it! You put the hangers in the closet the wrong way," and slammed the closet door shut.

"C'mon, Gauguin. I know you're having a hard time"—I stepped toward him—"but don't take it out on me."

He swung around. "What do you know? Your mother doesn't have cancer. I didn't know anything till now. My mother's dying in front of my face."

What could I say? I looked at him. His skin was yellow. His eyes were full of fear. "Is there anything I can do?" I asked. I knew there was nothing to be done, but I suggested making some chicken soup, if not for Alice, then for him.

"Nell, you can't help. No one can." Then he grabbed his jacket and headed for the front door.

"Where are you going?"

"I've just got to move. I'm going to walk around the streets," he said, zipping up.

"Want company?" I asked.

"No, not now." He opened the door and then called out, "Thanks anyway."

I nodded and bit my lip.

When he got home an hour later, I tried to talk to him again. "Gauguin, don't you think we should spend some time together?"

"Nell, my mother's dying—"

"I know."

"Nothing else matters." He turned to me. "You can't ask anything right now. Get it? Nothing."

"Yeah, sure." I turned and walked into the kitchen.

That Saturday morning, I went with Gauguin to visit Alice. I hadn't seen her in a week and I couldn't believe how thin she was. I reached out to take her hand then, frightened, pulled my hand back. My face flushed with shame. While Gauguin was in her kitchen making juice, she leaned toward me. I thought of our lunch at Tommy's Grill. She had tried to be considerate since then, even though she hadn't been sure how. My heart was filled with sadness. This was serious. She was dying. Any differences we had didn't matter anymore. I leaned closer to her. She wanted to say something.

"Nell, I know you have it hard. Gauguin's crazy right now. Forgive him. Last night he was here watching television with me, and an old rerun of the Beatles on *The Ed Sullivan Show* was on. He got all upset and said he should have been on there." Then she put her bony finger to her lips. "He's coming," she whispered.

"Hey, what's going on in here? Looks like a coffee klatsch." Gauguin walked around the couch, holding a tall glass of cranberry juice.

"Nothing, nothing," Alice said, and managed to smile at me.

I bit my bottom lip and raised my eyebrows in acknowledgment.

My December art show almost went unnoticed, because it was about that time that an ambulance took Alice to the hospital. She could eat nothing now and couldn't even swallow her morphine. We followed in our car. The ambulance parked in the oval drive, and two attendants carried her on a stretcher through the large swinging doors of the building. Her eyes were open. I bet this is the last time she will be outside alive, I thought to myself. The sun shone brilliantly that morning. Across the street were three redbrick town houses. In the basement of one of them was a small market with a glass window crisscrossed by metal bars and a thin neon sign spelling ICE CREAM. The E of ICE was broken off. I didn't know how much of this she saw. I looked down at the cracks in the sidewalk and said farewell to them for her.

For the next week Gauguin sat by her bedside, holding her hand and whispering in her ear to her semiconscious mind, "Alice, it's okay, you can let go." He'd read about saying that in a book on dying. He didn't know what else to do and he said it somehow felt right and true.

Mostly Gauguin seemed to want to be alone with Alice, but I went with him one other time. She was tender and wanted me to come close so she could feel the wool sweater I was wearing. I'd never seen someone that close to death before, and I felt a chill run down my spine.

Two days later, Gauguin came home and said, "I wish it was over. The nurses said they never saw anyone hang on so hard. I think she's scared. Telling her 'to let go' suddenly feels like bullshit. Hell, it's my mother! I don't want her to die!"

At that, he collapsed on the couch and started to sob. "Mom, don't go. Alice, please, I love you." He rolled himself into a ball and rocked himself back and forth.

I ran to get him a box of tissues. I wasn't sure what else to do. I sat down next to him on the couch and put my arm around him.

At 4:30 the next morning, Alice died. The phone rang twice. Gauguin climbed out of bed to answer. I heard his voice from the living room. "Yes, thank you. I'll be right there." He came back to bed and held me. "I have to go to the hospital. I wanted it to happen, and I didn't want it—now I can't believe it."

He held me close for at least a half-hour. He hardly spoke. I could only imagine what ran through his mind.

At one point he did say to me, "You know, she fished real well. When I was seven, we went fishing down on the Blackhawk River." He paused. "I'd forgotten all about it. It was a long time ago." Then he was silent again.

Finally he said, "I guess I should dress and go."

As he pulled away, I started to cry. "Can I come with you?"

He nodded, but when we got to the hospital room, he wanted to go in alone. I understood. I'd known her less than two years, and she'd given him his whole life. Gauguin told me later that Alice's body had been covered with a white sheet. He pulled down the sheet, bent over her face, and kissed lips that did not kiss back. "I love you, Alice. I'm going to miss you." Then he didn't know what else to say. He was facing his dead mother. He couldn't believe it. He began to cry uncontrollably.

When Gauguin emerged from the room, he was totally exhausted.

We buried her in the warmest January Minnesota had ever seen. A dense fog descended the morning of the funeral, and the grass was almost green. In the distance I could see the dark water of Lake Calhoun. Alice's one sister, who still lived in Iowa, did not come. She said she was sick. Several of her divorced and single girlfriends clustered near the gravesite. Rip stood by the grave weeping into his hands. Gauguin was speechless. He looked like a ghost. Afterward, we all went back to our house and ate roast beef sandwiches. People tried to be social, but no one seemed to have anything to say, and Gauguin was relieved when everyone left.

A month later, Gauguin and I visited Alice's grave. We could walk on top of the frozen snow. The headstone was buried in the drifts, but we stood near where we thought it was. Gauguin carried a bouquet of early daffodils that were already freezing. He placed them on the ground in an empty mayonnaise jar he had brought with him. Through the thin branches I watched the sun leave the city and sink behind the lake. The jar fell over and the yellow flowers lay in a field of white. Gauguin's lower lip trembled the whole time we were there, but he didn't cry. I noticed that he hadn't shaved in several days: Red stubble sprouted from his chin and cheeks, and he looked a lot older than when I had first met him in Taos.

That night at midnight I woke up, stone cold, and felt a deep crack from throat to groin opening inside me. In that instant I knew simply and clearly that I was experiencing the moment Alice had left her body. She wanted someone on earth to know how she felt, and she had chosen me because I was the other woman in the immediate family, and, I think, because she did not want to burden her son even further. It did not matter that it had been a month since she died. Time does not matter to the dead. It was just important that someone felt it, and I was chosen, not out of logic but out of connection. Though Gauguin was sleeping next to me, he did not wake up and I didn't ever tell him about it. I was afraid Gauguin would think I was crazy—or even worse, he might have regretted missing one last chance to be with her or been jealous that it had been me who was chosen.

43

Rip died two months after Alice did, on a yacht near the Madeira Islands off the coast of Portugal. Crushing a Marlboro into a clear glass ashtray in the lower cabin, he turned to his new girlfriend, Sarah, who was lying next to him with her blond hair spread out on the white pillow. "This is the last damn cigarette I'm ever going to smoke," he said. He reached for the silver cord to turn out the light and pulled it a little too hard. As the light extinguished, he let out a loud scream. That was it. A massive heart attack. He was already dead when he vomited. Sarah caught the scream and kept it in her mouth. She held its sound for a long time afterward. I bet some part of her is still tasting it.

The police packed Rip into a big black plastic bag and sat him upright in the window seat next to Sarah in the small prop plane that flew them to Lisbon.

We were at home when the phone rang. "Sarah! Aren't you on a boat?" Gauguin asked.

"Your father is dead." The words smacked Gauguin into another world from where he stood by our couch in the plain Midwest. His face twisted the way his father's had when he'd chewed at a cigar. I turned to watch a crow fly by the living room window.

"Rip's dead?" Gauguin said. The room exploded with the silence of gladioli. I walked across that silence to touch him, but he was breathing so hard that I knew nothing could touch his sorrow, and I stepped back.

The phone connection had a lot of static, so Sarah yelled into the receiver. I could hear her from halfway across the room.

"The Madeiras are Portuguese, so they won't let the body go right away unless we cremate it," she informed Gauguin.

"Bring my father home!" Gauguin screamed.

"He's dead. He's not coming home." I'd never heard Sarah be so honest.

Then Gauguin said quietly, "Do what you have to," and I saw in that moment he was thinking of Alice—that Rip had died in someone else's arms.

Two days later, we waited for Sarah's plane to land. Gauguin and I stood by gate seven and passed a can of Coke back and forth between us. The sky was overcast and even at midnight it felt gray. Through the window we watched Sarah's small body walk across the runway to the waiting room. In her arms she lovingly held a small square box. She bent four times to kiss it before she entered the brightly lit airport and handed the box to Gauguin.

"Here's your father," she said.

We drove Sarah home and sat at her kitchen table while she recalled every detail. "One of the last things your father said to me was, 'Honey, we're going to be together a long time.'" Gauguin threw his eyes down at the carpet. Sarah continued, "The day before he died, he navigated the boat." Sarah cocked her head to one side to see Rip better in her mind's eye. "Yes, he looked very nautical that day."

"Gauguin, it's getting late. We should go," I said to interrupt her. We kissed her good-bye, thanked her, and rode down the elevator with the box between us.

At home we put the box on the kitchen table and lit incense. It was wrapped in paper that looked like imitation wood. Gauguin just stared at it. "This is my father?"

"Do you want something to eat?" It felt like a dumb response, but I knew Gauguin hadn't eaten since lunch.

"Yeah." He looked up. "I'd love something."

I took some leftover chicken out of the fridge.

"Where should I put it?" I asked, holding a red plate of roasted wings and breasts.

"I guess over there." He nodded at the table where the box was.

"You sure?"

He shrugged his shoulders. "I guess."

We sat at the table in front of Rip's box and a huge hunger overtook us. We tore at the chicken with our hands.

"This can't be real," Gauguin said as he yanked a piece of meat off a drumstick.

The box was a strange dinner guest, a silent shadow of his father. We both were in a frenzy. No amount of food could fill us.

"This sounds nuts, Nell, but let's go to bed." Gauguin licked his greasy fingers. "What better way to make tribute to Rip?"

I laughed, a little hysterically. "Okay. What should we do with the box?"

"Bring it in?"

"You're kidding." My stomach turned. "I can't do that. That's sick."

"I can't either. It was a bad joke." Gauguin got up and blew out the candle. "Good night, Rip." His lips trembled.

He took my hand. We turned, leaving the box and the plate of chicken bones on the table.

I stopped. "Wait. We should clear the table. It doesn't seem right."

We carried the plates to the sink and then went into the bedroom. We crawled between the cold sheets and clung to each other. Gauguin was trembling. We made love desperately, urgently, as if it were the only thing that would keep us alive.

When Gauguin poured himself into me, I pictured beaver swimming upstream. I knew if I didn't get pregnant that night, in spite of the diaphragm, I never would.

Three days later, we buried the box at the veterans' cemetery near a 7-Eleven in Bloomington off Interstate 35. Camille rode a train all night from Indiana to come to the funeral. A thin rain fell and made the edges of the grave soft.

Camille kept asking, "Why isn't there a preacher?" We didn't have the heart to tell her Rip had been an atheist, though in her heart she knew, so we all clasped hands and sang the Lord's Prayer. We filled the hole with red carnations and each of us took a turn throwing in a shovelful of dirt.

Gauguin was first. Through the ceremony he had been dry-eyed, but when the dirt fell to the bottom of the hole, he started to sob. "Rip," he called down into the hole, "I love you."

Someone handed him a Kleenex, and an old friend of the family took the shovel from him and passed it to Camille, helping her scoop up some dirt.

I stepped forward. "Gauguin," I said.

He threw his arms around me and wept on my shoulder.

After the funeral, Rip's employees threw a champagne party at his architecture studio. Near his large white desk flicked slides of Rip at the Louvre in Paris, which he had visited two years earlier. There was Rip, standing by the Mona Lisa; there he was, by the Venus de Milo; and then in a flash he was contemplating Picasso's two-breasted, two-eyed twisted woman.

I sat by the window and looked across Washington Avenue at the Northwest Bank. Then I got up and walked into the other room, where platters of rolled slices of roast beef, ham, and turkey were spread out. I spied Camille at the center of a small group. Everyone wanted to meet her. Rip had talked about her all the time. She had never visited Minneapolis while he was alive. She cocked her head to one side and listened to whatever people said about her son, as if their memories could bring him back to life.

Suddenly, Gauguin approached me from behind. Breathing heavily, he firmly grasped my elbow and led me to the elevator. He pressed the tenth-floor button, and when we got in, he shoved me against the wall. We rode up and down the shaft with his body pressed against mine and his tongue deep inside my mouth. He was sweating so hard his white shirt became transparent. There was a yearning in him that could have walked through walls. Tears ran down his face and his nose was running.

"Nell," he said finally, "everything's over. My whole life. First Alice, now Rip. I can't work here—I don't belong in this state. Both my parents are gone. I'm all washed out." He leaned against the mirrored back wall and waited for the elevator to open. We'd already ridden up and down three times.

Gauguin had asked the authorities at the veterans' cemetery if his dad could have "artist" written on the gravestone—Rip had hated the army and during World War II had suffered a depression so strong, he'd been discharged at Camp Douglas. They said yes but they must have made a mistake, because when the stone was erected it read, "Raymond 'Rip' Howard II, Third Infantry, First Legion. 1915–1980."

When Gauguin saw the stone, he said, "Now it's up to me." His hand opened and closed in a fist.

44

I n the middle of April, Gauguin and I drove up to Gull Lake, near
Nisswa in northern Minnesota. The proprietor of the place where we
stayed couldn't believe that anyone would come farther north just when
the cold was breaking down in the Twin Cities. We were the only ones at
the resort cabins, and the canoes hadn't been taken out of the boathouse
yet.

We took photos of each other for the first time in our whole
relationship. We had never had a camera before, but now we used Rip's,
which had become Gauguin's. I took a photo of him eating breakfast the
first morning. Fried eggs and potatoes, Sara Lee coffee cake, sliced or-
anges, English muffins, and coffee were laid out on the table, and I
captured it all. He looked straight at the camera, his eyes weary and his
smile twisted to one side of his face. He was pale, so his freckles stood out
especially dark. I gulped, seeing him so haggard through the lens, and
snapped his picture.

We hiked in a nearby birch forest, where one tree duplicated the
next mile after mile. Gauguin walked in front, a slim backpack jogging to
and fro on his back. We stopped in the austere April woods and toked on
a joint. The monotony of trees only multiplied in my stoned eyes and
none of them sprouted leaves.

We made love every night of that vacation out of an old memory of our bodies. After that driven sex we had when Rip died, our passion seemed to evaporate. We were two human beings who didn't quite know what to do with each other anymore. We went through the motions of sex like a biology manual: Male genital organ is inserted into female organ until semen is secreted. The bed was soft in the cabin and Gauguin caved in on me.

On the last day we sat outside leaning against the wall of the cabin, gathering the pale sunlight into our faces.

"Nell," Gauguin said, and paused. "I've got to change my life. I feel like I'm dying just like my parents, going under with them. And we're dying, too—you and me. We don't get along anymore."

"No, we don't," I said, resigned.

"I've got to move out." He turned to me. "I've got to take some kind of action with my life." I knew it wasn't a threat. It was quieter than that.

I looked out at Gull Lake. It was still and blue and inviting, but I knew it was as cold as a refrigerator. I got up, walked off a little, pulled down my pants, squatted, and peed. The pee steamed as it hit the ground. Gauguin snapped my picture. When I heard the camera click, I turned to him with an already faraway smile. He clicked the camera again.

On the way home, we stopped at a small café in Barrows, Minnesota. We examined the menu. Among selections of club sandwiches and casseroles was a Reuben sandwich. Gauguin pointed to it and said, "This is for those of ethnic persuasion," and we both laughed. It was the only time we laughed on the whole trip.

Then Gauguin took a picture of me standing under the marquee of a closed movie theater that read, *"Gone With the Wind"*—the last movie that had played there. Next to the movie theater was a drugstore that Gauguin said was the perfection of the Midwest.

I looked at it—square, light green storefront, a red Rexall sign, and a gray sidewalk—and agreed. I snapped a photo of it.

Then we drove straight back to Minneapolis. The plum tree in our back yard was blooming. As we unloaded the car, Gauguin peeked through the white blossoms, wearing a green leather jacket that he had inherited from Rip, and I snapped our last picture. His lips were full, the way Alice's were when she was about to kiss, but his tender face was blown away.

45

As Gauguin carried his suitcases out the back door, I bent over the vegetable garden, dropping small round spinach seeds into the line I had made with my finger in the soil. I barely looked up. He carried the suitcases to the garage, opened the garage door, put the suitcases in the trunk of his car, and drove down the alley. I planted two more rows of spinach and one of carrots. When I went to get the hoe, I noticed he had chipped some yellow paint off the garage door frame as he pulled away. I thought of repairing it soon.

After the planting I washed my hands, and the dirt ran dark against the white porcelain sink. I turned on the living-room light, sat down on the couch, and picked at the already peeling white paint on the windowsill. Now that Gauguin was gone, the apartment seemed empty.

When the garden began to sprout a month later, it looked as if a child had planted it—there wasn't one straight row. Carrots popped up among the spinach, spinach grew in the broccoli, and many of the seeds never came up at all. Empty patches everywhere were eventually taken over by weeds.

For six weeks I was as dry and stiff as a bone. I came home from school and flopped onto the living-room couch. I stared out the window. The sky was gray, and it began to rain. I watched the drops hit the glass and run down to the sill.

I wanted to be out in that rain, to let it refresh me. I got up, put on a pair of worn sneakers and my old yellow slicker, and went out the door. I walked across the overpass to I-94 and onto Seward Avenue. The rain beat furiously on the asphalt and filled the gutter. I was completely alone for the first time in my life.

Let's see, I said to myself. Rip's dead, Alice is dead, Gauguin no longer lives with you. Come on, Nell, here's your chance to become a tragic painter. As I walked, I picked out colors and planned paintings in my head with them. Green, a meadow; blue, a sky; lavender, an iris. Oh, Nell, how conventional. Try again. Pink, a rabbit; lime, an avocado; white, a dead rat. As I stood on the corner, a woman walked by carrying a red umbrella. A whole world rippled through me: The red rose that unfolded before me on that first acid trip so many years ago, the red marble I stole for my sister, Rita, because her favorite color was red. My favorite color had been red, too, but I couldn't be the same as Rita. I'd told her my favorite was green.

As my legs carried me automatically, I developed a plan. I'd walk all the way up to Hennepin Avenue to Schlamp's Department Store. Only a town in the Midwest would have a store called Schlamp's. No one ever seemed to go in it to shop, and no one ever came out. I decided to go in it and see what they sold.

As I passed Portland Avenue, I began to feel an aching in my heart. It was the same old dilemma—Gauguin versus Taos—but now I didn't have either one. That thought stopped me dead in the middle of the street. Nell, go home, go paint, I told myself. There's really nothing else to do.

When I arrived home, I stood in front of the canvas for almost five minutes as my breathing became thick. Suddenly, a huge scream came out of me, and I grabbed the big wide paintbrush Gauguin had used to paint houses with in Boulder. I stuck it in black paint and smushed it in the middle of the white. I screamed and grunted as I flew at the black with red, then orange, and then a deep purple. Sight left me. I traveled on waves of grief and longing.

When I was finished, I fell to the floor, my face in my arms, and cried. I didn't care what the painting looked like. My marriage was over.

46

One Wednesday in early October I was sitting alone in one of the high wooden booths in the Meat Cleaver Café on Seward Avenue, eating a fat hamburger and sipping a Coke. I wasn't sure if I was alive or dead. Teaching had been hard that day. Maurice was in my class for a third year. His mother had gone crazy the night before and attacked her husband's girlfriend with an ice pick.

Maurice shook his head and out of the blue said out loud to himself, "But Mama promised me potato chips. A whole bag of my own. And I didn't get them."

Maurice bit his nails so badly that day, his fingers were bleeding. When the bell rang for lunch, he looked up hopefully.

I shook my head. "No potato chips today, Maurice, and I noticed you didn't finish your vocabulary test."

I was tough, because underneath I was crumbling. I couldn't stand sleeping alone at night while Maurice's father had two women.

I asked the waitress for a small bag of potato chips to go with my hamburger. I put the bag in my purse. I'd give it to Maurice tomorrow if he finished his vocabulary test. Heck, I'd give it to him anyway.

I overheard a couple in the next booth talking about musicians: Janis Joplin, Jim Morrison, Hank Williams. The man then said, "I sometimes think alcoholics are just more intense people that don't know how to cool out.''

That was a theory Gauguin had. I stopped chewing the hunk of hamburger meat and white bread bun that was mashed in my mouth. Was that Gauguin in the next booth? Naa, Gauguin wouldn't come to the Meat Cleaver. The sandwiches were too expensive.

The next booth was silent for a moment. Then I heard two beer bottles clink. A female voice said, ''Here's to you.''

I lifted my body just enough so my eyes saw the tops of the two heads in the next booth. Two redheads. My brain revolved like a slot machine in a casino. It stopped at the jackpot. It was Gauguin!

The mass of food in my mouth fell out. My nose began to bleed and my eyes watered. I stood up. I hadn't taken off my navy wool coat, just unbuttoned it. I turned and walked straight for the door as though I were in a trance. There was a crowd of people near the entrance. The expression on my face, the tears, the blood, must have caused immediate compassion, if not horror. They parted for me like the Red Sea.

I was outside. The cool night air was a great relief. I'd left my purse in the booth, but my car keys were in my coat pocket. I'd call the next day, pick up the purse, and pay for the hamburger. The truth was, if my purse were stolen, I didn't care.

A week later, Gauguin sat in our old kitchen. Daylight was already gone, but it was too early to switch on the electric lights. The white walls were blue-gray. I told him I wanted a divorce.

''What? Why?'' he asked. Then he put his head on the table and cried.

I flicked on the bulb.

Gauguin lifted his head off the table. ''I'm not sure yet that I want one,'' he said.

I looked him straight in the eye. ''I want a divorce,'' I said firmly, as though each word were a nail I was drilling into his forehead. I wanted to hurt him for that redhead at the Meat Cleaver Café. I wanted to pull the kitchen cabinets down, smashing everything I once loved.

In December I went to divorce court without him—as a favor. He'd been to court so many times to clear up Rip's and Alice's estates after they died that he couldn't face another judge.

Marian took the day off work and came with me. We drove in her car down Hennepin Avenue to the courthouse.

"Marian, this is really nice of you," I said. Her kindness always amazed me.

"What are neighbors for?"

That morning it seemed all of downtown was a parking lot. "Five Dollars for All-Day Parking, Three for Half-Day." After we parked in a dollar-an-hour lot, we cut across empty car spaces toward the ten-story courthouse. As we got closer, the building's shadow covered us. We entered, rode the elevator up to the eighth floor, and walked down a long carpeted hall. In the courtroom, Marian and I sat in the third row on a long wooden seat. Soon it was my turn to walk up to the bench.

The judge asked me to sit down. I took a seat on his left and looked straight ahead. "Now, why exactly are George Howard and Nell Schwartz getting divorced?" he asked.

The smell of sage swam across the courtroom. I wanted to tell him that when Gauguin played his sparkling trumpet, it was like water running in an arroyo, and that he and I had split cedar logs open with an ax, and that the logs had bloodred hearts and smelled like strong wind.

The judge asked, "Do you feel comfortable with the division of property?"

I looked at the white wall at the back of the courtroom and saw two eagles circling Taos Mountain.

"Do you agree to the dissolution of this marriage?"

I wanted to tell the judge that we loved each other. That we ate peyote one night in a white tipi and became fire drowning in stone. I wanted to tell him there is another place and it is not in this place.

"Please sign your name here. Ms. Schwartz, do you hear me?"

I heard water. It was running over the rocks in the Rio Chiquita. I heard coyotes in Talpa behind Blue's house and I saw stars climb over the Pedernal in Abiquiu.

When I got up from the chair and walked down the aisle toward the back door, I was no longer human. I had become a robot, drained of emotion. Marian followed me out.

"You did great." She patted me on the shoulder.

I turned to her and noticed that the muscles in my face that create a smile were gone. I saw her alarmed expression, but I didn't care.

I sat in the passenger seat of her car. "What do you want to do?" she asked.

"Take me someplace," I said. I looked straight ahead out the window.

We drove over the Mendota Bridge to a wildlife reserve on the Minnesota River. We walked through leafless bushes and trees. The sky was its usual gray.

"Nell," Marian called, and I turned to look behind me. Marian pulled a silver wrapper out of her pocket. "It's chocolate from Switzerland. I bought it at Dayton's Department Store."

Something in me stirred. "Chocolate?"

Marian opened the silver paper. The dark chocolate shone like an ancient god. Marian extended her hand, and I took two squares and carried them the five hundred miles to my mouth. As I moved them past my teeth and lips to my tongue, I remembered what had happened three Sundays ago.

It was three in the afternoon, and I'd been sitting on the living-room couch, remembering how good lovemaking was with Gauguin. It had been a long time since we had touched. Suddenly I walked across the room, picked up the phone, and dialed his number. Before that moment, I had hardly called him. If I bumped into him on the street, I was very brusque. It hurt too much to see him.

The phone rang twice. "Hello?" It was his voice. He lived in a one-room apartment four blocks away.

"Hello?" He said it again.

"Gauguin." I said his name.

"Nell."

"Gauguin, I want to make love with you. I thought I'd come over right now. We could do it and then I could leave." I couldn't believe what I was saying.

"Are you kidding?" he asked, incredulous.

"No." I was firm.

"Nell, I can't do that. It's opening a wound all over again."

"Please." I wasn't begging. I said "please" like a fact. I wanted him.

"No, I'm sorry." We hung up.

I went back and sat on the couch. My desire burned up the room. I knew he felt it four blocks down the street. The phone rang. I leaped up to answer it.

It was him. "Come over right now." I ran down the back alley, past garages, through dried leaves, and around barbecue grills to his redbrick apartment house. I rang the bell for 4C; 4C rang back and I let myself in.

Gauguin flung the door open. We were in each other's arms. We gulped each other up and ripped at each other's clothes. I had half a blouse on, and he had his red shorts around his left ankle when we finally landed on the nearby couch. We came together in the ecstasy of marble cat eyes, the red irises twirling around and around.

As soon as it was over, I said, "I have to go." I stood up and began to dress.

"C'mon, Nell. Give it some space," Gauguin pleaded.

"I can't." I buttoned my blouse and left, walking briskly back down the back alleys. My hair was wild and I carried the smell of smoked melon musk on me.

I closed my mouth around the two square chocolates Marian had handed me. The memory of Gauguin and me dissolved. There was only my closed eyes and the darkness behind my lids. I had no idea what I was going to do with the rest of my life.

47

I sipped a cup of Lipton's tea. Then another cup. I didn't even like the taste, but it had caffeine. I could have ordered coffee, but if I drank multiple cups of coffee, my blood would have buzzed like an old electric heater. Some caffeine was okay. Coffee was too much for my heavy heart. On the way to the Croissant House, I thought my heart would rip out of the casing in my chest and fall like a bowling ball at my feet. My only work in the two days since the divorce had been to lug around my heavy heart. It wanted to go nowhere. I finished my second cup of Lipton's and took the third bite out of my second chocolate croissant.

I read the *National Enquirer*. The way I felt, the *National Enquirer* seemed true. A man in Arkansas had changed his nagging mother-in-law into a milk cow. That seemed like a good idea.

A bat in Los Angeles had flown into the bedroom of Liberace and made love to Hector, his favorite purple poodle. That was a good idea. Why couldn't bats and dogs make love together? Maybe it would work out better than between two human beings.

A waitress in Kansas had discovered she was six months pregnant with an apple tree. After she found out, she refused to serve the apple turnovers the Grant Diner was famous for making. Her boss said, "We don't care what you do with apples after hours, but on my time you serve those turnovers." I liked her boss. He made a lot of sense. Business was business, after all.

I finished my croissant and eyed the muffins. It was ten in the morning. If I had been laughing as I read the *National Enquirer,* people might have relaxed, but because I read it dead seriously, they thought I was a pervert and circled far around my table when they passed.

I was devastated, not because of the tragedies in the *Enquirer* but because I was divorced. Everyplace I looked—at the man holding coins waiting for the public bus, at the young girl climbing onto the park bench, at the sparrow in the street—I saw death. I couldn't believe that half of America had gone through this and the country was still surviving.

I put down the paper. Anna, I thought. Anna. I'll call Anna. It was the first thought I had had besides death in forty-eight hours. My heart bristled a little at the edges at the echo of Anna's name, but it was more like the wings of a heavy bird, dead on the highway, whose feathers flutter a moment from the movement of a passing Chevy. When I stood up, my heart, against its will, rose with my body. I paid for the tea and croissants, then dragged it out the door. I drove home, dialed Anna, and didn't even care about there being cheaper long-distance rates after 5 P.M.

The phone rang loud and buzzy over the wires. It rang four times. I waited. I was going to let it ring until Anna answered, and I didn't care if that took half a day.

She answered on the sixth ring. She didn't like phones.

"Hello," she said.

"Anna!" I screamed. "I divorced Gauguin two days ago."

She didn't hesitate. "Get a road map right now. I'll go get mine."

I didn't ask any questions. I ran and got one off the bookshelf. "Now, let's see which town is halfway between Minneapolis and Dansville." I could feel her head bent over her atlas. She was quickly flipping pages.

"Nell, it's Lakestone, Minnesota. Do you see it? In the southwest corner."

"Yeah, yeah, I got it," I said with slightly more energy than a mosquito in the dead of winter. Something in me was alive.

"Okay, listen carefully." Anna then talked slowly and deliberately. "Today is Thursday. This Saturday, we are both going to leave our houses at 9 A.M. and drive to Lakestone. It will take each of us approximately four hours if we go around fifty-five miles per hour. Don't make too many pit stops. Lakestone is small—let me see, population: 3,140. Write this down, Nell. Look for the Standard station. If they don't have a Standard station, next look for a Shell station. Then a Seven-Eleven, then a Conoco, then an Amoco. If they have none of them, stand in the middle of Main Street and scream until I show up. Do you have the order down? Nell?"

I kept nodding, but I forgot to speak into the receiver. "Nell?" Anna asked again.

"Yes," I replied.

"Tell me the order," she demanded.

"A Standard, a Shell, a Seven-Eleven, a Conoco, an Amoco, and then scream," I repeated.

"Good. We'll spend the weekend together. There must be a motel there," Anna surmised.

"Anna, aren't you surprised about my divorce?" I asked feebly.

"Nell, last time we spoke, you were having a hard time. To be honest, I knew something was off when you stopped here on your way to be married. It just had to play itself out."

"Well, Anna, I did love him," I said defensively.

"Aw, Nell. I know you did. You still do. You're suffering." She talked more softly. "I want to help. I know how deep it was between you two."

"You do?" Suddenly, I got scared and paranoid. "I can't make love with you, you know."

"Nell, you're an asshole. I don't want to make love. I'm your friend. Do you think that's all I ever want to do?" Anna was hurt. She had a right to be. It had never even come up in conversation after that one time in Dansville. It was just that I didn't trust anything right now.

"Anna, I'm sorry." I started to cry. "I don't know where to turn."

"I understand. You need to be with people who have known you a long time, who know your history, who can reassure you that your whole life isn't all broken up." Anna was so smart. I didn't quite grasp what she meant, but I suspected she was right.

I recited Anna's words to myself over and over again as I drove to meet her. The sky was slate gray. The snow had melted, and everything looked soaked. Colors come out better when they are wet. The bark on the elm trees was browner, the concrete grayer, the red barns redder. Sadness became vivid to me. "Chew Pouch Tobacco" was lettered on the side of a barn. I thought of chewing gum, but desire fell through my feet. There wasn't anything left. There was just the car, the wheel I gripped with my two hands, the heat pouring out of the slots on either side of the front dashboard, and the jerking click of the second hand on the clock. I knew on that day that Minnesota would always be the land of sorrow for me. It would be about dying.

I drove through lost Lutheran towns, one after the other. I figured the devil must have left these towns because there wasn't enough pizzazz there for him. He abandoned the cows and the cats to fend for themselves. He knew that this kind of cold, this kind of gray, does not produce evil, only drunkenness; not the true darkness that glints off a black Cadillac, only a dead haze. In late December, people here didn't have the energy to work for the devil, and the heat of hell was a dream. All they knew was that winter would be here for five more months, and they surrendered themselves to it.

As I pulled into Lakestone, Minnesota, the digital clock on the bank blinked 1 P.M. To pull in, all I needed to do was make a left. Lakestone, with its two-block strip of brick stores, ran parallel to the two-lane highway.

I looked for a Standard station. No Standard station. I saw an Amoco at the far end of the street, but I had to go down the list. No Shell, according to a woman in a green parka with a fur-trimmed hood. No 7-Eleven, according to a teenager, who looked at me as though I had rabies. He was wrong. I was heartsick. Yet the smell of death was in my whole body. I pushed open the glass door of the five-and-dime store, and everyone stared at me. It felt as if I had just walked into a perfectly normal American store wearing a gorilla costume. Yes, I wanted to say, I'm Jewish. I'm dark. I do not live here.

I approached the redhead behind the cash register and asked if there was a Conoco station in town. She shook her head. In human language it meant "no." I was tempted to tell her I had a rendezvous with a six-foot-one-inch lesbian.

Well, then, Anna and I were going to meet at the Amoco. I left my car parked and walked down the sidewalk to the other end of town, where Anna would drive into Lakestone. I leaned against a sign advising you to get your car lubricated. I wasn't waiting in anticipation. I just waited. If she came the next day, I would still be standing by the lubrication sign.

I saw Anna's gold Volkswagen enter Lakestone. The road was empty, and she drifted in like a dream. She pulled up in front of me. She brushed the hair off the side of her face and got out of the car. She stood opposite me as tears fell down my cheeks. She didn't hold me or touch me; she just stood there. My mouth filled with mucus from my running nose, and my collar became wet from the tears running down my neck. My arms hung by my sides. I was a flower naked in her own rain. Anna faced me in silence.

"Anna, I loved him so much." There were no visions of peyote or mountains or tipis. There was just me crying in a Midwestern town with an old friend who had appeared from noplace. I don't know how long I stood there—maybe my whole life—before I choked, "I don't know what to do."

"You stand here," Anna said. "I'm going to the gas station for Kleenex."

"They won't have any," I cried. "Don't leave me."

She went back to her car, shuffled in the front seat, and found a crumpled paper towel she used to clean her window. She handed it to me, and I rubbed it across my face.

"You are beautiful, Nell." I don't know what she meant by that. "C'mon, we have to find a place to stay." I reached out to hold her hand and gripped it tight. At that moment, I was no longer a big sister. I was thoroughly helpless.

We found a hotel called the Brickman. It was four stories high. In the lobby, there were three old men sitting on a yellow plastic couch. One had on green striped socks. You could see the skin above his ankles before the gray flannel pants came down to cover his leg.

I stood behind Anna at the reception counter. "We want a room for one night, please, for my cousin here and me." At that moment, I thought Anna must have been a goddess, because they handed over the key for room 302 as she signed her name on the register.

"Thank you," Anna said. Anna knew how to talk human language. As we rode upstairs, I noticed a sign that said the elevator had a capacity of two thousand pounds. I was fearful that my heavy heart put us over the weight limit.

Room 302 had one window overlooking a silver grain elevator near the railroad tracks. Beyond that were lots of trees, all snarled up together. When I looked straight down, I saw two pickups and one station wagon parked at an angle to the sidewalk. This is a bustling town, I thought to myself. I was learning to be sarcastic.

Anna was in the bathroom. A picture of a white farmhouse hung over the bed, which sported a gray bedspread with threads hanging by the hem. The carpet was gold with a floral design and the walls were beige. Cheery, I thought, and threw my eyes to the ceiling.

"Nell." Anna stood by the bathroom door. "Do you want to wash your face?"

"No." I could start a fight with Anna. No, I couldn't. I went into the bathroom, picked up the white washcloth, ran it under hot water, and rubbed it across my face. I looked in the medicine chest mirror. My eyes were all swollen. I didn't care. I was the ugliest person in America.

Anna was sitting in a one-armed armchair when I stepped out of the bathroom. I'd never seen her so soft looking. I think she was worried about me.

"Anna," I said out of the blue. "Tell me about forgiveness."

"What do you want to forgive?" she asked.

"I don't know. There's this tight square in my brain." I pointed to my left temple. "If I could open it up, I think all the darkness I carry around would pour out." I paused, turned my head and looked at Anna. "I don't know what happened with me and Gauguin."

Anna was quiet for a moment, then said simply, "Let's go for a walk," and picked up a green canvas satchel. We walked along the sidewalk, past a feed store, sewing machine store, and drugstore. The drugstore's display of sunglasses had fallen on its side and looked like it had been lying that way for a hundred years. Across the street I noticed Kay's Luncheonette. I could get some meat loaf there with mashed potatoes and gravy. Then I could run up to our hotel room and vomit in the toilet.

I held Anna's hand as we walked. I looked up at her. Earlier she'd been my big sister, now she was my mother. The sidewalk came to an end, just like that. It fell off and after a parking lot there was prairie. Tall dried weeds and rolling hills.

We went up and down three of them. After climbing the fourth, we stopped and looked around. Occasionally, the sun peeked out from a crack in the dense clouds, and the hills became golden for a moment. Then they went back to being fields of dried weeds.

Anna nodded her head toward two flat rocks and we walked over and sat on them. In the distance, we could see a thin river snaking through a pasture. Closer to us was the town of Lakestone. Our hotel was the highest building.

Anna dug in her canvas bag. Uh-oh, I thought, now she's going to read me one of her short stories.

"Anna," I said, "I can't listen to a short story now."

"Nell, I have no intention of reading you my work," she said matter-of-factly. "I brought some poetry. It'll help you."

I looked at her. "Anna," I said, "I never realized you were so sweet."

"I'm not. Now listen." She opened a book of poems by Pablo Neruda and read me something about good-bye. I listened to it as though it were the wind blowing over me. Next, she read me a poem by César Vallejo, about how he was going to die on a Thursday in the rain in Paris.

"How did he know that?" I asked. I was stretched out on my back, my head on Anna's knee.

"How did he know what?" Anna asked.

"When he was going to die?" I answered.

"Poets know everything." She pushed an old fly from her face that couldn't believe it hadn't died yet. After all, it was December.

She read me a poet named Linda Gregg. She was divorced, too, and in the poem she was picking apples.

"Anna, I don't know what to do with my life," I said after she had finished reading.

"Me either." Anna looked down at me.

"No, really. What have you done alone all these years? I can't even sleep at night alone. I wake up around two and toss and turn for two or three hours."

Anna pushed the hair from my forehead. "I've always been alone. I don't know anything else," she said.

We went back to the hotel. In the lobby was an old red Coke machine that I hadn't noticed before. It said Coca-Cola in fancy white script and had a long thin glass door in the middle that opened to reveal old green Coke bottles filled with dark fizzy liquid that rots teeth and iron nails. I pulled out two bottles. They were cold and wet in my hands.

We went up to our drab room. I drew a bath. Anna poured in soap suds. She sat on the toilet seat and drank her Coke while I sat in the hot water and drank mine. When I wasn't tilting my head back with the bottle to my lips, I placed it on the ledge of the tub.

I talked all the way back to another life and Anna could follow me there because she knew that life. I told her about how Eugene made love funny, and how he sounded like a crow when he came. I told her about the kids I had taught at the Red Willow School, how we built a greenhouse one spring and went to an orchard in Velarde, where we learned about apple blossoms turning into apples. I told her how once when I visited my parents I had cried in the basement and didn't know why. I thought maybe it was because my life in Taos had become so different from theirs in Brooklyn and I was happy in mine. I told her how my mother had sent us an electric blender after she visited Gauguin and me in Talpa, how she refused to go to the bathroom in the outhouse. I told her about everything but Gauguin. I had no words anymore for Gauguin. There was nothing left to say about him, but I did tell her how crazy he had become with the death of his parents, how I knew I could no longer help him, how we had already died, and now I was just the wind blowing over our grave.

I told her how I thought it must hurt when you die, because Alice had held on so hard to life as it was pulled out of her. I told her about Rip and how we'd never understood his death.

I washed my underarms and then stood up in the tub. Anna held up a raggedy beige towel for me.

We went to Kay's Luncheonette in the late afternoon, and I didn't vomit. I had a club sandwich. Anna had a bowl of oatmeal. I could never figure out Anna and her tastes.

Anna told me that last month she almost went out with a man she met at the Dansville library. When she heard he hunted a lot, she decided she couldn't do it.

"What makes you a lesbian anyway, Anna?" I was suddenly curious.

"I've always been. I slept with a man once when I was eighteen—

my brother's friend—just to check it out. It wasn't for me. I love women."

"Yeah?"

"Yeah. I even had crushes on my female baby-sitters when I was eight."

"Do you like your father?" I asked.

"Sure. My father is a good man. Very reserved, though. He doesn't talk much," she explained.

We crawled into bed early. Anna fell asleep immediately. I lay on my left side, facing the window overlooking Main Street. A square of street light came in between the half-closed yellow curtains. It ran along the floor and up a quarter of the side of the one-armed armchair. That night I understood that stones, especially smooth ones, never sleep. They were just stone cold and awake. That was how I felt, but there wasn't any peace in it. My hands and feet were cold. I knew no socks or mittens would warm them. I kept looking at the square of light, listening to Anna's even breathing. I was glad she was there, even though she was asleep.

Sometime in the middle of the night I dozed and dreamed that I was completely white, even my eyes and hair. I was at the edge of a wood and the place was full of moonlight. Dead people walked past me. There was my grandfather. He hardly noticed me. There was an old janitor that used to work for my father, and a seventeen-year-old boy I'd met two years ago in Hopkins, Minnesota, who had just joined the carnival. All their faces were black. They had come out of their graves.

I burst out of sleep, my fists clenched and my heart squeezed tight. I let out a soundless scream, then Anna woke up and grabbed me. "What's wrong?" she yelled, frightened.

"I don't know. My heart hurts."

"Nell, are you having a heart attack?"

"I don't know." I paused. "No, I don't think so, Anna." I reached out for her. "I'm scared. I'm doing the best I can. I miss Gauguin." With those last three words, I tumbled over a waterfall and went under. I was swept out to where there was no one, where there never would be anyone, to the place I had always been afraid of. As my body went, my mind traveled through rock and desert. My mouth became dry. My hands were a thousand years old. My face was in Anna's shoulder. She was a skeleton.

"Nell?" she called me back. "Where are you?"

"Nowhere." I lay in that place, clutching Anna until, sometime before dawn, we both fell asleep.

Late the next day, we left each other. The sun tried to come out as I drove back to Minneapolis. It didn't make it.

48

I t was the second Sunday in February. I'd just come from working out at the Jewish Community Center and was pushing my shopping cart down the aisles of Lund's Market. I stopped in front of the Minnesota wild rice. As I reached for a bag, I remembered leaning over them once as they boiled in a pot and the smell of northern lakes filled my nose. That triggered the memory of our last vacation together up at Gull Lake. Tomorrow Gauguin was moving to California.

I put the rice back on the shelf and pushed myself over to an empty corner of the store where they sold birdseed. I stood there gripping the metal bar of my silver shopping cart, crying and facing the Dew-Hum bird feeders. To my left were the colored columns of eight brands of kitty litter.

I pulled in my last sniffle and walked over to the fluorescent-lit fresh vegetable section. I reached for a cabbage. I put it back. I looked at the brown misshapen bodies of the potatoes. They'd suffered enough, I thought, and pushed my cart past them. In pink and silver cellophane stood fresh gladioli, mums, and African violets. They reminded me of graves. I abandoned my cart in the middle of the store and walked out.

The day was cold. I was as crazy as I'd ever been, and instead of getting in my car I walked down Lake Street and turned right on Hennepin. I could go to the Croissant House, to the Rainbow Café, to Orr Books. No. I walked along Hennepin until it ended eight blocks down at the Lakeside Cemetery. I entered beneath the high iron gates.

The wind split my face apart. I trudged up one of the hills, past the graves of Philip Bates, Mary Bates, and the whole Bates clan. Past a sepulchre for Hudson Crews and a cement sanctuary for the Robinson family. I was headed toward Alice's grave. Suddenly, I broke down crying again, a dry hard cry like cornflakes without milk. I squatted near the gravestone of Elmer Johnson and leaned my back against his death marker. The ground was too icy for me to sit on it. In the distance, through the bare maple branches, out past the cemetery, I saw the Lyndale Butcher. Every once in a while, a car moved slowly down the street.

I got up, realizing I couldn't bear to find Alice's grave. There would just be a marker on the ground. I was consumed by an aching I had never known before. There was nothing to do for it, no place to go to relieve it. I headed for the exit. I'd go home and take a hot bath. Maybe that would help. Maybe it was the cold that was affecting me, I told myself, but I knew that wasn't true. I walked all the way back to my car, feeling that even the air pulled into my lungs was something strange and foreign.

As soon as I got home and took off my down jacket, I wanted to get out of the house. I felt like a desperate wild animal. Gauguin was moving away, and I couldn't stop him. I was frightened. I sat down on the couch. Then I jumped up, went to the refrigerator, grabbed the handle, and yanked open the door. There was nothing in there I wanted to eat. I slammed it shut. I went into the bathroom and turned on the tub water.

The phone rang. I hauled myself into the living room and lifted the receiver. It was Gauguin. "I'm heading out tomorrow early. I thought I'd pack up a few more things and come and say good-bye in about an hour," he said.

"Okay." I hung up.

In an hour I'd see Gauguin for the last time. I dropped my clothes on the bathroom floor and lowered myself into the white porcelain tub. Though the bath was hot, my teeth were chattering and I was trembling.

"Please don't go," I sobbed. I reached for a towel and buried my face in it.

My eyes were swollen by the time I was dressed again, sitting on the maroon couch, waiting for Gauguin to arrive.

The doorbell finally rang and I got up to answer it. Gauguin stepped in from the cold and stood by the couch. This was my last chance. I'd beg him to stay or take me with him—anything. Instead I was frozen. We stood opposite each other, maybe half a living room apart. He wore his old green army jacket, and his face, that face I loved, those thick lips, hazel eyes, freckled cheekbones—I wanted to reach out and touch them. I would be alone in Minneapolis, a city where I would never have lived except for him.

"Nell—" He started to cry. I glanced at his hand. That hand had touched my face, my breast, my ear. I would never find anything like his tenderness again. I began to sob.

"Please." I threw my arm across my face. "Please, please, don't say anything."

He kept crying. "Nell . . ." Neither of us made a step closer to the other.

". . . I'm so sorry we hurt each other." He finally got it out. A wide quiet space opened between us.

Then I couldn't bear it. Speechless, I motioned for him to leave. He opened the front door, stepped out, and closed it behind him.

49

"Nell, we're worried about you. Please come down. We'll pay for the ticket," my mother offered on the phone. "We're here for another month. It will be good for you. Uncle Harold is here, right nearby, and Cousin Sarah. It will cheer you up. Just because you're the only one in our family ever to be divorced, you shouldn't be ashamed. We all love you."

"Okay, I'll think about it. Easter vacation is coming up, so maybe I could make it." We hung up.

Three days later I made reservations to fly to Miami. I was lonesome and maybe my family could help.

After I bought the ticket I panicked. An entire week with my parents? I must really be crazy!

My father lunged at me as soon as I reached gate eight. "Nell, Nell, Nell," he moaned, and gave me a big bear hug.

My mother was there, too, along with two of their friends from the next condo who had come along for the ride.

"This is Shirley, and this is Max."

We greeted each other. "They live in New Jersey," my mother

said. "Nell, wait until you see the place we rented. You'll just love it. Very Floridian."

"Look at those palm trees. And you know Grandma is coming down the day after you leave. What a shame we couldn't all be here together," my father told me as we walked through the parking lot. "I love this semi-retirement. I was exhausted. Cousin Saul's learned the business so well that I can leave for two months."

We piled into the car, men in front, women in back. I was scrunched between Shirley and my mother. She held my hand and rubbed it, giving me sympathetic glances while she and Shirley kept up a constant banter, comparing notes on the price of bagels, the new Marshall's that opened nearby, and how much weight Selma in the next block had lost.

They drove me through the entire condo complex. It was forty miles from the ocean but had a clubhouse with an outdoor pool, tennis courts, and a Jacuzzi.

"Don't you just love it?" Shirley asked.

"My," I said.

It was late afternoon and a breeze cooled things off a bit. Almost on cue, people came out of their houses to walk or ride jumbo-size tricycles around the paved streets. It was good for the circulation, my mother told me.

As soon as we got to their place, my father settled into a big lounge chair.

"I don't do those things, Nell. Why walk all around the block to come back to your own house?" He grinned. "I'd rather go watch horses go round and round at the racetrack." He shifted his cigar from one corner of his mouth to the other and pressed the remote control button to switch the television on. "Come, sit with me. Your mother has to call everyone to let them know you arrived safely."

I settled down on the couch and together we watched Howard Cosell. The blinds were drawn against the sun. We sat in the light of the television screen. The New York Knicks were slaughtering the Boston Celtics.

Everything in the living room was white—the couch, the chairs, the rugs, the walls. A fat green schefflera plant occupied one corner and a ceiling fan whirled above our heads.

I got up during a commercial, took a chicken leg from the refrigerator, and ate it, standing by the kitchen sink. "Don't spoil your appetite, Nell. We'll have dinner after our walk. You'll come with me?" my mother asked, stepping out of the bedroom.

"Of course." I nodded.

She ducked back into the bedroom to put on her special brown walking shoes. When she reemerged, we went out. As she walked, she swung her arms. The walking instructor had said it was good for the heart. She liked going on her walk later than everyone else.

As we passed each house, she told me who lived there. "Oh, that's the Katzes'. The husband was a physician before he retired. They have three daughters. All married very well. One is married to an Israeli, and they live in Scarsdale.

"This is the Durantes' house. They're Italian, but very nice. They have two granddaughters who visited last week. The older one's a little chubby, but she has nice skin.

"Would you prefer brisket tonight? Or we could go out for dinner. Tomorrow your father and I start our diet. We read about it in the *Miami Herald*. We're only allowed lean meat twice a day. In the morning when we wake up and for dinner. In between we can eat carrot sticks. That's all."

"Mom, I don't really care what we eat."

We walked past small condo units, each with a green lawn, a hibiscus bush, a willow tree, and a forsythia. Wandering Jew plants were draped around the front entrances.

"Nell, isn't this paradise? Aren't these places cute? Look at that adorable flamingo statue on the front lawn." She stopped swinging and held my arm.

"My," I said.

We walked on in silence, my mother awed by the beauty.

At the corner she suddenly halted and turned to me. "So what happened? He didn't have a nice family?"

"No, it wasn't that. We were no longer compatible. I couldn't stand him playing music all the time and not being home," I said, hoping to satisfy her with an easy explanation.

"Nell, I don't understand. You knew he was a musician before you married him. That's the way they live." She was very logical. I was impressed.

"I guess I changed. And my painting—"

She interrupted. "He was a sweet boy. He just didn't look like you. That's all."

I knew she meant he wasn't Jewish. Could it be that simple?

When we came in the house, my father jumped up from his chair. "What took you so long? I'm starving. Let's eat a lot tonight since we have to start dieting tomorrow. Nell, I never get to see you. You arrive, and your mother takes you off gallivanting."

"I didn't take her gallivanting. We exercised. Something you should do." She tapped him on the stomach to remind him of his weight. He beamed with delight. He liked any kind of attention from her.

After dinner, my father and I settled into watching a late movie. My mother decided to go to bed early. She padded into the living room to say good night wearing a white cotton nightgown that ended above her knees. Her knees were brown and very round, like a young girl's. She kissed me, kissed my father, then padded back to their bedroom where she fell asleep to the crackling of the radio.

The movie was about a man in England who fell in love with a Russian spy. In the middle of the film, when the Englishman turned the corner on Trafalgar Square and barely missed a bullet aimed at his head, my father turned to me. "This movie is good, isn't it?" he said.

I nodded.

After the spy and the man ran off together, "The End" flashed across the television screen.

I got up to turn off the set. He raised his hand. "Don't do that. I like the sound." He shifted in his chair and fell asleep.

I crossed the living room to the guest bedroom. I stood in the bedroom for a moment, then turned and walked out the front door. I continued past the tennis courts and the artificial lake used for paddle boats. A thin moon rippled in the water and hung steady in the Florida sky.

I imagined that Gauguin and I were visiting here together. Gauguin would have sat for an hour in the hot tub and my father would have nagged me to tell him to get out. Lying on a chaise lounge, I would have said, "Leave him alone. His parents just died." In the morning, my father would have squeezed us fresh orange juice and my mother would have cut up bagels to go with the lox and cream cheese. Then both my parents would have sat and watched us eat. Gauguin would have made them happy by eating two bagels.

I headed toward the back of the condo village. I remembered something Gauguin had said about my parents when they visited Minneapolis. "They make you feel weird if you want to be alone, like it's an abnormal state."

I reached the high-wire fence that surrounded the condos. On the other side was forest. Shirley had said in the car that soon bulldozers would be knocking down the Australian pines to make way for the construction of Seagull Motor Park. I climbed the fence. No one was around to stop me. Everyone was asleep.

I dropped down into the soft dirt and pine needles on the other side. I walked far enough into the woods that the streetlights of the condo village were only a glow. I sat down, leaning against a pine tree. Even though there was a 7-Eleven a quarter of a mile away, it seemed like a wild forest, a place I could breathe. For the next fifteen minutes I tried to figure out what to do with my life.

There was nothing to be done. I sunk my back into the tree and felt the weight of my legs on the pine needles. The air was warm. It was hard to believe that Minnesota was still so cold. There must be a way out, I thought. I can't stay this unhappy forever. I wished it were ten years from the date of my divorce.

I walked back to the fence, climbed over it, and returned to the white square condo that held my mother and father. The television was still on in the living room, my father snoring in front of it. I tiptoed over to turn it off.

As soon as the television clicked off, my father stirred. "Nell, please, leave it on. I'm watching." I sighed and turned it on again. I didn't bother to argue that he had been asleep and at 1 A.M. there was nothing on but fuzz.

I went to my room, put the quilt on the floor, and slept there. The bed in the guest room was too soft.

My father shook me with his foot to wake me. He couldn't bend down to the floor. I looked up. "Nell, why do you sleep this way? We have a perfectly good bed. Come. It's morning. I squeezed you some orange juice."

"It's early. Let me sleep." I tried to remember my dream.

"You don't need to sleep. Your mother and I don't see you enough. Get up."

My parents began their special diet that morning. By the time I came into the kitchen, they had already eaten their quotient of four ounces of lean meat.

My father asked me, "Did you go out last night after I fell asleep? Nell, you shouldn't do that. There are rednecks in Florida. If you want to go for a walk, I'll come with you." As he spoke, I noticed my mother slip M&M's in her mouth from a dish on the cocktail table in the living room. I didn't tell my father.

That whole day they were grumpy and couldn't wait to go for dinner. They both planned to get a steak. They mentioned it often. We went shopping in the late morning. They wanted to show me the citrus groves and the peacocks that were let loose to wander among the orange trees. My father sat down on a nearby bench. "God, am I hungry! We should go home and change to get ready for dinner. There are big crowds at this steak house. We have to be early."

"But, Dad, it's only one o'clock. We have all afternoon. I want to go to the beach," I said.

He scowled. He couldn't believe dinner was so far away.

By 3:30, my father insisted we dress and drive out to the restaurant, which was only twenty minutes away. "We should be there when it opens at five. We can be the first in line."

I gave in. I went to my room and put on a sleeveless white dress and a pair of Mexican huaraches. When I stepped into the living room, my father was at the other end of it.

"You can't go to dinner like that!" he yelled.

I looked down. "Why not?"

"Those shoes—they look like you stepped out of the jungle. And you didn't shave your armpits."

"It's none of your business," I yelled back. I'd put up with him all day, and all of a sudden something in me snapped. "Get off my back!" I screamed, turned around, and went into my room. I grabbed my suitcase, threw open the bureau drawer, and tossed my clothes helter-skelter into the gray nylon bag. I zipped it up, reached for my sun hat, flung my purse over my shoulder, and stormed out the front door.

As I charged down the walk, my father shouted through the screen door, "Where are you going?"

"I'm leaving," I screeched back.

"Good riddance," he shouted again, and slammed the front door.

I marched through the gate of condo city. Outside of it there was only a highway. I crossed to the divider island and walked along it, heading west. I wasn't crying. I wasn't even thinking. I was blind and walking fast toward the airport fifteen miles away.

A white Buick pulled up. I turned my head toward the car as the man rolled down the window. It was my father. "Please, Nell, come home. Your mother is hysterical."

I continued to walk, my eyes straight ahead. "If she's hysterical, why doesn't she come get me?" I said.

"She can't. She's too upset. She wanted me to come," my father answered.

"Well, what do you feel?" I asked, still walking hard, suitcase in hand. He drove along beside me at three miles an hour.

"Me? About what?" he said.

"About me leaving?" I asked. He drove so slow that the car stalled. He turned the key and started it again.

"Nell, I'm hungry. Please, let's go to dinner," he pleaded.

"I'm not going to dinner. If Mom wants to see me, let her come and get me," I said.

A police car pulled up behind the white Buick. "What's goin' on here?" the officer drawled. "Is he bothering you, miss?"

"I'm her father!" my father shouted indignantly.

"He's not my father!" I yelled back at the officer.

"Come on, mister. Now move along here. Leave the little lady alone," the officer ordered.

My father turned so that half his body was now twisted, hanging out his open window. His right arm was wrapped around the steering wheel, and his left fist was clenched and pointed toward the police car.

"Nell, tell him who I am!" he shouted at me.

"I won't. If you don't know what you feel, go get my mother." I was beginning to break.

"Okay, I'll go get her. If you wait here!" he shouted.

"I'll wait here."

"Do you promise?"

"Yes."

I leaned against the guardrail and dropped my suitcase at my feet.

The officer called to me as my father pulled away. "Are you okay, miss? Was that your father?"

"Yes." I nodded my head. "I'm okay."

He pulled away. I bent my head. I cracked open inside and began to weep.

My parents pulled up. My mother jumped out of the car in a beige polyester pantsuit. She stood on the shoulder opposite me and screamed across the traffic, "Nell, what's wrong?"

My face was in my hands, but I had to say something. Right then, I felt raw and naked and knew I could only tell the truth. I couldn't protect them anymore. I looked up, tears running down my cheeks. "Mom, I'm lost. I'm lost since Gauguin left."

My mother broke down, weeping. "Oh, Nell," she cried.

My father stood behind her with the car keys dangling in his hand. He was embarrassed. "Please, can we go eat now? I'm starving."

My mother turned to him. "Irving, who cares about eating? Our daughter is lost."

"We can talk about it at the restaurant. I've been dieting all day. Please . . ."

A yellow Oldsmobile stopped. "Do you need help?"

"Yeah, take me to a steak house." My father made an attempt at humor. "No, we're fine."

My mother crossed over to the divider and touched my hair. "Nell, let's go home."

"Okay." I was spent. They knew the truth now.

We drove the one block back to their condo. I went in to wash my face. I didn't even look in the mirror.

At the restaurant my father drummed his fingers on the tabletop, waiting for our order. My parents were embarrassed around me now. I had exposed myself in front of them. They ate their steaks, and I picked at my chicken.

The next day the three of us took a walk along the beach. We progressed slowly. My parents had suddenly grown old. Every few hundred yards, we stopped and sat on a cement bench. In the distance you could see palm trees and mansions along the shoreline.

My father pointed. "That's a big house."

Yes, I nodded.

He reached his hand out to touch mine. We got up and walked at the rate of what seemed like two steps per half-hour. My mother needed to sit again. The sun was too hot. She wore a white bonnet and sandals on her feet. Her feet were calloused and there was a bunion on her small left toe. She pushed her foot through the sand. We were quiet and shy with each other, like swans. For a brief moment we hung suspended in the tropical air. I told my mother I loved her. She said, "And I love you." We looked at each other and then away. The warmth felt good.

The next morning they said, "Our Nell is suffering, we can't diet," and we all sat down to bagels and lox. My father squeezed fresh orange juice for the three of us.

The night before I left, my father and I watched television for a long time. There was a rerun of *Gunsmoke,* followed by a situation comedy, then a program about the Amazon River. We ate chocolate ice cream out of round white bowls. I spooned the last bit into my mouth and looked down at the empty bowl on my lap.

"Nell," my father said.

"Yes?" I looked up.

"Don't remarry out of loneliness." Those words drifted over to me across the chasm between his chair and the sofa I sat on. We looked at each other and I nodded.

"I won't," I said.

After he said that he fell asleep. He must have been thinking it for a long time. Just then, on television they showed the crocodiles on the river. It was the part my father had wanted to see the most.

The next day, I flew back to Minnesota.

50

Matthew from upstairs tied a blue cowboy kerchief around my neck. He said that that was what the Tibetans did to say good-bye. He and Marian stood at the curb and waved.

The sun was just coming up as I drove south on Highway 35. Just before the Burnsville exit, I pulled over to the shoulder, got out of the car, and stood with the traffic of bleary-eyed commuters passing me by in the opposite direction. The sky was streaked with pink and yellow, caught in fast-moving clouds. I looked back at the city and saw the IDS Building, Minneapolis's tallest skyscraper, the one that King Kong could not climb.

"Okay," I said to myself begrudgingly. "You learned a lot here. Go ahead and say good-bye." And I closed my eyes and wished the whole Midwest well. When I opened my eyes, I smiled and nodded. I waved my hand, then got back in the car and pulled into the traffic, heading away from all I had just said farewell to.

South of Albert Lea, I turned my car on the cloverleaf and faced west. I stopped in Worthington to tank up. The gas station attendant told me that I was standing in the Turkey Capital of the United States. I told him I was impressed as I surveyed the flatness all around me.

He said, "Yup, a town in Texas once challenged us. They had the nerve to say they were the Turkey Capital." He yanked the nozzle out of my car. "The citizens here got up in arms. To settle the matter," the attendant, now leaning against the pump and biting the tip off a cigar, continued the saga, "we had a turkey race down Main Street. Their turkey's name was Ruby Begonia and ours was Paycheck. We figured a paycheck goes fast. The whole town came out for the race. The schools shut down." He closed his thick-lidded eyes and shook his head, remembering. "It was fun. That dumb turkey of theirs flew to the top of a pole, and they couldn't get him down. Paycheck didn't take any straight route himself, but he had all the time in the world to win, since Ruby wouldn't come off the pole."

The attendant smiled. "We won. Yup, you're standing in the Turkey Capital of the World. You should be proud."

"Oh, I am, I am," I said, holding out a ten-dollar bill, hoping he would take it and I could go on my way.

He looked at the bill. "Where ya goin'?"

"Out west."

"Be careful." He handed me four dollars' change. "They're crazy out there."

"So I heard," I said as I lowered myself into the driver's seat. I shot my hand out of the car window at him, and as I pulled onto the road, I noticed through my rearview mirror that he was still watching me.

I crossed into South Dakota, and after a while I stopped in a town so small it had only eleven stores, seven on the west side and four on the east. There were two cafés on opposite ends of the street. One was open for lunch and one for dinner. I pulled into the town at three in the afternoon, so the dinner one had just opened and the lunch one had just closed. The dinner one was named Covey's. They sold postcards of the café, and while they set up the salad bar, I wrote one to Blue. "Dear Blue, I'm in South Dakota. I'm on my way. I'm sitting at the counter of the café you see on the other side. See you soon. Love, Nell. P.S." I drew a rooster. "How's old Sylvester doing?"

I paused, put the non-ink end of the pen in my mouth. Then I wrote under my signature another signature: Banana Rose. It felt good to write her name.

The salad bar was ready. I piled my plate high with cottage cheese and marshmallow salad full of bits of canned pineapple. This was my ride and I was going to enjoy it. I looked at the local newspaper, which came out of Sioux Falls. Heifers were going at a higher price. A little girl named Polly made eleven dollars selling lemonade on the corner of Eighth Street and Oak Avenue.

As I sat there finishing the last of a dish of canned corn kernels—you could go back to the salad bar as many times as you wanted—I knew I had to go see Anna. I hadn't planned to. Originally, I felt this trip was only about me, about my return alone to New Mexico, but now I ached to see her. I knew she'd be home. She was teaching summer school.

I headed for Dansville, and this time I knew how to get to her house.

I ran up the side steps and knocked hard, screaming through the screen door, "Anna! Anna, where are you?"

"Nell? Nell, is that you?" she called back. "Just a minute. I'm in the bathroom. Just come in. Door's unlocked."

Anna came running out and grabbed me as I let myself in. "Why didn't you let me know?"

"I just decided. I'm heading home." I had a big grin on my face.

"To Minnesota?"

"No, silly, that's not home. I'm going to New Mexico, Anna. I'm moving back."

"You are?"

"Yes." I nodded. Just then I noticed how thin Anna had become and that her eye had gone in. I grew quiet. "Anna, you're not going crazy again, are you?"

She sat down on a stuffed green chair. All the color drained from her. She picked at a thread on her pants. "I've been having a hard time, Nell." She paused. "That's why you haven't heard from me in a while. I don't think I'm going crazy exactly, just—I don't know." I knelt beside her and she tousled my hair. "My mother went into a home a month ago. She had another stroke and didn't come out of it. And before that we weren't getting along very well." She paused again. "Dad's feeble and a bit senile, but he still lives in the house we grew up in. Daniel keeps an eye on him."

"You and your brother still getting along so well?" I asked.

She perked up a little. "Yeah, and we've gotten even closer since my mother's illness. Daniel seems to understand that I'm different, and it feels so good to have someone in the family who really accepts me. 'Nam gave him a broader view."

"And how's your writing coming?"

She shook her head. "Not so good. I've been too depressed."

I grimaced. "Anna, are there any groups you could join? Lesbians? Writers?"

She shook her head. "Nell, you know I'm not a joiner."

"Well, why don't you join me and move back to Taos?" The idea sprang suddenly into my head, and I thought it was brilliant.

She laughed feebly. "That would be fun—but, Nell, I have responsibilities. I can't just leave with my mother in a home."

"But Anna, you have to save yourself—you're going crazy again. I'm serious. Pack up and get the fuck out of here." I stood up. "C'mon."

She brightened for a moment and then looked down. "I'm not like you, Nell. You always act on your pain. It gets you moving. Besides"— she hesitated—"I don't know if I want to leave Daniel. He might resent me moving away, leaving him to take care of Dad alone."

"Oh, Anna, you and your Midwestern stoicism. 'Rage, rage against the dying of the light'!" I thought I'd give her a little literary boost.

"Nell, Dylan Thomas was talking about death." I followed her into the kitchen area. "Want something to drink?"

"Got lemonade?" I asked. "I'll buy some if you set your booth up."

"I'll make some and for you it's free." She reached into the freezer.

329

"But, Anna, isn't it a kind of death you're living? I mean, you're unhappy and you're not writing. I couldn't stand that." I spun her around to face me. "Anna, you know what made me act? Not my pain. I decided that I was going to make it. I still don't know how or what that means. After Gauguin left, I was so down, I couldn't do anything. I knew I had to make something important enough to get me out of bed each day, so I gradually focused on my painting. And right now if there's one thing I'm sure of, it's that I'm going to paint no matter what."

I paused. "Wow, I never said that before to anyone, even to myself."

Anna studied me closely. "You've changed."

"My heart was pulled out of me. I didn't think I'd live. Gauguin was so different after Taos." All at once I didn't want to talk about Gauguin anymore. "Do you want to go out for dinner? That place we went last time—is it open at night?"

The next morning we drove to a secluded swimming spot Anna knew on the Elkhorn River.

We put down our towels and undressed. "Anna, it's so, so"—I looked around—"Midwestern. The summer, the trees. A wide and lazy river."

"Let's jump in. No hesitation." And then she dove under, her butt shining in the sun for a moment before it submerged.

I followed. My head surfaced, hair and lashes dripping. "Anna, you little shit. It's freezing! Why didn't you warn me?" I was treading water.

"If I did, you wouldn't have come in." She began doing the backstroke.

"I'm getting out. I'm freezing." Teeth chattering, I scrambled up the bank, grabbed a pink towel, and wrapped it around me. There were goose bumps all over my arms. A storm cloud moved over the sun. "Anna, look!" I yelled, and pointed toward the sky.

"Don't worry. We have time." She dove under again.

I dried off and sat down on my towel.

After a while she came out and joined me.

"Anna, quit being so athletic. Writers are supposed to be lazy and frail. You've got to get in the proper shape. Words have to ooze out of you. A firm body produces nothing." I was shading my eyes with my hand. The sun had come out again.

"Let's eat," Anna said, reaching for her bag. She pulled out a peanut butter and grape jelly sandwich.

"Hand me a peach." I reached out my arm.

She burrowed in her bag. "Nell, I'm so glad you came. I feel like a new person with you here."

I broached the subject again. "Anna, come back to Taos with me. You were happy there. You were writing there. People don't care if you're weird there. Everyone's weird."

She took a big bite of her sandwich. God, did I hate jelly. I don't know how she ate it. She chewed and chewed on that one bite until I thought her teeth would fall out. "I hear you, Nell," she finally said. "I'll think about it. I really will. I never thought I could, but now that you're going back, maybe it's possible."

"Really?" I sat up.

"Really," she said.

I grabbed her jar of lemonade and held it high. "I propose a toast: Next year in New Mexico!" Then I unscrewed the lid and took a big gulp.

As we drove back to town, it began to pour. At one point it was coming down so hard, we pulled under a nearby bridge and just sat there.

"I try to capture what this place is like in my writing, but maybe I'm too close to it," Anna said above the pelting water. Everything was green, greener in the rain. The wind blew and the trees bent without breaking.

"Can you put on some heat? I'm cold." I was hugging my arms, which were covered in goose bumps again.

"Here, I have an extra shirt." She leaned over the back of the front seat and brought forward a red zip-up jacket.

I put it on. "Anna, what's it like to write? I mean, how do you do it?"

"I don't know." She flicked the steering wheel with her nail. "I guess you have to tell it so people who read it understand. Otherwise you're not communicating. Isn't that the way it is with painting, too? It has to communicate."

"Yeah, even if you can't say exactly what it is you're communicating, a person has to feel something." Then I told her about the new paintings I had been doing back in Minneapolis. "I could hardly paint after Gauguin first left. I wanted to die. Then over time I began to paint from that place."

"What place?" Anna started up the car. The rain had eased.

"From death. First I did dark abstracts, and then I began painting things that looked alive—a tulip, a maple in full bloom—things that were alive now but that I knew could die." We pulled out from under the bridge. "I think down in Taos I believed we were all immortal, that we'd never die. Now I know that isn't true."

Anna nodded. "Open your window. Everything has been washed clean. Smell it?"

I rolled my window all the way down. "Yeah, I smell it." Leaves, road, grass, the end of July—I breathed in all of it.

I was supposed to leave early in the morning two days later, but Anna and I were having so much fun it was hard to separate. I think she gained five pounds while I was there. I kept encouraging her to eat. One night I roasted a chicken with potatoes and we ate the whole thing.

On the last day I made one more cautious stab at her moving down, and I could see she was serious about considering it. It made me happy.

I didn't leave until late afternoon. By the time I reached Maxwell, Nebraska, it was dark and I was tired. I unrolled my sleeping bag near a cow pasture, outside of town. The earth was dark and rich. To my left spread a field of corn, and above my head a blanket of stars.

In the morning, I got back in my car and looked at the road atlas. I decided to head for Boulder. I wanted to see Eugene, and I figured I could stay with Happiness. She lived there now and was also a Buddhist.

When I got to Fort Morgan, I asked directory assistance for Jane Berg's number. I telephoned her, and she said her roommate had gone off for a week camping, there was an extra room, and she'd be glad to have me. She gave me directions to her house. It was within walking distance from the downtown mall.

I thought of Jane as I drove toward Boulder. She was beautiful, always dressed in layers and layers of brightly colored skirts. I remembered when she named herself Happiness.

A bunch of us had been sitting around the kitchen table at the Elephant House, talking about our families. Jane came from Cincinnati. She said there were three kids in her family, and they were all happy except her.

"Yeah, right," Carmel had called out.

"No, really. I was the only maladjusted one around. My parents have always loved each other. My father is a banker who does good deeds for the community, and my mother is an amateur opera singer. She plays *The Marriage of Figaro* and *The Barber of Seville* on the stereo all the time. Into this happy house I would walk, carrying this cloud of gloom."

"You're okay now, aren't you?" I'd asked.

She nodded. Then she lit up. "Do you think I could change my name? I'm gonna call myself Happiness. This way I can be like my family —at least when I'm not with them."

"Huh?" Tiny looked confused.

"I'm happier when I'm away!" We all laughed, and then we baptized her, dripping lemon juice on her forehead.

I shook my head at the memory. We believed it all, didn't we? Banana Rose, Happiness, Neon—I got butterflies in my stomach. I was nervous to see him. We hadn't spoken since that day I left over three years ago. It's okay, I told myself. Eugene and I are friends. He's not mad at me for running off to marry Gauguin.

I passed the exit for Keenesburg. The thing about those years was that we had had so much *fun*. Everyone had wanted to play. Everyone, I thought, except Anna. Well, sometimes she would play, but she was always uptight about her novel. When she moves down, I thought, maybe I can get her to write about the hippie years instead. That will be a better subject than those damn depressing cows.

I pulled into Boulder at 8:30 in the evening. Everything seemed lush: Rose vines crawled over sidewalks; columbine, petunias, and zinnias were tangled together in gardens; and sweetpeas had draped themselves across people's front porches. Many of the houses were oddly shaped. Looking at Boulder at that moment, I appreciated it. When I had lived there before, it was my enemy. I'd blamed it for taking me from Taos.

Jane and I sat up until midnight, sipping tea and talking.

"You know, Light's here now too and Mark—oh, you knew him as Gum—everyone's changed their name back. We're all trying to be re-spectable citizens." She took a deep drag from a cigarette.

"Do you ever miss Taos?" I asked quietly, hugging my left knee, my foot up on the chair.

"Oh, sure, I still miss it, but when I think about it, I feel confused. How can I want to be there and here at the same time?"

"Do you ever think of moving back?" I asked.

"That time is over for me. There's no way I could make a living down there, and I certainly don't want to live the way I did. I'm older now."

"Do you think I'm crazy for going back?" I held my breath, waiting for her answer.

Jane paused. "No, in some ways I envy you. But it won't be the same; most of the old people have left."

"There are some still there," I said quickly, letting my breath out in a gush. "Like Blue."

"Yeah, she'll always be there," she said, crushing out her cigarette.

I paused. "I went through a hard divorce."

"I went through one, too, once. They're a bitch. Where's Gauguin, anyway?" she asked.

"In L.A."

"That sounds like a good place for him."

"Is Eugene still here?" I asked, trying to act nonchalant.

She looked at me closely. She wore makeup now. It was becoming. Blue eyeliner and brown mascara.

"Eugene became a serious practitioner of meditation and they made him head of the whole sitting program. It's a regular job from eight to five every day." She paused. "Hey, you ought to call him. He'd love to see you."

"Yeah, I think I will. Do you have his number?" I asked casually.

"It's 555-3802. He rooms with a close friend of mine." She glanced at the clock on the stove. "Nell, I've got to go to bed. I've got a job now in an office."

Jane had already left for work two hours earlier when I finally got up the courage to call Eugene. The receptionist answered the phone, "The Tibetan Center," and told me she would check, but she thought he was in a meeting. I tried to imagine Eugene in a conference room at a long table.

"Hello, Eugene here." I heard his voice.

"Hey, this is Nell Schwartz!"

He let out a laugh of delight. "Why, hello there! Where are you?" We decided to meet for lunch. I would pick him up at his office. He suggested we go to a restaurant across the street that served New Orleans–style food, "gumbo and all."

I waited for him on a bench in a long gold-carpeted hallway. On the far wall was a large oil painting of a black dragon spewing out blue fire. The dragon was wrapped around a gold snake and had a man's body gripped in its talons. The line from a Buddhist chant went through my head.

I turned and was amazed to see Eugene walking toward me in a suit, even though Jane had told me he would be. And he had on brown laced shoes with a design punched in the leather. Wingtips, they were called. Wingtips! I stood up as he approached me. He had a big smile on his face, and his arms were opened wide.

"Nell!" he said, and we hugged.

"Eugene."

He shook his head. I imagined his old curls shaking. He took my arm and steered me out the front door and down the five steps.

At Louie's, across the street, we sat at a table on the porch with a pink linen tablecloth. The sun was on my back, and it felt good.

We settled into our seats and looked at each other. He reached his right hand up to his lapel. "Like it?" he asked. "I found this suit in a secondhand store for thirty-five dollars, had it cleaned—good as new."

The waiter brought our drinks, and we clinked glasses, both of us laughing.

"So?" he asked me, leaning over, his elbows on the table.

I told him about me and Gauguin, about what it had been like to live in Minnesota, about Gauguin's parents, about our divorce. It felt easy to talk to Eugene, and odd—we hadn't seen each other in so long. Then I told him a bunch about my paintings. He nodded and just listened. I remembered he was always a good listener. I paused, looked down at my napkin, and then blurted, "Eugene, what do you think being a hippie was all about, anyway? All those years in Taos?"

"Love." He didn't hesitate. "It was about love."

"Where'd it go?" I asked.

"I hope it's still here. I'm still the King of the Hippies, even though I dress differently. What else is there but love?" I saw his crow eyes again, but I wasn't convinced. A lot of years had passed.

He leaned closer. "You know, a year ago I completed a special practice of a hundred thousand prostrations, and then I went back to Taos. I wanted to do two weeks of intensive meditation there. I remembered there was an old green 1949 trailer out back of Wisdom Mountain."

Yes, I nodded. I remembered it vaguely.

"It was small, just enough room to sleep one person, but it had

personality. Rounded roof, thin mahogany veneer inside.'' He showed me
the curve of the roof with his hand. "It was like an old roller skate
someone had left in the pines. I cleaned it out, set up an altar, and entered
fourteen days of sitting meditation by myself. I slept maybe six hours a
night. The rest of the time I sat cross-legged on a cushion. On the
thirteenth morning, I felt ready to perform the ritual that concluded the
hundred thousand prostrations. It requires extreme concentration, counting out a hundred grains of rice, placing them in a pattern on the altar,
destroying the pattern, counting out sixty-eight grains of rice, and so on.
Real complicated. If you miss even by one grain of rice anywhere in the
mantra, it is said that you could go crazy. That's why I sat so long before I
started it, to clear my mind. There was a chance that in doing it I could
burn through karma to pure, naked attention.

"Well, just as I laid out all the necessary incense, candles, and rice
to begin, I noticed a plastic bag under a bench. I pulled it out. It held a
small amount of white powder. I thought, 'Hey, this must be baking soda
or maybe cocaine.' I didn't know. There was only about a quarter of a
teaspoon in all. I decided to take it just for fun, as a celebration. The
amount was harmless. I licked it out of the bag. Within a half hour, after
counting out one hundred grains of rice, I was tripping my ass off. It
turned out that the powder was blue lightning acid. Someone must have
left it there years ago, and in that time, instead of deteriorating, it had
tripled its potency. The rice was dancing, the trailer was humming, and I
was on a locomotive sailing through time. I knew I had to complete the
ritual no matter what. It's said in the scriptures that once the Great Way
ritual is begun, it must be completed or death ensues. I tried to put all my
concentration into it, but of course I was tripping and had no concentration. The only thing I had to gauge it against was a clock. I continually
glanced at the clock as I performed the ritual in order to stay connected to
something and keep grounded. I knew that under normal circumstances
the ceremony took six hours.

"At sunrise the next day, I placed the last rice kernel in front of
the fifteenth candle in the exact direction to mark wisdom beyond

wisdom and vast eternity. On LSD, the ritual had taken me twenty-four hours!

"Yes, Nell, I'm still a hippie," he concluded. "I'm a freak, and I always will be."

I spooned saffron rice into my mouth. The sunlight glinted off my empty glass. I smiled at him. "I'm glad you're still a hippie. I think I am, too. It never really leaves us."

"Do you want dessert?" Eugene asked, wiping his lips with the pink linen napkin and then putting it on his empty plate. "Good place, huh?"

"A great place."

Then he wrinkled his forehead in consternation. "Uh"—he looked at his watch—"I better get back to work." He paid the bill for both of us. Then he hesitated, reached across the table, and took my hand. He wanted to say something and then decided not to. He got up, then sat down again. I realized Eugene was nervous. I had never seen him that way before.

"It's good to see you," he said.

I nodded.

"I missed you."

I nodded again. There was nothing else to say.

He got up once more, and I watched him cross the street and climb the steps to the front door of the Tibetan Center.

Back at Jane's, I was eager to move on to Taos. I planned to leave the next morning.

"Where will you stay when you first get there?" Jane asked that evening.

"Sam and Blue's up on the mesa. They have an old silver bus they're going to give me."

"Living in a bus, gonna be a hippie again?" Jane asked.

"No, not really. I just don't know any other way to live in Taos. It's temporary until I get my feet on the ground." I paused. I looked at her. "I'm going to be a painter now."

I dropped Jane off at work the next morning and then got back on the highway. Bypassing Denver, I headed south toward Colorado Springs and then past Pueblo. At Walsenberg I headed off the interstate, going west toward Fort Garland.

51

About ten miles from the New Mexico border, I stopped in the town of San Luis and parked in front of an empty storefront. Next door was a restaurant. In the window they advertised enchiladas and tacos for seventy-five cents. There was a little historical fiesta going on in the town. I crossed the street to go to the bathroom in the gas station.

On the way I passed a secondhand store and stopped to look in the window. There were three green melmac plates on a shelf, a candelabra —probably made of tin but painted gold—on the windowsill, and a pile of comics in a corner. There wasn't much to look at, but I kept looking. I touched the pane of glass in front of me. The glass became water under my fingertips and the sidewalk rippled. A breeze lifted the cottonwood leaves above my head and rustled my hair. Suddenly I remembered. Gauguin had bought a pair of khaki pants in this store once. They were from the 1950s. He got them for twenty-five cents. Banana Rose and Gauguin had been here. At that moment I thought I would never get those two names out of my head. The Midwest full of rivers rose in my face, the miles of highway, South Dakota, Gauguin's grandmother—I looked at my reflection. My hand was spread out on the glass. My hair was short. My sandaled feet were planted on the cement sidewalk. I breathed so deeply, a bouquet of carnations bloomed in my chest. I was full of sorrow and love and there was no way out of it.

I walked slowly toward the Exxon station. People dressed in festive costumes rode by on horseback. Everything passed me: color, wind, time. The bathroom was locked. I went to the office for the key. I'm returning to New Mexico, I thought, as I opened the locked wooden door.

South of San Luis the land spread out the way I knew it would. Lots of sage; naked, treeless earth; blue-gray mountains in the distance. Most of all, big sky and tremendous space. My heart flung open.

WELCOME TO NEW MEXICO. THE LAND OF ENCHANTMENT. That sign always made me smile. I pulled over, got out, leaned back against the hood of the car, and just gazed around, enjoying the sun on my face. I was home. I turned and walked off into the sage.

"Sage," I cried. "I haven't seen you in so long."

I picked a few thin twigs and brought them to my nose. That smell again. I inhaled it and my whole body dissolved into the land.

I went back to the sign, leaned against it, and sang the *Shehecheyanu* at the top of my lungs. I thanked God for bringing me to this day.

When they were released from the concentration camps, instead of grabbing guns and going mad, the Jews slowly walked past the barbed wire, came together in a bedraggled circle, and sang the *Shehecheyanu*. I was no Jew in a concentration camp. Still, I sang the prayer and held the sage up so I could smell it. When something as good as returning to New Mexico happens, there isn't much to say. The sky and the sage were better than anything I had remembered.

I realized that for a time I had thought Gauguin and New Mexico were one, so when he left, I believed I could never have it back. But the land was always here. It would be here after Gauguin was gone. After I was gone, too. But now I could return. I remembered a poem I had read by Pablo Neruda just before I left Minneapolis. It said, "Those who return never left." A part of me had always been here, moving among the chamisa, the Sangre de Cristos, the gorge. A part of me had traveled the goat path in Talpa, sat in the rain under a piñon, even as I waited for a bus in the brutal December cold on Hennepin Avenue. That part of me kept me alive, even while my marriage crumbled. I didn't know much else, but I knew this: I was not homeless. I had survived.

I got back in my car and drove to the mesa. When I got there, Blue was feeding the chickens. She put down the pail she was holding and cried, "Sugar, you're back! Got your postcard a few days ago. I thought you'd be here by now."

"I am here by now." I flung my arms open.

Blue hugged me, then paused. "I have some bad news. Sylvester ran off a day ago. I can't find him anyplace. I never heard of a rooster just running off—but you know Sylvester. He was very special"—she scrunched up her face—"and weird."

"I'm sorry," I said. "I'll help you look for him."

"Well, never mind." She waved her hand. "I got the school bus all ready for you, and then Lightning and his friends made a mess in it. I shipped him off to his father in Texas two days ago." We walked into the greenhouse.

"It's okay, I'll clean it up. I'm so happy to be back." I trailed after her into the house.

We had tortillas and beans for dinner, just the three of us. I was glad. It felt ordinary and natural, as if I'd always been there.

But then Blue said, "I made something special for you, Nell. Or should we call you Banana?"

I put my head to one side. "Let's stay with Nell for now. I have enough to adjust to."

"I made you a noodle cake." She went to the refrigerator.

"A noodle cake? Never heard of it," I said.

"It's Blue's original recipe," Sam said.

"Yes, it's spaghetti noodles. I cooked them, mixed them with lots of honey, and put them in a cake pan. Then I put it in the freezer. When it set, I frosted it with chocolate. Chocolate's still your favorite, isn't it, honey?"

"My, what a novel idea," I said. "Have you tasted it?"

"No, this is her first," Sam said, beaming at Blue. "She's an artist."

Blue brought the cake to the table. "I wanted to print 'Welcome Home' with jelly beans, but I didn't have any."

"That's fine. I understand." I took a forkful. "Hmmm, this is quite a taste sensation. Going to have it at your restaurant? What was the name of it?" I asked.

Blue laughed. "Something about unusual combos. You made it up."

"I guess this fits." Sam smiled.

"Blue's Babies." I snapped my fingers. "That was the name of your restaurant."

52

n the distance someone was whistling the most beautiful concerto. I knew who it was and I walked toward the sound.

"Remember me?" I asked old Joe Sandoval. "Do you have any of last year's dried apples?"

Joe was leaning on a pitchfork next to a ten-foot pile of straw. "Maybe so. I'll go look in the root cellar." Joe was sixty-five. He'd lived in Talpa all his life. He traveled to Taos, five miles away, about once a month. He'd been to Santa Fe, one and a half hours away, only three times in his life.

He reappeared. "Now I remember. You and that fellar lived down the road. He had some kind of instrument he was always carrying. Can't recall."

"A trumpet," I said.

Joe handed me a plastic bag full of dried fruit.

"Are these still the best?" I asked, opening the bag.

"Suppose so," he said, scratching his ear. "You look good. How many years ago was it?"

"Four, four and a half, maybe. Ummm, these are good. How much?" I took another bite.

"A dollar maybe."

"Sold." I handed him a bill. His fingers trembled. He'd been hit by lightning three times and lived.

We waved good-bye.

I walked farther down the road. I'd been back a week. Wild sunflower heads bobbed all along the road. Apricots were turning yellow-orange and under each fruit tree there were many that had already fallen. I looked over at Taos Mountain. Thunderheads were forming that would bring the afternoon rain. This land had not failed me. Each rock held a slice of eternity. I passed rose hips, not yet ready for picking. I turned and saw the elephant mountains. They were still kissing. I waved. Dark cloud shadows floated across their faces.

How could you ever leave? I asked myself. I'd left it for him. The letter was in my pocket. It had arrived yesterday. I took it out and read it again.

Dear Nell,

L.A.'s okay. A tough place. I'm trying to connect with the music scene. I'm still blasted from everything that's happened this year. I think about you, sometimes so much I want to burn you from my brain. Then I realize: You live in me. I have to let you be. I hope you are well and happy. I still love you.

Gauguin

I folded it up and put it back in my pocket. My heart was a dark prune. It became more wrinkled every time I read that letter.

"This is where we lived, Gauguin," I said out loud. "This is where we walked and kissed"—I passed our old house—"and made love."

All of a sudden I needed to get away from Talpa. I ran up to the reservoir where my car was parked, got in, and drove into town.

Lee's Bakery was next to the post office. I ordered Harvey's special there—lox, onions, and scrambled eggs—and from a rack near the

counter bought a card with a picture of the pueblo on it. I sat down in the
back room, and while I waited for my order, I wrote.

Dear Anna,

    I'm sleeping out on a platform Sam built—I can watch the
stars at night—and I'm using the school bus for a painting studio.
The mesa is still heaven. It's calling you. I hear it. "Anna," it
says, like a long low train whistle. I hope you come. I miss you.

XXX,

Nelly Belly

P.S. Treat you to a malt at Rexall's when you get here. No
vanilla.

    I didn't tell her that Rexall's had become a tourist place, but at least
they'd kept the soda fountain.

    When I finished my eggs, I dropped Anna's card in the mail slot next
door and drove back up to the mesa. Blue and Sam had been gone for
three days on a wood run near Tres Piedras. They'd be home this afternoon. I was glad. I was getting tired of being the only one up there.

    I parked beside Mohammed, Sam's 1940 red Chevy pickup, got out,
and looked around. Boy, this was big space. A person could get lost here.
Not me. I smiled. I'm going to paint.

    I went right over to the bus. Even though I could already see
lightning in the distance, I opened some windows. It was hot in there.

    Okay, I said to myself, we're inside, but let's paint what's outside.

    I drew a straight horizon line. Above it would be mountains. I'd
keep the bottom flat and full of sage. Yellow sage, I decided. Who could
ever capture the mysterious dusty blue-green color it really was?

    The painting pulled me in. I concentrated on a red mountain, then a
purple one. Rain pelted the hood of the bus. Lightning flashed. I drew a

jagged silver line half across the sky and half across the mountain. The
landscape informed me of what I should paint. There was no way I could
do an abstract painting here. The land demanded my complete attention.

Out of the corner of my eye, I thought I saw something moving. I
ignored it. What could be out in this rain? Even the jackrabbits had more
sense. I went back to the red, and then, surprising myself, I dipped the
brush in black. I wanted rain in this painting.

Something out there moved again. I put down my brush, crossed
over to a window, and shut it. Water streamed down the glass. Repeated
strikes of lightning lit up parts of the mesa. I squinted to see if I could
catch that moving object. I wonder if it's dangerous to be in this bus? Wait
a minute! I saw it again.

"Sylv—!" Just as I began to scream, lightning hit the ground right
in front of where I was looking. There was a blinding light and a huge
crackling sound like fat sizzling. Then it was gone. The sage on the side of
the bus was dwarfed and blackened.

I ran out. There he was, looking like a burned marshmallow. I
picked him up. Hanging from his body were those dinosaur feet. They
were almost untouched.

I heard a car and looked up. I could see its lights moving slowly on
the muddy road. It was Blue and Sam.

I ran toward them. My right sandal got sucked off in the mud. I
pulled it out and put it back on.

We met at the driveway. "Honey!" Blue yelled as she opened her
door. "What are you doing out in this rain?"

"Blue—" I held Sylvester at arm's length in front of me.

"Oh, lord!" She ran toward me and took the charred heap. "Sylvester? Yes, Sylvester." She saw his feet. She turned, showing the carcass
to Sam, who now was out in the rain, too. "It's a sign. It's a sign!" she
yelled. "Nothing that little and low gets hit."

"Of what?" I was cold in a sleeveless shirt, clasping my arms full of
goose bumps.

"I don't know. I'm not sure. An omen. Why didn't his feet sizzle? Let's get in the house. We'll toss the runes. We've got to do something! Poor biddy Sylvester."

We got in the house and Blue put the corpse right in the middle of her wooden kitchen table. "Now, Sylvester, don't you worry. As soon as this rain stops, we'll bury you out back next to Nijinsky and Mrs. Montoya in the poultry cemetery."

I began to feel a little crazy. What was going on here? In Brooklyn we ate chicken, we didn't have a graveyard for them.

"Sugar, why don't you go dry off? I'll heat up some soup."

I nodded.

She handed me a towel.

When I came out of the bathroom, there was hot tomato soup and grilled cheese sandwiches on the table where the chicken had been.

"Ohh, that looks good." I sat down. "Where's Sylvester?"

"I put him in the greenhouse," Sam said as he put the spoon to his mouth.

"Nell"—Blue took my arm—"that must have been a terrible experience. I threw the runes. It said, 'More darkness to come.' "

"Geez, it's already been raining so much," Sam said.

"Not that kind of darkness, Sam." Blue turned her head to me. "Nell, you better do some paintings full of light to ward this off." She shook her head. "Poor Sylvester. Wasn't he just the most special rooster?"

The ground was very wet when I walked back to the bus. The distant mountains almost looked navy blue and clouds still hung heavy. There would be more rain. The sage filled the mesa with its pungent aroma.

I stood in front of the canvas I had begun earlier. I had no taste for it. I took it off the easel and leaned it against a bureau. I sat down in the overstuffed red rocker I had dragged from Blue's shed a week ago and picked up a book of Mark Rothko's paintings that I'd borrowed from the owner of The Plaza Gallery.

I turned the pages. How could there be so much in a simple colored square? I looked at the thin line of black separating a white and a gold square on a background of red. Below the white space was a square of hot pink. I could swear God had crawled into that painting. How'd Rothko do it?

It was a thick book, and I got lost in it, lost in the same way as when I painted. Time disappeared. I even disappeared. I was all eyes, pulling color into my body. Nell Schwartz from Brooklyn was gone.

It began to rain again and the sound of the drops hitting the roof of the bus brought me back. I closed the book and then my eyes. The drops penetrated my skull and I felt sound. A moment ago I was square colors, now I was rain.

53

The headmaster blew his nose. "Excuse me, Ms. Schwartz. Yes, from time to time someone from Red Willow stops by, but I assure you Taos Prep is a very different place. I've heard about the old days. They sounded a bit crazy to me. A little on the wild side. Parents today want their children to be educated, to go to college. It's different now.

"However, I do see from your application that you have regular credentials." He shook his head. "Sometimes people come in here wanting to teach Sufi dancing or meditation. One fellow came in last year wearing a shirt with peace symbols pinned all over it. He wanted to teach, of all things, bread baking. We've worked hard to turn the reputation of this school around. Though it may be the same building, it's not the same institution.

"I'm sorry there are no regular openings, but we are looking for a part-time music teacher. Any interest?"

I shook my head. I couldn't wait to get out of there. "No, I'm a painter. I think I'll earn money this year doing individual tutoring."

"Suit yourself." His hands were folded in front of him on the desk.

I pinned up a sign on the bulletin board at the post office: "Professional reading tutor available for all ages. Inquire at Lee's Bakery next door.''

Lee said she'd keep messages for me. Blue had a phone, but it was in a box outside and you couldn't hear it ring unless you were walking right by it.

Then I looked for any notices for rooms for rent. I decided I'd live in town and keep my studio out in the bus.

I went to box 804 with my new key and peeked in the window. A white envelope lay on its side. I unlocked the door and reached in for it.

It was from Anna. I stood right in front of the box and opened it. There was a folded page ripped out of a lined spiral notebook. I unfolded it and read. Holy shit, I whistled under my breath.

Dear Nell,

My mother died a week after you left. She slipped away around midnight. No one was there with her. That's the part that bothers me most. I can't stop thinking of her lying there all alone. But otherwise I feel oddly relieved.

Last night I spoke to my brother. He said he understood when I told him I wanted to move back to Taos and that he didn't mind looking after Dad, that I should go where I can write.

Summer school's out. I'll head down to Beatrice to visit for two weeks and leave some of my stuff. Should be in Taos by the end of September—I can't believe I'm writing this! I have a little savings, so I won't need a job right away.

I'm going to drive down through Kansas. It seems romantic, Kansas. Where Dorothy lived. Daniel's number is 402-555-3068. He lives right near Dad. I'll be staying there in case you need to reach me.

All my love,
Anna

Holy shit! I said it again. She'll be here the end of this month! I leaned against the cool wall of the post office. My best friend's coming back. I stared at the sign across the way: Parcel rates have their UPS and downs. Theirs go up. Ours stay down.

Maybe I can't have Gauguin, but I'm getting something. My body breathed in a whole new kind of gratitude. I put the letter back in its envelope and walked to the car.

I've got to tell Blue. I headed for the blinking light and then took a left out to the dirt road. I passed a herd of sheep by the arroyo and two pure white horses. Farther down there were three black ones standing close to each other by a fencepost, and there was that mutt Cheesecake with his crazy red eyes, trying to bite my tire again.

It was early. As I pulled up, I remembered Blue had left soon after I did this morning for her walk in the mountains. She took their two dogs, Saltine and Chariot, with her. I wondered when they'd lost Bonnie. That was one dog I liked out of maybe a million.

I pulled my car right up to the school bus. I had a book with me that I had checked out of the Harwood two days before. It was filled with haiku. I sat down on the high green stool I had placed outside by the door of the bus and flipped through the pages.

Nothing intimates
How soon they must die,—
Crying cicadas.

Hmmm. I liked that one. I read it again. I read it a third time and then stared off into the distance. I stood up, book in hand, and walked directly into the bus and over to the easel. With gray paint, I wrote the haiku across the white canvas. Then I wrote the poet's name: Basho.

I waited for it to dry. Then I took charcoal and drew diagonal lines down and across the poem. I had no thoughts. I began to paint. Lots of yellow, every color green, a deep blue sky. An hour and a half passed.

I stood back. It was almost finished. I stepped forward and continued. After another half-hour, I was done. I had painted a big cottonwood I had passed on the side of the road this morning, its leaves shimmering in the light at the beginning of the end of summer.

And the haiku? It was completely covered. There was no sign of it, but it was my foundation and the painting's secret.

I stepped back. Suddenly I felt exhausted, as if I'd been hiking up a straight incline all day. I went outside and sat back down on the green stool in the shade of the bus. The sun had climbed to the middle of the sky. I must have sat there for twenty minutes. I was as still as a wood tick.

Then I went over to the house, drank a tall glass of water, and lay down on the couch. I must have been sleeping an hour or so when Sam slammed the door and woke me up.

"Oh, sorry, Nell, I didn't know you were here." He stood by the sink but was looking over at the couch.

"Oh, Sam," I said, raising my head. "Is Blue back? I found out that Anna's decided to move back. I'm so excited!"

"That's great. I've heard so much about her, I feel like I know her. Is that what made you fall asleep?" he joked.

"No." I laughed and shook my head. "Hey, want to come out and see my painting? It wiped me out completely. I'm not sure what it looks like, if it's good or not." I got up off the couch. "Hey, is that Blue's car?"

We both walked out to the car. "Hey, sweet things, I like this entourage greeting me." She reached behind her and opened the back door. Saltine and Chariot bounded out. "You bad dogs," Blue called after them. "They chased every chipmunk."

"Nell painted a picture this morning she wants us to see. Let's go over." Sam leaned into the car, kissed Blue, and nodded toward the bus.

When we'd climbed into the trailer, Sam let out a whistle. "Whew, Nell, that's the best thing you've ever done."

Blue was silent. Then she said, "It's lit from within. That's some tree. Nell"—she turned to me—"it's so full of light, it wards off any trouble that the other day might have brought."

"Huh?" I cocked my head.

"You know, when poor Sylvester fried. You created light out of darkness," she explained.

"Oh." I nodded.

"Nell, what do *you* think of it?" Sam asked.

"I . . . I like it, I think. I'm a little stunned. It's good, isn't it?" We stood there awhile.

Then we descended from the bus and headed for the house. "Blue!" I grabbed her arm. "Anna's moving back! The end of the month. I can't believe I forgot to tell you." I pulled the letter out of my pocket.

Blue's face lit up as she read Anna's letter. Sam looked over her shoulder. "That's great," she said. "Let's have a welcome home party for her. Should I make noodle cake again?"

I made a face.

"How 'bout an apple pie? They'll be nice and ripe by then."

I nodded. "Sounds good."

"I'm gonna leave you two ladies now. I have to work on the well." Sam began to step away.

"Sugar, we're women. Remember? W-o-m-e-n." Blue made a face.

"Of course, sorry." He waved.

Blue turned to me. "I'm starting a new book today. I'm so excited. I'm gonna take a bath and then begin reading."

"Uh-oh," I teased. "What is it?"

"*Shogun*. Tiny and Pebbles say it's great. It's about Japan. I love that little country." Blue shaded her eyes with her hand.

"I read it while I was with Gauguin. Trust me, you'll be out of it for a month. Knowing how you are, you'll probably start cooking teriyaki."

She laughed. "Do you miss Gauguin?"

"I feel him a lot here in Taos. Yeah, I miss him. Probably all the time. I don't know what to do about it." I leaned against the dome of the chicken coop.

"But now Anna is coming." Blue ran her hand along the rough surface of the dome.

I smiled.

"And that's not all," Blue added. "You've really become a painter, Nell."

"You think so?" I asked.

"I know so. Don't you remember back in Talpa how much you wanted it and didn't know how to do it?"

"I guess I've forgotten. It's in me now."

"It sure is, honey. That was a humdinger you did today in the trailer." She leaned back next to me on the dome. We both looked out at Taos Mountain.

54

"Yup, Anna should arrive any day now. I spoke to her a week ago at her brother Daniel's." I was sitting in Steven's Kitchen. It felt as if she might appear in the doorway any minute.

"That's swell," Tiny said. "Gee, Banana—I mean, Nell—it's so good to see you again. What do you want to order? The waitress is hovering."

"Hang on, let me look at the menu." My eye was on the green chile cheeseburger when I heard my name called from across the room by the door. Maybe it was Anna. I looked up. "Blue?" She didn't look good. "What's wrong?"

Blue crossed the restaurant quickly. "I thought I'd never find you. Anna's been in a car wreck. She's in Dodge City, Kansas. Her brother called. It looks like she'll be all right, but she's in the hospital. He can't make it down right away. I told him you'd go, not to worry."

I stood up. "Anna? She's hurt?"

"They say she'll be okay. I took all the information down. Here's the keys to my car. I got you some money." She handed me a white envelope. "You should leave now. Here's a map. It's about eight hours or so from here. You don't want Anna to be all alone when she wakes up."

"Anna?" My legs were following Blue out the front door. "Is she unconscious?"

"She was knocked out, but just for a short while. The doctors seem to think she's okay. Just a little bruised. I think her car's totaled, though."

"But you said, 'When she wakes up.' "

"Well, let's hope she sleeps tonight. That's all, sugar."

Tiny had followed us out. "Do you want me to come?"

"Thanks, Tiny." I touched his arm. "I'll be okay."

Blue handed me her keys as I sat down in the driver's seat of her red Subaru station wagon. "Sugar, be careful. Bring her back safely." She leaned down through the window. "There's a jacket in the back seat. You need to get gas. Don't forget. I didn't have time. I popped Van Morrison into the tape deck."

I nodded. I pulled out of the parking lot. I made a left at the light and drove down Kit Carson, headed out toward Cimarron.

I drove in a daze all the way to Springer, my foot on the gas, aiming straight ahead. I listened to "Into the Mystic" over and over as darkness crept in. I noticed the gas needle was past empty. I forgot to get gas. I prayed the car would make it to the next town.

It did make it, and by the time I hit Clayton, I had begun to cry. Anna, I hope you're okay.

I drove through the night and got to Dodge City in the early morning.

"Where is she?" I ran to the front desk of the hospital.

"Who, may I ask?" The nurse had spectacles down low on her nose.

"Anna. Anna Gates." I was leaning on the counter.

The nurse turned around to look at the roster. "She's in room 208, but it's too early for visiting hours."

"I'm her sister. I just drove in. She's been in an accident. I'll take responsibility." I ran to the elevator and went up to the second floor.

I didn't have a watch, but it was quiet on Anna's floor and I remembered the sun still hadn't peeked over the horizon when I pulled into Dodge.

I tiptoed past room 206. The next door would be hers.

There she was. Her bed was by the window. I walked over and sat by her side. I couldn't tell if she was asleep.

Just then, her head moved slightly, she turned a quarter of an inch toward me, and her eyes twitched. She opened them halfway, closed them, then opened them again. "Nell," she whispered my name, but it was emphatic. There was a bruise across her forehead. She wasn't on any life-support system.

I reached out and touched the bed sheet. I was afraid to touch her, that I might hurt her. "I'm here, Anna. The doctors say you'll be okay."

She seemed to rouse more. "I know. They told me yesterday." Her head fell back on the pillow.

"Rest now. I'll be with you." It felt as though there was no other time but this moment, no other place but this heaven with Anna. Taos, the long ride, everything fell away.

"My car's all busted." Anna began to whimper.

"That's okay. We can share mine. Don't worry."

"Nell, I almost made it."

"What do you mean? As soon as the doctors release you, I'll drive you the rest of the way."

She started to cry. I realized I'd never seen her cry before.

She shook her head. "No, it's not going to happen."

"Sure it is." What was she talking about?

"Nell, I see angels. They're coming for me. I see them."

I grew alarmed. She was hallucinating. "Do you want me to go get a doctor? What kind of drugs are they giving you?" I started to stand up.

"No, stay with me, Nell." I sat back down. "They're coming." She nodded her head and closed her eyes. "Nell, remember we'll always be together."

"Sure we will." I found a piece of gum in my pocket. I took it out and I began to chew it hard. It didn't seem to bother Anna. I stood up and began to pace. I was nervous. Maybe it was all those hours without sleep.

I leaned close to Anna. I took the gum out of my mouth and stuck it under her bed. "Anna," I called in her ear. "Anna."

She stirred slightly. She opened her eyes and smiled.

I smiled back and sat down again. It was so quiet.

Then I saw them too: five angels hovering over her bed. As I watched, almost a violet smoke came out of Anna. The angels lifted it like a veil and floated off. I kept staring but saw nothing except morning, its light, breaking outside the window.

I was suddenly afraid to look back at Anna. I stood up. My legs were shaking so much, I had to grab the chair. I glanced back at her as I ran out the door. She looked like she was sleeping. I ran down the shiny hospital floor and grabbed a man in a white coat.

"Please, I think something has happened." I could hardly speak.

"What room?"

"Two-oh-eight. Please." I turned and ran back to the room.

"I'll get a doctor," he called after me.

"Anna, oh, Anna." I knelt by her bed, put my cheek to her chest and my arms around her, and started to rock her. "Anna, Anna, Anna," I repeated over and over. I was crying now, low moans that came from deep down. I was still afraid to look at her face. I just kept rocking her.

Finally I looked up. I was right. She was gone. Her face seemed so peaceful, and her eyes were staring in the distance.

"Excuse me, miss." A nurse and doctor were behind me. The nurse put her hand on my shoulder. "Please let the doctor see her." The nurse led me out into the hall. I followed submissively. Other technicians ran in with machines, but I knew it was over. I'd seen the angels.

"She was my best friend," I told the nurse. "My sister," I trailed off.

"Yes." The nurse patted me on the shoulder. "Why don't you sit here on the bench? It will be a little while."

I sat down and waited.

The doctor came out. "A ruptured spleen. We didn't detect it. She's gone." He turned to me. "There's nothing we can do now. I'm sorry, miss."

"I'm her sister," I said. "I'm Nell Gates. Can I go see her again?" I was cool. I had a plan.

"Yes, of course. Take your time. Arrangements will have to be made. Do you want to tell your parents?"

"I'll call my brother." I was walking toward her room.

I went back in and shut the door behind me. "Anna," I said in my best schoolteacher voice, "now, listen. Just tell those angels to come back. Tell them to come back."

She didn't answer.

"Please, Anna." I softened. "Please. Tell them to bring you back. We'll go to Taos. I'll be a famous painter. You'll be a great writer. Please, Anna." I shook her arm. "Do you hear me?" I begged. "Come back, and I'll take you to Taos." I paused. My plan wasn't working.

The sheet had been pulled over her face. This couldn't be happening. There was a black fist in my stomach.

I sat down on the chair by her bed. I stared out the window. The sun was really out now. I saw a red semi in the distance. I leaned forward, put my elbows on my knees, and kept looking across the hospital bed out the window. She had died in Dodge City, Kansas. Not in Nebraska, not in New Mexico. Anna, my Anna.

I turned and lowered the sheet. "Anna, I promise I'll never forget you." I felt crazy. This couldn't be happening.

The nurse came in. "It's time to call your family. We have to make arrangements for the body."

"The body? Oh, I'll take it," I said matter-of-factly.

"Fine. You should call home and make funeral arrangements. You'll need to sign papers at the front desk."

"Of course." My head was empty.

I took out the envelope Blue had given me and sat down. There was three hundred dollars cash in there and a list of phone numbers, including Daniel's.

I looked up. Two orderlies had just walked in with a gurney. They lifted Anna onto it.

Oh, my god, they're taking her away. I stood up. "No!" I cried out.

They both turned to me. "We have to, ma'am."

"No. No. No." I shook my head back and forth. Now I was crying. Now I was crying real hard. "No. No. No."

They were pushing her out. "Wait." I held up my hand. "Where can I find a rabbi?"

"There's one on call. Ask at the desk."

"Can I see her again? I have to pray," I said.

"She'll be in the morgue. Go to the desk."

I started to pull at my T-shirt. I couldn't stop crying. I ran down the hall to the desk. "Please, get me a rabbi. My sister"—I pointed at the vanishing figures—"I have to take her home."

The nurse knew who I was talking about. "Yes, Ms. Gates. I'll call a rabbi. It usually takes him a while to get here. He's not exactly a rabbi—we don't have one in Dodge City—but he's a Jew. He'll come."

I nodded. "Where's the phone?"

I called Daniel. No one answered. I dialed Blue. The phone rang and rang. I thought of calling Gauguin. I didn't have his number. What would I say?

Nell, you are alone, I told myself. Take charge, the way Anna would have wanted you to.

I stopped crying. I composed myself and walked back to the desk. "How soon will my sister be ready to travel? I phoned my family and they're making arrangements. I have a station wagon."

"Well, it will take a while. You'll have to pick her up at the funeral home. Oh, and ma'am, the Jew can't come. His mother is very ill."

"Oh, that's okay. I'll say Kaddish when I get home." I was very calm. She gave me the funeral home's address and all the information I needed. "Where is a good place to eat?" I asked.

"We have a cafeteria downstairs."

"Thank you." I hadn't eaten since lunch yesterday.

I went down the elevator. Instead of going to the cafeteria, I walked straight out the front doors. Sunlight poured over me.

I looked down the street. A sign in the distance looked like it said, "Luncheonette." Then I realized it said, "Launderette." I scanned the street some more. There was Bell's. I walked toward it. Dodge City was the emptiest, loneliest place in America.

Bell's turned out to be a grocery. I went in, and right next to the piles of bananas and rows of fruit juices I put coins in the pay phone and dialed Daniel's number again.

"Nell," he said. "Oh, Nell, you're there. Dad got sick. I had to take him to the hospital. I was planning to try to come down tomorrow, but my hands are full." He paused. "How's Anna doing anyway? Nell, are you there?"

"Daniel, she's dead. She died at daybreak of a ruptured spleen." I paused for long time. "I'm sorry. They'll let me drive her up to Beatrice as soon as the body's ready. You'd better make funeral arrangements." There was a long, long silence. "Daniel, I'm sorry."

"My little sister? You sure?"

"Yes, I'm sure. I was there when she died." I breathed the words into the holes on the black phone receiver. "Anna's dead."

I began to cry.

"Oh, Nell, I've never met you, but Anna loved you."

"She loved you too, Daniel. What should we do?"

"I don't know. There's no family here but Dad. I'm afraid if I tell him—"

"Listen," I cut him off, "I'll drive the body up, and we'll decide then, together. Okay?"

"Yeah, that sounds like a good plan. When are you coming, did you say? Did she say anything to you?" he asked.

"That she'll always be with us." I wiped tears from my eyes. "That's what she said."

"Sounds like Anna." He let out a wry laugh.

"Daniel, Anna's dead." I had to say it again.

I bought two apples with a ten that Blue had given me and walked out the door, holding them in a small brown paper bag.

It was late September, but it was still hot. The sun seemed to bleach everything. The sidewalk blazed up at me. I passed a garbage can and threw the bag of apples into it. I didn't want apples. I walked on. I figured I had plenty of time. What were they doing to her? Shooting her up with formaldehyde. I winced. Anna wouldn't like that. It didn't feel like that was Anna anymore. The real Anna had flown off with the angels.

The noon whistle blew. I passed a steak house. That was what I wanted. I turned in. The lights were dim, the ceiling black, heavy curtains across the windows. The place didn't look too popular. I was the only customer. I took a booth in the darkest corner, opened the menu, and began to sob. I put my head on the table behind the menu and bawled. I cried as if a whole ocean were inside me. I couldn't have cared less where I was.

A waitress finally came over. "Is everything all right, ma'am?"

I just kept crying.

"Ma'am?"

"Bring me something, anything."

"A Coke?"

Yes, I nodded.

"A hamburger?"

Yes, I nodded again.

"French fries?"

"Anything you want." My head rested on the cool table.

She brought me the food. I looked up.

"My sister died." I pressed in my lips.

"Oh, honey," she said, and placed the plate in front of me. "Want some ketchup?"

No, I shook my head.

"Now, you just take your time," she said.

I nodded obediently and put a fry into my mouth.

Anna was finally ready to go. They wrapped her like a mummy and then put her in a body bag. While they placed her in the back of Blue's station wagon, I just sat in the driver's seat and looked straight ahead. The door slammed, and then a man came from behind and leaned into my window. "She's ready."

"Thank you," I said, and pulled away. I was afraid to look back.

With stony eyes I steered the car onto 56 North. The sign said "Scenic Route." Leave it to Anna to have picked this.

There wasn't much traffic. I thought of switching on Van, and then I couldn't. Anna was dead in the back seat. After about twenty miles, I pulled over to the shoulder and fell over the steering wheel. Sweat was pouring down my body. C'mon, Nell, get a grip, I said to myself.

"What are you doing?" It sounded like Anna.

I sat up. I looked around me. No one was there.

Then I looked around again. There she was, in the passenger seat. Not in the flesh. More in the form of smoke. "Nell, turn around. Take me to Taos. You promised to get me there."

"Anna!" My eyes were bugging out of my head. "You're dead. What are you doing here?" I was shocked but not afraid. It felt like Anna, not like a devil or anything. "You're dead, Anna."

"Quit all this crying, Nell. Turn this car around. I was headed for the mesa. Now finish it. Take me there."

I started to cry all over again. She grabbed my T-shirt at the collar. "Listen, will you?"

I jerked up—this was a strong ghost. "You're serious, aren't you?"

"Nell, take me where I belong and quit bawling." Yup, that was Anna, no-nonsense, Midwestern. Then the smoke disappeared through a crack in the windshield.

"No, wait," I called. "Wait, Anna. Talk to me."

"I did. You heard me." Her voice was like a distant echo.

I turned my head and looked in the back of the car. The body was still there. She was still dead.

I took a deep breath. "Okay, Anna," I said. I spotted a break in the divider and spun the car around. "We're heading home." I gassed the car up to 85, opened the windows, and put on Van at full blast.

55

aniel had arrived two days ago. He was even taller than Anna and had the same color hair, almost the same length, but his eyes were brown. You could tell they were related, but Daniel was more awkward with his big size and clumsy about his manners.

"It's okay that you hijacked Anna." He broke into a big grin. It was Anna all over again—her heart-shaped face, her wide cheekbones, her rugged mouth. He reached out his hand to shake mine.

For a moment his sister was present again in the flesh. I had to turn away as I offered my hand.

We kept Anna in the pyramid Sam had built years ago after he read that pyramids had magical powers. When I arrived from Dodge, Sam made a simple pine coffin for her.

I visited her every day. First I'd recite the Kaddish, then I'd tell her everything I could remember about who she was and about times we had spent together. I'd sit on the ground real close to the coffin; my voice, echoing in the pyramid, sounded as if it were reciting a litany. I told Anna about how I admired her for caring about writing and how I had never known anyone from Nebraska before. I even told her that sometimes I wished I were as tall as her.

One morning I asked her, "Anna, do you remember when we hung the sage to dry all over the vigas on your ceiling? And then we sat under that beautiful smell and ate scrambled eggs fresh from Mel's chickens." At that I ran outside and picked armfuls of sage and hung it all over the inside of the pyramid. It was cool in there, and the sage made a good smell.

I accompanied Daniel on his visit to Anna. When we opened the door of the pyramid, the sage smell filled our lungs. Daniel walked right over to the coffin and opened the lid. He knelt down and picked Anna up in his arms. "Sister, sister, sister," he whispered over and over, rocking her in the body bag, his eyes closed, his face trembling.

He laid her back gently and closed the lid, rested his forehead on the pine wood. I knelt beside him, and he reached for my hand and clutched it. I stroked his head.

He glanced up, his cheeks wet. "This is like 'Nam all over again." I nodded. "Let's get some air."

We walked out into the sunlight. Daniel blinked a few times. "I gotta move," he said, and took off running across the mesa. I stood watching until he topped a distant mound and then disappeared.

On the morning of Anna's funeral, I thought of taking a walk when I woke up, but instead I went straight over to the pyramid and sat with her until lunch.

Daniel came to get me and we walked back together.

"You ready for this evening?" he asked me.

"I guess. It's probably best. We can't go on this way," I said, and took his arm.

"Yeah, it's still hard to believe. I feel like I have to do something to mark her passing. After lunch I'm gonna shave my head."

I nodded. We went in the house.

Blue had made a beautiful salad and fresh lemonade.

"Did you know Anna sold lemonade in the summer when we were on the farm?" Daniel lit up when she poured him a glass.

"No—yes, I'd forgotten—but maybe I didn't." Blue sat down and smiled.

"Want to hold hands?" I asked, reaching out my arms.

We sat with our eyes closed.

"Anna, I really miss you," my voice choked.

"Me, too." Daniel squeezed my hand.

We began to eat. There were only the four of us. We had decided to keep it small since we were pretty sure what we planned to do that evening was illegal.

After the salad plates were cleared, Blue brought out the most beautiful two-layer white cake I'd ever seen. There was one big candle in the middle.

"Daniel, do you want to blow it out?" she asked as she placed it on the table. "Make a wish."

He stood up, closed his eyes for a long time, and then blew it out.

"Give me a big piece. I deserve it," I said. "I always made fun of Anna for liking vanilla."

After I finished it, I said, "I still don't see what she saw in that flavor. It's got no punch."

We laughed and then a tremendous sadness swept over me. I looked around and knew the others felt it too.

All afternoon Sam and Daniel piled up piñon and cedar. I helped for a while but had no will for it. They understood and I walked over to the bus.

You're going to paint now? I asked myself. I didn't know what else to do. Anna would have liked me to paint.

My eye glanced at the haiku book on the floor. I squatted down, closed my eyes, and picked out a page. My eyes fell upon:

The first snow,
Just enough to bend
The leaves of the daffodils.

My whole chest took in the haiku. Basho again. He knew some stuff.

I stood up, picked up a brush, dipped it in blue and wrote on the top of a big piece of paper, "FOR ANNA AND NELL." Then I dipped my index finger in red paint and wrote the poem in big letters. Then I picked up a paintbrush almost half the size of my fist, dipped it in black, and held it over the top of the page so the color ran down to the bottom. As I waited for it to dry, I searched through a big wooden chest at the far end of the bus. I found what I wanted—a clear plastic box full of silver and gold stars.

I licked the backs of them and stuck them all over the red writing and the black drips. As I did it, I said aloud, "Excellent, Nell gets an A. Anna gets an A-plus. Excellent, excellent. The two of us excelled. Congratulations."

I must have glued at least a hundred of them on. "Yeah for Nell and Anna! They were great and wonderful. They were A students." Then I glued colored sparkles all around the edges of the painting. I stuck a picture postcard of the Virgin of Guadalupe in the center, and then in the upper right-hand corner I painted a white Star of David.

"Voilà!" I made a smacking noise with my lips. "Anna and Nell are full of Glory!" I yelled as loud as I could for anybody to hear.

At evening, we burned her. The flames were so hot and big, they could have been seen from a hundred miles away. We watched them all night.

Past midnight—I don't know quite when, the night was so long—I stuck the corner of my Anna and Nell painting in the flames, held it up, and watched it burn against the dark sky. The heat got close to my hand. I hesitated a moment. Then I threw it in.

I didn't need anything to remind me of her anymore. Anna was in me—she was in the mesa, the sky, and every cell of our bodies. She was true to her promise. ''Nell, we'll always be together.'' She couldn't have left if she tried.

EPILOGUE

I f you became Anna's lover, I'm pretty sure it would be her kisses that you would remember, how they led you way out into the open as she turned herself inside out in giving them to you. When she finally decided to kiss me that evening in her apartment, everything came with her, like a house collapsing, with all the hinges giving in. And it wasn't even that she had such great lips—one of her teeth was crooked, and her bottom lip sometimes stuck out stubborn—but when she wanted to give, the heavens opened up. She wasn't always that way, but she was when she kissed, and a lover of hers, a real one, would remember her kisses years later and would wish Anna well, no matter what awful things had fallen between them.

I also imagine there could have been some awful things, because Anna could get mean and silent when she wanted to. She once pinned me to the ground. She was strong, with wiry muscles. I thought she was kidding, but she wouldn't let me up, even when I said I wasn't playing anymore. I got scared, panicked, and bit her on the wrist. For a long time afterward, she had teeth marks in her skin. After that I studied her biceps. She was always lifting something heavy to see if she could do it. I didn't know women could have muscles like hers. And her hands, too. Broad and blunt. Before I met Anna, I was ignorant about how far a woman could go.

I never paid much attention to Gauguin's muscles. And his kisses? They weren't all that memorable, though sure, I liked kissing him. It had more to do with water. The first time I saw him, even before I spoke to him, I felt it. Then, over the course of our relationship, I felt all kinds of water: a slow river, shallow and muddy, like the Green River flowing through the red canyonlands in Utah; the hard sparkle of water in a creek after the snow has melted and it catches the sun or even the moon's cold light; also the kind of water that would come out of the faucet in my family's place in Brooklyn. I'd stand in the kitchen, leaning on the sink, waiting for the water from the spout to run clear, and then I'd fill a tall drinking glass with it. As I drank, I'd smell fresh green parsley sprigs. All of this about water woke in me when I first laid my eyes on Gauguin.

He got married two years ago. When Gauguin called to tell me his plans, it was a Tuesday and I was baking bread, the first bread I'd baked in six years. My hands were full of flour when the phone rang. It was a short conversation; he told me, and I lied and said I thought it was great. I got off the phone and dumped the bread dough in the garbage.

Finally, I was able to accept it. I drove to Blue's and slept over. That night I had a dream. I was lying in bed in a motel, and Gauguin and his new girlfriend walked in and stood at the foot of the bed. I turned my head to the wall. Then I said to myself in the dream, Nell, you have to look, so I lifted my head off the pillow and I looked. It hurt like hell, but I saw them, and they were perfect for each other.

The night of their wedding I was in Jerome, Arizona. I excused myself from friends in the restaurant and looked for a pay phone. There was one outside, against the brick wall of the building. I called Gauguin and left a message on his answering machine. "Congratulations," I said. This time I meant it. "I had a dream, and in the dream you were perfect for each other." I hung up. It felt cold out and I never wanted to visit Jerome again, though it wasn't the town's fault.

You know I'm not a writer. Anna was the writer, but I had to write this. I had to tell this story. We all have to tell our stories. We lived those years. We know them better than anyone else. We can't let other people tell it for us. We each have to tell about those times, so we can remember how we believed in love and carry that belief forward.